NYT AND USA TODAY BESTSELLING AUTHOR

TIJAN

Edited by The Word Maid and Paige Smith

Proofread by: Allusion Graphics, LLC, Chris O'Neil Parece, Kara Hildebrand, and Pam Huff

Formatted by: Elaine York, Allusion Graphics, LLC
www.allusiongraphics.com

To Erica Adams, and so many others!
I wrote *Home Torn* (the original version) sooo many years ago. I dreamed to have Home Torn as one of my first novels published. One agent even showed interest in it, and that meant the world to me. This book is so dear to my heart. I truly hope it'll be close to yours as well, and remains so for those who continued to support this book and myself over the years.

You guys truly inspire me.

1

Bells that were hung over the bank's door jingled as Dani O'Hara stepped inside, and five seconds later she heard the first intake of breath.

"Oh, my God."

Well, shit. That hadn't taken long.

Ten years. That was how long it'd been since she was home. Craigstown's population was only a little over two thousand, so maybe Dani had been a little delusional? She thought she could come in, deposit her checks, get some cash, and slip away unseen. It might've felt surreal to another person, but it wasn't to her. In fact, it was the opposite. It was too real. Dani didn't want to feel or deal with any of the storm going on inside of her, so she shoved everything down except for wariness.

She could feel wary. That was a safe emotion to handle, or the safest out of the others. And with that last thought, she needed to face whoever whispered that first greeting. They were about to be her first reunion.

Kelley Lynn.

Dani recognized her right away, and *of course*, it had to be her. If it wasn't the person who was the reason why Dani left in the first place, it made complete sense it'd be that person's sidekick. No irony there at all. None whatsoever. Nada. Dani wasn't funny, but even this situation was making her insides shake slightly with laughter.

"Kelley," she greeted, folding her hands in front of her. "How are you? What are you up to now?"

Simple questions. They were the polite response, but Kelley was floored. Her mouth was still hanging open. Then again, Dani had been prepared for this type of reaction. It was everyone else who wasn't. Dani studied Kelley. She seemed to be struggling with a response.

Kelley was the popular girl in the grade below her. She was friends with Dani's youngest sister—the actual reason, or kind of reason, the more-or-less reason, fuck-it-it-was-complicated reason why Dani left ten years ago and never returned. Correction—they were best friends. She remembered Kelley being blonde, beautiful, and the typical bitch 'mean girls' were portrayed as. Looking at her now, she looked like a grown-up version of the same person. Her clothes upgraded from the too-tight tank tops to the just-right cleavage underneath a cashmere sweater.

"Is it you?" Kelley blinked. "Dani?"

"It is. It's me."

"It's you!" Squealing, Kelley wrapped her arms around Dani. "We all thought you were dead. I mean—you didn't come to Erica's…" Kelley glanced down before lifting her head again. "We didn't know what to think when you didn't come to—" she jerked up a shoulder, "you know."

Five seconds before someone gasped at the sight of her, and now the invisible elephant had just been alluded to. Her sister. That took a whole minute. Then again, Dani realized *she* was the second elephant in the room. It made sense the rumors were that she was dead. Ten years and not a word from her, but for the first elephant…Dani wasn't ready to talk about it, not yet. She would, but not with her sister's best friend. She was glad Kelley hadn't had the balls to actually say the words of what 'it' was.

She spoke before Kelley changed her mind. "I was on location for my job. Julia and Aunt Kathryn didn't get in touch with me." Though, if her oldest sister and aunt could've, she didn't know if they actually would've.

"You're home? For good?" Kelley Lynn was still holding her hands, as if she feared Dani would run away.

"For a bit, yeah."

"Me and Dave are having a grill tonight. You should come." Her eyes lit up, and she squeezed Dani's hands tighter. "Yeah. You should come. Julia's bringing Jake. It'll be the old gang, all back together again."

Julia and Jake? Dani felt a pang in her chest. It had been Erica and Jake.

"The old gang?" Dani frowned. There'd been no 'old gang,' at least not one where she was included.

"Oh." Kelley's smile lessened. "We all kind of regrouped, you know, after Erica's thing." Dani could almost hear an elephant trumpet in the background. Kelley was saying, "Julia, me, Katrina Lloyds, Heather Carlile, and some of the others all formed a clique. Kind of like in high school, but all we really do is get together for dinners and have a few beers around the campfire. Sometimes the girls will go shopping. It'd be great if you came."

Yeah. Dani's smile grew painful. "I'll think about it. First night and all, you know…" They both knew she wouldn't go.

"Oh." Kelley's smile was almost gone by now. "Well, you're welcome, you know that. I want you to know that. Gosh. Have you been home yet? Have you seen Julia and Kathy?"

"Not yet. I wanted to take care of some business first."

"They're going to be so excited. I just know it. Julia's going to die happy tonight. I'm sure they've been missing you so much."

"Well, they thought I was dead. So," Dani's eyes slid away. "There's that."

"Okay." She cleared her throat, gesturing to the door. "You know, I should get going. Dave needs all the steaks and brats before long. We have to start up the grill before the guests start arriving, and we need time to prepare everything." A few steps away, she stopped and turned back. "It really is great to see you, Dani. Really."

Dani held up a hand in response as Kelley left, but she wasn't smiling anymore. There was no reason.

Maybe Kelley actually was happy to see her, but it wouldn't last. She had been on Erica's side back then and Dani had a hard time imagining things would be different now. If Julia was in her group, Dani knew things *definitely* wouldn't be different. A line would be drawn, and sides would be chosen. Kelley wouldn't choose hers, so the jaded side of Dani knew what was genuine wouldn't last. It was just a matter of time.

And with that thought, Dani moved forward to the counter.

She was officially back home.

After opening a new account (her last was closed because of the whole 'dead' thing), Dani headed to see the one person she thought would be happy to see her, and would never change that status.

Her other aunt.

And she heard as she headed inside Mae's Grill, "Well, hell, the barn cat dragged something in here worthwhile, for once."

Mae slapped her bar towel over her shoulder and hurried around the bar counter. Dani had two seconds before she was hauled in for a bear hug. Fifty-three and Aunt Mae was still the feisty strong woman she always had been. When she was let go, Dani moved back so she could really see her. Steel-toe boots. Silver hair pulled into a haphazard ponytail. Checkered button-up shirt with a lacy tank top underneath and a tease of cleavage peeking out. And faded jeans.

Same old Aunt Mae.

There'd been a time when Mae was the only one Dani could lean on, and then there were times when the woman wasn't anywhere in her life. She was glad that it seemed she got back the first version of Mae again. Dani hoped it would last, and she couldn't hold back a grin. She had missed her. "Hi, Mae."

One of the regulars looked up from his drink. "I didn't know you had a cat, Mae?"

"I don't. It's a saying, Barney." Her hands rested on Dani's shoulders, shaking her lightly. "Christ's sake, it's about fucking time you got your skinny little behind back to these parts. It's been so long. Too long!" She threw her head back. "This calls for a celebration. What'll you have? On the house!"

"You don't have a barn, Mae. How's you can have a barn cat?" Barney mumbled, dipping over his drink.

She rounded on him. "I got a barn. Why don't you go look for it?"

"Where's it at abouts?"

"Right behind here. Go take a look-see. Tell me when you find me that barn cat of mine. I'd like him back someday."

"Are you joshing me, Mae?"

"Barney," she sounded tired, "when do I ever josh you? You'd have to be sober for me to do that. Now git and find me that cat of mine." She scooted around the counter, giving Dani a wink.

"Mmkay, but if your barn cat scratches me, and I have to get me some tetanus shots, you're paying, Mae. Just laying the law down there." He almost fell off his stool as he got to his feet.

He was a keen negotiator.

As he stumbled out the back, another guy at the bar lifted up his beer. "Mae, that was cruel even for you. You don't have a barn, or a cat." He was hunched over, sitting toward the middle of the counter. Dani couldn't see him clearly since half the lights were turned off inside the bar, but she could make out a flannel shirt, dark hair lined with grey strands, and a small beard on his face.

"Shut it, Jeffries, and drink your beer while I'm still giving it to you."

He saluted and drank. "Shutting it."

"So, what finally brought your ever-pretty mug back to these whereabouts? And don't think you ain't getting off that easy. I know you don't like to say much, never did, but you better start yapping or your Aunt Mae is going to get pissed. Might have to make a phone call to my sister." She cringed. "Never mind on that. I couldn't handle Kathryn when you were here. I know I won't be able to now." She winked and then sobered, leaning closer. She softened her voice. "Seriously, I'm glad as hell that you're back. About time, if you ask me. How are you going to break the news to that sister of yours? She'll have some words for you, especially since you missed your sister's funeral."

Your sister's funeral.

When Mae kept going, not giving her time to answer.

Kelley's words from the bank echoed alongside. *You didn't come to Erica's...*

There it was.

But I thought...

Mae was still talking. "—She's going to light into you. You better have a good excuse ready, though I don't think it'll work."

Yeah. A good excuse. Dani cleared her throat. "I didn't know about Erica's death when it happened. I couldn't come for the funeral. I'll tell Julia that when I see her."

"That's not going to fly. She's going to say you didn't tell anyone where you were, and it'll be your fault. They'll turn everything on you. You know that." Mae had a keen eye on her. "Well, I'm guessing this isn't the first you heard about your sister's death. You'd be shaken and you're not. How *did* you find out?"

That was a whole other conversation as well. "Just heard around, you know. What's done is done."

"That why you're here?" Aunt Mae continued to study her niece.

"Just time to come back." Dani motioned toward the liquor bottles. She was suddenly parched. "I'll have a rum and diet."

"Ah hell, don't go breaking your aunt's heart. You'll have a beer on tap, not some diet soda crap."

Dani grinned. "I'll take one of those then. Whatever you have on tap and need to get rid of."

Mae slid the drink across the bar. "That's my girl." A pause and a tap on the counter with her fingers. "So, you going out to see that sister of yours after this?"

"I was wondering about a place to stay. I wouldn't feel right about imposing on Julia and Aunt Kathryn."

Dani was lying, and Aunt Mae knew it. She wouldn't step foot in that home if it were the last habitable place in the world.

Mae nodded, approving. "You've grown some teeth. I can see it. You look good, too."

Dani flushed.

She was fit and trim. Clear skin. Doe eyes, or that was how they'd been described to her by a boyfriend once and eyelashes that models would've killed for. Dani knew she looked good, but she also knew it'd cause problems. It was another reason to steer clear from her last remaining sister, but that was a problem for a different day. "How about a place to crash for a while?"

"There's my place. You're always welcome there, but if you're looking for some privacy, the cabin's open, too."

A three-bedroom, log cabin on a corner of Loon Lake and protected by miles of woods on both sides. It was out in the middle of nowhere, and that sounded perfect. It was exactly what Dani needed.

"Sounds good. Thank you so much." She sipped the rest of her drink.

"Do me a favor." Mae rested a hand on the counter, pointing to where Dani was sitting. "I remember how you used to be, always ready to go off on your own, but stay a while. You only got fighting to look forward to right now."

Put that way...Dani stayed sitting.

A settled atmosphere ascended the bar for a moment, but the front door opened up. Sunlight lit up a path inside, hitting right onto Dani's back, and the peaceful feeling was suddenly gone. She tensed, and then the door slammed shut. The room was cast into darkness for a moment.

"Hey, Mae."

The voice was smooth and silky, and Dani recognized it immediately. Jonah Bannon.

He was the badass in high school, always ditching class and fighting when he *was* there. She didn't know much about him because they ran in different circles. She *did* know that even back then, he'd been gorgeous. He was literally a lean mean machine, and glancing from the corner of her eye, Dani saw that hadn't changed. There was a bit more recklessness built into the twitch of his jaw. His hands were tan and strong. Firm. A bit rough from working, but a person could tell the fitness underneath those clothes.

Jonah's infamous body couldn't be hidden.

The only other difference she could see was that his ruffled curls were shaven for a clean-cut, buzzed look. They had been rich and thick before.

The new haircut agreed with him.

"Can I get a beer?" Putting some money onto the counter, he hopped on a stool three down from Dani. "And who owns that Mustang in your parking lot?"

Aunt Mae reached for a bottle. She glanced to Dani underneath her eyelids as she set it before him, then waited a minute before commenting, "No can do, Jonah. My loyalties lie elsewhere on that topic."

He had reached for the bottle, but held it suspended in the air now. "You kidding?"

She shook her head. "Nope. 'Fraid not. I know for certain that owner won't want you bothering *him*. Can't tell you a thing."

The back door slammed shut, and a second later Barney appeared, holding a bleeding arm to his chest. "Mae, I didn't find a barn back there, but I'm pretty sure I found your cat. He didn't take a likin' to me. You might need to pay up on that tetanus shot you offered."

Mae cursed, grabbing his arm. "I don't have a barn cat. I was just messing with you."

"You were?" He sounded like an insulted four year old. "But you said you weren't."

"That's the whole point. You don't admit to it when you're doing it." She started probing his wound.

"Ouch, Mae! That hurt."

"We need to clean this so you don't get an infection. Jeffries, watch the bar for a while?"

He lifted his hand in the air. "Sure thing, Mae." Then he pretended to zip his lips. "And look, still shutting it."

She rolled her eyes, pulling Barney to the back. "Come on. Let's clean this up."

"You make sure that's all you're cleaning up."

"Thought you were shutting it, Jeffries?" Mae shouted over her shoulder.

"Doing so again. It was a temporary error." He saluted and took another drink.

As they disappeared into a back area, Jonah asked, "Hey, who owns that Mustang out front?"

Jeffries shrugged and took a drink. "You got me there." His eyes slid toward Dani and a hint of a smile lingered there, just a hint. "I haven't seen a vehicle like that around for a long time, not since Mae's little niece took off."

Jonah frowned. "You mean Erica and Julia's sister? That niece?"

Jeffries waited till Jonah glanced to where Mae had disappeared before winking at Dani. "That's the one."

Dani glared at him, knowing she took a seat purposely in the shadows. If Jonah fully looked around, he would've seen her and maybe recognized her, but he was more interested in Mae. Feeling a knot start to tighten in her stomach, Dani knew it was time to head out to the cabin. Jonah would have more questions if he spotted her and she was still hoping to put off giving those answers.

"What was her name?"

"I dunno. Didn't talk much, but Mae thought the sun set around that girl. She went in a slump for a good few months after that girl took off."

Dani stiffened again.

"Yeah, I remember that. Whole town was in an uproar because Erica and that guy started hooking up. No one seemed to like that couple," Jonah murmured, his voice slightly distracted.

And that was enough. It was time to go. Dani slid off her barstool. No one noticed as she made her way to the door, and just as her hand reached to open it, she heard Jeffries say, "It's a damn shame, too. Mae was hoping that girl would come back for the youngest's funeral. When she didn't show, Mae fell apart for a few months. That girl broke Mae's heart."

She stood frozen, her hand still on the doorknob and she looked back. Jeffries was staring right at her.

She hadn't realized...

Ten minutes later, Dani pulled up outside Mae's cabin.

Small and nestled among the trees, it looked like a fresh coat of white paint had recently been applied. Dani didn't go inside right away. First things first. The lake beckoned to her and after pocketing the hidden key from behind the grill, she went straight for it. Conflicting emotions were inside her, but she nudged them aside again. No matter her damned history, she still yearned to be around water. The dock looked like a rag tag line of wood, all thrown together, but she was surprised to find out how sturdy it was.

Mae had been taking care of this place.

Dani was still sitting there when she heard a car approaching. Standing, she walked back around the cabin, and had another shock in store. She thought maybe Mae came behind her with food, or even Julia heard about her and tracked her down. She was wrong on both accounts.

A police cruiser was parked beside the Mustang. There were two men sitting in the front, but she couldn't tear her eyes away from the driver. Sitting there, in a crisp uniform was the other reason why she left town.

Jake Cairns.

Her best friend from childhood. Her middle school crush. Her boyfriend in high school. He was her other half, until he chose her younger sister over her. Now he was a cop, and he was with her other sister, too—the one who was still alive, anyway.

"Hey, Jake."

She supposed it was now or never. She had hoped to put off seeing him, just like everyone else, but maybe it was better to deal with him now. Deal with her sister later.

"Dani," he rasped out, stopping a few feet from her. The blood had drained from his face and he looked like he just saw a ghost.

"How's it going, Jake?"

Dani felt stupid saying those words, but what else could she ask? He was her ex. He chose her sister over her. He ripped her heart out, but he was also the only thing keeping her in Craigstown. In a way, she should thank him. He let her go free, and what a journey she had been on. Then again, remembering the reason why she was home, maybe she should curse him out too. This new heartache, this numbness she was experiencing—she wouldn't have any of that.

She suddenly felt herself wanting to ask how life would've been if he hadn't chosen Erica? Would she have stayed? Would they have married? Maybe they even would've had kids by now. She sucked in her breath, feeling an invisible knife plunge into her chest.

Maybe she shouldn't be thinking about any of those things, and needing to change her thoughts, her eyes trailed past his shoulders, landing right onto Jake's companion's laughing eyes. Jonah Bannon.

Fuck.

As if he could read her mind, his mouth twisted up in a smirk. He remained back with the car, but she saw the challenge in his dark eyes. He wasn't going anywhere.

She sighed. She could already tell he was going to be a problem.

Jake shifted on his feet, pulling her attention back to him. "I didn't believe it. Jonah told me he thought you were back, but damn." He could only stare at her. "Dani."

That one word, one name from him. Her heart twisted. It was the same soft tone he used when they were kids, right as he kissed her lips and moved to her neck. She clenched her jaw. Maybe she shouldn't have come back after all?

He kept going, his hand at his jaw. He just held it there, like he didn't know what else to do with it. "Julia knows you're back." His hand fell back to his side. "I didn't mean to tell her, not till I saw you myself, but she was on the other line when Jonah found me. She overheard." He paused, his lips pressed together. "You can't stay at the house, if that's what you were thinking. Then again," he turned to take in the cabin, "I can see you liking this place better. You always did, didn't you?"

"Jake." She didn't want to talk about Julia, or that he remembered she loved this cabin more than her home. "Why'd you come here? Did Mae tell you I was here?"

"Nah. It was a guess." He seemed to remember Jonah, and looked back, but focused on her once again. His eyebrows pinched together, like he was distracted. "You never called, when Erica died. Did you know? I thought maybe you'd come for the funeral."

She didn't want to talk about it, but she heard herself say faintly, "I knew."

"So you just didn't care?"

It wasn't that. It was… she didn't want to think about it.

"Jake…"

She didn't want to remember when she found out.

"No." He held up a hand. "I didn't mean to attack you. That's not why I came out here, but uh," his hand grabbed the back of his neck and remained there, "I should let you know that Julia's got a lot on her plate. Kathryn's in the nursing home now. Did you know that?" He didn't let her respond, speaking to himself, "No, I suppose you wouldn't, but Julia's got too much going on. I don't think she can handle seeing you right now. Her Aunt Kathryn either."

Dani had no plans of seeing either, but she couldn't help herself. "*My* Aunt Kathryn."

"What?"

"She's my aunt too."

"Oh." A wrinkled line in his forehead increased. His eyebrows pinched even harder against each other. "Yeah. Yeah. I know."

And then suddenly, as quick as the fight came to her, it left her in one sudden whoosh. She was tired, all the way down to her bones. She didn't know another time in her life when she'd been this exhausted.

She knew there'd be a time when she and Jake should talk. They never did, not after he told her he was leaving her for Erica, and she took off the very next day, but that time wasn't today. It wasn't now.

"Look, Jake." He lifted his head, finding her. She added, "You go back and let Julia know that I got her message." It was better if Julia thought she was adhering to her command, and not that she was staying away because Dani didn't want to see Julia or Kathryn. Julia was just one of those people. It was her way, not someone else's, but Dani didn't want *that* fight on her doorstep either. "I'll stay away."

"That's it?" Jake frowned.

She shrugged. "What else do you want me to say?"

"I don't know. I just—" He cut himself off. "You're right. Maybe there's nothing else to say." He clipped his head in a nod, returning to his car. "I'll let Julia know. I'll tell her you send your best to her too." He was at the car. She went with him, and he reached for the door handle. Jonah had moved. Dani didn't see him, but she knew he was around. She could almost feel his presence, but she was focused on this ghost from her past.

"Jake—"

She didn't know what to say. There wasn't anything, not at that moment anyway. It was too soon.

He ignored her and said instead, still turned toward the car with his back to her, "I best be going now, Dani. I'll let Julia know you're okay with staying out here."

"Thank you." She nodded.

He opened his door, but suddenly looked back up at her. "Where've you been these ten years, Dani?"

Why are you back now? That was the unspoken question in the air.

She didn't answer. She didn't want to and she couldn't find the words anyway. Jake waited a beat, but when there was no response, he didn't look surprised. He got inside, started the engine, and pulled out of the driveway.

There was an extra heaviness on her heart, but ignoring it, she turned for the cabin and there he was. Leaning against her door, Jonah

Bannon flashed her that smirk again and dropped his arms that had been crossed over his chest. His hands slid into his pockets and a dimple in his right cheek winked at her. "Now, about that Mustang of yours…"

"No." Dani shook her head. "Why were you with him, anyway?"

He laughed. "When he heard you were here and he was coming with or without me. I just hitched a ride."

"It was a wasted trip." She stepped around him and pulled out the key. Unlocking the door, she stepped inside, but turned around to block him from following her. She placed a hand against the doorframe. "You should've gone back with Jake, because I'm not letting you in."

"Are you serious? I just want to—"

"I remember you from school, but that doesn't mean I know you. And I'm not talking about my car. It's not for sale and no, you can't take it for a ride if you were going to ask." She jerked her chin up, indicating behind him. "If I remember right, it's a long walk from here to your place. You should get going if you want to get home before dark."

Then she shut the door, locked it, and forgot about him, or tried to forget about it. She didn't really. He was in the back of her mind, but what she said had been true. She didn't know Jonah Bannon. She didn't owe him anything either. He wanted her car, that was obvious, but it wasn't until she got ready for bed that she started wondering if she'd been too hard on him. He came into the bar asking questions and not respecting the answers he was getting. He was like a tornado, but she had enough of those storms in her. She could only handle one at a time, and lying in bed, she hoped some of them were staying at bay.

She needed to sleep. Badly.

It was the screams first.

Then the babies started crying.

People running. It was so silent, but those footsteps. They were pounding on the pavement. People were rushing for their lives, and then an eerie moment of silence, and the water came down.

Gasping, Dani jerked awake. She moved to the edge of the bed and dragged in some air. Deep breaths. One in. One out. In. Out. She kept going, her eyes closed, and waited for her body to remember. She was safe. She wasn't there.

Safe.

I'm safe.

Dani could still hear the sirens in the distance, and she flinched, gritting her teeth.

"Hell." Dani cursed, catching a glimpse of the clock. Three in the morning. She'd gotten five hours of sleep. It had been almost three months since she had a full night's sleep.

She'd been given a card for times like this. If the nightmares kept coming, she'd need to talk. But that was the problem. Dani didn't talk unless it was necessary, but her hand still reached for her purse and pulled out the card. The number was bold and black, emblazoned for easy reading.

"You've been through an awful and horrible event in your life. You'll need help, and when you want it, it's there, Dani."

Fuck that. She'd get through this, like she got through everything else. Crumpling up the card, she stuffed it back in her purse. She stretched her neck, kneading the sore muscles there, and moved to the kitchen to get a bottle of water.

As she opened it and took a sip, she heard another voice in her head. This one was a dark baritone, and he'd only been trying to help her. *"I'm here if you decide to stop running. I'll always love you. You know that, but I can't keep following you around."*

Her hand twitched now, spilling water into the sink.

Her eyes caught sight of her bare finger and she held still. She couldn't look away. That man, that voice—he hadn't asked for what she did to him. Shame hung her head, but then she put the water away and glanced at the clock. Mae would probably still be awake.

A drive to Mae's Grill would help clear the nightmare from her mind.

After dressing, she headed out, but coming to the main highway, she let the car sit and idle a second. Just over the ditch, running alongside the highway was the town's livelihood.

Falls River.

It encompassed their entire state and wound its way through the next two and into Canada. Most of the workers who settled in Craigstown worked at the dam, not far north. It kept their town with food and fuel. And life. Many nights she remembered jumping off a certain bridge, not three miles from Mae's place.

Tenderfoot Rush was a bridge where everyone, every teen and every adult, had jumped off naked, dressed, or in swim trunks. Everyone did it. It was the favored pastime of the summer. If you couldn't find anyone in town, and it was over 100 percent humidity, just check Tenderfoot Rush. They were always there. The place was built on memories—from everyone. And so many decided to make the trek to Mae's Grill, just three miles south. Many tubing trips started at Tenderfoot Rush and pulled out at Mae's Grill.

There were still a few cars in the parking lot when she got there, and she heard yelling from inside as she opened the door. "Barney, get the hell out of here before I do something I'll regret. You hear me?!"

"Aw, come on, Mae. I don't got nowhere to sleep tonight. Can't drive. You made sure of that when you took my keys."

"I don't care. It's not my problem. If you get annihilated and think I'll let you drive out of here, just inviting a lawsuit against my bar— you're a fool. You drink, that means you're not driving, but you're still not my problem. Now get out of here!"

"But, Mae." He was slumped on his stool at the bar when Dani went inside. "I don't have anyone to call."

Mae slapped a towel on the counter. "Don't make me call that future nephew-in-law of mine. He'll arrest you."

"But I don't got no place to sleep, Mae." He whined again, settling his forehead on the counter again. He snorted. "Yeah, you call your nephew. He's marrying the side of family that don't want you around."

Barney had a death wish.

A second later his words penetrated his skull. His head jerked back up with wide eyes, and his cheeks lost color. "Oh, gosh—I didn't mean... Mae, that didn't come out right. I'm sorry—"

"You. Get. Out. Now." Her hands wrapped around the towel and she was wringing it, envisioning it was his neck.

"I's going, Mae. I didn't mean nothing by what I's just said. I mean it, Mae. I speak without a brain. I'm sorry, Mae." He made a scramble for the door. He turned back and opened his mouth, but nothing came out when he saw Dani standing just inside the door.

Mae heard his pause and turned, too.

"She sure is purrty, Mae."

Mae threw a bottle at him, which he ducked. It shattered against the wall, and Barney was out the door in a flash.

Mae's chest was heaving. Her nostrils flared. "Every damn night it's the same thing over and over. I'm getting tired of it. He needs help." She began wiping the counter, her hand moving in quick, savage circles.

Dani remained in one spot. She was still so damned tired, but she was thankful her aunt wasn't paying her much attention. She was still cursing under her breath. Dani tried to warm her hands and rubbed at her cheeks. She looked in the mirror before she left, and knew she looked like a ghost. She could still feel the nightmares. They clung to her like a wet blanket, but she needed to get rid of them. She needed to look alive when Mae really focused on her again. After hearing what Barney said, Dani was thinking she needed to be the one there for her aunt and not the other way around.

Mae was grumbling. "I should just make Jake kick him out of town. Barney don't got no family here, and he doesn't have a job. He's got nothing. Jake could take him out of town in his cruiser and let him hitchhike to the next town. He's got a soft spot for him." She kept going. Her hand moved faster and faster.

"Mae."

"No." Mae shook her head. "No, girl. You sit and help yourself to some coffee. I brewed a fresh batch not long ago. It takes all my energy to argue with that damn drunk. He's so stubborn, but no more. He always says he won't be a problem if I let him have the bottle, but he's always harping for a place to sleep."

Dani poured herself a mug and sat down. She couldn't help wondering if it was Barney who Mae was even talking about now.

"He don't got anyone. Why's he here?" She stopped scrubbing, brushing some of her hair off her forehead. "Yeah." Her voice was quiet now. "He should go, but he never does. Never will." Then it was like she remembered Dani was there. Mae blinked a few times, dropped the washcloth on the counter, and looked at her. "What are you doing here at this hour?"

Dani went for the easiest answer. "Jake stopped by earlier."

"He did?"

"Yeah." Dani took a sip as Mae leaned against the counter right across from her. "Julia doesn't want me out at the house. She doesn't even want me to see Aunt Kathryn."

Mae pushed back up from the counter with a sharp movement. "That—!" She heaved a deep sigh to calm herself. "Can't say I'm surprised. She's not going to like you being home." She eyed Dani. "She'll be worried you're going to take Jake away."

Dani felt there was a little more to that statement when Mae said it, and she put her mug back on the counter. "Is she the only one thinking that?"

Mae lifted up a shoulder. "People are talking. They're wondering."

"People are wondering about me?" Dani leaned forward, resting her elbows on the counter. "Or are you wondering?"

Small towns meant big mouths. Dani knew that. She'd always known that, but this gossip had been fast. Then again, she ran into

Kelley Lynn. Maybe she should've expected it after being in town only for one day.

Mae grabbed the washcloth again and began cleaning the counter where Dani sat. "I did before. I don't anymore. You're not the same you from before."

"What do you mean?" She reached for her coffee, but only sat there. Her hands grew cold, even holding that hot mug.

Mae shrugged again, finishing up her cleaning. She tossed the washcloth to the back kitchen. "You're not the same girl who left these parts ten years ago. I can see it in you, and I'm guessing that you've seen some of what life has to offer. I'm betting it's not the side that goes to operas and sings church hymns. It's big news when the middle O'Hara comes back to town after vanishing ten years ago. It's even bigger news when she left a slip of a girl and comes back a stunning young woman. Even if others can't tell, I can. You've got a backbone now. And this is the same girl who holds the title First Love on Jake's love life, but the question isn't how is Julia going to handle you being back." Mae watched her steadily. "It's you, so what are you going to do Dani? Is Jake the real reason you came back home?"

The air grew thick with tension.

Dani cut some of that tension as she said, "I didn't come back for Jake." That only answered part of her aunt's question, and the other part was a question she was starting to realize maybe others had as well.

Was she going to take him back?

Dani and Mae had a nightcap, and a conversation that was purposefully kept light-hearted, though Dani made sure to get some information on Jonah Bannon. She wanted to know whom she was dealing with, but after a second drink, she was able to sleep a few hours on Mae's couch. And it wasn't long after when she woke again, but this time it was from jet lag. No nightmares. Hearing Mae's soft snoring from her bedroom, she didn't want to wake her as she let herself out. Knowing she had no food at the cabin, other than what Mae always kept stocked there, she was in the grocery mart when she heard Jonah Bannon's slow drawl again. "Milk, eggs, cheese, yogurt, and, let me guess, you can't forget the chocolate. Every female I know has to have chocolate." He was right behind her.

His hair was wet like he just showered. He was clean shaven, and those same dark eyes that had been laughing at her yesterday still held their distinct cocky twinkle. Wearing a black hooded sweatshirt that molded perfectly to his form, Jonah looked good in the early hours of the morning, but Dani wasn't surprised.

She had a strong suspicion that Jonah *always* looked good.

"Please." She opened the freezer for a bag of frozen vegetables. "Mae told me you used to be a big shot head hunter before you came back to town. That means you're smart. I'm sure you could identify five food products every female has to have, but maybe stick to something that's not so stereotypical. We need to have our chocolate for our periods, right?"

Jonah cut a grin. "I heard you were the nice, shy O'Hara. You're not nice and shy now."

"My nasty side tends to come out when I have a thorn in my side. You, Jonah Bannon, are becoming that thorn."

She moved to another aisle, and he kept pace with her. "Okay, okay. I'm getting the message. The car's not for sale, but what about a ride?"

She stopped and shot him a look.

He held up his hands. "I know what you said before. No rides. But man, that is a seriously sweet car. You don't understand the agony of seeing it out and about, and not being able to give it a ride. Can you really blame a guy for trying?"

She grabbed a carton of milk, and started forward again.

Jonah got in front. "Put yourself in my shoes."

She frowned at him. "Is this really about my car? Or is there something else going on?"

"Huh?" He lowered his hands.

She was being paranoid. "Nothing. Sorry. I started to think you were another one of my sister's minions."

His eyebrows shot up. "You're funny, too. I've never met an O'Hara who was funny." He shook his head. "No. I'm not here because of your sister."

Their eyes caught and held, and an undercurrent passed between them. Dani couldn't help but murmur, "Not that sister, anyway."

Jonah sobered, resting his hands on the end of her cart. He said, quietly, "I wasn't sure if you remembered."

She nodded. Her insides swirling again. "I remembered." He dated Erica for a week. It hadn't been long, but Erica shouted it from the rooftop. It was one of the only arguments she had with Julia. Their oldest sister hadn't loved having Jonah Bannon dating their littlest. She kept claiming it was because he was a bad influence. Everyone knew it had nothing to do with that, and everything to do with her own jealousy.

"You didn't think Erica was funny?" Dani remembered his earlier words. "*Everyone* thought Erica was funny."

"Erica thought she was funny. That's good enough for most."

"But not you?"

His grin slipped a notch. "Are you trying to trip me up? Is that what this is?"

"I just want to hear some truth. Everyone raves about my sister. I didn't think there existed a person who didn't."

"Besides you?" Jonah searched her face. "And no, I didn't think Erica was funny. That's my truth."

"You just went up a notch, but only a notch." She bit the inside of her cheek to keep from grinning as she passed him to the checkout counter. "And I'm still not selling you my car. That's *my* truth."

He groaned, falling in line behind her. "A ride? One ride?"

They heard a gasp, and both looked over. The clerk had her hands pressed over her mouth, but she slapped them on the counter and came around. "If it isn't... Oh my goodness. I heard you were in town, but I didn't quite believe it. If it isn't little Dani O'Hara!"

Dani paused, eyeing the clerk for a moment. She was in her forties and it took a little bit for Dani to recognize her. "Mrs. Tatums." She taught piano to all three O'Haras. Julia and Erica excelled. Dani quit.

She grasped Dani's face in her hands and shook her. "I cannot believe it! It's been ages! How are you?" She pulled her in for a hug.

"I'm good." Dani's mouth was pressed into her shoulder.

"Oh dear!" She gushed again as she pulled back and held Dani at arm's length. "Mmmm mmm mmm. The rumors are indeedy true. You, my dear, left an ugly duckling and returned a swan. I can't get over this."

Then her eyes fell on Jonah, and went flat. "What are you doing here, Jonah?"

His grin was easy. "Early morning breakfast, Karen. I loved that coffee cake so much I ate it in one sitting."

"Stop playing with a married woman." Her cheeks reddened. "I have my mother's talent. The best coffee cake in seven counties now. It won champion at the fair last year, you know."

"Let's hope it wins again."

Mrs. Tatums tried to look disapproving, but the coffee cake won out. "Oh, you, Jonah. So charming." She returned behind the counter and began ringing Dani's things up. Her eyes slid to Dani. "You better watch out, Dani. If you're seen with the likes of Jonah Bannon, there's going to be other rumors spread around." She winked at her. "If you know what I mean."

She didn't, but she could guess. Dani's smile was a little more forced as she waited to pay for her things. She held her tongue, waiting as everything was bagged up. After paying, she waved to her old piano teacher, and headed for the door. She muttered under her breath, "Now I remember why I quit after five lessons. You old bat..."

She trailed off, seeing Jonah right behind her.

His smile spread a little wider and he held his hands up. "I didn't have anything to buy, and I have some advice for you." His head leaned forward an inch. "If you want to get out of a conversation with her, just bring up Mr. Mells. You can say anything about him, but he was her competition in town. Both taught piano lessons and she hates him. If she thinks you're going to start gushing about him, she'll end that conversation real quick."

"Thanks. I'll keep that in mind."

She stowed her things in the back seat, and reached for her door. She paused. "Um." She looked back up. "You haven't said anything to make me think this, but just in case your interest really isn't about my car, I'm not here to compete with either of my sisters." Before she knew what she was saying, she heard herself being more honest with him than anyone else. "I left a really great man behind and I didn't come back to find a replacement for him. I'm not home for any of that."

She got inside, or attempted to. Jonah stopped her. Just as she was about to close the door, he caught it. "Hey. Wait."

Before he could say anything more, she added, "That might not be what's going on here. I know. I could be speaking out of turn and you might really *only* want to drive my car, but it doesn't matter to others." She pointed around the street and sidewalks. "They're already talking about me, and as much as I hate to give that Old Bat some credit, she is right about one thing. If people see us talking, or you driving my car, you know what they're going to think. I didn't come back to deal with any of that either."

He shifted closer to the door, lowering his voice. "I know what my reputation is and sometimes it's earned. Other times it's the furthest from the truth. I get what you're doing, but here's my advice to you—you don't have a reputation yet. People can't figure you out right now because you're not the same as when you left. That could be bad for you. They'll give you a rep you might not want. Your ex, for one. People are going to assume you're here for him, until you show them you're not."

"I'm not here for Jake either."

"Okay." He pointedly nodded to the car. "Then let yourself be seen with me. Being seen with me will counteract any other rumor." He leaned even closer to her. "If it's not me, it should be someone else. It won't hurt you to be seen with someone other than Jake Sullivan."

"Jake was my best friend all my life."

"He's engaged to your sister, and you're going to need friends."

"That's what you're offering?"

"If I can get a joyride in this magnificent piece of machinery, then yes." He tapped her car door. "I'm offering."

"You sure your reputation is only half-true?" Dani grinned as she got inside and started the engine. Jonah closed the door for her. "My aunt also said you're a ladies' man. Been with half the town."

He grinned down at her, and Dani ignored the little flutter she felt. He winked at her. "Let me come by the cabin later and I'll show you how much of a gentleman I can be. You know I'm itching to get underneath this hood."

Her body grew warm, and was getting warmer the more they talked. She schooled her features so they were almost a glare. Or she was trying. "You better be talking about my car."

"Of course." That dimple was winking again at her. "What else would I be talking about? I'm a gentleman, remember?"

She groaned, but then she heard herself answering, "I'll be around this evening." What was she doing?

"Sounds good. See you around six, and I like my steak medium-rare."

Steak? She had to cook for him now? He held a hand up and headed across the road. She was about to pull out into traffic when she heard the short warning signal of a cop's sirens.

She looked over.

Jake had pulled up next to her.

Shit.

Dani cut the engine and sat back to wait. Jake had a partner in the passenger seat, but when he climbed out, his partner stayed. And it wasn't Jonah this time, but a woman. And judging by the glower on his face, he didn't look like he wanted to have a few words. He looked ready to rip into her about something.

Before Jake could say anything, she nodded at his car. "Who's your partner?"

"My partner."

"Yeah. Got that. Who is it?" Dani craned her neck, trying to get a better look around him.

"Oh," Jake remarked, a bit sheepish. "That's Kate Daily."

"Kate Daily's a cop?!"

Kate Daily was the female version of Jonah, or her reputation claimed. She probably felt the counselor and principal's office were second or third homes to her own. She'd been known for cutting class, smoking on school property. Thinking back, Dani knew the girl had been into more than just sex, cigarettes, and skipping school. The tracks on her arms announced it to the world.

Kate Daily was now a cop. Dani was stunned.

"Yeah."

"I didn't know small-town cops got partners."

"It's new. We're trying it out."

"Julia likes that you have a female partner?"

"Dani." He shook his head. "Don't start."

There it was. The old Jake and Dani. He spoke to her, using his soft voice, how he used to when they dated. And like back then, she answered. The wall fell, and for a brief moment, they were eighteen again. Dani watched him, her head against her seat's headrest, and a silence fell over them.

Jake began to drum his fingers on the door.

Dani grinned. That was his thing whenever he was anxious, but didn't know what to say. His fingers would strum up and down on whatever surface they were resting on. Jake always prided himself on being a stellar poker player, but it just wasn't true. She knew all his tells.

He cleared his throat. "You sleep good last night?"

"I slept alright."

"I know that cabin is a good distance from civilization." He tugged at his collar, hunching his shoulders forward. "If you're ever scared, you know, just give me a call."

"And wake Julia? And have her know that you're running off to help me?" Julia would throw a fit, and they both knew it. "So the next time I wake up at three in the morning, I'm supposed to call you, and Julia will be okay with that?"

"Don't play this game. I know what you're doing. You're pushing my buttons, and you're trying to piss me off."

"Is it working?"

"It's too early for something like this. I don't want to play games with you."

"Well, tough." Dani expelled a deep breath. She was over Jake, had been for years, but a bubble of anger rose up in her. "You screwed me for years, screwed Erica after that, and now you got Julia. You don't want to play, you should date outside the O'Hara pool."

"What happened to you?" He took a step back. "You were never this bitter before."

"I come home and find that you're still playing puppet to one of my sisters. Don't act outraged that I'm tired of it."

"Dani—"

"Let's get some things straight. You asked where I was, but we both know you want to know why I left. You were part of the reason, but you weren't the total reason." She narrowed her eyes. "And when I say you were part of it, I'm meaning that you're the one who kept me here. Once you were gone, I was gone."

Jake glanced over his shoulder. Kate had gotten out of her seat and approached the car. She looked good. That was Dani's first thought. The Kate from her day had been skinny, dressed in goth, and had a chip on her shoulder telling the world to go to hell. This Kate had gained about ten pounds, had a soft smile, and even smoother skin. She looked happy.

"So the rumors are true." Kate waved a hand. "Hi, Dani. It's been a long time."

They'd never talked except for one time. Both had been ordered to the counselor's office. In the lobby, Kate cursed at her, and Dani moved down a seat. That had been the extent of the interaction and their history.

"Kate."

"How you holding up against the Craigstown scrutiny?"

"Oh, you know, the power of one eye twitch can go a long way."

"Yeah." Kate laughed, resting on one hip. "The nonverbals in this town are legendary. I remember in school. I'd walk through a store, and by the time I finished making one trip, there were twenty different stories made up. I was either going to to rob the place or blow the owner's son. Those were the two main ones."

"Kate, do you mind?" Jake gestured to Dani before his hand fell back to rest on his holstered gun. "We were in the middle of something."

Dani held up a hand. "Ignore him. I'd rather talk to you."

"Dani."

Kate's gaze skirted between the two, then she glanced in the direction Jonah had gone. "So, is it true? Are you and Jonah Bannon an item? That's what I heard from one of the regulars at the Piggly Squiggly. Everyone is talking about the two of you."

"Kate!"

"What?" She looked at Jake.

The ends of his mouth turned down in sharp disapproval, and he crossed his arms over his chest. "I can't believe you listen to that stuff. That's just all rumors and gossip."

"Say what you want. You get the best dirt there." Kate shrugged. "So, is it true, Dani? You and Jonah Bannon?"

"Kate." Jake's laugh came out sounding forced. "Dani and Jonah? Seriously. If those two aren't the oddest and complete opposites, then I don't know who is—"

"Like you and Julia?" Dani interrupted.

Jake fell silent.

Kate remarked, "And opposites sometimes attract, Jake."

"Or you and Erica?"

Jake shook his head. "That's completely different."

"How come?"

Kate closed her mouth as her eyes darted between the two. She edged back a step.

"Dani."

"Jake."

"Come on." He now laughed. "What are you—are you serious? You and Jonah? Jonah Bannon?"

Jake had no right commenting or speculating on her love life. He'd been a part and played his part well, but he was out. He'd been out for a long, long time. He had no place passing judgment, no matter what was the truth.

She lifted her chin up. "Maybe."

He went still. "Are you serious?"

Kate commented out of the side of her mouth, "I think you should be asking yourself why you care so much."

"Kate." Jake shot her a glare, and it shut her up.

Dani sighed. She was suddenly done with this conversation. Jake was jealous, but that was old news. He'd been jealous in high school too, and there'd been no basis for it then. She loved him, completely and whole-heartedly, and seeing him yesterday took her back there. It'd been brief, but hearing that same shit from him now, she was over it.

She was grateful to him for one thing, and that was realizing she truly *was* over what they had. She could safely answer Mae's questions if she was going to get Jake back. She didn't want him. Julia was welcome to him, but as for the rest of her aunt's questions: Dani still wasn't ready to admit them even to herself.

Her sister had been buried. She had been clothed, prayed upon, and blessed. She had been put into the earth's dirt. It was something that Dani was beyond familiar with. Feeling the same emptiness that haunted her at night, she heaved a deep breath and shook her head clear. She couldn't expel the shiver that ran down her back, putting the hairs on her neck straight up.

"Hello?"

Startled, Dani jumped and cursed.

"Sorry." Jonah poked his head through the open door.

Dani realized that she'd forgotten to shut it. After leaving town, she went to the cemetery. She hadn't planned on going, but she found herself parking along the gravel driveway. That was as far as she got, though. She stared at the set of tombstones where she guessed Erica was buried. She would've been put next to their mom's grave. And sitting there a full thirty minutes, Dani couldn't make herself get out. When she got back to the cabin, she couldn't remember what she did for the rest of the afternoon. She remembered making coffee, and with a jerk, she was still standing in her kitchen.

Her coffee was cold now.

"What time is it?"

He checked his watch. "It's about six-ish. You were going to let me drive the car, remember?"

"Oh, yeah." She frowned. "I, uh...sorry. I was just..." She pushed away from the counter and dumped the coffee into the sink. "I got busy and forgot all about tonight."

"That's okay." He produced a package from behind his back. "Two steaks. I wasn't sure if you went back in the store for them after this morning, so I did."

"Thank you."

"Yeah." Jonah nodded and moved to her side. "Do you want to spice those up? I'll go and light the grill."

He was out the door as her hand came up to take the steaks from him. He'd already placed them on the counter, and she could hear him removing the cover from the grill outside.

Her mother once told her that spices attracted the best magic. They each had their own purpose. Garlic protected the soul against invading temptations. Oregano protected against cynicism. Parsley protected against old age. Her mother would go down the list, and Dani would sit there, mesmerized by everything her mother told her. She remembered lying in bed that night, and as she would look up at the ceiling, all the spices danced above her. They each twinkled, protecting her against the world.

Dani believed that for the longest time.

As she took the steaks out of the wrappings and placed them on a plate, Dani perused Aunt Mae's old spice rack. Her eyes fell on the ginger, and for a moment, her fingers lingered. She knew the truth by now.

There was no magic.

There was no protection.

"Those steaks ready?" Jonah called from outside.

Dani went outside. "I don't like my meat spiced."

"Okay." Jonah cast her an easy grin and flipped open the grill top. As he put the steaks inside, he asked, "You got anything else in there that you want grilled? I know some folks like a roasted corncob every now and then."

A moment later, with slabs of butter placed inside the corn's husk, Dani sat on the porch's step as she watched Jonah flip the meat and everything else on the grill. She grabbed a few more vegetables and put them in tinfoil for the grill.

"You know," Jonah began, his back turned to her. "The steaks look like my best work, if I have to say so myself." He glanced at her and flashed a grin as he began to fill the plate with their food. Placing it on the porch's table, he asked, "Got anything around here to drink? Maybe even some utensils?"

She'd forgotten to prepare the table.

She'd forgotten about a lot.

"I'm sorry. I was just..." Dani trailed off and saw that he wasn't even waiting for a reply. Jonah had already ducked inside and emerged with most everything they needed. Plates. Forks. Knives. Butter. Salt. Two glasses and a pitcher of water.

She took the plates from his hand, and they arranged the table with the food in the middle. When she sat down, Jonah still stood. She cast a questionable grin his way, and Jonah chuckled, pulling out a bottle of beer from his back pocket.

"We can share, if you tell me one thing."

"What's that?"

"Why you love that car so much."

She'd been to hell and back, and that car was the only thing that still stood intact. "I bought that car with money I earned and because my sisters hated it."

"I bet their boyfriends loved it."

"That made them hate it even more." Dani grinned. It was true. Julia had thrown more than her share of fits. She threatened, she pleaded, she cried, and every time—Aunt Kathryn and Erica would get pulled into it. Aunt Kathryn hated that car almost as much as Julia and Erica.

"I know I did."

Dani looked up. *Erica...*

He pulled back the parted husks. "I'd never been to your home except one time. I saw your car, and I asked Erica about it, if it was hers, who owned it. Questions like those. Your sister blew up, literally just—she went off like a firecracker."

"Bet that made her hotter."

"No." Jonah laughed. "I guess I was always grateful in some way."

"What do you mean?"

"I don't know." He shifted and leaned his elbows on the table, holding the corn just before his mouth. "I think—when I asked those questions about your car, your sister's lid flew off, and I always thought that I got a window to the future. I saw a little into your sister. Scared the shit out of me. I tucked tail and ran."

"She was so mad, too," Dani noted, grinning. She still hadn't moved to place any food on her plate. Her hands hadn't left her lap. "You never dated Julia."

"Ah nah. She was always kinda quiet around my crew, but some of the guys were into her. I wasn't. Nah—I wanted to know who the owner of the Mustang was."

"How come you never said anything?"

"We were at the Rush one day, and I saw you pull up to pick up Erica. I was going to come over then, but when you got out of the car..." Jonah shrugged. "I just...you had this look about you that..."

"What?"

"When I saw you, I recognized you from around town. I never really took notice of you, but that day at Tenderfoot—it looked like you wanted to be anywhere but around there. And then Erica snapped at you, and she made you wait for her."

Erica wanted to finish hearing about Kelley Lynn's date with Ted Foster. Dani knew from previous experience that Erica would make her wait for hours. Dani hadn't wanted to wait. So when Erica turned her back on her, after chewing her head off, Dani turned right around and got inside the Mustang.

She laughed now at the memory. "I left her. She screamed my head off that night. I got the silent treatment for two weeks." Those two weeks had been a vacation.

"Yeah." Jonah grinned over his corncob at her. "Your sister was pissed."

"You never introduced yourself to me because of that?"

"I never introduced myself because I saw why you didn't want to deal with the rest of us. Every time I saw you, you were always walking away from something or someone."

She left. She did it her entire life. She just left and walked away. She left her family. She left for ten years.

I'm here if you decide to stop running…

She left everything that she had in the last ten years too.

Jonah began cutting into his steak. "I always felt that I would've been pestering you if I ever said hello or something."

Dani's plate was still untouched. Her hands had yet to leave her lap.

He added, holding her gaze, "Truth is, you kinda intrigued me after that day when you ditched your sister. I thought it took balls for someone to do that to Erica O'Hara. No one did that. All those girls worshipped the ground your sister walked on, but I thought you must've had steel in that spine of yours to do what you did."

"I was her sister." Her voice grew hoarse. She didn't know what compelled her, but she heard herself saying, "When I left, I traveled a bunch. I wanted to be something else than what I'd always been here. I worked here and there, but there was this group. I got involved with them, and at first it was great. We laughed, we drank, we…they were nice to me." Then things changed. "This one girl, her name was Parker. She—she had this thing for this guy who started traveling with us."

I'm here…

She swallowed a lump in her throat, and kept going. "She was a little like Erica. She got all the guys, but she wanted this one guy and he wanted me. So she started to hate me, and then the group did too."

"Hi." He had dark eyes, dark hair, and a warm smile. He looked like Jake, but he wasn't Jake. He offered his hand, and said as she shook it, "I'm Mitch, but call me Boone."

Boone chose her.

"I went off on my own again."

Boone went with her.

She remembered when she shook his hand. It was sturdy, the tiniest bit rough like he wasn't used to manual labor until recently, and she blushed that night. She felt her cheeks now. She was blushing again. "Sorry." She ducked her head, laughing softly. "I don't remember what I was talking about."

"What happened to the guy?"

Boone had fallen in love with her. "Nothing." It didn't matter. She left him, too. "I'm a walker. That's what I do. I walk away."

"I know."

Her breath caught in her throat. She stared into those eyes. He was serious, but there was depth there. "You're not what everyone says you are, are you?"

"That depends on what they say?" He gave her a half-grin.

"You're a ladies' man. You can charm your way into anyone's pants. You're a heartbreaker." But as she was saying that, she couldn't remember if those words had been used to describe him or if it was her own memory. She remembered what Mae said about him that first night over their nightcap. "Mae told me you're dangerous to a hurting heart."

His half-grin lessened. "Really?"

"I think that was her way of warning me to steer clear of you. She said you moved back to Craigstown a few years ago."

"A few, around three. I take care of the river now."

"You were a big head hunter before."

He nodded, half-grin was almost gone. "I worked for my father's company for a bit. Yeah."

She frowned. She couldn't remember anything about his parents from before. "Your father?" She remembered he had a sister.

"My sister and I grew up here with my mom. She let us believe that our dad didn't want anything to do with us, but that changed when she died. Lawyers had to involve him and suddenly he wanted back into our lives again. I was a junior in school. Aiden was a senior. I went to college on his dime and worked at his company for a while." His eyes grew downcast, and he cleared his throat. "I didn't like who I was becoming, so I decided to change. I've never regretted it for a second." He looked up, looking right into her eyes. "How about you? Anything you regret?"

So much.

It was on the tip of her tongue. She swallowed those words and instead said, forcing a small laugh out, "I know one thing that people think I'm going to do, but I'm not. I'm not going to break up Jake and Julia, and I'm not going to regret not doing that." She laughed again, this time it was less forced.

"That's good to know, but I'm not here to find out that information either."

"You're here for my car."

"Not really."

"You're here for a ride."

"That'd be nice."

There was a different look in his eyes. Something more. He didn't react to her comment about the car, not like before. It was like... She cocked her head to the side. "You're not here about the car, are you?"

He shrugged. "I'd still like to take it for a ride, but no. The car was an excuse. The fair's tomorrow. You going?" He moved his fork around his plate and sank it into his last piece of meat. "I think you should go. You can go with Aiden if you want."

"Your sister?" Dani asked in surprise.

"Yeah. She and Kate are going together. They're good friends." He rolled his eyes. "Kate usually shows up Friday nights, and the two of them gossip about every girl I've ever dated. That's what friends do, right?"

"Gossip?"

"Yeah."

"I wouldn't know."

"You should get some." Jonah placed his cup on the table. "You're right, you know. Everyone thinks you're after Jake and Julia. I know that my presence is supposed to help assuage that, but it'd be good if you were friends with my sister. Kate also."

"And why's that?"

"Because Aiden is not friends with Julia." He cleared his throat. "And that's all I'm going to say. I'm not getting anymore involved."

"What?" She heard herself tease. "Too good for the gossip scene?"

"Exactly."

His eyes darkened. "Come to the fair. I honestly think my sister would love seeing you again."

"Are you going to be there?"

His grin deepened. "I might be around, but I have to warn you." He'd finished eating, and he stood with his plate in hand. He said, before heading inside, "If you don't agree to come, either my sister or Kate is going to show up to help convince you." He disappeared beyond the door, but she heard him call back, "Don't say I didn't warn you!"

She *had* been warned.

Jonah stayed to help with the dishes, despite her reassurances she didn't mind cleaning up. He only shook his head and filled up the sink. He washed. She dried, and he kept asking her questions about her travels. Once he was done, he helped finish with the drying, and then gave a wave as he repeated his warning once again about the fair. He said, "Don't be surprised if one of them show up tomorrow."

And it was a day later, after she'd gotten her first good night's sleep in a long time, when she heard a car honking from the driveway. Dani moved to the front door to see Jake scowling from his squad car. He stayed sitting while the passenger door opened.

"Hey, Dani!" Kate got out and approached, a friendly smile and wave.

Dani was holding a cup of coffee and raised it in the air as a greeting. "Morning. Would you like a cup?"

Kate groaned, closing her eyes a moment and swaying on her feet. "That sounds amazing." She jerked a thumb over her shoulder. "I've been dealing with cranky ass all morning. I need caffeine since I can't have anything stronger till I get off-duty. And I have to tell you," Kate began as the door slammed shut behind her. "I swear that Julia is a greyhound. It's like she can just sniff out whiffs of you on his uniform or something. Whatever she said must've been a doozy."

Dani held out a cup. "I didn't realize the power of my presence."

"Are you kidding me?" Kate snorted, taking the cup. "I might have to deal with Crabby out there, but trust me when I say that this is the most fun our town has had in a year."

"Really?"

"Oh, hell yeah." Taking a sip, she continued, "And speaking of the town, that's why I'm here. I know Jonah mentioned the fair, but I don't think you have a complete understanding of what's going on." She raised her cup toward Dani. "I'm here to fill you in."

Dani hid her smile.

Suddenly a more reserved expression came over Kate's face. The little spark dimmed in her eyes, and her mouth moved into a serious line. "I'm taking some liberties coming to you and talking about this, but I hope that's okay with you. Also, I feel like I'm already involved because of my sour-puss partner out there."

Dani prepared herself. "I'm ready." She nodded at Kate, folding her hands on her lap. Her own coffee was left on the table. Dani had a feeling she needed to hear this head-on. No distractions.

"Politics. That's what this town is about. Small. Town. Politics. And you, my dear, just threw yourself smack in the middle of it. You see, most of this town worshipped your little sister, blessed be her name, but...your other sister—she's been walking around this town like she's got a crown on that head of hers." A hardened look entered Kate's eyes. "Most of us are tired of it. Really tired of it, and that's where you come in."

"Me?"

"Yep, because you are going to take Jake back from her. We all know he was rightfully yours in the first place." She leaned forward. "And when you do—"

Ah. Kate *really* didn't like Julia. Dani nodded, filling in the blanks. "Julia will be a puddle."

"Exactly." Kate lifted her cup in a salute. "And her group will be knocked out of power. People like Jake in the community, but they don't like him with Julia."

"And I'm supposed to be the one to break them up."

"Exactly." Kate beamed at her, missing the sarcasm in Dani's voice. "Except that I have no intention of getting back together with Jake."

"Really?" Her eyes rounded, like a sad puppy dog. "You don't?"

"I don't."

"Are you sure? I thought I saw a flirt going on yesterday."

"No flirt."

"No?"

Dani shook her head. "No."

"You sure?" Kate asked again.

"I'm sure."

"Can I ask why not?"

"I didn't come home with an agenda for small-town politics or to knock my sister off her throne. I came home...just to come home."

"Well, I'm disappointed." Kate sighed, leaning back in her seat with her shoulders slumped. The battle just defeated her. "I was so hoping. You stole my entire thunder I had going all day yesterday. I had everything worked out in my mind and there'd be 'happily ever afters' all around for everyone."

"Why don't *you* steal Jake from Julia?" Dani would've laughed if she hadn't been taking a sip of coffee as she saw the horror come in to Kate's eyes. "Or not."

"Hell no. I like him as my partner, but that's it for me. Man." She sighed again, the corners of her mouth dipping down. "This just means that Julia has him for good. Jake's never dated outside the O'Hara gene pool. He's doomed forever."

"Maybe he's actually happy with her?"

"No. That can't be." Kate shook her head. "I was so hoping to get you on board."

"You said the rest of you are tired of her. Who's the rest of you?"

"Me. Aiden and Bubba. Oh, those two married. Her and Bubba Meadows. And Robbie Gray—he's a lawyer, you know. And it's perfect because Kelley Lynn is his secretary. Sometimes we ask him to find out what they're all planning."

"Robbie Gray? Wasn't he—"

"Tall, skinny, and nerdy? Yep. A social misfit just like the rest of us, except that he's tall, dark, gorgeous, and rich now. He's not a social misfit anymore, but he remembers his roots. He's a good friend."

Catching a note in her voice, Dani grinned. Kate had a thing for the attorney. That was interesting, and she could handle interesting for someone else, just not her own issues. She needed to be uninteresting.

"Why don't you ask him out?"

"Jake? We already went over this."

"No. The other guy. Robbie." Dani picked up her coffee, but only held it, frowning. "Or did I get that wrong?"

Kate's own frown was almost a glower. "No. You got it right, but Brooke Richter and Lori Hayden are duking it out over him."

Dani was pretty sure they both had been cheerleaders, or on the dance team. "Are they still...?"

"They're still gorgeous."

After Kate's high school transformation, she now looked almost average. The brown hair fell to her shoulders, and she was no longer the skinny skeleton she'd been back then. She filled out, and while some guys loved the wholesome, healthy look—most guys either went for the dark hair, dark eyes, sensual lips kinda look, or girls who looked like Brooke Richter and Lori Hayden.

Kate slapped a hand on the table, excited again. "What about Jonah Bannon?"

The coffee was lowered back to the table. "What about him?" Dani sat back, her frown forming again.

"I was joking yesterday, but *is* there something going on between you? That'd be great. Jonah's better than Jake. I'd love watching my partner squirm. I didn't know he had it in him to snipe so much as he did yesterday. Bannon this and Bannon that. All I heard yesterday." Kate continued, "And Jake's worshipped the ground Jonah walks on, until yesterday. That all changed now."

"Kate."

"Huh?"

"I'm really here just to do my own thing. Nothing else."

"So, no Jonah?"

"No Jonah."

"Oh." She sighed. "Okay. I'll get over it. You should still come to the fair tonight with us. I even made Robbie promise not to bring Brooke or Lori. It's a date-free night, except for Bubba. He doesn't count anyway since he's Aiden's husband, and Julia's going to be gone for the weekend. She's at some clinic or conference, or something. She won't even be there."

"Who's all going?"

"Me, Robbie, Aiden, and Bubba, and I think Stilts is coming, too."

"Stilts?"

"He migrated from Northway, but he's fun. Just the group. Jonah will probably be with his crew. Hawk, Gee, Cory Lyles, those guys. I don't know if you remember them from school, but they're all still friends. Badasses back then. Badasses now. Well," she amended, "they're more responsible now, but no. They'll be at the beer gardens, and it's a little disgusting to watch women fall over themselves for Jonah. Although, Aiden likes to rate them all later when we're at her house. Jonah doesn't much appreciate it, especially when she gives the reasoning for her ranks too. If you want entertainment—that's funny!"

Did she want to go? No.

Should she go? Yes.

"When and where?" She accepted her defeat.

"Seriously?" Kate broke into a wide smile. "We're going around eight thirty to check all the barns, and we'll end up at the beer gardens later that night. This is great, Dani. What's your number?"

Dani wrote her number down, and around nine that night, she was at the beer gardens. It was set up inside a white barn, with two large green-painted doors opened. Picnic tables were spread out all over the inside, with a section in one corner where beer was being sold. From where Dani stood, she could see a thick crowd had formed as people waited to pay for their cups. Some left with a pitcher filled and a stack of plastic cups in the other hand. The entire place was still warm. Dani's hair stuck to the back of her neck. She knew it'd be even hotter inside, but two large barn fans were set up outside the entrance and she spied another one by a side door. Even over the fans' loud noise, she could still hear loud murmurs of conversations, laughter, and cheering inside.

She wondered if she should try the side door. She could sneak in and see if she spotted the rest, but Kate called earlier and said everyone was running late. Dani came a bit later than she had planned. Kate instructed her to look around the beer gardens first. The group was going to congregate there before going through the animal barns. She hoped to avoid walking into the beer gardens alone, but looking around—"Hey."

Jake was behind her, dressed in a blue polo and jeans. His hair was wet, and he ran a hand through the wet locks. He was dressed for the evening, but that wasn't whom she saw. He held a confused look in his eyes, like he was still wondering if she was staying or going and Dani didn't think it was about being at the beer gardens. His shoulders slumped forward, he put his hands in his pockets. In that moment, she saw the little boy who'd been her best friend. The boy who always shuffled behind her, kicking rocks ahead with his hands stuffed in his front pockets.

She felt an ache at the memory, but he jerked his head toward the corner. "You going in there?"

"Thinking about it."

"Yeah. Me, too." He itched behind his ear. "Look, You and Jonah— you two are so opposite. I just...it kinda spun me. The thought of you with someone else. I know lots of years have passed, and realistically you've probably been with other guys, but it feels like we just broke up last week. I don't know if that makes sense. We broke up and you were gone the next day. I didn't have time to..."

"Adjust."

"Yeah."

"I'm not here to take you away from my sister."

"I know."

Did he? Because she didn't want to deal with him thinking that, or saying something to her sister so she thought that, too. Good gracious.

She had enough on her plate. She studied him a moment, but didn't push it. She supposed that was an issue she'd have to wait and see how it played out, and hearing an outburst of laughter, she gestured behind her. "I think..."

"Okay. Yeah." Jake nodded as he stayed put.

"You're not coming?"

"I'm going to sit tight for a little while."

Dani took a second look. He was exhausted. He either didn't want to be seen going in with her or he wanted a moment to collect himself. The Jake she knew always liked those brief seconds before. He liked to ready himself.

"Okay." Dani nodded and turned the corner.

Maybe she should've taken a page from Jake's book and gotten prepared, because once she stood in that doorway, she was *so* not prepared. It was like in the movies. People saw her and the room grew quiet. It sounded like a collective hush, and Dani knew the cause. She began to turn away. It was instinct, to run, but she stopped herself. That wouldn't help either.

Someone laughed in the corner and stood up, starting a slow clap. "The rumors are true, and our mysterious friend has returned home!"

The lighting inside was dim, but Dani thought she recognized Aiden Bannon.

The clapping took off, slow and tentative at first, but then thunderous and fast by the end. Dani was fighting against rolling her eyes. She didn't want to piss people off further. Dani's ears were ringing from the clapping.

She waved both hands in the air. "Okay. Stop. Please."

It took a little bit, but when it was quiet enough, someone yelled out, "Where you been, Dani?"

"Looking good!"

"Damn good!"

A few wolf whistles and laughter broke out, but Dani ducked her shoulders and moved to the back corner where she thought Aiden was located.

She was right.

Around a table in the back, she spotted Aiden, Jonah's sister, with her husband. (His massive bulk hadn't changed or gotten softer over the years.) Kate sat alongside who Dani figured was Robbie Gray (Kate was right—tall, dark, and gorgeous now). And another guy with a medium build and dark hair pulled into a ponytail.

"Hey, Dani!" Kate called out, coming toward her. She hooked her elbow, pulling her closer to the table. "Let me introduce and re-introduce."

She turned toward Aiden and Bubba first. As they were introduced, Dani couldn't help but think how these people had never been her friends, yet they seemed to want to be her friends now. Growing up how she did, with whom she did, she instantly wondered what their agenda was, but no. Jonah didn't operate like that, and this was his sister. Kate might've had her own goal, but Dani told herself to relax. Aiden was always known to be kind. Dani searched for any malice intent in her wide and soft eyes, but she couldn't find any. Jonah's sister shared his genes. While he was dark and lean, she was blonde and petite, but both had the same striking eyes. They shared the same cheekbones as well.

"Dani." Kate pointed to ponytail guy. "This is Stilts. I told you that he migrated from Northway—"

"I'm not a goose or a bear, Katey. I didn't migrate. It's not like I go north during the summers and south for the winters."

"You're my big teddy bear, Stilts." Aiden laughed as she leaned closer to him, resting against his shoulder. It was obvious they were close. He gazed down at her with genuine affection, his eyes warming.

He said, "Then you can say I migrated, but not you, Kate. I'm not a damn goose."

"Everyone from Northway should migrate to Craigstown. You're just the only goose in the town with a brain." Kate laughed, unhooking her elbow from Dani's.

Robbie reached around her laughing form and extended a hand. "Hi, Dani. Remember me? I know we didn't know each other that well, but times change. Thank goodness, right?"

"Hi, Robbie. I *do* remember you."

"Take a seat." He pointed to the empty stool on Kate's other side. "It's good to see you again."

"Dani!" Kate pointed. "Please tell Stilts that he kinda looks like a goose. See, his mouth and chin could be a beak, you know—one of those long, black beaks."

"It's nice to meet you, Dani." Stilts offered his hand. "Don't mind these guys. Not only are they drunk, but their maturity levels return to high school where it must've been cool to pretend everyone was some form of bird. And speaking of, Kate, if you're going to liken me to poultry, at least let it be something cool. Like—"

"A turkey!" Aiden shouted, giggling.

"This is going from bad to worse."

"I know." Bubba leaned forward, and everyone quieted. "You could be one of those flamingos."

Aiden and Kate shrieked, throwing their hands back.

"The goose was better." Stilts groaned. He said to Dani, "They've been drinking. You can't tell at all, right?" He winked.

Dani noted the eight empty glasses left on the table. They'd gotten there earlier than expected.

Robbie thumped him on the shoulder. "Chin up, mate. Kate told me I was an opossum the first five months I got back."

"She has to be an animal." Stilts pointed to Dani.

"Uh..." Dani was caught. She was half-amused and half-horrified.

"She's a swan." Kate smiled. And Dani blinked at the sincerity in that smile.

Then everything was interrupted.

Jonah drew abreast the table, and his sister lunged for him, hugging him. Three other guys followed him—Dani remembered Hawk from high school. They'd been the bad boys everyone wanted be with, or just to be like. Jonah had been their leader with Hawk as his best friend and enforcer. With the same Mohawk, an even bigger muscular build, and tattoos covering his neck, Dani shuddered. He looked like he was *still* the best enforcer.

"Oh—" Jonah grimaced as he caught Bubba's gaze. "My little sis is drunk. Good job, brother-in-law."

Bubba shrugged and grinned. And took a large gulp of his own drink.

"Oh." Aiden swatted at her brother, and missed. "What are you all crabby about?"

Jonah looked up and caught Dani's gaze, but he answered, "Nothing." He shrugged off her hold. "Take my sister, Bubs. I gotta get a drink."

Kate gasped. "How many tonight, do you think, Aiden?"

"You guys." Jonah groaned.

"Oh." Aiden scrunched her face, concentrating. "I'm thinking...five girls tonight."

"Yep." Kate gave Jonah the once-over. "Definitely five—at least. He's got the trendy jeans on tonight with his white T-shirt. He'll get, at least, five tonight."

Jonah rolled his eyes and left with Hawk. The rest followed behind.

"I hate my brother. I hate how he got the good genes in the family."

"Excuse me?" Kate asked in disbelief. "Do you not see yourself? You're gorgeous, Aiden. You know the one girl who is so beautiful that she's above scrutiny from anyone else? That's you." She snorted. "Thank God you're nice. Otherwise you'd be a bitch."

"Oh, please." Aiden rolled her eyes.

"Dani." Kate looked to her. "Tell me that you agree."

"Kate's right."

Aiden snorted, gesturing to her. "Have you looked in the mirror, Dani? You've got one of those stunning serene looks that make men just drool. Literally." Aiden stuck out her tongue. "I'm not like that."

Bubba wrapped his arms around his wife and murmured something in her ear. Aiden blushed and turned to whisper back.

Kate shook her head, a fond smile lingering over her mouth as she watched the married couple. It was evident how close everyone was, and Dani had a feeling this conversation had been brought up a few times.

Finishing his drink, Robbie stood up, and asked her, "Dani, what do you drink?"

"Nothing. Not tonight, anyway."

"Come on. That's why we're at the beer gardens. Fair only comes once a year." Kate held up her glass. "You know my drink."

Robbie gave her a similar fond look that she'd just been wearing, and he took her glass. "Only a few more, then you had too many."

"Come on. I'm off-duty tonight."

"Are you ever really?" Dani teased, but she caught sight of Jake finally coming inside. He was looking around the place, his jaw clenched and he was moving stiffly. A stiff Jake never meant good things. And when he reached behind him, his hand extending to someone else, she let out a quiet breath of air. A knot started to tighten in her stomach. "On second thought, I'll take a whiskey."

"Alright." Robbie nodded his approval before disappearing in the crowd.

Stilts whistled. "You *have* changed, Dani."

"Says the one who never knew you." Kate barked out a laugh.

But Dani was still watching Jake and after a moment, a feminine hand touched his. That's when Dani knew for sure—Julia hadn't gone to some clinic for the weekend.

"Hey, Dani."

Kate was saying something to her in the background, but a buzzing sound filled Dani's head. She felt the blood draining from her face. She knew, but she hadn't, not until she actually saw her sister step inside. Julia was thin before she left, but she looked even more now. Her cheekbones, nose, and chin were similar to Julia Roberts'. It'd been a laugh in their family, because of the similar names. It was maybe a bit more pronounced since she'd lost some weight. She was wearing a white cardigan, with a billowy skirt and white top underneath.

As Dani studied her sister, Julia pulled the ends of her sweater closed. A normal person might've assumed she was cold from that gesture, but Dani knew better. Julia was guarding herself. That cardigan was like her armor. She did the same when they were children, always needing something to cloak her. Dani used to think it showed her insecurity, but that never mattered. Julia would slink to the background and whisper her complaints in Erica's ear. Erica was larger than life. She had no problem doing whatever she wanted, wearing whatever she wanted. Julia was almost the exact opposite. She was too controlled.

Dani was staring right at her sister. She got a few moments to study her before everyone else realized what two presences were among them. A second hush fell over the room, and her sister looked up, her eyebrows pulled together. She glanced to Jake, then followed his gaze all the way to—Dani readied herself. She knew it was coming.

Julia saw her. Her eyes widened, and her chest rose in a jerking motion.

Both sisters stared at the other.

"Oh," Kate murmured.

Aiden laid a hand on her arm. "Dani."

Dani wasn't sure what she was supposed to feel. This was a moment that was supposed to be lived in infamy, but all she felt was emptiness. Gone. Ten years past, and it was like she never left. The same derision and superiority lined her sister's shoulders, making them straighten as she stood to her fullest height.

Anger filled Julia's eyes. She whipped around to Jake, and her hand lifted. She was shaking it in the air, in sharp quick motions.

Jake tugged her closer. His hand was in the air too, but he was making a soothing movement. When he bent his head down, then snuck a glance to Dani from the corner of his eyes, she went into motion. They were talking about her. She could already imagine it. Julia was saying, "How could you? Why is she here?" Like her own sister was a dog to her, underneath her, asking for her crumbs.

Dani pushed through the crowd. "Oh no, you don't."

Julia snapped to attention, and her eyes widened, seeing Dani still covering the distance between them, and coming in fast. She looked panicked, but Dani didn't care. It was going to happen sooner or later. Dani'd rather have it done now. She wanted a fight.

The beer gardens remained quiet.

Julia tried to hide behind Jake, but Dani reached and hauled her in front. "You do not hide behind him."

Julia snapped to attention—and there was the Julia Dani remembered—eyes blazing. She shoved at Dani's hold on her arm. "Excuse me? Don't touch me!"

"Then don't get Jake to fight for you." Dani squared up to her. Their noses were almost touching. She could almost breathe on her. "You sent him to tell me to stay away. I'm right here. Say it to me yourself now."

"You can't come home and expect everything to be the same—"

"When?" Dani shot back. "When did I demand for things to be the same? Because I'd rather be gone again than have things the same. So when did I, in your imaginary conversation with me, demand things to be the same?"

"Excuse me?"

Dani wanted to go back at her, a smart-ass comment on her tongue. She swallowed it. The emptiness that she had been feeling before was gone. It was filled up with years of anger. This wasn't how she hoped her first conversation would go with her sister, but it was happening nonetheless. Her sister would run any other time. She couldn't this time. They were in public. People would talk about how she'd been the coward of the two O'Hara sisters.

"I have as much right to see Aunt Kathryn as you do."

Jake frowned.

Dani knew that he knew. She didn't really want to see Kathryn. She just didn't want Julia to think she could make commands and she'd obey.

"You do not." Julia's eyes were blazing again. "And she doesn't want to see you."

"Then the house."

Julia quieted. "What about the house?"

"I want to come and see if any of my things are still there."

Julia snorted. "Yeah, right. Erica trashed all of your stuff, and what she didn't, I did." She was smug, taking pleasure in her words. "We had a bonfire one night. The rest of your crap got burned." She leaned back against Jake. "If you don't believe me, ask Jake. He was there."

Guilt filled her ex's gaze before he looked down to the ground.

Dani gritted her teeth. She wasn't surprised, but she *was* surprised at the added pang in her chest. "I want a picture of mom."

"No."

"Why not?"

"Because you left for ten years. You're not owed one."

"So there *are* some pictures left?"

Kathryn got along with their mother as well as Julia got along with her. If her sisters burned her things, she wouldn't have been shocked to find her mother's sister doing the same to her remnants.

"I don't know, okay?" Julia confessed, some of the fight leaving. She quieted her voice, and her shoulders loosened a bit. "We didn't burn her stuff on purpose. There was a fire in the house. A lot of stuff was lost, but I remember seeing a few pictures of Mom. I can't recall where they're at right now."

Julia was fidgeting with her fingers, and her throat was moving, she kept swallowing. She was lying. Dani saw it. She knew her sister's tells and she was reading them right now.

Dani wanted to call bullshit on her sister, but she refrained. It was their first meeting in ten years. There'd been no hugs, no handshakes, and no tears of happiness. There hadn't even been a 'welcome home.' Julia hadn't said she missed her, and Dani didn't think she missed her sister back either. There was so much they needed to say to each other, or maybe they didn't. Maybe they could go through life not talking at all. No. Dani considered it. It was tempting, but she knew at some point they'd have to talk.

Jake. Erica.

But Dani wanted to focus on one thing right then. She wanted a picture of her mom. And whether Julia was going to give it to her or not, she was going to get it.

One way or another.

She was sitting on a bench toward the north end of the fair's pond. It'd been man-made so it wasn't large, and it couldn't be classified as a lake, but it wasn't the typical mud-like pond that Dani always thought when she heard that word. No. This body of water was serene, and calm, and there were lights set up all around it. A path circled it with a few benches set up so people could sit and enjoy the view.

Because she was sitting at the north end, she saw Jonah coming long before she would've heard the quiet crunch of his shoes on the path. Not that she would've heard much. He was silent, and almost ghost-like. He sat beside her, leaning back to mirror how she was sitting.

She kept her gaze trained on the water. It always soothed her. Any water. She needed that soothing at that moment too. She slid her hands inside her pockets. "I'm good. I just needed a breather."

"You know what I do, right?"

She nodded. "You take care of Falls River for us."

"I'm in charge of the town's water front. I oversee everything. So if someone wants to build on the river, I'm the one who gives permission to their permits or not. There's a lot of other stuff I do, but the one area that I get a kick out of is when I check on the park. There's always this whole line of little kids there. They're all lined up. One by one, shoulder to shoulder, just throwing rocks into the water. You think they'd get tired of it, but they never do."

He bent down, scooped up a rock, and tossed it in the pond.

"They feel powerful when they do that." Dani watched the waves ripple. "My ex-fiancé was a psychologist with the Red Cross. He told me that one time. He tried to explain to me why the kids in the orphanage always wanted to go to the ocean."

She was talking, and she had no idea why. She'd barely acknowledged Boone, and now she was talking about the orphanage? Maybe she should've been shocked at her confession, but she couldn't put the brakes on what she was saying. She frowned. Maybe she was getting tired of holding everything in?

Jonah glanced at her. She saw it from the corner of her eye. She still didn't turn to him, even when he asked, so quietly, "You were engaged?"

She nodded.

"I'm sorry."

Dani shook her head. A sad laugh slipped out. "I thought you'd talk about the orphanage, not the guy." She looked now, a grin teasing at her mouth. "We'll go with him. I'd rather have that conversation than the other one."

Jonah grinned back. "Now I don't know what to ask." He laughed softly. "So you were engaged, huh?"

Her head fell back and she laughed with him. It was the first genuine laugh she'd had, and then she sobered because she couldn't remember the last time she laughed for real. She sighed. "That felt good. I haven't done that in a while."

She waited for the line. She looked good laughing. She should do it more often. It was always that same message: be happy. Don't be sad. Or at the very least, don't show you're sad. Be fake. When Jonah didn't say either, and she waited a beat to see if he would then and he didn't, she murmured, "Thank you."

"For what?"

"For not telling me to laugh more. For not telling me to be fake."

He shrugged. "Trust me. I get it. And I like reality, not fake shit."

"My family's the opposite. They want fake every day." She gestured back where the beer gardens were located. "Julia's not changed. She's lying to me, too. I asked for a picture of Mom, and she said she couldn't 'recall' where she saw they were. That's bullshit. She knows exactly where they are. She just doesn't want me to have any."

"Why a picture of your mom?"

"Because I don't have any."

Because she'd been stranded in a place for so long and she didn't know if she was going to live or die. Because she kept thinking about her mom, kept feeling her presence, and she just wanted to see her face one more time. Dani felt her throat closing up, and some tears threatening to spill. She didn't want to cry. She couldn't remember the last time she did that either.

"I get that." Jonah nodded. "There were a few things I wanted of my mom's when she died. They were small things, but they were damned important to me. One was a picture of her and me, the other was a picture of her and Aiden. It was nice to have a picture of my mom in my wallet. Comforting. It helped, especially when I was around my dad's family. They're like sharks. Always circling for blood in the water."

Water...

She spoke without thinking. "I was in a storm. I took a job as a teacher at this orphanage, and we got stranded in this building. The storm wasn't too long, but when it was over—"

It was all happening again. She was back there, and she heard that eerie silence.

"Some of the kids were outside playing."

She ran out and grabbed whom she could. The first wave was coming down—she couldn't grab them all. A lump was sitting in the back of her throat. It was blocking her air, and she could barely grasp for oxygen again.

"The water slammed against our building, and the bottom floor was swept away. It was there and then it wasn't. Part of the wall maintained, and we climbed over to the next building. Then the wall collapsed. We were stuck in that second building."

They couldn't get out.

No one knew they were there.

"Once it was over, it was a while until we heard the search parties. We could hear them, and we'd call out."

She blinked a few times, feeling the tears falling free. "They didn't hear us for the longest time. We were so weak, and a lot of the kids couldn't move. Some were injured from running into the building. Some got hurt trying to get into the second building. Some were hit when the wall collapsed against where we were."

She was in that room again. Her throat was burning. Her stomach was hurting. The smell of urine was so thick in the room. They were throwing up. And then nothing... "They all just fell silent."

"You were in a tsunami?"

"It hit a small island where we were."

"A tsunami's not a storm. It's a natural disaster."

"No one knows about where I was." Now the shock started in. She hadn't talked about it with anyone, even Boone. Mae. No one. Panicked, she turned to him. "Don't tell anyone."

"I won't. I promise."

He patted her hand, or it might've meant to be a pat. His hand touched hers and began to leave, but she turned hers over quickly. She grasped onto his hand, and held it. "Thank you." Dani was staring right into his eyes. Only a few inches separated them, and she felt her lips lifting in a half-grin. "Erica was right. She once said your eyes could spin a rock into a frenzy. I see what she meant."

His eyes darkened. "That was a long time ago."

"I still remember." Dani saw the dreaminess of his eyes. They were a dark brown, and they were almost black when he felt strong emotions, like he was feeling now. They could smolder, burn, get heated, but she saw something Erica hadn't. There was a calming effect to them, too. Peace. She saw a refuge in them. "You're not the guy everyone thinks you are, are you?"

"No." He regarded her with a faint grin. "I know one of your secrets. Now you know one of mine."

She sat on the bench for another ten minutes after Jonah left. He asked if she wanted to go back to the beer gardens with him, but she didn't have it in her. When he left, it was an odd feeling that settled over her. She felt comforted, but also exposed. One of her secrets wasn't a secret anymore. She hadn't gone into detail, but he knew about the storm. Her head was down as she walked the rest of the path around the pond, circling it toward where her car was parked.

"Dani."

She looked up now and saw Aiden waving to her. The group had moved to one of the farthest tables outside the beer gardens. It was the closest to the where the cars were lined up.

Jonah sat at the end of their table, with a redhead trying to hang on him. His arm wasn't around her. He wasn't even paying her attention, instead listening to Hawk across the table, but Dani could tell the redhead wasn't giving up. Hawk had his own woman, clad in black leather, and they seemed perfect.

Aiden separated from the group, crossing to her. "Hey, are you leaving?"

"I think that's for the best. I don't want to air any more dirty laundry, and I will if I see Julia again. Apparently, I'm in the confessing mood tonight. I think it's time to turn in."

"Look." Aiden's tone turned serious. "I wasn't outside when you talked to your sister, but in case you're leaving because of Kate, I want you to know she's not always this power hungry. She told me about your conversation earlier today and how she wants you to break up Julia and Jake. She's not using you or anything, if that's what you were concerned about. It's just she's affected more than the rest of us. I have Jonah and everyone loves Bubba. Robbie's accepted no matter what, you know? Everyone thinks Stilts is the most hilarious thing that's come to town in a long time. So for most of us, yeah, we're affected by the small-town politics, but it's more for Kate. She's—"

"Not accepted." Dani could relate.

"Yeah." Aiden looked guilty. "Kate was so excited when she heard you were back in town. Julia has made her life hell. She's gone out of her way to be cruel to Kate and everyone knows it's just because Kate is Jake's partner. She thinks he's going to leave her for Kate or something."

"Kate's not an O'Hara." Dani rolled her eyes. "Doesn't Julia know? That's a dating requirement for Jake."

"Try telling that to your sister's jealousy. It rears an ugly head sometimes."

"I have in the past. Never works."

Aiden laughed and then gestured toward the parking lot. "We're all going to go to Mae's Grill. Would you come with us? I know it's going to be crazy busy there, but the whole group would like to get to know you better."

She remembered Jonah's warning. It didn't hurt to have friends in a small town, so Dani found herself agreeing to meet them there. Once inside the Mustang, she didn't start it right away. She rested her head against her seat and let out a deep breath.

What the hell am I doing?

Friends? That's what she was doing now? Trying to be included by a group? Dani never belonged in crowds like those. She didn't have friends. She wasn't even sure if she knew how to be a friend now.

Thump! Thump!

Jumping, Dani gasped and saw Jonah grinning at her through her window.

He motioned for her to unlock the passenger door, and he climbed in once she did. "You looked like you were sleeping? Did our talk wear you out?" He winked. "Or maybe it was holding my hand. I know it must've been overwhelming to touch these glorious things." He held his hands in the air, turning them around like he was modeling.

She groaned. "There's the old cocky Jonah from high school. I was almost convinced you were a nice guy."

"Hush now. No spreading that secret around. You were supposed to have forgotten all about it?" His laugh grew more serious. "Jokes aside, what are you doing?"

"I'm waiting for the parking lot to clear out. What are *you* doing?"

"I need a ride to Mae's."

Dani shook her head even as she started the car. "What is it about you that everyone loves? It's like you have some billboard on you that says 'Like me, I'm adorable.' Does everyone do what you ask of them? 'I need a ride,' so therefore, I must give you a ride? Is that how it works?"

But even as she was grumbling, she knew how it worked. He was a good guy, but he was also charming, charismatic, and he had a hell of a body. She knew not many could resist when he asked for something.

Oh good God. I'm becoming one of them.

"What?" He seemed genuinely puzzled.

"Nothing."

"You know." He narrowed his eyes, studying her. "You're not like everyone else. Some girls act all tough and are mean right off the bat because they're protecting themselves. I get that. I do, and I know that women like me. And then there are the other girls who—"

"Throw themselves at you."

"Don't get me wrong. Sometimes it's nice and it's what I need after a hard day at work, but to be honest, I think you have so much crap to deal with, you couldn't ever see me in that light." He lowered his voice. "*That's* why I like hanging out with you. That's part of the reason I showed up yesterday for dinner and sat on the bench with you tonight."

It made sense, but she wanted to make sure he understood. "You're not responsible for me."

"Yes. I am."

"No—"

He softened his tone. "Let me be responsible. Let one person care for you."

"I didn't tell you that stuff to make you feel like this."

He shrugged. "You tell that person something, trust them, and they have your back. You do it back. Friendship. It's part of the package."

She held in her breath, a knot forming in her gut. She didn't know what to say to that. "Friends?"

He grinned. "Looks like you're stuck with me."

And as she headed out of the parking lot and followed behind the rest to Mae's Grill, she realized she didn't even want to argue against it. That horrified her the most. Or it should've.

Aiden called it.

Mae's Grill was filled to the max. And it was a mix between the fair's beer garden inhabitants, the regulars, and tourists who traveled up during the summer for Tenderfoot Rush. All three groups came together at Mae's Grill, and Jonah was right.

Jonah tapped her hand and asked, leaning close to her ear, "What do you drink?"

"Just a water. Thanks."

"Are you sure?"

"Yeah."

"Okay." He nodded toward the corner. "Gang's over there."

When Dani arrived, Aiden and Kate moved to her side. "Where were you?"

"I was about to send Bubba out to your home."

"I held back and waited for the parking lot to clear."

Shifting on her feet, Kate glanced over her shoulder. "Did I see you come in with Jonah?"

"Yeah. He wanted a ride." Dani shrugged. Seeing Robbie on the dance floor with someone, she asked Kate, "Is that one of the girls he's interested in?"

Kate nodded, making a face. "That's Lori. She was here, just waiting for him once we arrived."

"Then, in that case," Dani nodded toward the pool table. "Want to play a game of pool?"

"Love to!" Kate looked so relieved. "Thank you, and maybe we can flirt it up with a couple guys over there."

Dani added, "Robbie won't know what hit him."

"Damn straight!" Kate laughed, ducking around Jonah as he returned from the bar. "Hey, Jonah. I'm stealing your ride. She's going to be my sidekick the rest of the night." She tapped on his shoulder and pointed to a table of women, all eyeing him up and down. "Just a word of advice, avoid that table. They look a little crazed tonight."

Dani grabbed the water from Jonah's offered hand, but Mae showed up at that time. "We're swamped. Can you help behind the counter?"

"Yeah?" Dani glanced to the rest of the group. "You guys wouldn't mind?"

Kate waved her ahead. "And have our own personal bartender? Go. Now! We won't have to wait in line anymore."

Dani just laughed, then waved to everyone. She moved through the crowd, bypassing Robbie who was heading back to the table with Lori in tow.

Dani used to help bartend when she was younger, before her mom died, and Aunt Kathryn took over. Mae seemed to vanish from their lives then, but Dani worked behind the bar in her travels. It was a job where she could pick up some extra cash whenever she needed it. The crowd was insane, but she didn't think it'd be too hard before she picked it back up, just like old times.

Aunt Mae yelled in her ear, patting her on the shoulder, "Hope you didn't go rusty with your time away."

Dani merely shook her head. "Never!" Then she began filling an order, and the first hour went fast. The rest of the night passed just as quickly, but the last thirty minutes were always the worst. The drunk got drunker and the one-nighters became more brazen with sharing their numbers.

Jonah had taken residence at the end of her counter space. Every time a girl approached and her hand lingered down his arm, he'd shoot Dani a look and she'd move in. The first few were deterred when Dani announced that he'd come with her. And then one took it as a challenge to throwdown, and Dani changed tactics. Now she merely slid them a watered-down Coke and pointed across the bar. She told 'em it came from the gentleman in the blue.

There were too many gentlemen in blue to count.

The girls loved it, didn't notice it was watered-down soda only, and went off in search for their mysterious gentleman. After the fifth girl, Dani slapped a towel in front of Jonah and suggested, "Must be hard. Having to literally fend them off, huh? Or having another chick to do it for you?" His rich laugh was her reward, and she rolled her eyes. She gestured to the towel. "If you really want to get rid of them, just get busy. I'm sure Mae will need all the help she can get to clean up."

Robbie heard the last words as he approached the counter. He noted Jonah, who was leaving to start clearing tables. "You and Jonah seem to get along."

"For now." She winked at him. "What'll you have?"

"Water and a Diet Coke."

"Lori's had enough, huh?" Dani murmured as she filled the glasses. Robbie lingered afterwards, gazing back to that table where the group was still hanging out. "Something wrong, Robbie?"

"Yeah." He hunched over the bar, folding his arms on the counter. "Can I ask you a question?"

"Sure. Although we really only met tonight."

"That's why I want to ask you. You're objective. You might have a different set of eyes." He leaned closer. "Do you think...coming from your first impression, do you think Lori would make a good mother?"

"Whoa. What?" Dani slid a drink to another customer. "I barely remember Lori, and I haven't talked to her at all since getting back here. It's only been a few days."

"Yeah, but look at her. Does she look like good mother material?"

"Uh." Lori was pretty. That's all Dani thought. "Look, I can only tell you what I do think, and if you're asking the bartender about the girl you're dating, you're probably dating the wrong girl." Kate was watching them talk, but trying not to make it obvious. She ducked behind Bubba.

Dani let out a breath. "Go for the ones who scare you. Maybe there's a reason they scare you."

"You think?"

Dani lifted a shoulder up, picking up a washcloth to dry out a glass. "I don't think I'm one to give advice. Trust me." Two men. One who left her, and one she left. And speaking of, karma wasn't on her side.

Jake walked into the bar.

He and Robbie crossed paths, and did the whole guy head-nod thing, and kept on walking. Spotting her, he slowed, an unreadable mask falling over his face. "Mae likes an extra hand at closing time." He nodded to Mae as she came down the counter. "Heya, Mae."

"Jake." Her eyes skimmed over him and Dani, then slapped the counter. "You know, thanks for coming tonight, but I think we'll be alright. Jonah's here, and Katie's over there, too."

Kate laughed at something Bubba said, slapping him on the shoulder. She looked at Robbie, who was standing by Lori, and missed the first half of Bubba's huge shoulder. Her hand slipped off, and she fell off her bar stool.

"Yeah, Kate's drunk. I think I'll stick around for a bit." He jerked his head toward the kitchen. "Got some coffee back there?"

"Help yourself!" She moved to close tabs for waiting customers.

Dani kept drying glasses, and Jake returned, holding a white Styrofoam cup. "You seem to be getting along pretty well with some folks."

That wasn't what he wanted to talk about. "I don't want to talk about Julia."

"Noted." He glanced around, frowning. "Is that Jonah wiping tables?"

"Yeah." Dani grabbed another washcloth and tray. "You can help him." Then she headed to the back, and she stayed there washing dishes the rest of the night. Jonah came to help at one point. She loaded up the trays of dirty dishes, put them through the cleaning machine, and he'd pull them out. She tried to tell him he didn't need to help, but Jonah just ignored her as he began putting the dried dishes where they belonged.

Dani said, "I'm okay, you know. If that's what this is all about, about the storm. I'll probably join my aunt for a nightcap and crash at her place."

Jonah just laughed as the machine beeped it was done. He lifted up the doors and pulled out another rack of clean dishes. "You think this is all about you? Maybe this has nothing to do with you. Ever thought about that, Miss Natural Disaster?" He winked. "Maybe I'm the one using you. Maybe it has nothing to do with making sure you're okay."

"You're using me?"

"It can happen. People use people all the time. Why do you think I'm any different? Like," he paused. His eyes rolled upwards, thinking. "Ah!" He snapped his fingers at her. "Take this one: why do you think I rode with you? Huh? Hung out at the bar with you, and why I'm here right now? Maybe I'm avoiding my sister. You know, she's always after me, wanting to set me up with a good girl. But if I'm hanging out with you, someone who probably doesn't want to deal with any of that love stuff, then what can she say?" He whispered behind his hand. "She can't say shit because she doesn't know the truth about us."

"The truth?"

"Yeah." He went back to piling up plates before carrying them to their spot. He said, coming back, "We're friends. No one needs to know the specifics."

Dani didn't feel a flutter in her chest when he winked at her.

She wasn't noticing how sexy he looked when he was waiting for the machine to finish. He didn't look lean or gorgeous when he crossed his arms over his chest, or when his dimple only half-showed she found herself wanting to make him laugh so she could see the whole dimple.

No.

Nothing like that was happening.

And she certainly didn't drop a few glasses when she was trying to put them in the tray. Nothing like that at all, but Dani heaved a silent sigh of relief when Kate came to the doorway and hollered they were all leaving. Her gaze lingered on the two of them. Dani ignored Kate, and her relief was short-lived. Jonah waved Kate off, and ten minutes later the two of them walked out to find the entire bar empty except for Mae.

"Is my sister here?"

"They all took off, said you had a ride." Mae jerked a thumb over her shoulder. "Do me a favor? Shut the door tight after you go? Everything's locked up." She nodded toward the back. "I got some things to take care of, so I'm heading to the office. Have a good night, you two." She kissed Dani on the cheek before repeating her good nights and disappearing to the back.

Jonah groaned as the two walked outside. "I thought Aid would come and ask me. Hell, my sister probably did this on purpose. She probably thinks that I'll go home with you..." His eyes lit up, and he flashed her a smile. "What do you think?"

"No. I'll just give you a ride home."

"It's not worth it. It's 3:30 in the morning. I have to be on the river early. I live thirty minutes away. Come on," he persuaded. "Loon Lake has a channel to the river. I can crash on your couch. You won't even know I'm there. I'll just have one of the guys shoot a boat down to pick me up in the morning. I've got a change of clothes at the station in my locker."

"Falls River runs into Loon Lake?"

"Yeah. The channel is gorgeous. I'll take you on a boat ride sometime. Better yet, you should just canoe through it."

Why was she entertaining this? No, she knew why. Someone else would be there. That meant no nightmare. Maybe. They weren't as bad when Boone was with her. Then again, he was in bed with her. Still... maybe it was worth it?

She heard herself saying, "Fine."

Jonah grinned and nudged her hip with his. "Thanks, Dani. Who knew we'd have such a great friendship?"

Friendship. She fought against rolling her eyes, but couldn't stop her own grin.

When they got to the cabin, Dani crossed to the patio and flipped on the lamp in the corner. She didn't want all the lights on. If the whole place was lit up like a Christmas tree, that wouldn't help her fall asleep. One light cast a nice relaxing glow through the room.

"Drink?"

"What do you have?"

"Knowing Aunt Mae—probably everything."

"Beer then. Nothing fancy."

Dani pulled out two bottles and walked outside to the screened-in patio.

Jonah glanced around the place as he sat down. "This is nice."

"It's Aunt Mae's, but if you ask her, she'll say it's mine." Dani uncapped both bottles and slid one over to him. It ended right in front of him.

"Nice."

Dani grinned and took a sip. "Bartending is like breathing to me. I helped out in Mae's bar for years." Then she heard herself saying, "Boone never knew that about me." As soon as the words were out, she faltered. She wished she could take them back, but she couldn't.

No, that wasn't true either.

She didn't want to take them back. In fact, she wanted to say more.

"Boone? That's his name?"

"That's his nickname." She frowned. "And I have no idea why he was called that. He never told me."

Jonah stretched his legs out, getting comfortable. But he was looking at her, and she was feeling him, and she knew she shouldn't have been. Then he murmured, almost too quietly for her to hear, "I'm guessing he didn't know where you're from."

"What makes you say that?"

"He's not here," Jonah stated. "If you were my girl and I proposed to you, nothing would keep me from you. I'd follow you, and I would take you back. Nothing."

She looked away, and ignored how her heart picked up again, or how she felt a little breathless in the chest. She hadn't felt something like this in a long time. It was alien to her, but it probably wasn't what she thought. She wasn't attracted to Jonah Bannon. They were friends, weird friends, but friends.

Putting her thoughts away, she focused on what he said. It was true. There *was* so much Boone didn't know about her. So much that she had chosen not to tell him. It wasn't a conscious decision. It was just...that was how it was. She just hadn't told him all those details about herself.

"The gang liked you tonight." Jonah tipped his head back and took a large swallow. He was watching her over the tip of his beer.

She averted her gaze. "I liked them, too. Lori was a bit iffy, though I didn't talk to her."

"Lori *is* a bit iffy."

"Robbie asked me if I thought Lori would be a good mother."

"What?" Jonah laughed. "He must've been drunk. What'd you say?"

"I told him that if he was asking a stranger, he probably knew the answer."

"Robbie knows the answer. He's just comfortable with those girls. Kate's so far-off on that guy, but he's clueless."

"Most guys are," Dani noted. She set her bottle on the table. "What *else* do you know?" She returned his gaze, almost like a challenge. She lifted her chin up, just half an inch. "I feel like there's a lot more you know than you let on."

Jonah let out a small grin. "I know that my sister worries about Kate. I know that my sister feels guilty because she's always been accepted, and Kate has to fight for it. I think Robbie might develop a little crush on you if you give him attention."

She held up a finger. "Noted. No nice attention to Robbie."

Jonah's grin deepened and he kept going, "I know that Bubba secretly loves it when Aiden and Kate drag him onto the dance floor. I know that Stilts has a thing for Lori—you can't say anything about that, by the way—and I know that Aiden and Kate both really like you."

Dani held her breath, but Jonah continued, a slow drawl, "Kate feels a camaraderie with you because you weren't accepted by your family like she wasn't accepted by everyone in town. And she idolizes you because you stood up to your sister."

"I did?"

"You're not hiding from your sister. In Kate's mind, that means you're standing up to her, and you are."

Dani was starting to feel warm. She glanced to the beer. Maybe it was the two sips she took.

Jonah's voice was beginning to feel like a soothing caress. "Kate was scared of Erica and she's scared of Julia. And I think Kate and Aiden are both relieved they don't have to talk with Lori or Brooke anymore. There's another female around, so it's not as obvious when they want to snub Robbie's girlfriends." He pulled his legs in, set his beer down, and turned to face her more squarely. His baritone softened again. "I know that Kate has a little crush on me, but she'll never act on it. And I know that you let me come here tonight because of a reason. I'm just trying to figure out what it is."

They didn't know her. Kate. Aiden. That group, but they wanted to and Jonah knew things she hadn't even told him.

She looked down to where he was holding his beer, still sitting on the little table between them. "It's a little alarming how intelligent you are."

Jonah chuckled. "So, Dani, what's the reason you let me come back here with you?"

She held her breath. Her hands tightened around her beer. She looked back up, saw that he was even closer. His eyes held hers captive.

He asked again, "What's the reason you brought me here tonight? Do you want me to hold you and keep the nightmares at bay? Is that it?"

She didn't move. She didn't dare. Her body was already heated, and her lips became parched.

He leaned forward, and his eyes were downright smoldering in the soft lamp glow. "Or maybe you want me to screw you? Do you want me to make you forget that other guy?"

A normal girl would've gotten pissed. But, Dani wasn't like other females and pushing the lust at bay, she saw right back into him. She said, "You're either a dick who pretends to be a good guy, or you're a good guy who can be a dick. Because right now you're being a dick no matter what."

"You haven't picked."

God. Those three words.

Her heart was racing.

"No." She shook her head, trying to calm her body's reaction. "Maybe you're pushing on me because you want to know more truth from me. Is that it?"

He remained cool. He lifted up an eyebrow, and smirked. "What do you think?"

He was an asshole. His words struck deep. Then again, maybe that was his intention in the first place. To go deep, make her feel something. Well, she was. She was feeling all sorts of things, and she didn't know if she should ask him to screw her or—she went with the other choice.

"Nightmares." The words tumbled from her. "I get them, and I hate them. I honestly hate them. If I could murder and destroy them, I would, but they're in my mind. I can't destroy that. I'm tired of hearing water rushing down on us and screams as everyone is running for cover. I'm *really goddamn* tired of hearing the sound when someone gets trampled. Have you ever heard someone get stampeded? You can hear the bones cracking under the weight, and then it's nothing. It's a dull sound after that, like they're a sack of potatoes. But that's not even the worst. The breathing stops. They're gasping for breath. They start to wheeze. It turns into a gasping sound until they choke on their last breath. Then nothing."

She didn't talk about the other type of breathing, the kind where it's quiet. Like when someone is sleeping. You know they're going to die. They haven't eaten, or drank anything in days. When they stopped emptying their stomachs. When they just lay there, and you can't help them. You can't make it go away. You can just lay there with them, and listen for the next soft breath because when they stop breathing, that's when you know you're lying next to a dead child.

She didn't talk about that sound because it was the worst of all.

Jonah murmured, so damned gently, "A buddy of mine told me once that he could handle the nightmares. He always knew to just expect them, but it was the flashbacks that got him. He said they'd rip through him like a scorned tornado."

Scorned tornado. She felt her mouth curve up at that. "What happened to him?"

"A kid went under. He tried to save him, but the undercurrent swept the kid out of his grasp. The body had moved farther down the river by the time he got to him, it was too late. He said when they found the body he couldn't get the eyes out of his head. They were glossed over."

He wasn't looking at her, but staring out the screen to the water. The moonlight shone down on it, and the wind was making small ripples over the surface. Was he thinking of that kid right now? Imagining him? Or was his buddy actually himself? Jonah must've seen more than his fair share of dead bodies, but it was true. One minute, life was there and the next there was nothing. No life. No soul. Nothing. A person would keep looking, expecting them to suddenly become alert, life would come back to them, but it didn't happen.

Once they were gone, they were gone.

Her voice dropped to a hoarse whisper. She was holding onto her beer like it was a life preserver. "They stopped breathing. They stopped moving, even the slightest twitches. Sometimes the fingers were the only things that moved, and I just knew when the little pinkie stopped moving. I couldn't bring myself to look in the eyes after a while."

She'd never admitted that before, not even to herself.

"Can we not..." Her voice was hoarse. "Can we not talk about this anymore?"

"Want to get piss drunk instead?"

"Yes."

That was what they did. She remembered asking him to hold her when she got sleepy. She remembered holding his hand, and saying, "Boone would hold my hand sometimes in the hospital."

She remembered him asking, "Did that help?"

She didn't remember what she said after that, except he stood up and held out his hand. "Come on."

He pulled the bedcovers back. Dani crawled under the covers, and she remembered him holding her. He was wrapped all around her.

She remembered asking, "Why are you doing this?"

"I don't really know." He pressed a kiss to her shoulder. "Go to sleep."

And she remembered curling her fingers around his.

Dani slipped out from underneath Jonah's arm. Six in the morning. They'd slept for a few hours. Not long, but enough for her. After the bathroom, she went to the kitchen for coffee, and rested against the counter.

She hadn't had the nightmares, but she dreamt of Erica instead. Her little sister had been at the end of her bed. She smiled, beautifully, and Dani remembered feeling the love from her sister. It was warming, and it felt pure. When Erica turned and left, that was when Dani woke up. And the weird part was next—she wanted her sister to be there.

It felt so real.

"Hey."

Dani started, seeing Jonah in the doorway. He asked, "Did you have a nightmare?"

"No, I woke up a few minutes ago."

"It's a little after six." Jonah yawned as he raked a hand through his hair. "I'll need to go in, but that's not for a bit. Come back to bed. We can sleep a little longer."

It sounded wonderful, but her hands curled tighter around her coffee cup. "Jonah, I..."

Jonah waved her off. "I know."

She didn't say anything more and followed him back to the bed. He crawled in first and held the covers up for her as she slid in. He pulled her against his side, but stayed on his back. Within seconds, Dani heard the slow methodical breathing from him and knew he had fallen asleep. She stayed awake, but remained tucked under his arm.

She kept her eyes open.

Just in case...

But no Erica came again, and when she knew she couldn't sleep, she slid out of his arms again. Instead of heading back for more coffee, she went for a quick run. He was on the dock when she came back.

She waved from a few yards away. "I'll stop here. Don't wanna foul-odor you to death."

Jonah grinned. "Much appreciated, but I'm a man. I've smelled worse, guaranteed."

"Don't tell me I didn't warn you."

Jonah moved to sit on the end, his toes in the water, and he patted the seat next to him. There was enough room for two between the posts. "How far did you go?"

"Far enough."

Jonah shook his head. "How far?"

"Three miles."

He whistled softly. "Must've run pretty hard to get back when you did."

"Think I was trying to outrun my problems," Dani admitted ruefully, kicking her feet lightly in the water. The water felt good, but that just meant the day was going to be a scorcher.

"What woke you the second time?"

Dani knew he wouldn't buy a non-answer, but she shrugged. She didn't want to talk about it. "Nothing."

She stared ahead, but Jonah stared at her.

She felt his appraisal, and she held her breath, knowing he'd continue with his questions. It wasn't that she didn't trust him. She was beginning to. It was that she didn't want to voice the words. Once she did, once she heard them out loud—there was no going back. Half the battle was accepting the haunts, and talking about her dead little sister, who was one ghost she didn't want to discuss. Not yet, and then an approaching boat interrupted them.

Dani almost leapt to her feet, alongside Jonah as he waved them down. She felt a knot unravel, just a little bit inside of her.

The boat veered toward them. A second later, Dani stood and saw Trenton Galloway grinning back at them, one hand over his eyebrows to help see against the rising sunlight.

"Trenton Galloway works for you?" He was another memory from high school. He'd been in Jonah's rough group of friends, but also ran for student council. She was pretty sure he was one of the basketball captains, too.

Jonah grasped the boat's front and climbed inside. "I run the river. Everyone works for me. They just don't know it."

"Hey, Dani." Trenton lifted a hand, already reversing the boat. "Heard you were back."

"Sure am."

But her gaze was on Jonah as he helped push off the dock. Grinning at her, he held her look until they turned the boat around and sped back through the lake's canal. The waves slowly melted, and the lake shone smooth once more. A glass reflection from the blue ocean above.

Good riddance. Dani took a deep breath as she held on to a steel post on the end of her dock. The floorboard creaked and protested as she shifted her feet. She'd never allowed Boone a window into her soul. The shutters were always drawn, but he'd never asked. She'd let Jonah share her bed, hold her hand, and comfort her.

He'd done more than Jake and Boone combined. Well, almost.

Dani shook off the unsettling thoughts and moved back inside. The coffee had been good, but she craved some tea. After a shower, a change, and a quick inventory of the kitchen—she only had enough for that day. She'd have to go back to town again, and as she drove past some fields, a cow was in the ditch on the wrong side of the fence.

It had a black body with a white-tip nose. Dani knew the nearest home belonged to Mrs. Bendsfield. There was a billboard positioned at the end of the driveway. It was supposed to proclaim the owner's age, and every year she got older, Mrs. Bendsfield bought a cow. The number read fifty-two, but the paint was faded. She wasn't going to hold her breath that the number was repainted until there was a new owner. Dani glanced at the rest of the cows standing on the right side of the fence, and eyeballed more than fifty-two, but if one could get out, others could follow.

Dani tried finding the hole in the fence, but couldn't and she ended up turning into the driveway. Rounding a bend in the driveway, the farmhouse came into view and Dani parked just before the garage. A small picket fence closed in a garden, greeting the house's frontside. Except for a smattering of oil-streaked rags piled on the front porch, the two-story, white house looked clean. It looked like it had recently been painted. Dani never got a tour of the place, at least not at any age she could remember, but she remembered visiting with her mother a few times. She mostly remembered the chocolate chip cookies. After her mother passed, Mrs. Bendsfield was nice, but she'd never been 'on good terms' with Aunt Mae. So the visits stopped, and so did the chocolate chip cookies.

Not many of the upstanding citizens of Craigstown acknowledged a friendship with the owner of Mae's Grill, one of the busiest businesses in Craigstown. It didn't matter. Her Aunt Mae's background of boozing and floozing still set the precedence, and so any friendship that might've been there would never see daylight.

Aunt Mae never cared. Dani thought she actually preferred it because she could do what she wanted and say what she wanted. Folks would keep coming to Mae's Grill no matter what. It was too popular among the tourists and locals.

But Mrs. Bendsfield was on the different side of the tracks. She wasn't one of the upstanding citizens, but she wasn't one of the 'other' citizens like Aunt Mae. Mrs. Bendsfield just lived in her own little world.

Remembering all of that, she wasn't sure what she was in store for as she knocked on the screen door. "Hello? Mrs. Bendsfield?" It was loose, so it rattled in the doorframe with each knock. Dani was hesitant to knock harder. She didn't want to bust through the screen on her first adult visit. Not hearing a response, she turned and walked to the backyard. Nothing. Dani checked the garage. Two vehicles were inside.

Mrs. Bendsfield's van, the world's largest daisy painted on it—Dani saw it had just been given a fresh covering, just like the house—still sat in the same place Dani remembered from her visits. A red Volkswagon was next to it, with a foot thick of dust.

Dani didn't want to intrude in the house, so she tried the barns next.

The shed was empty, only home to an antique tractor and grainbinds.

The main barn was unlocked and Dani stepped inside, finding herself in the milking room with the aroma of drying milk inside. Heading down a small hallway, she opened the door and a bunch of cats scattered in every direction. Expecting to find feeding stalls, she saw instead that half of the interior had been renovated into a pottery studio. The left side still had the stalls where the cows were fed and milked.

"Mrs. Bendsfield?"

Her voice echoed across the barn.

"Huh? Who there?" Mrs. Bendsfield called back, her voice shrill.

Dani couldn't locate her. "It's me, Mrs. Bendsfield's. Dani O'Hara."

"What? What you say? I thought a moment you said Dani O'Hara, but that can't be right. That girl's been dead a long time." The voice was still distant, and both voices kept echoing.

"No. No, it's me, Mrs. Bendsfield. I came back home."

"No, no. It's me. I'm just fooling in the head again. Little Daniella O'Hara was taken by that cancer. I know because her mother came crying to me. Thirty-four back then."

Dani caught her breath. She hadn't heard words spoken about Sandra, ever. It had been an understood rule—no one talked about her grandmother.

Mrs. Bendsfield mused to herself. "Oh no. I know you's in my head. Little Daniella O'Hara died long while back, left three rabbits behind, and her mother just sobbed and sobbed. No one knows what to do. No one knows what to do. Little Daniella O'Hara was the minx and angel, I tell you. Half-minx and half-angel, that one. No one knows what to do."

Dani took a hesitant step forward. Crossing toward the pottery studio, she continued to hear Mrs. Bendsfied mutter, and realized she was in a back room where a heavy plastic curtain was hung from the ceiling.

"I knows I'm just hearing my own voices. Memories, that's what they are. Little Daniella O'Hara, always came around these parts. She just took a liking to Oscar, that she did. No one knows what to do. Her mother always cried to me. Thought I was supposed to know what to do, but I didn't. Clueless. Just like the rest of them! Oh no. That girl's just back to haunt me. Always knew it was coming. Always knew it was coming."

Dani paused at the doorway and saw Mrs. Bendsfield's petite figure. She wore a loose long-sleeved shirt, as big as the old woman was, and she was bent over a pot. Mrs. Bendsfield was circling with a paintbrush in hand, pausing sporadically to lean forward and make a dab. She was adding detail to the pot.

Dani saw herself staring into an oncoming ocean wave. And she suddenly felt, literally felt, the waves coming for her.

Choking in a breath, she steeled herself. The waves crashed back, and she heard the first scream—"Daniella O'Hara?"

Mrs. Bendsfield stood frozen, hand raised, clenching a small paintbrush.

"Uh..." Dani blinked, pushing the memory away. "Mrs. Bendsfield, I came in because I saw—"

"No." Mrs. Bendsfield interrupted, waving the paintbrush at her, stabbing the air. "Do you know what you've been doing to me? Years of guilt, girl. Years of guilt, and here you are, living, breathing, and part of my delusions. I want you out! *Out!*"

"No. No. Mrs. Bendsfield, it's me. Dani O'Hara. I'm Daniella's daughter. I came in because I saw one of your cows got loose. She's in the ditch."

Mrs. Bendsfield sniffed and crossed her arms. The paintbrush smeared paint across her face and arm, but she didn't notice as she stared intensely at her. She circled Dani's form, studying her from every angle. Then she murmured, "You're the best damn delusion I've ever had. I must've had an extra dose of mushrooms in that last batch."

The lady wasn't senile. She was high.

"Mrs. Bendsfield, I am not a delusion and I am not my mother's ghost here to haunt you. I am here because one of your cows got loose." Her head inclined forward an inch. "A cow."

"Oh." She waved the paintbrush in a dismissing manner. "That's GoldenEye. She wanted to go for a walk, so I let her loose. Don't worry. She'll come back."

"Mrs. Bendsfield."

"No, no." Mrs. Bendsfield turned back to her pottery and hunched down on her haunches. She returned to painting. "GoldenEye always comes back. Always has, always will. You can either take off or you can sit and entertain me a bit."

Dani sighed.

"Don't get snippy with me. You're *my* delusion."

Dani glanced back to the door, but sat on an empty chair in the corner. She'd never known that Mrs. Bendsfield knew her grandmother. She wanted to know why her mother's ghost would be haunting the potter.

"Why would I be haunting you?"

Mrs. Bendsfield sniffed, wrinkling her nose at Dani. "You know why. Don't play that game with me. Not with me, girly ghost."

"I'm here and I'm haunting you, but I don't know why. I'd at least like to know why. I'm an amnesic ghost."

Mrs. Bendsfield fixed her with another hair-raising stare. Then she shrugged. "Because you loved my Oscar and I wouldn't have any of that."

Oscar Bendsfield was Mrs. Bendsfield's son. He went missing thirty years ago, and the story was that he fought with his mother over his absent father. He wanted to find him. She didn't. But he swore he would and that night, he walked to the woods and never came back. The story was told over campfires and during sleepovers. The moral had been to avoid empty threats. Some argued he hadn't made an empty threat. He was still searching for his vagabond father, but some thought he'd gotten snatched and murdered. Still, others always said Mrs. Bendsfield killed him in a rage because he dared defy her word.

Dani always rolled her eyes every time she heard the story. It was a stupid rumor created by mothers to scare their children from using emotional blackmail, but she found herself asking, "Did he love me?"

"Delusions are supposed to be all-knowing, not all-stupid," Mrs. Bendsfield said matter-of-factly, dabbing away.

Dani held her breath. She waited a beat. "Did he father my children?"

Mrs. Bendsfield froze. Her hand stopped mid-motion and then, after a second, she stood slowly and rotated on her feet to stare at Dani. "Oscar Bendsfield was my son, and he was no father to any of your children. You get that in your head and stop showing up around these parts! I took a shovel to you thirty years ago, and I'll take a shovel to you today."

Dani stood slowly, hands fisted at her side. "Are you sure he wasn't my father?"

Mrs. Bendsfield blinked, but remained in place. She shook her head and muttered, "Don't need these headaches. Don't need these delusions. Headaches and delusions. I have to lay off those mushrooms..."

"Did you hurt my mother?!" Dani's voice rose, quaking just a bit.

"Stop playing with me. We both know what happened. Your mother's been in the insane asylum since Oscar took off. You should've gone with her for all the foolhardy things you were saying. My Oscar would never touch a piece of filth like you. We both know that. Just get on raising those bastards of yours."

Dani stepped forward. "Bastards? Bastards of whose? I want to know!"

"It was the other vagabond. Although he wasn't no vagabond by my standards. Kept coming back to sire the last two, didn't he? Vagabonds come and go. That's how they do it. That's how my Oscar was born."

"You kept your son from being my father?"

Mrs. Bendsfield frowned and stepped back as Dani stalked forward. One step by one step. A slow and menacing game of cat and mouse.

"Where's my grandmother?"

Confusion crossed the elder woman's features a moment, and she answered, "Your grandmother's in the grave, Daniella. You know that. You held my hand at her funeral."

"Where's my mother?" Dani asked instead.

"The asylum. I already told you, but you know that. You kept it from your two sisters, remember? A secret to the grave, that was our agreement."

"What asylum? I don't remember."

"St. Francis over in Petersberg. You've been visiting her all your life. I don't know why you forgot that. Don't make no sense. Delusions don't make no sense." She bent back over her work, muttering to herself, "Subconscious, my ass."

"Mrs. Bendsfield," Dani said firmly.

The old lady turned back, slightly irritated at the intrusion.

"I am not a delusion, and I am not the Daniella O'Hara that you remember. I am her daughter, *Danielle*. I was named after my mom and I *will* be back. Be sober when I do. I want some answers."

She knew Mrs. Bendsfield would just shake her head, convince herself it was a weird hallucination, and go back to painting. Dani didn't care. She remembered her mother with dancing spices and magical powers. Mrs. Bendsfield remembered her mother with suspicion, hauntings, and secrets to the grave.

Dani didn't like knowing that her mother would take a secret to the grave.

She drove until she found GoldenEye. As she drew closer, the cow didn't move. She had a halter on with a strap attached, and didn't bat an eye when Dani led the cow back down the road. A gate wasn't too far away. Dani unlatched it, led the cow back inside. Once inside, she unclasped the halter and took it off, draping it over a post as she headed back to her car.

Just before she was about to get in, Dani turned and looked back toward Mrs. Bendsfield's home.

She had walked this road many times, driven the same gravel, and she even cried here after a few fights with Jake. She never thought about the older woman, but she noticed now that the home lay underfoot of two massive oaks, as if protecting it with giant hands shielding the sun's rays. It always had a peaceful air to the home.

Or she used to think.

Dani was on her dock that evening when Aunt Mae arrived. She didn't have to look back to know who it was. Only one person could walk that irritated without sound.

"You need a damn cellphone." Aunt Mae plopped beside her and tugged the afghan Dani had on her lap to cover her as well.

"I traveled, Aunt Mae. The whole point of me leaving was not to get in touch with anyone back here."

Aunt Mae sat silent, then harrumphed, "Well, that's all done. You're here. You're staying, and it's time you got one." She patted her leg.

"You think so, huh?"

"I sure damn do—stop with the bait and hook game. I'm too irritated to bite the bait."

Her word was final, set in stone, and passed by legislation.

Dani chuckled silently to herself. "I love you, Aunt Mae."

"I love you, too."

"And I'll go get a cellphone tomorrow." Dani waited and added, "Right after I steal my mother's picture."

She didn't have to wait long. It only took a second before Aunt Mae sputtered and exclaimed, "You're doing what? From where?" She frowned. "I'm surprised any still exist. Kathryn was always a bit irrational, and she could be mean. I thought she would've tossed everything out."

Dani held her breath, remembering Mrs. Bendsfield's proclamations. "Why was Aunt Kathryn so irrational? Was your mother like that?"

"Oh." Aunt Mae's frown deepened, and she plucked at the blanket on her lap. "I suppose. Your mother and Kathryn never wanted to talk about your grandmother, but I got enough black sheep in me to handle it. No. My mother had all these ideas and grand schemes in life. She'd either be on top of the world or she'd be thinking the world was on top of her. No, no. Your grandma wasn't alright in the head at times. I'd like to think Kathryn got more than her fair share of our mother."

"What part did my mom get?"

"She got the dreamer. Kathryn got the scheming part, some of her paranoia, too."

"And you?"

"Oh." A smile warmed her face. "I got the wild streak. But I got some of her demons. Too much boozing, too much whoring, and too many life lessons learned the hard way. That was me—yep—up until the day your mother asked me to take care of you."

Dani caught her breath.

"I stopped living your grandmother's dreams, thinking they were mine, and I turned serious. I think she knew you wouldn't take to Kathryn."

"Aunt Kathryn didn't take to *me*."

"No, no. That wasn't it." Aunt Mae's voice was firm. "I'm betting your mother knew Kathryn wouldn't mold you, so she came to me. That's back when she found out she was going to go, and Kathryn wasn't accepting it, you see. I think Kathryn lived in denial of your mother's sickness."

"Why didn't you guys ever talk about Grandma?"

"Oh," Aunt Mae sighed softly. "It was more about what she didn't do than what she did do. I lived through it, but I was the first out of the home, so I guess I didn't see the worst to come. I heard about it, and I always thought Kathryn and your mother got a little brainwashed against me. Your grandmother and I used to fight. Those was ugly fights. Nasty."

"You said it was about what she didn't do?"

"She didn't love us. Not the way it's supposed to be, you know. She put herself first. I think a part of us all came from your grandmother, but I'd like to think I partied my selfish streak out of me. I knew enough to know when my little sister Danny came to me that meant my universe shifted. I needed to change, and she informed me of that. She said she would not have my lifestyle influencing her children, and I needed to straighten up if I wanted to be a part of your life."

Another memory tinged with a bitter lining. Dani remembered standing at her mother's funeral, staring at that casket in the ground. Julia and Erica were huddled against Aunt Kathryn's sides with her arms holding both, all three with tears on their faces. Dani stood alone. She'd yet to throw her pink rose inside, but she bit her lip to keep from crying.

Then Mae was there, and she nudged her hand with her own.

"You held my hand at the funeral."

A hoarse chuckle ripped from Aunt Mae's throat. "I'd been standing in the back, all self-conscious and not knowing what the hell I was supposed to do. Your mother only spared one conversation with me in years, but you looked so lost and lonely. A little puppy that just realized her mother wasn't coming back for her."

"You picked me up, and Aunt Kathryn thought it was the most horrible thing that could've happened. I remember that."

"Ah—Kathryn has some of our mother's jealousy, too. She was clueless, didn't know how to even speak with you, but she couldn't stand the thought that I might know. You and me, Dani, we speak the same language. Your two sisters, they speak Kathryn's language. Your mother knew that."

Her mother had known her. Her mother had looked out for her. Dani blinked her own tears back, holding tighter onto the blanket.

"Your mother was a good one." Aunt Mae's voice rasped out, thick with emotion. "Life's not been easy for you, but you had one great mother. You got a good start in life."

Dancing herbs and magical spices. Dani closed her eyes, but chuckled. "Erica used to sneak into my bedroom. She'd tell me that it was because our mom came to her. She wanted Erica to check on me, make sure I was okay." Dani grinned fondly. "Erica was scared of the dark. She slept with me for three years."

"Erica loved you. She looked up to you."

Not when she used her.

Not when she betrayed her.

Not when she forgot Dani was in love with someone.

Erica hadn't idolized her then.

Dani pointed out, "Until she was eleven. It was Julia after that."

Mae's hand came down over hers. "Erica was an idiot." She squeezed lightly. "Pure and simple, tried and true. That girl was an idiot. She loved you, and I knew she loved you. She worshipped the ground you walked on."

A tad dramatic, but Dani enjoyed her aunt's flair.

"I know you think I'm just exaggerating, but I'm not. Your sister, your littlest sis, she—Erica was a lot like you, more than you think. She kept the world away, like you do, Dani. You keep the world away. Erica did that. She gave one face for everyone to love, but she had another face behind her. Your little sister, I watched her. I saw it. She wasn't the Erica everyone thought."

"What?" Dani asked. "She wasn't really as self-absorbed as I thought? She didn't want to be a goddess like everyone deemed her?"

It was laughable. And it was bullshit.

"Why do you think she fell in love with Jake?"

Dani frowned.

Aunt Mae added, "I never talked much to those two, but I saw plenty. Julia with her nose in the air, prancing in Kathryn's shoes. You skulking wherever you thought no one would look, and Erica was the youngest. She watched, too. She got by. She played the part Kathryn wanted, but she kept you in her rearview mirror at all times. Your little sister, she idolized you no matter what you say. I know it." She continued, "Little Erica was smart. Smarter than Julia. She had everyone in town wrapped around her pinkie, but by my thinking, she hadn't counted on her fatal mistake."

Dani wrapped her fists in the blanket now.

"She fell in love with your Jake. And your Jake fell in love with her."

Dani closed her eyes as if to ward off the impending assault.

"She loved him because he loved you. I've had a few years to ponder the two of them. I've come to my conclusions, and I've got to say that Jake loved her. Hook, line, and sinker. It was the part of you that she had inside of her. That's who he fell for."

Dani caught her breath and released it slowly.

"Erica took a part of you that she loved and she made it a part of herself. That's who Jake fell for. And I know it'll hurt, but Jake was needed by Erica."

"What?" The words cut from Dani's throat. "You don't think I needed him?"

"No." Aunt Mae continued, "Not like she did. Jake was her soul. You were his, but he was hers. She needed him. You didn't, and that's what reeled that boy in. You didn't need him, Dani. You didn't need anyone."

Did she need Jake?

What about Boone?

"That boy didn't know what train was coming his way. Erica was the train, and she barreled over him, but she didn't know. She didn't have no stupid driver. Erica was playing life just like the rest of us. She was going forward, but she couldn't stop. She had no idea until you left."

Dani stood, holding the blanket around her. "I don't want to hear any more."

"You got to." Aunt Mae scrambled to her feet. "Because you have a sister in the grave you haven't mourned yet. You have to mourn her. You got to make right with her."

"She's dead!" Dani snapped. "She's dead! She doesn't give a rat's ass what I think."

"*You're not!* That's what I'm getting at." Aunt Mae was right there, right in her face. She didn't blink an eye. "You're alive and you've survived hell, though you don't speak about it. I know! I know the look, but you're standing, and you're alive. You survived, but you ain't living."

Erica wasn't either.

Dani couldn't breathe. Her chest was constricted.

Erica was dead. She hadn't felt her sister leave, yet she'd felt the children die.

That was the point.

"You got to make right with your ghosts. Erica didn't mean to fall in love with Jake, but she needed to."

"How can you say this?"

Erica had Kathryn. Erica had everyone, but Mae was her aunt. She was supposed to be on her side.

"Because I know you better than anyone else." Aunt Mae grabbed Dani's shoulders. "And I know how strong you are, how courageous you are, how beautiful you are. You left holding your head high because you lost your boyfriend. You and Jake were together all your life. News alert: if you didn't need your boyfriend for that long, he's not the one for you."

"I loved him!" The words ripped from her throat. "I loved him, and she took him."

"You're not fighting Julia, Dani. You're fighting Erica. She's alive, and she is a ghost to you right now. Her body's in the ground, but she's around. She will be until you're finally at rest with her."

Where had this come from? Where had any of this come from?

"You feel guilt," Aunt Mae murmured, quieting. "You gotta push that aside and start living. It's stopping you from living. I don't know what you're guilty about. If it's Erica dying, your mother dying, I don't know. Or that you didn't fight for Jake. I don't know, but I see those demons in your eyes. Me, finding you here, sitting alone and damn near chilled—that pisses me off. You should have a husband beside you, and you should be happy, not a numb robot."

"What is this? An intervention on guilt?! Don't come here and tell me what I'm messed up on, who I'm fighting. It wasn't my fault that she up and died." Her voice cracked and it took a moment for her to regain it. "Erica is supposed to be here, and she is supposed to be apologizing to me! I'm not in the wrong. It's not me who should be apologizing to her!"

"She apologized, Dani. It took about two years, but she did. She came and talked to me. She changed because of you. Erica knew what she did, that she lost you."

"I don't want to hear this." Dani started for the cabin.

She did what she did best.

She left.

She grabbed her keys and was down the road within a second.

Dust skirted underneath her tires, spitting the gravel behind her. She drove without thinking, and when she parked, she found herself on a cliff that overlooked Falls River. She closed her eyes, drawing in a breath. Another painful memory. Two trails led down to a pool of water below the cliff. There was a small cave that was underneath.

It was where she and Jake first made love.

Dani climbed from her car and moved to a trail. It looked the same, but brush had grown over it, nearly erasing the trail. It was years of remembrance that highlighted the trail as she made her way downward. It seemed a bit steeper, but flooded topsoil may have had a hand. As she came to the bottom, two buckets were placed near the bank with one containing different mussels and shells.

The cave hadn't remained a secret

A large bubble popped the surface, and a dark shape quickly followed. Two heads broke the surface, complete in diving suits and snorkeling equipment.

"Hey!" A smile broke out as he peeled off his goggles, and his mouth dropped the snorkel mouthpiece. Still attached around his head, it fell to his neck and Dani found herself meeting Jonah's dark eyes. "What are you doing here?"

His colleague peeled off another pair of goggles. It was the same Trenton Galloway who steered his boat to her dock. He waved before ducking back underneath the water. Jonah hoisted himself up and sat on the bank.

"What are you guys doing here?"

Jonah shifted through the bucket. "We found this cave a little while ago."

"What's with the—?" Dani gestured to his hand.

"It's a freshwater mussel we found. This was supposed to be extinct, but Trent thinks we've found the next greatest discovery since the Red River ran north."

"What?"

Jonah studied the mussel and replied, distracted, "It's a river on the Minnesota and North Dakota border. It goes up where all the others go down."

Not what she meant. "Why are you here? How'd you find this place?"

"Oh—Jake told us about it. He said he used to come here all the time as a kid—oh." Understanding dawned in his shoulders as he suddenly glanced up, wide-eyed. "This was..."

"I found this place. Not Jake." Dani sat beside him. Rolling up her pants, she slipped her feet into the water and felt it's warmth against the cold air. This was a day when one shivered as they came up for air. The water served as a warming blanket.

Jonah continued to watch her. "Any consolation, but this mussel's going to be on the cover of *Rivers and Streams*. It really is a find. There's a research team coming to town in a month just for this sucker."

"And they're going to violate my cave."

"Sorry."

"No, you're not."

"You're right. I'm not. But I understand, if that's worth anything."

"This was my spot with Jake." It went without saying. Jonah was quick on the draw, but she felt the need to say it.

Trenton decided to reappear that moment and grinned at them. "This is awesome, Jonah. Another load and we'll have a good enough find to get some grant money for this river."

Jonah shot a cautious look in her direction.

Trenton waved at her. "Ah, it's Dani. She won't say anything. Besides, it'll go public in two months. Plenty of time to solidify our ownership before any freshwater pirates join up."

"Freshwater pirates?"

Trenton hoisted himself on the other side of Jonah. "When a lot's been found like this and it has some serious scientific finding, there's always going to be someone else trying to cash in."

"Which isn't necessarily a bad thing in the scientific world."

Trenton shrugged. "Yeah, but we want to make sure all the new grant funds are going to come through our department. When the magazine comes out, the word will be officially out. Research teams are going to pop up around Craigstown like ticks in the summer."

Dani cringed and started itching. "Thanks for that thought."

Trenton laughed and rifled through the bucket, still in Jonah's hand. "What are you doing here, by the way?"

Dani shrugged. "Felt like a drive down memory lane."

Jonah's eyes sharpened, and Dani knew he hadn't bought it.

Trenton looked up. "Huh?"

"This used to be Jake and Dani's spot."

"Oh." Trenton grimaced. "Sorry, Dani. This spot's going public from now on."

No doubt.

"So, what's so special about these mussels?" If she was going to lose her secret spot, she might as well know what the sacrifice was for. If it was worthwhile.

Trenton flashed another blinding grin, and Dani remembered why he'd been their prom king, but he remained silent, letting Jonah do the explanation.

"There's a few different benefits from this find." Jonah started out, and Dani realized how truly excited he was. He really did love this river. "The first is that this mussel was thought to be extinct, and this bed is the largest bed of mussels I've ever heard about. That's huge for Falls River because it means it's pretty damn healthy considering the dam blocks up the water's travel. The more mussels, the healthier the water system. Plus, they have a natural grey pearl inside. The financial market's going to go crazy over the grey pearl."

It was a bit astounding how one piece of shell could ensure a river's safety. Dani lifted one of the mussels out of the bucket and held it up.

"It looks disgusting." Its shell was slimy, black, and repulsive. A dead fish hung off the side of it.

Jonah and Trenton laughed.

Trenton piped up, "That's its decoy for fish. Fish bite onto it, thinking they're about to have a meal. The glochidia are released inside, and voila, the mussel just landed itself a plane ride for its little babies. The female mussel has her eggs transported into this glochidia stuff. The fish carries it downstream until they drop and form little baby mussels."

"Smart little buggars."

"Nah—they're just another part of nature." Jonah stood up and kicked off his diving fins. "Nature's pretty damn miraculous if we wouldn't stop killing it."

Dani glanced up, a little startled at the vehemence in his tone. Jonah had always been charming. A good ol' boy who drew the ladies in like bees to honey. She'd heard of his ruthlessness in business dealings, but she'd never seen him angered. She heard it now, laying just underneath the bitterness.

"I never would've thought the two of you would become nature lovers." She asked, "What do you need to help this research study go faster?"

"What?"

"You said you only had two months. What do you need? Volunteers? Money?"

"This needs to be as quiet as possible." Jonah held up a hand. "We don't even know if this is the mussel we're thinking about. The research team is going to identify it, no matter what species it is."

"Why wait a month? Why can't they be here before then?"

"That's as soon as we can get the funding for their travel arrangements. They're coming out on our request, but getting the okay for their travel and hotel accommodations takes a while. Red tape can be a bitch."

"How much money?"

"I don't know. Probably twenty thousand, at least. More like fifty thousand."

"I'll pay." Dani wanted to help. In that moment, she needed to do this. Forget all the damn tragedies that happened in her past. This was her way of helping. This project could potentially mean more than their whole town. She wanted on board.

"No, Dani, we can't take your money."

She had money. They just didn't know how much, or where it came from. Both stories she wanted to keep quiet about, too. "I want to help. Consider this an investment."

Jonah studied her, gauging her commitment. Dani knew what he was doing. He wanted to make sure this was a clear-headed decision, not an emotional one. There *was* emotion underlying, but Dani clamped down and let her professionalism shine through. Boone always said there was no room for emotion in the boardroom.

"I'm single, young, and I've already got a home. I can invest my money how I choose. This is one of them, and this is a good investment."

"This might not be a profitable investment."

"Nonprofit grants are great tax write-offs." She had no clue.

Jonah hid a smile, but Dani saw it. She won and she held her hand out. Another second pause, but Jonah reached out and shook on it.

"I'm going to be swimming with you guys, at least some of the times. Part of the deal."

"Fine by me," Trenton added, slipping back into the water. "We need all the help we can get." He took the bucket, saying, "I'm going to swim these out to the boat. It's almost quitting time anyway."

Dani studied Jonah, as Trenton left. "So this is what you do on the weekdays."

"My job description is flexible. I'm supposed to protect the river. Science is slower than business deals. Weekends are an easy sacrifice if it means what I think it'll mean." Jonah checked his watch and murmured, "Aiden informed me to *inform* you, that you have to be somewhere tonight. They're emceeing a talent show, and your presence is required." His eyes traced her face and slowly slid downward.

Dani's mouth was suddenly parched.

"I won't push you right now, but I can't help but wonder what other secrets you got hidden?" His eyes darkened, lingering on her lips.

She'd been right. He hadn't bought the lie.

16

Kate and Aiden were dancing a jig on the stage.

Dani skimmed the crowd. Robbie was waving his arms, seated at a round picnic table. As she neared, Dani saw Jonah at a nearby table with Hawk, his arm around a woman with pigtails, and another two guys who Dani recognized from high school.

"Hey, Dani! We saved you a seat." Robbie kicked out the empty chair on his left. Stilts was on her other side, with his arm around another girl. Lori sat on Robbie's right with both their chairs turned toward the center stage.

Kate was saying, "...we were given an announcement to make from the baking committee. They wanted to let you know that due to the sale on lemon pie filling at our wonderful sponsors, Deano's Supermarket, there has been an influx of lemon meringue pies for the pie contest." As the crowd started to laugh, Kate kept on, "So they're going to divide the contest into two sections. One section will be just the lemon meringue pies while the other will be the general pie contest. They will award two winners because of this event."

Aiden laughed, dipping closer to the microphone. "Please still bring lemon meringue pies next year."

Kate commented as she tried to muffle her microphone, but the crowd still heard, "My pie's one of those. I'm so embarrassed."

The crowd went wild.

Kate blushed while Aiden patted her friend on the back. "Don't worry, Kate. There were twenty lemon meringue pies this year. We hit a record!"

Another scream filled the air. At the same time, Kate began to announce the next act, but Aiden's microphone caught her. "Bryant, you will drop your sister's hair now!"

Kate started laughing in the middle of pronouncing the act's name.

Aiden flushed this time and murmured to the crowd, "Sorry." She left the stage, and everyone heard, "Leave your brother alone! Or no pizza tonight. I mean it!"

Kate shook her head, still grinning, as she departed on the opposite side.

Dani sat back and listened to their fantastic attempts at a high E, but she saw Jake and Julia on the opposite side, surrounding a similar table to their own. Kelley Lynn and the rest filled the other seats next to them.

Jake had been watching her and nodded. Dani waved.

Julia frowned.

That bothered her, and without thinking, Dani got up. She began to walk around the crowd. Julia's eyes widened when Dani kept walking her way.

She stopped right in front of her. "Can I talk to you? Just you and me?"

"No crowd to cheer you on?"

Dani flinched. "You and me? Please?"

Julia stood, and Dani led the way.

Why was she doing this? She wasn't sure, but it felt right. They were center stage. All eyes were on them, but Dani didn't care. She was starting to care less and less, and when she found a private corner between two horse trailers, she turned around.

"When did we become enemies? Sometime in our childhood? When Mom died? When?"

Julia looked down at her hands. She was fidgeting with her shirt. "Why are you doing this?"

"I don't know," Dani admitted. "Maybe because I'm tired of hating something, but not knowing what I'm supposed to hate. Maybe because I'm tired of this supposed 'fight' between us. I don't hate you, Julia.

You're my sister." Her words hung in the air. She repeated them, "You're my sister. We share so much."

"Like what?" Julia snorted.

"We both lost our mother. We both lost a sister. We both weren't taught how to love each other. And we both loved the same man."

Julia looked away and turned her back. Dani saw her wrap her arms around herself. It took a second, but she heard, "I love him. Present day. I love him now."

"And I remember my love for him."

Julia's shoulders arched upward. Dani heard the soft sniffle from behind. Her sister was crying. Her supposedly heartless sister was crying.

"I don't want Jake back." Dani took a breath. "I left that night and he and I, we haven't gone through the process of seeing each other again when we weren't together. Does that make sense? I've thought about him with someone else, but now I'm back. We have to go through that process of seeing each other *not* together for closure, but I don't want him. I don't love him anymore."

"But you used to." Julia turned back, her hand to her face, as if just waiting to swipe another tear before it trickled down.

"I did." She had loved him *so* much. "It took an entire year before I didn't think about him when I woke up in the mornings. A year."

"You left us."

Dani stiffened.

Julia lifted her chin up, challenging her. "You didn't tell anyone. You have no idea what you put us through."

"Put you through what?" Dani narrowed her eyes. She must've heard her sister wrong. The sister who never wanted her around. The sister who always took Erica's side in every fight. The sister who barely talked to her, even when they were children. She would come in the house, laughing, and look around for someone to share whatever had made her laugh. She'd see Dani, and that light would dim in her eyes. Every time. She'd find Erica or Kathryn to tell, and Dani would hear them laughing together from the next room.

"Ten years, Julia." She closed her eyes. "I went through twenty-two years of torture from you and Erica. Twenty-two to your ten?" She shook her head. There was no comparison.

"It was a selfish, thoughtless act that you did. You have no idea what you put Erica through—"

"What I put Erica through? Erica?!" Dani cocked her head to the side. Maybe her hearing was actually going? "Erica was probably the first to celebrate I left. She wasn't this perfect little princess everyone pretends she was. She might've changed at the end, but she wasn't perfect. She was far from it."

Julia paled. "You don't even dare—"

"She stole boyfriends."

Julia gasped.

"She cheated on her boyfriends."

"Shut up."

Dani pressed, "She lied. She backstabbed. She called the cops on at least six of her friends' parties. She stole money from you, Aunt Kathryn, and me—she probably stole from friends. She sent one girl to a psychiatric hospital. Erica wasn't a saint, and I'm tired of you acting like she was."

Julia refused to look at her. She turned to the side, and raised her head even higher. If she'd been looking at Dani, she would've been literally looking down her nose at her. "You shouldn't say those things, not about Erica. She's not here to defend herself."

"She doesn't need to be."

"We all know why you left. Stop blaming Erica for everything. So what? Yes, she stole Jake. Well, I have him now. Are you going to talk about me how you're talking about Erica? I'm alive, Dani. What are you going to say about me when I die?" A shrill laugh slipped from her.

"I just told you that I'm not here for Jake."

"Then why'd you come back?" She whipped back around to face Dani fully. Her nostrils flared. "Why are you here? We were fine without you."

Dani felt slapped in the face. The real Julia just stepped forward. "Not even thirty seconds ago, you were saying how could I have left and

105

put you through...what? What did I put you through? You're mad I'm back, not that I left. That's the truth. Isn't it?"

"Stop it, Dani." Julia hissed. "You know what I meant."

"Yeah," She bit out. "What I *just* said. You're mad I came back."

"This isn't your town anymore."

This wasn't her home.

"Jake's mine."

Not yours.

"Aunt Kathryn wants nothing to do with you."

She never had.

Julia's eyes were irate. Her skinny arms and hands pressed against her side. If she'd been a violent woman, Dani would've braced for a slap. She was wary, waiting for it, but Julia started crying again. She didn't sniffle this time, or make a sound. The tears slid down and Julia didn't react. Dani wondered if her sister even knew they were there. And in that moment, she felt farther away from her sister than when she'd been on the other side of the ocean.

There was a river of secrets, lies, and alliances between them. One stood on one side, the other across from her.

Dani saw it all, and felt an undercurrent of exhaustion sweep underneath her. It pulled her down. "I asked to talk tonight because I don't want to be your enemy."

Julia's eyes twitched. Her lips pressed together. She said nothing.

"But maybe that was wishful thinking?"

The crowd clapped in the background. Whatever act had been performing, must've been a hit, and the crowd roared again in approval. Her lip curved in a sad smile. Maybe that was her cue to walk away.

Dani raked a hand through her hair. "Look, you have my word."

Julia turned back to her.

"I do not want Jake. I can't promise that we won't talk, but I can promise that we won't be friends. We won't hang out together. We won't be anything. All we'll be is two people who grew up together, and two people connected through you." And Erica, the silent ghost still haunting them. Dani didn't mention her. "And for what it's worth, I did tell someone."

Julia didn't ask, but her eyes sharpened.

"I told Kathryn I was leaving. It was her choice not to share that information."

17

The show went off without a hitch.

A few acts stumbled, but Kate and Aiden covered for them, a smart joke delivered with tongue-in-cheek. The last act finished with a bang, a literal bang of the cymbals. One of the lemon meringue pie winners marched onto the stage banging a pair of cymbals together. Kate asked her to stay as the rest of the winners were announced, and each time the cymbals led the applause.

When the last winner was called up to the stage, Dani wanted to avoid any conversation so she moved through the animal barns. She hadn't had the time to visit the night prior amidst the beer and angry outbursts.

Heading into the beef barn, she saw Jake at the opposite doorway. He stood, leaning against the doorway, hands shoved in his pockets. He was in plain clothes, and he looked good. As she walked to him, slowly, Dani saw why each O'Hara had fallen for him.

It wasn't just his outside. His heart was on his sleeve, and he gave it wholeheartedly.

The straw crunched underneath her feet as she stopped before him. The fans whirred in the background, shooting streams of air through the barn. Even though it had been chilly and raining earlier that day, the barn's insides were overheated from machinery and too many bodies.

Just behind Jake, a tiny Jersey calf laid her head down. Her long, oval, doe-like eyes closed, and her gleaming rubbery nose nestled against her mother's leg.

"What'd you say to Julia?"

She fought back a grin. He wasn't wasting time. "I said a little about some stuff and nothing about a lot."

"You're not going to tell me?" Jake sighed. "Julia's in a mood. We were supposed to go to Mae's Grill tonight, but now she wants to go home. She wants to get the house cleaned for Kathryn tomorrow. She's visiting from the nursing home."

"Julia and I are fine."

"Then how come she's been twitching like she's got Tourette's?" Jake rubbed a hand over his jaw.

"Julia's guilt has nothing to do with me."

"What does that mean?"

"You can think on it."

"Are you going to be at Mae's Grill?"

"Probably. Maybe not. I haven't planned my evening."

"That group of yours will be there."

Dani heard the tone. He wasn't talking in a general sense. He was talking about someone in particular. She didn't hold back her grin now. "If you're talking about Jonah, then I wouldn't know. I haven't talked to him tonight."

"Not *yet*."

"Maybe. Maybe not." She leaned forward. "It's really none of your business. Your job is to make Julia happy. Go. Make *her* happy."

"Way she's going, she's just going to work herself into a frenzy."

"Well, you'll do what you do and you'll calm her down. That's your role, right?" She suddenly had no idea why she was even talking to him. There was no reason. "Did you have something to say to me? I came in here to avoid talking to people."

He didn't answer. He just looked at her.

She nodded, moving around him. "Go find Julia, Jake."

The talent contest was done, and others must've had the same idea as her. The other barns filled up, and she grew tired of trying to push her way through another to see the poultry. She surrendered and headed for the beer gardens. It wasn't long before someone spotted her.

"Hey!" Kate waved her arms. "Dani!"

Aiden laughed, then groaned, touching her forehead. "Ooh—I shouldn't have had those drinks in between the acts."

"It added entertainment. I liked it." Bubba curled an arm around his wife.

Kate already had a beer for Dani when she got there. She nudged it across the table. "Drink up! You're behind! I have the night off. Jake's on call, so he can't drink. But I sure can. And after that gig, hell yeah, I'm drinking tonight." Her gaze trailed beyond Dani's shoulders, and she snorted.

Jonah was at the entrance, and a toned brunette rubbed against him. Jonah remained still, leaning against the wall as he watched. Her coy smile added in the seduction, but Hawk and another friend seemed to enjoy the show more.

Aiden groaned. "Where do these girls come from?"

As if by some unspoken agreement, all heads turned in Dani's direction. She knew they were looking at her. She could tell from the corner of her eye, but she couldn't move. She was frozen, her own eyes glued to a person who pushed his way through the crowd. Four others followed behind, and Dani felt her world shut down.

Her arms started to tremble.

Lori grabbed her hand. "Hey." She leaned closer, lowering her voice. "You okay?"

"Dani?" Both Aiden and Kate were watching. Their smiles faded, as did everyone else's. Kate asked, "Dani, what is it?"

Aiden followed Dani's gaze, but turned back with a frown. "Who is it? Is it Julia again?"

"Worse." She bit down on her lip, and her mouth dried up. "My ex-fiancé."

Boone had just walked into her beer gardens.

It wasn't one of those moments when a person feels the eyes. He didn't look up like he sensed her presence. He looked up to skim the room, and his gaze passed over her. He crossed the room, heading into the parallel corner of where she sat. The room started to swim, Dani felt like she was being pulled under the surface, but her eyes fell down the length of his arm. He was holding hands with a woman, a redhead. Dani's lips curled up in a sneer. Boone looked so happy. An empty table opened, and his group quickly nabbed it. The redhead sat beside him and caressed his arm.

Dani needed to look elsewhere. The woman slid her hand to his waist. He sat sideways to where Dani sat. She was getting the whole view. Then the woman's hand dipped even more south, and that was enough.

Dani shot out of her chair.

Boone. He was here.

She started for them, but rational thinking clicked back in, and she took an abrupt left. She went outside instead.

He was so happy. He was—her chest felt tight—what she wasn't.

"Hey, wait up."

Dani ignored Jonah, almost sprinting for her car. Just as her hand grasped the door handle, Jonah grabbed her other arm. He whirled her to him, her back now against the Mustang.

"Whoa." He caught her face. "Whoa. Whoa."

She tried to look away. He didn't allow it. He forced her to look up at him, and what he saw—he cursed. "Hey." He gentled his tone. "What happened? Tell me. What's wrong?"

"I can't."

Dani tried to shove him away, but he grasped her other arm and leaned against her, trapping her.

He murmured next to her ear, "I'm really sorry to do this. This is against my character, but letting you drive out of here in this state is worse. I can't let you do that, not until you talk to me. What happened in there? What did you see that the rest of us didn't?"

Didn't he know?

Dani tried to slide out the side, but Jonah trapped her again. He settled his legs on either side of her. Every inch of his body was plastered against her now.

Dani's chest rose up in short breaths. "You know." She tried to shove him back. He didn't budge.

"I don't. I was at a different table. Remember?" His breath teased her ear, and Dani couldn't suppress the full-body shiver. "What happened back there?"

Her voice hitched on a sob. "Let me go."

She was crumbling. She was under the water again, sinking deeper and deeper.

"You're going to run." He was soothing her. His thumbs began running up and down her arms. "I don't want you to run. Tell me what happened in there."

"I'm fine."

"Dani." His hands slid down, landing with hers. His fingers slid down hers and intertwined them. "Tell me what happened."

"Really." She pulled her hands from his, and tried to push him back again. "I'm fine."

Even she didn't believe herself.

Jonah cursed. He tipped his head back and met her gaze. Then his eyes slid to her lips, and Dani was hot all over. She felt the cut of his jeans, his hands as he caught her hands on his chest, his abdominal muscles. She watched him, her body responding on its own. Jonah slid one of his hands up her arm and curved against her back, moving its way underneath her shirt against her naked skin.

Dani glanced from his eyes to his lips and back.

His eyes never moved, they were steady on her lips. His other hand had started a slow pattern on her back, and Dani closed her eyes, feeling his hand brush against her shoulders and back down to circle her waist. It moved to the front and rested atop her stomach.

He leaned in.

She sucked in her breath. This... This wasn't what she expected to happen.

Jonah touched his lips to hers. Gently, they tasted each other. A slight nip and then another. Dani tasted back and felt her arms move of their own volition. They wrapped around his shoulders. He deepened the kiss, and she felt his tongue slide inside.

Her insides were melting, but a sudden burst of laughter drenched them like a bucket of cold water. They were both brought back to reality.

Jonah moved back. Dani let go, her hands falling back to her sides.

She raised her fingers to her lips. "Oh God." Her voice ripped from her throat. She had forgotten about Boone.

"Not really, but close."

"Not that." Dani flushed. "It's—my fiancé is in there."

"What?"

"My *ex*-fiancé is in there. He just walked in with another woman." How? Why? Who—so many questions ricocheted in her head. "I don't know how he knows I'm here. We never talked about our histories."

The memories were slamming back to her, all at once. Her last night in the hospital, when Boone whispered his love. *"Dani." He held her hand, cradling it like it was the most precious thing against his chest.*

He asked her to marry him.

She said yes.

His friends burst in from the hallway. They all wanted to celebrate.

She murmured now, to herself, "I was too weak."

"Dani? Too weak for what?"

She heard Jonah's voice, but she was still in the past. "I tricked him. I lied, and then I convinced him to go out with his friends." She felt horror sliding through her veins, chilling her. She focused on Jonah. "He asked me to marry him, and I said yes. I didn't want to marry him. I made him go out for a beer. He didn't want to go, but I was in the hospital. I said he needed to celebrate. He was only going to be gone for thirty minutes, enough to appease his friends."

She left him that night.

She left a note on her bedstand.

"What is he doing here?" Her mind was buzzing. Her lips were still tingling from Jonah's kiss.

"Do you want to go talk to him?"

"No."

"What do you want?"

She looked at him, *right* at him. "I want to steal something."

And he held her gaze. "I'm in." He didn't blink, not once.

Jonah had given her his confident, cock-sure smirk when she handed over the keys. She hadn't wanted to drive, to tell the truth. She wanted to sit back, not think, and watch the stars and trees fly by. Any other moment in her life, Dani would've been unsettled by the contentment that sat with her as Jonah drove beside her. Any other moment, but she wasn't thinking about that.

"What are we stealing?"

"There's a photograph of my mother in Julia's house. I want it."

"A picture? Are you serious?"

"Very," Dani said. "Julia said a bunch of her stuff was burned, but I think there's a picture somewhere."

"I'd hide it in the flour container if it was my place. Don't know too many guys around these parts who bake with flour. Now, a fish fry is a whole other story."

"You're not a chef?"

Jonah shrugged. "Who am I to say anything? But this is Craigstown, remember? We're not real 'with the times,'if you know what I mean. I get flack for the river. I'm supposed to be a firefighter or a cop or...I don't know, a lumberjack."

"A lumberjack?"

"Manly jobs, not snorkeling for mussels. Last Thanksgiving, my grandmother sat me down and informed me it's time I go into the family business. I should be competing with those CEOs and not be a nature-loving hippie." He shook his head with a sad chuckle. "I love my grandmother, but she's crazy."

Family business? That's right, she'd forgotten about his father. "What's the family business?"

He signaled and turned the car onto a gravel road. "My dad has a few different companies, but his biggest one is construction. He does commercial."

"Bannon Corp."

She blinked rapidly a few times, startled. The name was posted on billboards, at building sites, and sponsored just about every charity event in the local area. They owned a good portion of the nearby metropolis.

"Yeah," Jonah said dryly. "It's not really something we advertise around here. When Mom died and we lived with our dad, I learned that we were considered the black sheep of the family. And when I went into my field, I became the family's disappointment."

"I can't believe I never put two and two together."

He shrugged again. "Bannon Corp is so big, I think people get immune to it. It's just there, and no one's really noticed it. Plus, I've never said anything. Only one girl asked me if we were related to that company."

"Did you lie?"

"Didn't have to. Aiden lied through her teeth for me." The pride in his voice was unmistakable. Sibling protecting sibling.

"But all these companies that want to build on Falls River, do they know who you are? They have to run in your father's circle."

"Some of them know it upfront. My dad's warned them about me or something. I've gotten a few job offers. Mostly from guys who are looking to get into dad's social circle. But," his eyes sparked, "some don't believe it until afterwards, when I've ripped their proposals to shreds. One guy commented that I had the Bannon streak in me after all."

"Your father is a billionaire."

"My father and my grandfather and my grandfather before that. Not me. Trust me. I'm very much not a billionaire. I'm content where I am. Besides—Aiden wouldn't ever talk to me again if I went to the dark side."

"The dark side." Dani had a sudden image of Aiden scolding her brother, hands on hips as she yelled at Bryant to stop picking on his sister.

"It's kinda how we grew up thinking. Learned later that our mom was ostracized when she left our dad. We didn't know, you know." He glanced over. "We thought our dad was dead."

"And here I thought it was only my family that was screwed up."

"I think most families are messed up in some way. Wouldn't be a family if they weren't." As her old house came into view, Jonah asked, "Should I cut the lights? Is anyone home?"

"I don't think so." Dani squinted, trying to see her house clearer. It was her house, but it wasn't. Half the house looked new, but it was still her home. The other half still supported the building she grew up in. "Jake mentioned he was going to Mae's Grill. The house should be empty."

"Do you have a key?"

"I know where Julia hides the spare."

For all of the perfection Julia and Aunt Kathryn proclaimed, they kept losing their keys. All throughout their lives. Dani could never figure out how they'd lose 'em, but they did. Erica thought it was hilarious, and whenever (the little it happened) she fought with Julia or Aunt Kathryn, the spare key got moved.

Dani felt a grin tug at the side of her mouth. She forgot. Erica had been funny at those times.

She told Jonah to pull the car in the back and into a partial road that was hidden by a cluster of trees. If anyone arrived home, her car would still be hidden from sight. It had no way out except through the driveway, but that could be done without light.

Making sure not to slam the doors shut—just in case—neither spoke nor whispered as they approached the darkened home.

She was scanning everywhere. She wanted to see what was still familiar to her, what had been there when she was.

The broken swing still hung from the tree. The treehouse still stood, but the bottom looked like it had fallen out. And as they approached the back door, the same porcelain frog was nestled among a bunch of flower pots.

Dani knelt and opened the frog's ear. The key was right inside.

Dani took Jonah's hand and pulled him inside once she unlocked the door. His fingers slid between hers, and neither flipped a light switch. The house sat on a hill and could be seen two miles in the distance. They didn't need to proclaim their burglary. And, knowing Jake, his job wouldn't allow the possibility of a forgotten light. But, she used this to their advantage and drew open the curtains. The moonlight lit up the inside, enough for them to make their way around.

The flour was tried first. Nothing. The sugar—nothing. Jonah was convinced it was in a baking container, so they broke apart. He was digging in the coffee grounds when she ran her hands along a picture frame's edge. Still nothing. She went into Julia's bedroom, but only did a cursory look over the dressers and bedstands. Going back to the living room, she checked in a few books, anywhere that wouldn't need to be moved on a daily basis. Julia wouldn't want to keep moving the picture around.

Dani chewed on her lip, thinking.

The piano was still in the corner, but no. Julia hadn't been fond of piano, even though she suffered through her lessons.

A picture of Jake and Julia.

A picture of Julia and Erica.

Then Erica...

Dani kept going. There were more pictures, no—she swung back to that picture of Erica. The frame was thin, but her picture looked a little more pressed against the glass than the others. Dani went over, opening it up, and slid a hidden picture out from behind Erica's.

There it was. It was her, their mother.

Dani stood there, taking in everything about her mother's smiling face.

She must've made a sound in distress or awe because Jonah moved and wrapped his arms around her waist. He pulled her against his chest, propping his chin on her shoulder. Both stared at the picture.

He breathed next to her ear. "She was beautiful."

Her eyes sparked intelligence. A heart-shaped face surrounded perfectly plush lips. Slender shoulders showed strength and fragility. She'd been graced with the same almond-colored eyes as Dani, and her hair was almost a silvery brunette.

Dani was her mother's reincarnation.

A ragged breath escaped her. "I don't remember her like this." She traced a finger over the picture, over her mother's eyes. "She looks sad." But her mother *had* been sad, Dani realized. She just hadn't realized it at the time. "She was always so alive. Her eyes were warm, loving. She laughed. Erica had the same laugh."

A lone tear slid down. Dani wished for her sister, she wished with all her strength. To hear that laugh, just one last time.

"We gotta go," Jonah suddenly said. "Did you want to snap a picture of it on your phone? Or—"

"No." There was no question. She wanted the real deal. A copy wouldn't do it. "It's going with us."

"Okay." He moved around her, put Erica's photo back, and closed the picture frame. His hand found hers. "Come on. A car's coming. If we go now, we can be on the road before they turn in."

Dani followed, in a daze.

Jonah replaced the key. He pulled Dani to the car. Without turning the lights on, he drove around the house, and down the driveway. They turned onto the road. He waited a good distance before switching on the lights. Just then, another car pulled over a hill, slowed, and turned into the driveway.

Julia hadn't stayed at Mae's Grill long. Dani didn't really care. She had what she wanted. They drove in silence until Dani looked up. He drove them to the cabin. "No Mae's Grill tonight?"

Jonah turned off the engine. "Figured you'd want to put that somewhere safe."

Oh.

He added, "Didn't know if you were up to the crowd anyway."

Boone.

She'd forgotten about him. Then again, that'd been the reason for their burglary mission, but there'd be questions if they didn't go. Hell, there'd be questions if they did go. Dani had a sudden wish to hear Kate's laugh and Aiden's shriek as they mercilessly teased Robbie or Stilts. Dani wanted to hear Kate rate the sleaziness of the girls who propositioned Jonah. Which reminded her...

"Do you really just have to stand in a bar and get hit on? I mean, I've seen it, but really? Like you stand there and here come the pick-ups?"

A sheepish look came over him. He cleared his throat, tugging at his shirt's collar. "Uh, well...yeah, I guess. I mean...I don't sleep around, and I don't take those girls home. I'm not a manwhore, if that's what you're thinking."

"You really don't even have to work for it?"

He laughed. "Trust me. There are some girls I have to put in overtime." His gaze fell to her lips, staying there. "Where did these questions come from?"

"That girl was grinding her *entire* body on you."

His eyes flicked to hers. A cocky grin appeared. "You noticed, huh?"

Her eyebrows rose. "Was I supposed to?"

He shrugged, his grin widening. "Nice to know you noticed, but I've found it's easier to let the girls do their thing and think they'll get what they want. Hawk or Carl would've hit on her eventually, and she'd get tired of me, and start liking the attention from them. She was one of those girls who gets more aggressive if you put 'em off, you know?"

"Right." She mocked in disbelief. "That was her not being aggressive."

"I don't think I want to have this conversation anymore."

"Why?" Her voice was mocking.

"Because." He gripped the back of his neck. "Not with you."

She'd never seen the infamous Jonah Bannon uncomfortable and self-conscious. It was a sight to behold. She was grinning so hard now.

"What? Why? Unless it's not true. Are the girls actually hitting on you? Maybe they're a show?" He was squirming, and she was loving it. "I bet you don't sleep with any of them, do you? Just like that one girl you had Hawk take home and you were hiding from."

"I'm not a whore."

She pretended to gasp, opening her eyes wide. "What if it's the opposite, and you don't sleep with any of them?"

"Dani." He groaned. "Look. I'm healthy, I'll just say that."

"I bet you don't even like sex, and you bake! With flour!"

"I don't—" He broke off and shook his head. "I like sex."

"Do you do kinky stuff with flour?"

"Where in the hell did this come from?" He scowled, getting out of the car. Dani followed, and she led the way inside. When the lights turned on, the words died in his throat.

Dani frowned, confused at the sudden speechless look on his face.

A slow smile spread across his face. "You look happy."

She was. Dani frowned. How could she be happy? She turned away sharply.

"Don't." He grabbed her arm and pulled her back. "Don't shut down because you're experiencing a moment of happiness. You got your mom's picture."

Dani looked down to her mother. It was like the world righted itself, just for that moment. "She died when I was nine. I just have these little bits of memories of her. I think we were happy. Her, me, Julia, and Erica. The four of us."

"I bet you're just like her."

"No." Dani shook her head. "Erica was like her. Everyone loved my mother. She had this warmth about her." That was what Dani remembered. She'd been the dreamer, but she inspired everyone else to dream. Erica had the same charm. "I think I'm like my father, whoever he was."

She placed the photograph on her dresser. She'd hide it the next day, but she wanted to see it before she slept and when she woke. She wanted to see her mother bathed in the morning's sunshine, no matter how cheesy that sounded.

Jonah was waiting in the doorway.

Why was he different than Boone? Why did she allow him to see her when she shut out everyone else?

Caught in a spell, Dani stood there and held his eyes. Slowly, his eyes moved back to her lips. Dani caught her breath. Neither moved.

And his phone rang.

She jumped while Jonah cursed. "Yeah?" He turned and moved back into the living room.

Dani sat on her bed and exhaled. Lying down, she closed her eyes and listened to Jonah's one-sided conversation. Aiden wanted to know where he was and if he was going to Mae's Grill. Jonah didn't know. Why not?

Dani grinned as she heard Jonah successfully block that trail of questions when he asked if Robbie was bringing Lori or Brooke. Even from the bedroom, she could hear Aiden go off, ranting about both of them.

Jonah moved to the doorway and watched her back. That phone was pressed to his ear, but his eyes were on her. Hers were on him, and for a moment, Dani knew what she wanted. She sat up, still holding his gaze, and he murmured, "No, Aiden. I don't know. I'm working tomorrow."

Aiden's voice was even clearer. Could he barbeque with Bubba? You know it's Bryant's favorite meal. And he hasn't seen you for a few days.

"Aiden," Jonah interrupted. "I don't know. I'll try. I took Bry and Amalia swimming recently."

She knew, but she was just saying. Bryant misses his favorite uncle.

The guilt trip worked wonderfully because Dani heard Jonah sigh, "I'll come for dinner tomorrow night. Yes, I'll barbeque." He cleared his throat. "I have to go."

He had never looked away from Dani. And he murmured now, tossing his phone onto her dresser, "I always fall for it. She dangles my niece and nephew, and I do whatever she wants."

Dani heard him, but she wasn't listening. She was paying attention to what her body was saying, what it wanted.

There was a pause that hung between them.

Jonah asked, "Do you want to go or...?"

She knew what would happen if they stayed, and drawing on strength that she didn't know she had, she stood up. "Let's go to Mae's Grill."

Two shots equaled...

No. That wasn't right. She had more than two shots. How many? Her fingers would tell her. She knew it. They never lied. How many fingers did she have?

"There you are."

When they got to Mae's Grill, Kate declared it was Shot Night, and the title was self-explanatory. Shot after shot after...shot...after...Dani lost count. She hadn't meant to take them, but they ended up down her throat. Somehow. And now the world was all fuzzy, but not Jonah. He bent down in front of her, and she could only smile at him. "You're so pretty. Do you know that?"

He chuckled as he slid his arms underneath her, lifting her in the air. "Up you go. It's time for bed."

She touched his face. It was so smooth and so masculine. His jaw was one of those that made women melt. Strong. Square-like. Oh yes. He was very delicious. She understood why that woman rubbed herself against him, like a cat. She said, "You're not hairy. Cats are hairy."

"Yes. They sure are, and I'll tell you what I am. I'm sober." He carried her back to the parking lot, putting her in the front seat of his car. Then he pointed to the backseat where Kate was. "Unlike you and Kate. Come on. I'm driving you both home."

Dani turned around. "Hey, Kate!" She frowned. "You're not hairy either. That's good."

Kate groaned, her voice muffled against the carseat, "I love him. Why do I love him?"

"Who do you love?"

But Jonah answered, getting into the car, "Because Robbie is intelligent, good-looking, and he's the yang to your ying. Right, Katie?"

"That's right." She sniffed against the seat.

Dani frowned. "What are you crying about?"

"I love Robbie, and he doesn't love me back."

"Robbie doesn't want Lori," Jonah clarified, pulling out of the parking lot. "He just thinks he does, but he doesn't."

"What do I do, Jonah? What do I do?"

"You flirt with him, and then you flirt with someone else. You go on a date with someone else."

"I don't want to go on a date with someone else. I want to go on a date with Robbie. I want to have sex with Robbie." She giggled. "S.E.X."

"Trust me. Date someone else and Robbie will wake up."

"You promise?"

"I promise."

Kate sighed. "I'm so glad you're around lately. You've been around a lot more than usual. Nights like these you'd usually be off getting s.e.x." She laughed, hiccupped, and groaned. "Not again."

Dani laughed and then clamped her mouth shut. Vomit. Vomit was coming. She couldn't speak, but she patted Jonah's arm.

Jonah swerved to the side. "Shit!"

Dani shot through the door and emptied her stomach onto the county highway's pavement.

"What's going on?"

"Nothing. Go to sleep." Jonah moved around the car, kneeling beside Dani. His hand began to brush her hair back and he sank down until he was sitting. "Okay. That's not good. Get it all out, Dani. You'll feel better afterwards."

She didn't need to be told. She was already doing it, or her stomach was doing it. Over and over. And over. There was nothing left inside when she finally stopped, breathing raggedly. Her hair was a mess. She had puke breath, and she was sweaty all over.

"Fuck." She moaned.

Jonah chuckled softly, rubbing her back. "You think you're done?"

She shook her head, so weak. She knew there was more. Her stomach was already cramping. A groan came from her, and soon she was going once again. Jonah sat with his back to the car. He pulled Dani onto his lap with her head hanging off to the side, far enough to not splatter either of them.

After another round, she asked, spitting extras from her mouth, "What's Kate doing?"

"She passed out."

"That was fast."

"The booze helped." Jonah rubbed her shoulders and arms.

"I can't feel my arms. I can't feel my legs. I can't feel my lips. Nothing."

"But you can still feel him, can't you?"

"Yes," Dani relented. "God, yes."

Oh yeah. That was how those shots got down her throat. She went to Mae's Grill and saw that woman Boone had been with. He wasn't there, but damage done. She didn't wait for Kate to offer the first round of shots. A tray was brought to the table, and Dani grabbed one and threw it back.

Boone. She felt him all night, which was so ridiculous. She'd been making out with Jonah earlier. Ooh Jonah. She lifted her head up and looked at him. He was so pretty. And his kisses were amazing, and she couldn't have any of them that night. She was a mess. He wouldn't want to kiss her again.

She was going to ask, to make sure he wouldn't hold this night against her, but nope. Another round was knocking on her throat's door. She lurched again.

Jonah just kept rubbing a hand down her back. "Is that why?"

"Yes." She collapsed against Jonah's chest and pulled his arms tight around her. She was done. Her stomach was finally settled, but Boone was there. He was in town, and he'd been holding that woman's hand. "I keep people away."

Jonah's arms tightened.

"I'm drunk and telling you my biggest problem. There's probably cows over there."

Jonah stroked her hair, kissing her forehead. "You're telling me because I know all the other secrets. What's a few more?"

"I barfed."

Dani closed her eyes as he kissed her cheek, her jaw. He avoided any area close to her mouth, though. "That's not a secret. You're drunk, and I'm going to put you to bed after we drop Kate off. You're going to sleep it off, and you're going to hurt so much tomorrow that you won't want to move."

"Sounds heavenly."

"I'll bring you hangover food tomorrow."

"Ugh. Food. No." Dani lurched forward. Jonah let her go. When she was done, he helped her back into the car. She murmured once they were on their way again, "Jonah?"

"Yeah?"

"I'm messed up when it comes to guys." It needed to be painted on a billboard.

Jonah took her hand and entwined their fingers. "You've just got some of the puzzle pieces messed up. That's all."

"I mean...I can't..." She fell silent. The words escaped her.

"I'm not asking, Dani."

"Okay."

She fell asleep like that, still holding his hand.

Dani woke, gagged, and immediately covered her face with a pillow. Her entire body felt like it'd been rubbed raw against a tree. Her throat had digested the bark. Beside her, she heard a low chuckle as Jonah turned and pulled her against his side. He hid his face in the crook of her neck and shoulder.

"Not funny," Dani rasped out into the pillow.

"It is." Jonah lifted the pillow away and grabbed Dani's hand as she tried to cover herself. He lifted his head and grinned down at her. "Aren't hangovers the best?"

Dani curled away from him and hugged her pillow.

Jonah fitted himself behind her, entangling his legs with hers, and leaned over so his face was beside hers.

Dani's breath escaped her as Jonah's body blanketed her.

"Aren't they?"

"You suck." Dani breathed on him, letting him have the full force of her hangover breath.

Jonah laughed. "I brushed your teeth last night so good try."

"What time is it?" She looked. Seven thirty in the morning. "What time did we go to bed?"

"Around three."

Dani groaned and tried to pull her blanket over her. Jonah blocked her efforts and tucked her underneath him. She was captivated by the spark in his eyes. It was instant, and just like that, one look from him, and she felt like sunlight fell over her, warming her from the inside out. Startled by her reaction, she blinked a few times as he moved to straddle her. He braced himself with an arm on each side and looked down at her.

"What are you doing?" She felt the tingles starting. Her fingers enclosed over his as he touched one of her hips. It was an inviting touch. Dani held his eyes. He was asking for permission, and just like that again, one touch and her insides were engulfed with longing.

She wanted him.

She nodded, so slight, but it was enough. He bent down and pressed his lips to her stomach.

Dani closed her eyes.

Jonah lifted her shirt and pressed a second kiss to her flat stomach. Then he shifted so he lay between her legs. He glanced up, held her eyes, and lifted underneath her waist to fit her against him.

Her heart was thumping hard, pressing against her chest, and she bit down on her lip. She had woken in pain, but with a few touches he took over her body. She was in a different pain, but she was waiting. She was anticipating. She wanted him to do more.

She couldn't wait.

And she sighed, surrendering to what would happen. It felt right, and she didn't think about it. She answered his body's urgings because her own was switched to autopilot. She wasn't going to think of the ramifications, consequences, or what-ifs. She let her body take over. Shutting everything off, she wrapped her legs around his waist.

"Dani," Jonah murmured. So soft. She heard his own aching, and then he was pushing her shirt the rest of the way. She sat up, letting him slip it off. They both paused, suspended in the air, chest-to-chest, face-to-face. It was just the two of them, and whatever was happening between them. Then he dipped his head to take her lips in a soft kiss. They paused again, their lips on each other's, and she felt he was asking for permission once again. A groan came from her, and it was enough. His tongue swept in.

Yes.

Dani laid her arms on his shoulders, falling back to the bed as his hand helped guide her. She pulled him with her. Then he was kissing her neck, the corner of her eye, her lips again. Jonah was weaving a spell only her body could answer. His fingers swept around her breast as another caressed her leg.

Heated sensations speared through her, all the way to her little toes. They curled, and she gasped, just wanting more. The aches and pains vanished. A throbbing replaced them, and pleasure had her body writhing. She needed more. Desire like she'd never experienced had her answering his body's urgings, meeting her lips to his, and demanding her own entry.

They kissed, caressed, and teased each other until finally the ache was too much for both of them. Time stood still for a moment, when he paused right before sliding inside. He looked up, poised at her entrance, and her hand tightened over his arm.

Then he moved inside of her, and she came alive.

The rhythm built between them. She was blind, turning to him for everything she needed, every touch she wanted, her body feeling an addictive high. She sought his mouth, and he met her. Their mouths fused together as he continued thrusting into her. She trembled, meeting him, answering his strokes with her own. She was right with him. They were riding this moment together, until she arched her back, coming to the edge. She sucked in air, and still Jonah kept going.

As they climaxed, he pulled her tight against him. She clasped on, and both shuddered as their bodies were feeling the waves crashing over them. Dani sighed and curled into Jonah. He ran his hand up and down her body, a soft and tender caress.

Nothing was allowed in her mind.

It was only the two of them, and their pleasure and heat. She moaned, reaching for his hand. Their fingers entwined again, and Jonah laid his arm across her body, one leg rested over hers.

Her body was humming, and soon her eyelids closed. A peace rested over her. Later, much later, she woke. The bed was empty as she glanced behind her. Jonah's welcoming weight no longer sheltered her. She yawned, but her body felt alive.

She felt alive.

A grin tugged at the corners of her mouth, as if she'd been given a secret no one else was worthy to know. Filling a mug, she returned to her bed and pulled the comforter over her. She could still feel him. She wanted to savor that, but her eyes moved to her dresser...

...to her mother's picture.

A conversation came back to her.

"The asylum. I already told you. A secret to the grave, that was our agreement... St. Francis over in Petersberg. You've been visiting her all your life."

She remembered Mrs. Bendsfield's comments.

Maybe it was time she found out some other secrets.

She didn't make a conscious decision, but she was soon dressed and back in her car. She wanted answers, and she was going to get some. She wasn't going to hide from this part of her life, unlike Boone. She could bask in bed all day, but somehow Jonah had become entwined with her family and her need to find out more answers. Maybe she got an extra amount of strength from Jonah, but she headed to Petersberg and on to St. Francis.

Three employees sat behind a large counter when she entered the bricked hospital. Her sandals echoed against the tiled flooring, and a middle-aged woman with graying hair and a nametag that said Marge looked up with a pleasant smile. "Good morning. How may I help you?"

"I'm here to see my grandmother."

"What's her name?"

"Sandra O'Hara."

Marge turned to the computer, and a moment later, she murmured, "And your name?"

"Dani—Danielle O'Hara."

"Right." She placed a blank nametag onto the counter alongside a black marker. "You need to put your name on here. The staff will know you're a visitor then. You'll head straight back down the hall, and at the elevator, you're going to want to go to the second floor. Phyliss should be at the front desk. She'll help you from there."

"Okay." She took a breath. Her hands trembled. She didn't move.

"Your grandmother's quite popular around here. This will make her day."

Might've helped if she had known her grandmother. She didn't, but Dani dragged in some more air and headed forward. A lady wearing a nametag that said Phyliss smiled at her when she got off on the second floor. A woman was in the corner, hunched over in a seat, and humming. Her eyes, glossy and glazed over, snapped to where Dani was. They didn't move.

Phyliss cleared her throat. "Who are you here for, sweetie?"

"My grandmother. Sandra O'Hara."

Phyliss nodded and stood up. "Follow me. I'll take you to her."

The lady was still humming.

"Um...is she..." But Phyliss was walking away, and Dani followed. She glanced over her shoulder. The woman's eyes followed her.

Phyliss said once Dani caught up, "You'll have to excuse Henrietta. Sandra's nothing like that one. She just sits and hums. And watches. That's about it. Sandra's—well—you'll see for yourself."

They stopped at a closed door, and Phyliss knocked twice. She opened it. "Sandra? You have a visitor."

Dani heard something fall inside the room and frowned. There was a quick shuffling on the floor, and Phyliss stepped back. The door opened.

Sandra O'Hara had the wrinkles that artists loved to capture. Long white hair was pulled into a messy braid, and her eyes were like Dani's. Almond color. No, Dani had her grandmother's eyes. For a moment, the two looked and studied each other. Raking each other up and down. Not a word was spoken.

She was short, like Erica.

"Who are you?"

Dani saw intelligence then. She heard it in her voice. Clear and strong. "I'm your granddaughter." She tried to match it.

"Which one?"

"I'm Dani O'Hara. Daniella was my mother. She—"

"My daughter's dead. I know that much." Sandra gestured to Phyliss. "I'll visit with my granddaughter in the reading room. Can you get Lawrence out of there?"

Phyliss patted Sandra on the arm. "Of course. Of course."

"How'd you know I was here?"

"I heard you were crazy."

Sandra barked out a laugh. "Oh—I'm crazy. Crazy, senile, and old, just not today." She raised her head to Dani. "You're my granddaughter. Spitting image of your momma." She turned and sat in a chair. "Let's hope you ain't nothing like your momma."

"And why's that?"

"Because she had awful taste in men, that's what. She died, leaving you young'uns alone. And because she wasn't alright in the head either. A little cuckoo, and that's coming from a crazy lady." Sandra leaned back in her chair. "So, what are you doing here?"

"I found out about you from Mrs. Bendsfield. I never knew you were alive."

Phyliss knocked on the door. "The reading room is open, Sandra. I told the kitchen where you'll be, and I ordered an extra tray."

Sandra heaved a deep breath, standing up. "Come here." She waved impatiently for Dani to move closer and clasped her arm. "You can help walk me there. Make sure I don't go face first and break a hip."

Dani was looking for the craziness. She was looking for why her grandmother was locked up and never spoken of, but the elder who sat before her was sane, logical, and a little too intelligent.

She said, "You don't seem crazy."

Sandra snorted and patted her granddaughter's arm. "I am, girly. I am. You're just seeing me on a good day. Trust me. These days don't come by so often. Believe it or not, I'm needed behind these white-ass walls."

"You talk like Mae."

The smile vanished from Sandra's face. "Yeah. Guess I do."

The reading room was a small library with two coral plush couches on one side. Three bookcases framed the walls with a narrow window above them. In one corner, a light-stained wooden desk stood bare with two moss-green lounging chairs placed before them. The upholstery's stitches were coming apart at the seams, but Sandra didn't mind as she dropped down on one of the chairs. She motioned with a brisk hand to the other chair. "Sit."

"The couches look more comfortable."

Sandra shook her head, a grimace adding more wrinkles to her face. "I can't get up when I sit on those. I'd rather be able to stand than look like a fool when I break a hip."

Dani sat. "I have your eyes. And you're short like Erica."

"She's the one who died? Philly read me the obituary. She was young, wasn't she?"

"She had just turned twenty-two."

Sandra clasped her seemingly frail hands together. "I got two daughters who don't speak to me. The one who did is in the ground. And I used to have three granddaughters who didn't know I existed. One of them's already dead." She laughed to herself. "How is it that the crazy grandmother is outlasting them all?"

"Why don't they talk to you? Kathryn never talked about you. Neither did Mae."

Sandra studied Dani for a moment. Her eyes seemed to pierce straight through, like her grandmother was trying to read inside of her.

"Let me guess," Sandra mused, her lips pursed. "You're closest to Mae, huh?"

"How'd you know?"

"Because I know my daughters. And I know how they don't enjoy each other. You talk to Mae. That means you don't talk to Kathryn."

"I thought my mother got along with Kathryn." They always had. She could remember Sundays spent together. Holidays. Birthday parties.

"Nuh huh." Sandra leaned forward and grabbed a pencil awkwardly. Her hands shook, but she managed to keep a hold on it. "Kathryn, Danny, and Mae hated each other. No, that's not right. Mae loved Danny, but Danny knew who she could be around and who she couldn't. Your Aunt Mae was wild back in her day. Too wild, but she never listened to me. Hated me, she did."

"But Aunt Kathryn and Momma..."

"No." She waved the pencil at her. "Kathy and Danny had two things in common. Presentation. And their taste in men. Their taste in men was awful." Sandra sounded disgusted. The loose skin under her chin was wiggling as she kept waving the pencil in the air. She nodded to Dani. "I see how you been raised. You been raised like Mae. You look like your momma, but you handle like Mae. Not much Kathryn in you."

"Why didn't I know about you?"

Her grandmomma lowered the pencil to her lap. "You have to come for a second visit for that one."

Dani leaned forward. This grandmother spoke of 'Danny,' not 'Dani.' Dani knew Mae was careful when she talked about her mother, but they shared the same name. She knew they shared the same nickname, but it felt different coming from this woman. This was almost a stranger, and in a way, Dani hadn't felt closer to her mother than she did at that moment. She wanted to hear more about 'Danny.'

"Why were you kept a secret if my mom came to visit?"

She snorted. "I'd like to know why your momma stopped coming to visit. I'd like to know what my granddaughters were like. I'd like to know how my daughters are doing, if they're happy or miserable. I'd even like to know if they're living on the streets. There's a whole hell of a lot more that I'd like to know than you, I guarantee that." She paused, then abruptly asked, "You a drinker?"

"What?"

"I know what Mae was like. A drunk and a whore. You got a little of that in you?" She didn't sound accusatory, just curious.

Dani flushed. She rarely drank, but got drunk the previous night. And she rarely had sex, but had it that morning.

"No." Her grandmother answered her own question. "A drunk and whore wouldn't blush like that. You ain't no drunk and whore. Tell me." She leaned forward. "Mae still like that?"

What kind of family did she come from? Kathryn would've fainted at the nerve. Dani had a hard time understanding her Aunt Kathryn had lived with this woman, as a mother.

"No."

"What is she then?" She barked out. "What she doing nowadays?"

"She owns a bar. She's really successful. You should be proud of her."

"What's the name of it?" Her grandmomma had hawk eyes. They followed every twitch, every swallow like a mouse two miles away.

"Mae's Grill."

"Are you serious?" Dani was startled by the sudden smile that spread over her face. All the wrinkles were pushed back, and her face distorted into a happy human being.

"Yes."

She tipped her head back and laughed. "All the workers talk about that place. They love it. Once a week they put in orders, and James drives down and gets them. Her food is good. Damn good. Just like my own momma's cooking. How is Mae?"

"She's good. She owns the house next door to the grill, and she's letting me stay at her lake cabin. She's happy and sober."

"Still got the men, I bet." Sandra harrumphed, but there was no condescension behind it. "Tell me about Erica. I want to know about the one who died."

"I don't really know who Erica was when she died."

"Why not? You're her sister."

"You don't know about your own daughters!"

"No." A breath. "No, I sure don't, and I'll tell you next visit why I don't know them. I want to know why *you* don't know your sister now. This visit."

"Because I left town. Erica was spoiled, a brat, and obnoxious when I left. When I came back—"

"Let me guess." Sandra didn't miss a thing. "She changed?"

"She was dead."

"Death changes you."

"What?"

Sandra waved at her. "You said you left. She lost you." The food was brought in. Sandra started with her pudding and then grabbed the ham sandwich. "This is good food. You don't want to eat?"

Dani shook her head.

"I'm the crazy one?" Sandra laughed to herself. "You're crazy for not eating, but to each her own."

Dani had to ask, one more time, "Why are you in here?"

Sandra's white hair flew around her as she finished her milk. She shook the carton to make sure every last drop fell into her aged mouth. "Because I get real sad. Sometimes I get real angry, and other times I get real violent. I used to hurt myself on a regular basis. I had someone always watching me. They'd sit on a chair and stare at me for all hours of the day." She put the milk down and frowned. "They changed my meds a few months ago, and I'm a little better. I'm real good today, got a visitor to boot." She patted Dani's knee with a shaking hand. "This is a good day. That's all it is." She kept going, "I'll tell you a little something, just enough to whet the appetite. I want you to come back so you can hear the rest. I wasn't a fit mother. I wasn't. I'm not going to say there are two sides to the story because I should've been my little girl's momma. I wasn't. I know, now, that some of it's from my own momma and her momma before that. You got a different momma, and judging from the looks of you, whatever my little Danny did—it was right by you."

"Who is my father?"

Sandra shook her head and stood. She shuffled to the door and yelled out, "We're done in here. Lawrence, you can have my granddaughter's food. She didn't eat a bit."

Lawrence was inside in a flash. Dani thought it wasn't for the food, but for the room. He grabbed her sandwich and pudding and escaped to the farthest corner.

"That's your next visit," Sandra informed her granddaughter. She held out her arm, and Dani sighed. She grasped the arm and walked alongside her grandmother. As they walked past the humming lady, Sandra stuck her tongue out. Dani was shocked to see the lady harrumphed as she stuck her own tongue out.

"She's a feisty one. She always tries to take my cigarettes. Got the damn staff fooled, thinking all she does is hum. She don't sit and not think. She's a feisty one. Smart, too."

At Sandra's room, Dani held back in the doorway.

"Next visit, I'll tell you why you never knew about me."

Dani waited.

"And the visit after that—I'll tell you who your daddy is." She sat down and rearranged a blanket over her legs. Then gave Dani a pointed look. "You can always ask Kathy. She knows who your daddy is, too."

"Kathryn doesn't like me much."

"That's not surprising. You look like your momma. She didn't like your momma either."

Dani left feeling more confused than when she arrived. Not normal. That was what Dani had thought she was, but maybe she wasn't.

Maybe she *was* normal after all?

Jake was waiting at the cabin when she got back. She motioned for him to head inside, but showered first to prepare herself. She didn't know what this visit was about, and when she went back out, he was at the kitchen table.

She sat across from him. "You and I don't do visits. Why are you here?" There was no sense in beating around the bush.

"What's going on between you and Bannon?"

"Since I've become friends with both Bannons, you need to be more specific."

"You piss me off, Dani." Jake shook his head and growled, "Jonah Bannon. And you. What's going on?"

"Why is it your business?"

He stared at her, studying her. Dani was used to it and especially with him. She knew Jake better than anyone. Something was brewing underneath his surface, and she wanted to know.

"Bannon's gotten mixed up in some business that could go dirty. I don't want you hurt in the crossfire."

"What kind of business?"

"You know Bannon."

"No. Not really." The significance wasn't lost on her. She heard some, she saw a little, and she'd felt a bit more than she wanted to admit. In the end, though, she actually didn't know much of his business. If it was a fight, she doubted Jonah wouldn't back down.

"Another fight is brewing over that river of his. A conglomerate wants in. They want a piece of our land, and Jonah's got his heels dug in. He doesn't want them here." Jake leaned forward. "I know these guys. I've heard of their family, and their dad is a shark. One scent of weakness and this could get bloody."

"Are you talking about illegal stuff?"

"It's been known to happen. Bannon means good. He really does, but he works for us. We gotta watch him so he doesn't end up dead one of these days."

"He works the river. How dangerous could that be?"

"Very," Jake said. "Falls River is a huge money market. And, especially because we're so close to Tenderfoot Rush, everyone wants in. This is prime tourist land. People all over the nation come to visit here. You know this, Dani. Think about the multimillionaires who want to get richer, and they're being told by Jonah that they can't. They roll over people. It's happened before."

He was right, but... "Come on, Jake. You're talking about physical safety. Like Jonah's going to get assaulted or something. That's not going to happen. This isn't the Wild West. There are laws."

"Laws that those millionaires pay a lot of money to get around." He stood and crossed his arms over his chest. "He's gone and worked himself into another one of those battles. There was one too long ago that had the whole town riled up. This company is worse than them."

"What company? What are their names?"

"Quandry, Inc. Drew Quandry's the head of it."

Dani recognized the logo. They'd manufactured about a third of her belongings in that cabin, sponsored charities for the tsunami victims, and even awarded her some money that no one knew about.

"Oh."

"Yeah." Jake shook his head. "Look." He started to walk, but turned back. "Jonah's going to get himself killed one of these days. I understand why he does it. I even understand why he loves that river so much. But he's going to end up gone one of these days. I really, really, don't want to be the guy to tell you his body has been found. I see it between the two of you. Everyone sees it. Don't try and tell me it's not like that with you two. When you talk to Jonah, let him know I talked to you."

"So you can mark your territory?"

"What? No."

"Look, Jake." This business thing could be that dangerous, but it didn't feel right that it was Jake telling her this information. She was going off a hunch. "According to a few around town, you used to worship Jonah before I came back. You're not going to use some business deal that could turn bad as an excuse to have a go at him because you're really pissed about whatever we might have going on."

"It's not like that, Dani. I'm worried about you. I just don't want to see you get hurt."

"Bullshit!" she said. "You didn't care ten years ago, and you don't care today."

Jake froze. "That was different."

"It's not. You tore me in half. You didn't have the decency to break up with me and not date someone. You were with me when you were with her. You broke up with me *to go* to her that night."

"Dani."

She saws his hands in clenched fists. She saw the tension in his shoulders, and she saw a wariness in his eyes.

She didn't care.

"Don't. This isn't about you and me. Believe it or not, but I *am* here because I care about you. I don't want you to get hurt. Stop hanging around with Bannon."

"Fine," she clipped out and crossed her arms. "You stop banging Julia."

"Excuse me?"

"I'm serious." It was reasonable. "You tell me what to do, so I get to tell you what to do. I call an even trade. I'll stop talking to Jonah, and you stop screwing your fiancé."

Jake gaped at her. "Who—who are you? You *never* would've said something like that before."

"A lot's happened from then to today. Catch up."

"Like what? How? You won't tell anyone where you've been. You won't say a damn word." He spread his arms wide. "And the one time that you *are* upset, you tell me to get lost."

"You're not the person I confide in anymore." She narrowed her eyes. "Not anymore and if that person is Jonah, it's going to stay that way. You have no right to come here and order me around. So get out!"

Jake stood still, his eyes frozen on her.

"I'm not changing my mind, so stop waiting for it to happen."

"I want you to stop seeing him."

"Tough shit."

Jake stuffed his hands into his jean pockets. He turned his back to her, but he didn't move to the door.

Dani watched him from behind. "You know, as well as me, that Jonah can take care of whoever he wants to. That's just who Jonah is. He's always been like that, and I'm guessing he'll always be like that. You might worry about me, and it might be justified, but this right here—between you and me right now—is not because Jonah's into something that could turn bad. You're here because you don't like seeing me with him."

Jake remained silent, then left, slamming the door behind him. Dani closed her eyes. She stood in place and when her phone rang, finally let out her breath slowly. Smoothing her hands down her pants, they were sweaty, but she didn't move to answer her phone. She saw it. She had placed it on the kitchen table, but she just stared.

Her mind was still on that door, seeing it slam again and again in her mind. It was that night when he told her about Erica, except she slammed the door. Not him.

When the phone kept ringing, she answered. Mae didn't wait a second. "I need your help at the grill. We're packed."

"I'll be right there." Dani hung up, changed again, and headed back out, ignoring the knot of dread that had taken root in her stomach. She took two steps outside of the cabin before she realized another car had pulled up.

She saw him first.

He was right there.

His mouth was moving, but she didn't hear. Not right away. Her heart stopped, and then she heard Boone say, "Hello, Dani."

He looked even taller than she remembered, but he couldn't have grown any more than his six-five. He'd lost weight, maybe twenty pounds. His brown hair still curled just over his forehead and framed his angular cheekbones. His blue eyes still pierced through her.

It was funny. She hadn't taken in the details when she saw him at the fair. Shock glossed over everything then, but she was soaking it all in now. "Boone."

It felt like an invisible hand reached inside her, and gutted her.

Boone took in a deep breath, stuffing his hands into his pockets. "It *was* you who I saw before." He looked around the cabin. "This is a nice place."

The moment was surreal. She'd left him when he'd been out celebrating their engagement. And he commented on her cabin? "How'd you..."

"What?" His eyes whipped to hers. "Find you? Find this place? How'd I track you down like a hunter?"

She felt a headache starting. "Stop it."

"I didn't come to Craigstown for you, if you're wondering that. This visit right now is about you, but not me being here, in general. Just so we're clear." His tone was clipped, bitter. "I asked around. Turns out that Dani O'Hara is quite famous around these parts. And she lives in the 'most wonderful cabin' on this godforsaken secluded lake."

"Are you...did you...?" She just gave up.

"This was supposed to be my trip to get *over* you. My brother's here on business, and I was just supposed to tag along. Heal my heart, something like that." He sounded exhausted. "Can I come in?"

"Oh. Yeah." She stepped back, letting him in. As he sat at the table, she asked, "Your brother?"

"Quandry, Inc."

Dani connected the dots. "You're the guys. You want to build here, but Jonah doesn't want you to. I was warned about you."

Boone shot her a confused look, but didn't say anything. He rubbed a hand over his face. Exhaustion came off of him, from his slumped shoulders to the bags underneath his eyes, and even how he breathed. They were shallow breaths. Almost as if he weren't capable of deep breaths any longer. They took too much energy.

"I don't sleep, you know."

Dani closed her eyes and shook her head. She thought she was getting better, but with this—with Boone in her kitchen. She stopped thinking. She had no idea now. Dani turned and poured two cups of coffee. "Cream or sugar?" She needed something to do.

Her hands picked up a creamer for her cup.

"No, but you'll take one cream."

Her hands paused.

"You used to."

Dani finished and put both cups of coffee onto the table. Both were black, without cream *or* sugar. "What are you doing here, Boone?"

He stood and began to pace around the room. Hands stuffed in his jean pockets, he walked around, looking at nothing. "I never told you this, but my grandpa used to call me that. It was his nickname for me and when you just started calling me that—I liked it. It made me feel connected to him again. My family doesn't remember that. I'm Mitch to them."

Mitch Quandry.

"They call me by my first name." He chuckled. "It's like...I don't even know. I hear that name, and I think of you, because I'm supposed to be called Boone. That's what our friends called me, but it's like you claimed it. Boone's my name from you now."

"I'm—"

Boone cut in, "Don't say that you're sorry. You're not sorry, Dani. If you were, you would've said something to me and not left a goddamn note on the table. I read it when I was drunk, and I thought it was a joke, a horrible, sick joke." Another bitter laugh slipped free. He gripped the back of his neck. "I kept thinking you were in the bathroom or something. I passed out thinking that."

Dani took a deep breath and stared at her coffee. The steam had stopped rising.

"What are you doing here?" He expelled a ragged breath. "What are you doing *here*?"

"I grew up here. This is where my family is from."

"That's right. Erica O'Hara. Julia, Kathryn, Mae, Dani. You guys are like the perverted small-town Brady Bunch or something. I feel like I'm drunk again, and I'm reading your Dear John note all over."

"You have a right to be angry at me."

"You're damn right I have a right to be angry."

She flinched. "I wasn't right, and you proposed. I didn't know what to do. Everything was—" Everything was swirling around her as she lay helpless. She didn't have a grasp of what was going on, but she knew she needed to stop it. "I had to get out. I wasn't right, Boone. I was barely holding on as it was."

She was under the surface.

Sinking.

Falling.

Drowning.

It was happening all over again.

A knock sounded on her door, and before Dani could open it, it opened itself. Jonah stepped through, an easy grin on his face that disappeared immediately. He looked at Boone. "Uh..." His eyes held a question for Dani, one that she was still helpless to answer.

She wanted to laugh. This was hilarious, in a sad and twisted way. She woke up with Jonah, was warned off by Jake, then Boone was at her table right now. It seemed fitting that Jonah would come back around, complete the odd circle in a way.

She knew a slight edge of hysteria was in her voice. She held out a hand. "Boone, this is Jonah Bannon. Jonah, this is Mitch Quandry, my ex-fiancé."

Boone cursed.

"I've met your brother." Jonah's tone was cold. "His company's here to build where the mussels are."

"I don't know much about it, to be honest." Boone nodded and shook his head. "Wow. This is all messed up. I—uh—I should get going. This isn't the time for this."

Jonah stepped aside as Boone moved toward the door. Just before he stepped outside, he stopped and looked at Dani. "I..." The words died in his throat.

Dani didn't say anything. She could only watch him back.

"Nevermind." He shouldered through the door.

It slammed shut behind him, too.

"They're here because of the mussels?"

Jonah nodded. "It's a lot of money in those pearls. Everything will go up in worth now."

She couldn't digest that, but Jonah didn't say anything else. There was silence for a beat. Dani inhaled it in like she was starving. Her insides were trembling. The tsunami was back, it was inside of her, and she couldn't focus for a moment. She only heard the waves, the cries, the screams, then the silence. A gasp for breath. Then nothing again.

Her heart was going crazy. She felt that it actually wanted out of her. She looked down as if to see if it was still there, still inside of her.

Jonah was sitting down. She recognized it in the background, but the sounds were distant. He was saying something. A question. She frowned, trying to concentrate more. Oh, yes—he was asking, "You want to talk about that?"

That was the last thing she wanted. "No."

"Okay. Come on." He nodded, then started to lead her toward the bedroom.

"I'm not tired."

"Liar." Jonah chastised and he turned back the blankets. Dani crawled in and looked up at him.

Jonah stood, uncertainly, as he held her gaze.

"I don't want to have the nightmares."

The decision was made. Jonah toed off his shoes and he slipped in beside her. Dani tucked her head in the crook of his arm and shoulder. He reached down, caught her hand and a moment later, her eyelids weighed down.

Jonah wasn't there when she woke the next day, so she went for a run, and ended up at the end of Mrs. Bendsfield's driveway. She wanted to go inside, see if she could find out more answers, but...it was Mrs. Bendsfield. Dani doubted she'd be as open this time around, but still. She found herself migrating there, and she went past the house, right to the milking barn this time. The cats scattered just inside the stable door, and Dani saw the owner wasn't in her pottery studio that day.

The designs were beautiful and intricately made. Why didn't she display her work? Why else does an artist create if not for someone else to view?

Her eye caught on one pot in particular. It was large and oval with dolphins carved around the top brim. Lilies and daisies were between each of the dolphins. They were Erica's favorite flowers. They were her mother's favorite flowers, and now, Dani remembered that she always saw Mrs. Bendsfield with those two flowers. They were embroidered in her shirts, pants, sweaters, or socks. She had them painted on her van. Even her sign that proclaimed her false age—it had with a border of lilies and daisies.

A memory came back to her. Her mom was hugging her at night, and she whispered, *"If you find any lilies or daisies, hold on to them, Dani. They grow with love. Lots of love."*

"What are you doing here, girl?"

Dani heard the harsh voice, but she also heard a slight tremor in that voice.

She turned slowly. Mrs. Bendsfield was there with her chin raised high, a shaking hand on the milking room's door handle. It was as if the door was for her protection—her way of escape. She wore another over-sized white shirt, stained with paint all over. Her white hair was pulled up in a messy bun.

"Why lilies?"

"Why you wanna know?"

The elderly woman's eyes were intelligent and clear. Dani knew no hallucinations would give her answers today.

"Why lilies? Why daisies? What do they mean?"

"Just flowers. That's all."

They weren't that easily dismissed. Dani caught the flicker of emotion in the older lady's eyes.

"Why them?"

She shrugged this time, uneasy. "Don't matter." She crossed her thin, aged arms over her chest.

"It matters to me."

"It don't to me."

"Are those your favorite flowers?"

"Not mine. My husband's." Her voice was sad.

"What do you mean?"

"They're just flowers, girl. It ain't no unsolved mystery. My husband picked those flowers for me. I had them wild daisies and lilies in my bouquet on my wedding day. But, they just flowers."

Memories weren't just memories. And anything that stood for a memory, sparked a memory, meant something more.

"My son ain't your father." Mrs. Bendsfield surprised her again. She added, "I know what you thought when you left that last time. I know that I wasn't myself, but my son took off long ago. I ain't seen or heard from him in over forty years. He's long gone, as far as I'm concerned."

"Why'd he leave?"

"Ain't your business."

"I think it is."

"I think not," Mrs. Bendsfield rasped out. "He's my son, and I have to mourn his absence every day. I don't 'have to' explain anything, least of all, to one of *her* rabbits."

That was the second time Dani had heard Mrs. Bendsfield call her that.

"Is that what you thought of my mother? That she bred like a rabbit?"

Mrs. Bendsfield snorted. "She might as well have for all the trouble she caused around these parts. Your mother wasn't alright in the head. Took damn near an earthquake to get her to see reason one time." Her gaze fell away, clouding over.

Dani jerked in reaction. "You said that you took a shovel to my mother. Did you hurt her?"

"What?" Mrs. Bendsfield looked again, her thoughts in the past, and murmured, "No, no. Just a phrase—that's all I meant. It might've helped if I *had* taken a shovel."

"I don't believe you."

"My son ain't your papa. You can believe that!"

"Might so, but you know something about my family, and I want to know what that is. I think I have a right to know."

"You got no right except to live your life. That's what all you O'Haras are supposed to do. Just live your lives and leave everyone else in your dust, hurting like my Oscar, like..." Her voice trailed off, then she shook her head. She snapped back to attention. Her hand tightened on the door handle. "My Oscar ain't your papa. If he were, I'd rather kill myself and dig my own grave afterwards."

"Would it be so terrible? If your son was my father? Would that really be such a terrible thing?"

She expected anger or hot denial, but the fight seemed to evaporate. Her hand slipped from the door handle. Her shoulders dropped, and her head hung low. She whispered, "Yes. Yes, it would, little Dani O'Hara. In ways you can't possibly conceive."

Dani stood still. The world was whipping around her.

Mrs. Bendsfield moved to look out the window.

Dani was transfixed on the lilies and daisies. And the dolphins. Her mother always talked about the magical dolphins and their healing qualities. They were the protectors of the ocean. They guarded everyone.

Her mother talked about the white dolphin that rode atop the white clouds in the sky. She said that when it was your time of dying or healing, that white dolphin would appear and you only had to grasp her fin and she'd pull you home. Dani thought home meant *their* home.

It wasn't what her mother meant.

"My mother wasn't bad."

Mrs. Bendsfield swung back around and gazed at her, blinking a few times, like she'd forgotten Dani was there.

Dani added, "You talk like my mother was awful, but she wasn't. She was a good mother."

"Child." Mrs. Bendsfield's eyes were hollow. "I don't care if your mother was good or not. All I know is that the pain wrecked my family, and that'll stick with me till my dying day. My Oscar's gone, and it's because of your mother."

"What happened? Tell me what happened." She insisted, "Tell me what you're *not* telling me."

"I can't."

"Why not?"

Mrs. Bendsfield looked at her as her white hair slipped out of her bun. The strands framed her aged features, and her old eyes seemed to sigh on their own.

She murmured, "It ain't my secret to tell."

"It's not my mother's. She's gone. She's dead."

"Your mother ain't the only one in this secret. There are others involved, even though they don't know it or not. It's more their secret than mine." She nodded. "You get it from them. Not me."

"But—"

"I've had enough of your family. I don't want anything more from anyone with the name of O'Hara." Mrs. Bendsfield harrumphed, and she took a faltering step toward the door.

"Wait."

She looked back, right in the doorway. "I know who your daddy is, and he comes around every now and then. He checks in on you three. He was at your little sister's funeral."

The milking door, white and rickety, shut behind her.

"He checks in on you three."

Mrs. Bendsfield was outside, GoldenEye was eating grain out of her hand. Their eyes caught and held, and Dani knew she'd never come back. Whatever secrets were still there would remain there. She'd find out from someone else.

She just had to find out whom that someone else was.

She headed for the cave, knowing she would find Jonah there.

Trenton spotted her first as he popped up from a dive. He flashed a blinding smile, even more striking against the backdrop of his black wet suit. "Hey, Dani, you come to help us dive?"

"Maybe," she murmured and sat on the edge with her toes dipped into the water. She rolled up the ends of her pant legs and waited as Trenton dove back down, and a second later, Jonah popped up in his stead.

"Hey." Jonah grinned as he hoisted himself up beside her. "What are you doing here?" He moved his bucket between them and rubbed off the dirt and grime from the mussels. He dunked them in the river to further clean them.

"Jake stopped by yesterday." He knew about Boone, but they hadn't talked about her other visitors.

Jonah paused in his washing.

"He said you have a fight brewing. It's with Boone's brother, isn't it?"

"It is." He nodded, the teasing left in a flash. "But I can't talk about it. I can talk about how this mussel is going to save our town's economy. I can talk about how we don't need to keep exploiting the river, but about that—I can't. I'm sorry, Dani."

Dani nodded. She understood.

Jonah frowned. "How'd Jake know about that anyway?"

She shrugged. "He said the police make it their business to know what's going on, in case they need to protect someone."

"That's bullshit," Jonah cursed swiftly. He kept washing off the mussels. "Jake's interested because you're my business. He's never cared before, and if he says the police are involved, that's even more bullshit. The police force around this town don't want anything to do with my 'battles.' They want the conglomerates to come into town because it means more money and they can hire more staff."

"I don't think Drew Quandry is going to threaten me. Boone wouldn't want that."

Trenton broke the surface again. "Man, I just hit another bed."

"You did?" Jonah transferred the mussel he'd been holding to Dani and jumped into the river.

Trenton dove after him.

Dani spotted a loose pair of goggles and snorkel. She grabbed them without thinking, shimmied out of her pants, and dove in after them. It was dark in the water, but she followed the trail of bubbles, and within another moment, she saw Jonah's and Trenton's floating figures as they ducked inside another cave of the river.

Dani kicked her legs and put forth a burst of speed until she was behind Jonah. She tapped on his shoulder, and when he whirled, his eyes widened when Dani pointed to his mouthpiece and her own.

He nodded, took a deep breath from his oxygen tank, and removed it.

Dani expected him to give her the oxygen mouthpiece, but instead Jonah fused his lips over hers and breathed out his air of oxygen. His lips lingered over hers before he gave her the oxygen piece, and Dani drew in enough breaths to tide her over.

He took a few breaths before handing it back over. They traded evenly. Trenton tapped Jonah's shoulder and jerked his head toward the bed again. He skimmed it with a flashlight. Dani's eyes widened at the vision of black mussels upon black mussels. There were possibly twenty dozen, and they were blanketed by fish who were trying to eat the decoy fish.

Dani caught a flash of something and swam to grab it.

Her hand pushed through the swarm of fish. She felt the cool slide of mussels against her hand, but her fingers dug into the river's bottom until she felt what she thought was a pearl. Grabbing it, she swam back to Jonah and lifted up the grey pearl.

Both men nodded.

Trenton gave her a thumbs up as Jonah handed over the oxygen again. Once she took a couple breaths, he took it back, then placed his hands on both sides of her face. He leaned in and touched his lips to hers. He kissed her hard.

Dani softened, her arms went around his shoulders. They fit together, and Jonah continued to kiss her. She was content to let him, her lips moving against his. She could've kissed him forever. The heat enflamed again, as it had before, but Jonah pulled back. His hand found hers, and he tugged her to the surface. Their heads came up, inside an air pocket in the cave. There was a large slab of dry rock in the corner. A bunch of bags were stored in the corner.

Jonah noticed where she was looking. "We keep stuff here. Blankets, dry clothes, whatever we need if we don't feel like swimming all the way back to the opening. Brought 'em in with bags to keep everything dry."

Dani grinned at him, water streaming down her face. "That pearl must mean something."

Jonah's hand slipped to her hip, and he pressed her closer. She felt him fully and heard his response, as his mouth bent just beside her ear, "These pearls will bring a lot to Craigstown and Falls River. That's what this means."

"Hmm mmm?"

"And what about right now?"

Jonah dipped and tugged her under the water. Delight coursed through her, buzzing her blood. She clasped tighter to him. And before she knew what was going on, he kicked off with a burst of speed. He was swimming back, leaving Trenton behind, and then they broke the surface again. They were back at the entrance. He trapped her against the edge, his arms braced on both sides of her. Leaning forward, he nipped at the side of her mouth, then trailing kisses along her chin to her ear. One of his hands curled around her hip, and he pressed against her. "Remember when you called me 'God' before?"

She didn't, but she was going with this. She wanted to know where he was going to take her. "Hmm mmm?" She tipped her head and Jonah's searching lips found her neck, sending new shivers of lust ricocheting throughout her body.

"I'm going to make you call me that again."

And once they got back to her cabin, he did just that.

Jonah spent the night that night, but Dani remained awake. Once she saw the clock said it was three in the morning, she slipped from the bed. Wrapping a blanket around herself, she went to the porch. A bonfire was still burning at the Smith's home across the lake and after she propped open the door, laughter greeted her. A faint smile graced her features. It felt good to hear that sound. Sinking back in her chair, she closed her eyes. She was content to sit there and listen to their family's happiness.

It felt less lonely somehow.

"Hey." Jonah yawned and padded to the lounger beside her. He reached for the bottom end of her blanket and tugged it over his lap. "Did you have a nightmare?"

"No." Dani moved in her seat to turn his way. She rested her head against the back of her seat and watched him in the moonlight. It filtered over him, accentuating his chiseled cheekbones and soft bedroom eyes. "I have come to the conclusion that my life is a mess."

Jonah grinned. "How's that?"

"I'm sleeping with you. My ex-fiancé is in town. My childhood boyfriend is jealous, and he's engaged to my sister."

Jonah snorted. "That's not a mess. That just sounds like a small-town soap fest. It's something Aiden would love to hear. You'd make her day if she got ahold of your drama. She'd sit for hours and help you fix everything, and in the end, you and I would be married in my sister's fantasy."

"I've never done the friendship thing."

"What do you mean?"

"Isn't that what someone's supposed to share with their friends? All their problems?"

"I guess." Jonah shrugged. "I talk to Trenton sometimes about issues, but they're usually about work. Hawk's not exactly the 'emotional-sharing' type. He likes sex. He thinks that's his entire reason for being on this Earth."

"He sounds stellar."

"Hawk has good qualities. If I ever need anything, he'll drop everything to help."

"Even a threesome?"

Jonah barked a laugh. "Aiden called me tonight. She wanted me to remind you that they have their Friday Night Poker Showdown this week. I'm supposed to drive you. I think Aiden wants you to get drunk."

"That might be a possibility."

"Oh, and to warn you, Jake was invited. That means Julia will be there. I guess it'll be pretty big because some of her new friends were invited, too. Aiden doesn't even know who all is coming, but she's planning for thirty."

"How many play poker?"

"Eight tables are set up. Everyone watches until the winning table faces-off against each other. It takes all night, so plan on sleeping it off the next day. Most people just go to drink, laugh, and lose some money." Jonah ran a hand over his face, yawning. "It's pretty fun. Aiden and Kate wore these ridiculous hats last year. They pretended they were the next generation of Red Hats. They wore red and purple all night. Even their poker tables had to have a red or purple tablecloth."

Dani could imagine it.

Jonah tugged at the end of the blanket. "Not to change the subject, *but* to change the subject." He leaned closer, his eyes darkening. His voice dropped low. "Are you naked under there?"

Her heart spiked, and she felt a coy smile tug at her lips. "Maybe."

Jonah stood and moved to her. Sliding his hands underneath the blanket, he made an approving sound as he felt silky skin underneath his fingertips. He lifted her legs to wrap around him, and he stood between them. Her body grew warm. Her blood started to buzz, and she felt a tingle spreading right where his hands were moving. They went under her thighs, and he pulled her tight against him.

He bent, kissing the corner of her mouth.

Dani was beginning to ache for him, and she couldn't help but ask out loud, "How do we fit?" She wasn't talking about their bodies. She knew exactly how they fit, like perfection.

"We just do." Jonah pressed another kiss, hard, to her mouth.

She slid her hands down his back, delighted in the shiver he couldn't suppress. "Is that it? We just do this without rules?"

"No." Jonah bent and met her lips again. He murmured against them, "When something happens and we need to clarify rules, we do it then. Until then, I'm all for just having fun." He hoisted her up in his arms, her legs wrapped more firmly around his waist. He asked, "How about you?"

"I'm thinking I like how we fit."

Jonah walked them inside and to the bedroom. He laid her down, pulled the sheet free, and leaned just above her with one knee braced on the bed. His other leg was still on the floor. He held his weight, resting on a hand next to her shoulder so he was half over her, half holding her captive. Her heart was picking up speed. She wasn't so sure about the 'captive' part. Biting down on her lip, she fought against pulling him on top of her. Her eyes darted to his.

"I like how we fit, too." He traced her lips with his thumb, then cupped the side of her cheek. He lowered himself down at an aching pace until his lips softly found hers.

Dani slid her hand down his chest, savoring the hard contours of him. He was hard in all the right spots. She felt his strength, especially how he was still holding himself above her. Smoothing her hands down to his waist, then around and up, she felt his back muscles rippling. They were shivering from her touch, and she wrapped one leg around his thigh. The ache was there and growing deeper each moment he held himself away from her. She started to pull him down with her leg.

Now.

This.

She wanted him on top of her. She wanted to feel his weight. She wanted to feel every inch of him.

It wasn't long before his kiss deepened, and she was writhing, gasping, and begging until he slid inside. She woke later, and felt his searching lips and fingers on her once again.

Jonah was gone when she woke again.

It was nine in the morning, and she'd been a no-show two nights ago. It was time to find Mae. She had an apology to issue. The bar was almost empty when she entered, but the restaurant side was bustling. Mae was knelt down behind a stack of boxes on the bar counter.

"Hey, ho."

Mae popped out. "Did you just call me a whore? And after you not showing up the other night? I thought you were coming to help out."

Dani grimaced. "Sorry about that. Some stuff happened." She indicated Barney and a few of Mae's regulars. "And I was making a lame joke. You kinda have six dwarves who sit in your bar, and you take care of the seventh back at your cabin." She pointed to herself. "Me. You take care of all of us."

Mae frowned. "You're not a dwarf." She nodded to the others. "Neither are they, but I'll take the Snow White reference. It's a compliment compared to what I used to be called." She eyed her. "Where'd this good mood come from?"

"I have surrendered to the chaos in my life."

She made the decision last night. Her life was a mess. She was going to embrace it, and she ended up embracing Jonah right after. That was a sign, right?

Mae barked out a laugh. "That just means you have a life." She slapped a hand to her hip and sashayed a two-step. "Folk like me are supposed to have 'messes' for lives, but I don't. I got no life except my favorite niece, this bar, and that restaurant. Sometimes I think this business got a better life of its own than mine." She narrowed her eyes, studying her niece a bit longer. "If I didn't know better, I'd say you have a glow. You're glowing." The ends of her mouth tipped down. "Why?"

Subject change. Dani reached for one of the boxes. "Can I help with anything here? What are you doing anyway?"

"No." Mae slapped away Dani's hand. She pulled some of the towels out from the first box. "I'm not letting you turn yourself into an unpaid volunteer who works here full-time. If you work, you get paid. My rules."

"Then pay me or consider this in exchange for the cabin's rent."

Mae cursed. "That cabin is yours. It's been yours for a long while. You're just never around to be told that. You're not working for rent. I pay well for my staff."

"Fine. Pay me. Put me to work. I've got nothing to do right now."

Mae was putting the towels under the counter, but stopped. She leaned against the counter and cocked her face to the side. Her arm rested on top of the box. "You know." She gave Dani a knowing look. "I came by the cabin the other night. Real late that night. Wanted to check on you, since you didn't show."

Well.

Fuck.

Her aunt knew. And she knew that her aunt knew, so now Mae knew that she knew that her aunt knew. Still. Dani rolled her shoulders back. She was going to do a Mae. She was going to try and bullshit her way out of this one. "Yeah?" Her tone was casual. "I was up. You could've come in for a drink."

Mae snorted. "Stop lying." She grabbed hold of more towels from inside the box. "I know what you were doing last night. Don't think I didn't notice when you changed the subject five seconds ago either."

Dani held her breath. It was out. "And?"

"And what?" Mae shook her head. "And nothing. About time you got underneath that man. He's like a stallion, just asking to be ridden. Besides, have you forgotten who I am? Sex is healthy. I know that more than others." Mae paused, and her face softened. "Just watch out, though. I might not know what you went through, but I know you went through something. If your heart's vulnerable, guard it wisely."

And Dani was melting on the inside. "Aunt Mae." She placed her hand on the bar.

Mae covered it with hers, giving it a light squeeze. "You know I love you. I trust you, just couldn't take seeing you hurt even more."

"I'm the runner, remember?" It was meant as a joke.

Mae barked out another laugh. "True. Of the two of you, you're the runner. I said my piece. I'm done. Consider the Aunt's Obligation fulfilled. As long as you're being smart, have all the sex you want." Her voice picked up at the end, carrying through the bar.

Dani cursed silently, catching movement from the corner of her eye. The other dwarves looked over. "Thanks, Aunt Mae."

Mae shrugged, picking up the boxes from the counter. "What do you expect? You're in the town whore's bar?" She winked, then nodded toward the restaurant side. "Your sister's over there, along with her hoity-toity friends. Save yourself. Every O'Hara for themselves." She laughed, dipping into the back.

Dani stayed back.

Her aunt was wrong. This wasn't the 'town whore's bar.' This was her aunt's bar, and the rumors might've been horrendous and widespread, but they were wrong. Mae probably hadn't shared her bed with a man in years. And she really probably hadn't done it if the guy also wasn't in her heart.

Dani felt a dip in humility. She was proud to come from the same family as Mae.

Dani was about to follow her when someone coughed behind her

Jake had on a half-scowl, and her eyes tracked to the right—she gulped. Boone wore a full-scowl.

Shit.

They knew each other.

Jake pointed next to him. "Dani, this is Mitch Quandry. He's—"

Fuck's sakes. She was about to be introduced to her ex-fiancé.

"You can call me Mitch."

That was all Boone offered. No handshake.

She muttered under her breath, "Oh, boy." Then nodded. "Hi. I'm—" This felt wrong. Neither knew who the other was, or she didn't think they did. She was pretending right now, and when it would come out. The truth always came out eventually.

Jake cut her off. "This is Julia's sister." He nodded to Boone. "This is Jenny's boyfriend. Jenny is—"

Boyfriend? Dani gulped again.

Boone cut Jake off a second time. "Jenny's a friend of mine."

"Oh." Jake frowned at him, scratching behind his ear. Then he cleared his throat. "Okay."

"Boyfriend." Dani couldn't stop herself. She shouldn't care. She *soo* shouldn't care. The caring was burning in her chest.

Boone's smile was tight. "It's nice to meet you. Julia seems lovely."

"Yeah, uh—" Jake coughed a second time. "They're not real tight, but they're sisters. They care about each."

Dani hissed, "He gets the picture." She clenched her teeth.

Jake shut up.

The air was tense. Jake was frowning still, and still itching behind his ear. Boone was staring right at her, like he wanted to drill holes into her skull. She focused on the counter. It needed another washcloth over it, but unable to stop herself, she flicked another glance up. She looked right smack dab back at Boone, and he adjusted. He clipped his head to the side, as if he'd never been staring.

"Where'd Mae go?" Jake looked around the grill. "I wanted to introduce him to her."

No! That was Dani's first thought, but she couldn't say that. She saw a rag under the counter, and reached for it without thinking. Her hand tightened around it. "Really?"

Mae was hers. Why was Jake introducing Boone to her? Boone, who suddenly had a girlfriend? Whose girlfriend was friends with Julia? Mae was hers, not Julia's.

Jake's head dipped down under her stare, still holding her gaze. "What's with you?"

"She's a thief." Julia came around the corner, along with another female. She moved to link her elbow with Jake's. "That's what's wrong with her."

This day couldn't get any better. The only ones missing were Erica and Aunt Kathryn. Hell. Throw in the crazy grandmother, too.

She turned to her sister. "Excuse me?"

She tried not to study the other woman, who stood a little too close to Boone. All-white clothing molded to the slim redhead, with white pearls circling her neck and wrist.

"I called you a thief." She said to Jake, "Arrest her."

"For?"

Jake was frowning.

Julia's eyes flashed. "I want Mom's photograph back."

Dani kept looking at Boone, and the hand that was resting on his arm. A part of her wanted to snatch it off him, but that wasn't her place anymore. Feeling jealousy that she had no right to be feeling, she shoved it all down and concentrated. Her sister was trying to get her arrested—what a shocker.

"What are you talking about?"

"You know what I'm talking about." Julia stepped toward her.

Jake hauled her back. "Whoa!" He clamped a hand on her arm. "You don't take a threatening stance here. That's not how anything's going to get resolved."

"There's nothing to resolve. She stole a picture of my mother—"

"*My* mother."

"Excuse me?" Julia's eyes narrowed, her entire body went unnaturally still.

"My mother." Dani didn't move from behind the bar, but she wanted to. Letting go of the washcloth, her hands flattened on the counter. Her head lowered. Her eyes narrowed, mirroring her sister's. "She's mine, too. Maybe whatever was taken belonged to me as much as it did to you?"

"She did it." Julia pointed at her, turning to Jake again. "You can arrest her. That was a confession."

Jake tugged on his collar. His eyebrows bunched together. "That wasn't a confession of anything, and this is a picture. You two are fighting over a photograph."

"It's something that's priceless. It's mine, and I want it back."

It was more than priceless. It was a memory. It was a time capsule. It was the last item Dani had of her mother's, and it was going to remain in her possession until she could pass it along to her children.

Jake let out an aggravated sigh. He raked a hand through his hair, looking at Dani. "Did you take it?"

A look of familiarity passed between them. He was remembering the times when they snuck into the creamery and stole candy, or when they sold candy at the football concession stands and pocketed a few items they shouldn't have. He might've been a cop now, but he hadn't always been above the law. Most those times were with her.

"Dani, come on. I'm not going to charge you. It's your mom, too. I get it, but Julia has a right to know if you took the picture or not."

She felt Boone observing the entire exchange. Her fingers curled into the counter, her nails pressed down. She couldn't have taken away the way Jake just talked to her, how it spoke volumes of unsaid history between them. If it were her, she'd be hurting, but she didn't dare sneak a peek at Boone.

She didn't want to see what was there.

"Yeah." Her tone cooled. She straightened up, her hands falling back to her side. "I took it." Her eyes met her sister's. "I'm not giving it back."

"What?!"

Dani shrugged. "Sometimes we don't get what we want."

Julia's reaction was immediate. She sucked in her breath. Her eyes widened, looking like they were going to pop out, and her cheeks reddened. She started forward again, saying, "You did not just say that!"

"He—hey!" Jake tried to haul her back. Julia kept coming. He jumped in front, holding both of his fiancé's arms. He braced himself, holding her in place. "Stop! Julia. You can't assault your own sister."

"Watch me." She lunged again, but he caught her in half of a hug/half of a hold. "Okay. We're leaving." He glanced over his shoulder.

"Dani, stop pushing your sister's buttons. We're going, but I'd strongly advise you to give that picture back."

She pressed her lips together. Fat chance of that happening.

Julia continued to protest, but Jake carried/dragged her out of the bar, leaving behind another awkward ex-couple. Dani pressed a hand to her forehead. She couldn't imagine what Boone was thinking, and glancing to him, under lidded eyes, a wind swept through her. It took all her fight in one blast.

He was looking at her like she was a stranger. His top lip lifted in a small sneer. She was a stranger he didn't like.

"Mitch, honey," his friend started, patting his shoulder. "Maybe we—"

"Jenny." He interrupted smoothly. His hand caught hers, holding it against him. "Why don't you go see if your friend is okay? I'll be right out."

Surprise lined her eyes. She looked at Dani, then Boone, then the door. "Uh. Okay." Her hand slid out from under his and she reluctantly walked for the door. She looked back twice before finally slipping outside.

"Boone." Her eyes fell back to the counter. She didn't know if she could bear looking at him again, see the disapproval or even the distaste in eyes that she once thought she loved. "I—"

"Don't." He gentled his tone. "Please, don't." His Adam's apple moved up and down. "I came to see you, and it's been two days."

"What?" She looked up now.

He was hurting. A vein stuck out from his neck. "I thought you would've found me, so that we could've done this in private."

She hadn't.

His voice was so quiet. "You never did."

Oh. She laid her hand on the counter again, and spread it out. Her palm rested flat. She needed it for balance. It was like an anchor for her. "I—"

"You should give the money back."

"What?"

"The award my family's company gave you. You should give it back."

Her eyebrows pulled in together. She was given that because she tried to save a house full of orphans. Her mind was buzzing. "I didn't know that came from your family's business. You used a different last name. I didn't know you were a Quandry until you showed up in my cabin the other night."

But maybe he was right? She'd been hailed a hero, even though so many children died. She had no doubt the money came to her because of him.

"You have money. I thought you didn't have anything."

"What?" She had money? Well, she did now. "I have money because of the award. I didn't at the time." He was right, but that didn't matter. She'd get a job. The money wasn't important.

"No. The settlement. Jenny's become friends with your sister. She told her. You led me to believe you left home with nothing. That's not true." He tilted his head to the side. "Right?"

"*What* settlement?"

"Oh, hell."

She twisted around. Mae was in the doorway behind her, another box in her hands. She had the door propped open with her leg, like she caught the tail end of their conversation and stopped abruptly. Blinking a couple times, her shoulders lifted up and she dragged in a deep breath of air. "Okay. Um." She came out, placing the box on the bar beside Dani. The door swung shut behind her. She raked a hand through her hair. "Hello, I'm Mae O'Hara. I'm the owner of this place." She waved a distracted hand around the bar, then resting on Dani's arm. "I don't mean to be rude, but I need to have a word with my niece."

Boone nodded, giving both of them a second appraisal before leaving.

Both waited until the door closed behind him. They spoke at the same time.

Dani: "What settlement?"

Mae: "You and that man have history."

Dani pressed her hands to her forehead. A migraine was coming, but she couldn't ignore Mae's words. "What?"

"You and that man." Mae waved a finger in her face. "I came around before, but it looked too intense. I snuck off to the side to watch."

"You were watching?" Dani had to laugh. Of course her aunt would watch. Why wouldn't she? "Did you have a snack? Popcorn, perhaps?"

Mae ignored that. "Who is he?"

Dani had another retort to deliver, but swallowed it. She closed her mouth. "He's no one."

"Danielle O'Hara."

"He's...no one important."

Mae spoke again, her voice patient and calm, "Who is he, Dani?" There was a grave expression in her eyes. "You need to tell me."

"He—" It was painful to say these words. It was different with Jonah. He listened. He didn't judge. He didn't have questions afterwards. She knew there'd be questions now, and answers she didn't want to give. They would be pulled from the depths of her, and she would feel split open when she gave them.

"Dani." Another low warning.

"He was my fiancé."

She closed her eyes. She waited. The barrage was about to happen. Nothing.

She opened her eyes again. Mae was staring at her. There was no judgment, no anger. She lifted her chin up, slightly. "Did you love him?" There was nothing in her voice that Dani expected. It was kindness, and compassion.

Tears pricked at her eyes. Dani swore under her breath. Why would she start crying now? She flicked a hand over her eyes. "I did, but the timing was wrong. And..." She'd been a mess. An absolute, complete mess, and she still was.

"When did this happen?"

"Before I came here."

"That's why you came back." There was new understanding in her aunt's voice. "You came back to heal. Didn't you?"

There was no holding the tears now. They fell, but she kept her eyes closed. She could try and slow them down.

"Oh, honey." Mae drew her into her arms. She tucked her head into the crook of Dani's neck and shoulder. Her voice came out muffled. "If I'd known, I—" She let out a shaky laugh. "I have no idea. We would've gotten drunk more often?"

Dani laughed. It split through some of her pain. She felt the pressure behind her forehead lessening, and she stepped back. "I'm fine, Aunt Mae. I am." She used both palms to wipe the rest of her tears away.

Mae knew part of the reason she came back. She didn't know about the storm, or the children. Dani wasn't ready to share those ghosts, not yet. "What settlement was he talking about?"

"Oh." Mae cursed to herself. "Erica won a big settlement with the hospital a long time ago."

"What settlement?" Her voice hitched on a high note. How many times did she have to ask?

Mae bit down on her lip, looking around the room. She was looking anywhere, but at Dani, then she stopped. Her eyes found Dani's again. She dropped the bomb. "The hospital screwed up some of her lab results. They told her she was pregnant, and Erica stopped the chemotherapy. It was a mistake. She found out later there was no baby."

The ground shifted under her.

Dani asked, her voice a hoarse rasp, "How much later?"

"She was sick a lot. She thought she lost the baby. Julia asked them to retest the blood from before. It wasn't until after..."

She knew, but Dani wanted to hear the words. "After what?"

"After she was already gone. She never was pregnant."

Her stomach dropped. It was her sister, hearing about an unborn child she never had, but Dani was back in that building. The first child died. The second. They just kept dying. She couldn't stop them.

Mae continued, her voice sounding from a distance, "Julia pushed for the lawsuit. I think if Erica had chemo during that time, she'd be alive." Mae paused a beat. "They settled for two million."

Julia was rich. Good for her.

Erica thought she'd been pregnant...Dani ached inside. There were no words. It was her child's life, or her own. She chose her child, and in the end it'd been for nothing, but Dani knew that Erica would've made the same choice if the same lie had been told to her. She knew, because it was the same choice Dani would've made, as well.

Dani left Mae's Grill, went to the lake cabin, wrapped herself in a blanket and sat on the porch until it got dark. She cried that night. She didn't know if she could stop, but it wasn't just for her sister. She cried for all of them.

Her mother.

Her grandmother.

Mae.

Even Kathryn.

She cried for Erica. For Julia. For herself.

She cried for everyone. And when she stopped, she was raw and scraped hollow inside, but she cried even more.

Jonah found her like that. Her face was streaked with dried and fresh tears. Her blanket was a sopping mess. She had a Kleenex box beside her, half emptied because she used them all. He took one look at her, tucked his phone into his pocket, and he carried her to bed. She told him a little of what had transpired that day. He knew about Boone, but he hadn't known about the settlement.

She lifted her head from his chest. "You didn't know?"

He shook his head. His hand rubbed another tear from her eyelid. "I didn't. I'm surprised, small town and everything. It must've happened before I came back."

She rested her head to him again. It was time to talk to Julia. She didn't care about the money, but finding out the reason, she hurt for her sister. Julia must've been there. She must've held Erica, maybe how Jonah was holding her, as Erica made her choice. Maybe not. It was probably Jake who held her, but did it even matter anymore?

For the first time since she left, Dani regretted leaving. She hadn't been there for her family when she should've been.

She woke the next day with the same decision. It was time to face her ghosts, but she wanted more answers. A second trip to see her grandmother was in order.

The drive didn't seem as long as her prior visit. Marge was at the front desk, and after one swift glance, she produced the same blank nametag and black marker with a smile. Dani filled it out.

Phyliss stood when she got to the second floor. She regarded her with reluctance "I don't know if she's up for a visit. Unfortunately."

"What do you mean? What's wrong?"

"She's pretty weak and down right now. She's been bedridden for the last three days."

"Is she sick?"

"She's not physically sick. It's part of her mental illness."

"What does she have?"

Phyliss smiled. "You wouldn't understand if I just gave you the clinical term, but I can talk in laymen's terms since she gave us permission to talk with you. Your grandmother gets real sad at times and real happy at other times. You got her on a downward cycle last time, but now she's fully at the bottom. It might take a while for her to come out of it."

"I thought there were meds for this stuff."

"There are." Phyliss nodded. "But sometimes the meds aren't enough."

"What about therapy?"

"Your grandmother won't do therapy. She says it's hogwash. Truthfully, I just think your grandmother doesn't want to talk about stuff that happened in her past."

Dani accepted it, but she asked anyway, "Can I see her? Just for a little bit?"

"I wouldn't want to see my grandmother as yours is," Phyliss advised her. "But, if you'd really like, I could see if she wants to see you."

Anything. She just wanted to see her again. "That's fine with me."

"Okay."

Dani glanced around. The humming lady had been sitting in the corner when she got off the elevator, but once Phyliss left, she stood and shuffled her way over. Dani held still, stiff, as she poked her arm. She shook her head, hummed, and poked Dani again.

Dani didn't say a word.

After a third poke, the lady turned and shuffled back to her sitting spot. She shook her head and went back to humming.

"What's your name?" Dani asked.

The humming stopped, and she gazed over. "Henrietta."

"What are you humming?"

"I'm not humming," Henrietta clarified. "I sing in my head."

"Why don't you sing out loud?"

"Because they wouldn't understand."

"What do you mean?"

"The voices. The angels. They wouldn't understand."

"What wouldn't they understand?"

"The angels are dead, but I'm singing about live folk. I can only sing in my head so that the angels don't get mad."

Henrietta glanced down the hallway and went back to humming. The volume rose a notch as Phyliss rounded the corner.

"She said you could come in for five minutes, but that's all she has in her." Phyliss nodded, and they both turned down the hallway. Outside of Sandra's door, Phyliss knocked once and poked her head in. "We're coming in, Sandra."

Dani heard a creak and a rustling of bedsheets before she stepped around Phyliss and saw her grandmother. The white hair hung limply off her scalp, and the bedsheets seemed to overcome her grandmother's pale form. She had a hospital nightgown on, and her eyes were numb.

Dani swallowed.

Phyliss had been watching her, gauging her reaction, so Dani smiled. "Thank you."

Phyliss nodded and left the room quietly. She gently pulled the door shut behind her.

"You can sit."

The order came out in a monotone voice. Her personality seemed washed out of her grandmother. Dani missed her already.

She sat, and the chair's plastic creaked slightly underneath her. The back unyielded, and Dani's skin molded around the seat's back. She folded her arms, unfolded them, and finally just laid them on her lap as she tucked her legs underneath.

Sandra chuckled. "They're damn uncomfortable, ain't they?"

Dani smiled abruptly. There was the Sandra she remembered from her last visit.

"Something like that."

"You come for your second visit today. I suppose you want what I promised you."

"If you're up for it."

"What do you care?" Her question came out like a bark.

"I care." And Dani realized that she *did* care. Very much.

"*I* don't even care. How am I supposed to believe that you care?"

"I've learned recently that there are people out there who do care. And I think I'm a little like you, but I've learned not to look a gift horse in the mouth."

Her grandmother studied her intently for a moment before she sighed and lay back down on her bed.

"Have you always been like this?"

No answer.

"Is this why my aunts don't talk to you?"

There wasn't an answer. Dani waited, suddenly filled with an uncanny calmness. Strength filled her. She didn't know where it came from, but it was there. She felt similar strength as she held one of the children in her arms. It came from nowhere, at a time when she should've broken. She learned that day she could feel strength and weakness at the same time. She could feel surety and terror at the same time, too.

She waited, like she had during the storm.

Finally, Sandra O'Hara broke the silence. "My daughters don't talk to me because they don't know I'm here. I only told one person I was here."

Dani bit back the inevitable question.

Sandra answered it anyway, "Their father. No one else knew I was here. With him gone, I'm in the system. The government pays my bills."

"That doesn't make sense." Dani shook her head. "How'd my mother know you were here?"

"Because she was told by someone else. I got a guess who that was, but it ain't for you to know."

Dani leaned forward. "I think it is my business. I don't think it's right to have secrets in families."

Her grandmother snorted, sounding so much like Mae that Dani felt a pang in her chest. "Yeah, well, we got so many generational secrets, I don't feel it pertains to us. We don't pretend to be a family anymore. We got broke long ago."

"Who's my grandfather?" Dani had asked a different question on her last visit. She had asked for her father, but now she wanted to know who lay at the start of the roots. She wanted to understand how the branches had grown as they did.

"Your grandfather ain't around anymore. He's long gone."

"Did you love him?"

Sandra's movements stilled in the bed. As quiet as she grew, Dani would've easily believed death just took her grandmother's breath. And so her answer was even more eerie when she replied, "That was the problem. I did love him."

Dani frowned.

Her grandmother mused further, "The two of us together broke a lot of folks. We weren't supposed to love each other, but we did. I loved him and he loved me, and it wasn't right. We were supposed to stop, but we never did. I got pregnant three times from him. That's another secret." Sandra laughed a bitter laugh. "Everyone thinks my babies were born of different daddies, but they weren't. Whole-blooded sisters, they were. Same thing with your mother. She had the same sickness as me. All of you had the same daddy. I'll tell you that bit."

"You're not going to tell me who my father is, are you?"

Her grandmother didn't respond, and Dani knew she wouldn't.

She saw the emptiness in her grandmother's eyes. She knew some of it was inside her, too. "What happened to you?" Dani asked, but she didn't expect a response. Hell, Dani wasn't sure to whom the question was directed. Herself or her grandmother. "What happened to us? All of us? What happened to my mother?"

"We fall in love with the wrong men."

"What if we don't fall in love?"

"Then we don't live."

"Are you alive?" The question was an afterthought.

The answer was whispered in return. "No." Sandra continued, speaking to the air, "Sometimes I don't know where I am. Sometimes I don't know what time it is. I don't know what's real or what's from my head. When I met him, he made me feel alive. I got an anchor to the world, like I belonged somewhere when he held me, even though we both knew it wasn't right. I could've stopped it, but he could've too. Neither of us stopped because I needed that feeling. It's why I'm in here. He left me and my sadness came back. I stopped living the day he went away."

Dani heard a hallowed wistfulness in her grandmother's voice. She didn't dare move. She didn't dare interrupt whatever else she was going to hear.

"You don't got the same sickness as me, Daniella." Dani knew her grandmother wasn't whispering to her. "You ain't sick in the head. You just sick in the heart. But you got a wall inside of you. I made sure to install that. I made damn sure. You need a wall or people gonna take you for a ride. They tried with me. Hell, most think your daddy did take me for a ride, but I went with him. I'd go again if the chance arose."

Dani bit her lip and held still. Her grandmother forgot who sat in her visitor's chair. She thought she was Dani's mother. It was the same voice that Mrs. Bendsfield had used as she spoke to a ghost.

Her grandmother whispered, "I'd love to go again."

Dani's fingers bit into the plastic seating of her chair.

"You raised those girls right. I hear how you talk about them. Julia sounds real proper, like she's going to be a queen or something. Erica— she'll be the sweetheart. You believe me, right now. Erica's gonna wrap everyone in that hand of hers. She's gonna make hearts thump."

Her grandmother fell silent for a moment.

"And Dani." She sighed, stricken. "She's the one who's gonna walk her own path. Julia'll wear the crown, but Erica's going to rule the lands. Dani's just going to walk right through them. She's got it inside of her to make it. I know it."

Sandra laughed.

She was laughing with a ghost.

"You gotta make Mae clean up her act. And you can do that. I know you can. You might not think it, but you just get her at the heart. You promise her one of your girls, and she'll turn about. Mae can't have kids, and that's where most of her partying comes from. She's mourning all those unborn babies of hers, but you promise her one of yours. She has to earn it, though. She's gotta walk the straight and narrow."

Dani jerked in the chair.

"You promise her one of yours..."

Dani tasted salt at the corner of her mouth. She'd started to cry. It couldn't be... She shook her head. That couldn't mean what she was starting to think it meant.

"You give Julia to Kathryn. Kathryn can speak Julia's language. They the same, but Dani—she's different. You give her to Mae. Mae will teach her how to stand. I guarantee that. Mae will raise her right. Erica, you best give her to Kathryn, too. Erica's a mix of both her aunts.

She's like you, Daniella. She got your spirit. I know. A mother knows. A grandmother knows even more. You do what I say."

Dani pressed a hand to her mouth. She was shaking. Her hand was trembling.

"No, no." Sandra O'Hara soothed her daughter. "You be fine. That sickness will work its way through you, and you'll find peace at the end. You loved him true. I know you did. And, even though he's not around, I know Emmy. He'll be back. He'll check in on your girls, but he'll know that they ain't his girls. Your girls will be fine, Daniella."

Dani took another breath. Then another.

"Okay," Sandra whispered in a short breath. She sounded drowsy. "You best be going. I'm getting right tired now. I gotta get my strength for tomorrow. You call and tell me how your doctor appointments go. I want to know."

She reached over the bed, grinned distantly at a ghost, and grabbed Dani's hand. "I'll see you when I pass away, too."

❦ ❦ ❦

She drove to one place.

She parked.

She walked in.

She ignored everyone sitting there.

The one person she came to see straightened. "What's wrong?"

She asked Mae, "Did you adopt me?"

Dani saw the answer before Mae responded. It hit her smack in the chest, and it was like a bomb that imploded. It was true. Everything her grandmother said was true. Dani never knew. Lies. Had *everything* been lies? Had *everyone* been lying to her?

"I can't." She turned away. Her heart was splitting open.

"Dani!" Mae rounded the counter and approached her, slowing at the end as if she were an injured animal. "Maybe we should talk about this somewhere quiet."

"I don't want to talk about it." Dani removed her arm from her aunt's touch. "I already know."

"There's a lot that went on that you don't understand."

"No, there's not. There's the simple fact that you kept something from me. You lied to me."

"It's not that simple. It wasn't about lying or holding back the truth or..."

"Yes, it was. I was a child who wasn't loved by her caretaker. And the person who did love me, who could've taken me in, chose not to. That's how simple it was."

"Dani—there's—there were stipulations. There were things that your mother wanted done before I could even think of making your adoption legal."

"But you did. Somewhere down the line, you and Aunt Kathryn signed me over, and both of you never told me." Dani felt it in her gut. It made sense why one aunt wanted her, and the other hated her. "That was wrong."

"Dani."

"I don't want to talk about it."

Dani started to move away, but Mae caught her elbow and kept her in place. "You will not run from me, not from this. There are a lot of things that you aren't aware of. Before you pass your judgment on me and run, you best be hearing all the facts before you judge me."

Dani stared at her. The two stared at the other. Neither looked away, but it was too much for her. Dani pulled away again. "This isn't a trial. This was a lie you kept from me."

"You don't run."

"I wasn't planning on it." But that wasn't true. It'd been there in the back of her mind, but it wasn't strong. There were more reasons to stay than run.

Pain flashed in Mae's eyes. "Fine. I'll tell you."

"*Everything.*"

"I'll tell you everything."

Dani saw who else was in the Grill then. Jake. Kate. Aiden. She ignored all of them, and walked away. Just outside, she stopped short because Boone and another man were studying her Mustang.

She said, "It's mine."

She guessed this was Boone's brother. They looked similar. Both were tall and lean with the elder Quandry outweighing the Boone by twenty pounds. Those pounds had been lost in mourning, and Dani stood there, plain as day, as the catalyst for that weight loss. An emotion flickered in Boone before he masked it and straightened stiffly. He slid his hands into his custom-made suit pants. His brother arched an eyebrow, raking Dani up and down.

He held out his hand. "Drew Quandry." He gestured to her car. "You got a nice vehicle. A classic."

"I'm aware." She was tense, ready for another fight, for another onslaught of emotion that never seemed to stay away for very long.

"Drew," Boone spoke up.

Dani tensed again at his wary voice.

Drew turned and frowned in surprise at his little brother. "What?"

Boone sighed. "This is Dani."

Drew jerked back to her, new comprehension in his eyes.

"This is my ex-fiancé."

"Oh." Drew reared back. He raked his brother with worried eyes, then turned to Dani. Sudden suspicion, and anger sparked there.

"I haven't told anyone else." Boone spoke to his brother, but he watched Dani. "I don't know what you've said..." He trailed off, letting her answer.

She did. "Two people."

Drew Quandry was silent. He watched the two exes a moment before saying, "You broke my little brother's heart."

"Yes."

"And you're sleeping with our enemy."

A lump formed in her throat. She heard his condescension. "I don't know how that's any of your business." Dani made sure she was looking right at Drew when she spoke. It was Boone's business, but not his brother's. "And with all due respect, your brother's relationship is with me and him. Not you. And you don't know a thing about me except that I left your brother."

"You walked out on him when he was celebrating your engagement." Drew narrowed his eyes. "I know that, too. And I know that you're the reason my brother's half the man he used to be."

"Drew!"

Dani studied Boone. "Is that true?" she asked softly. "Are you half the man you used to be because of me?"

Boone closed his eyes. He ran a weary hand over his jaw. "I don't want to do this here. Not with my brother here. You've got something going on. I can tell. What's happened, Dani?"

Dani flinched. Of all the people to ask, it was him.

Kate called out Dani's name at that moment, with Jake right behind her.

He was beaming, and he clasped Boone on the shoulder. "I didn't know you were out here." He nodded to Boone's brother. "You must be Mitch's older brother?"

Boone gestured toward him. "This is Jake, he invited us to a poker tournament Friday night."

"Oh, yes!" Drew held his hand out for a handshake. "Jake Cairns, you're the deputy who's engaged to *Julia* O'Hara." Drew slid a sideways glance underneath his eyelids to Dani. "Susan was impressed with how you carry yourself. She said you were a good man to have on the team." He seemed to remember. "Oh, sorry. I should explain. Susan's my fiancée. She and our father are flying in Friday. Mitch and I won't be able to make the poker tournament."

Dani tucked that information away. Jonah would probably want to know, if he didn't already.

Jake nodded, like it made sense, like he had friends flying to Craigstown every day. "Family before pleasure. That's what I always say."

Kate's mouth opened an inch. She gazed dumbfounded at Jake. She turned to Dani, but she shook her head. Dani was giving her a silent command to let it go. Kate got the message, but she gave Jake another incredulous look. Her eyebrows were arched high.

Drew caught the look between Kate and Dani, but held his hand out again to Jake. "Not to cut it short, but we should be heading out. It was a pleasure to meet all of you."

He shook Jake's hand, then turned and left. Boone glanced back, looking at Dani briefly before the two got in an SUV.

"Yeah." Kate held out her hand and pretended to shake an invisible hand. "It was a pleasure to meet you, too, Mr. Drew Billionaire and Gorgeous Quandry. A huge pleasure." She let out a sigh, her hand resting on her hip. "Man. They're always taken. That Mitch guy's taken, too. I've seen the red bombshell on his hip around town." She looked at Jake. "You're friends with them?"

Jake was studying Dani. "What? Oh, yeah. Uh." He scratched behind his head. "Julia is. Her and Jenny hit it off yesterday at a tea party."

Kate snorted. "A tea party? Are you kidding me? You're going to marry someone who attends high tea at noon?"

"It wasn't at noon, and, I guess." He asked Dani, "You okay?"

Kate cursed under her breath, whirling around. "Oh, shit. I'm sorry. That's why we came out before we were distracted by Mr. Hoity Toity here and his new golfing buddies." She jerked a thumb over her shoulder at Jake. Then softened her tone. "We heard what you asked Mae. Is that true?"

Dani sighed, accepting the inevitable. It was fresh, but so was her resolve to stop avoiding. She looked right at Jake. "I don't know about the adoption stuff, but I do have something I need to tell you."

Jake grew quiet.

She felt a lump forming in her throat again. "You asked me a long time ago why I came back. I was in a relationship, and he asked to marry me. I left him, and that's why I came back home. I came back to heal." He needed to know the rest, or most of it. "You warned me about being with Jonah because he's going against the Quandrys, but they're not going to hurt me. Mitch was the guy who proposed to me."

"Whoa," Kate said under her breath.

Dani was only worried about Jake's reaction. "Jake. I'm sorry."

He jerked back a step. Raw emotion etched over his face. His eyes looked strained. His mouth tightened. "No. I mean, good job. You got one over me."

"Jake."

But he was gone. He was already halfway to his squad car.

Kate laid a hand on her shoulder. "I'll talk to him. He'll get over it. Men are stupid sometimes. They don't realize that when they break up with a girl, that girl is no longer theirs anymore." She gave Dani a quick pat. "Honestly. Don't sweat Jake. If anything, this is good for him. Maybe make him rethink some of his hoity-toity choices in life." She murmured before following her partner, "And for the record, holy shit, woman! Mitch Quandry." She whistled. "Blows Julia's money out of the water."

Their car's back lights turned on.

Kate groaned. "I gotta go before he leaves me. And he says I'm the emotional one." She laughed. "Please tell me your secret. I must learn from your amazingness. You're like a goddess with men." She took off, getting in the passenger's side. Jake reversed the car out of the parking spot, bringing him almost right in front of her.

He wouldn't look at her.

Jonah came over later, and she filled him in on everything that happened. He was gone when she woke the next day, so she figured he was off to work, and she was just sitting down with her coffee when someone knocked on her front door.

It was Aiden, and she wasted no time. "I need your help."

Dani readied herself. "What with?"

"My father is coming into town tonight, and he wants to stay at my home."

"Whoa." Jonah hadn't said a word. "What? Your dad?"

"You don't understand. My father. Is coming. And he wants to stay— at my home. At my house. My house, where I'm supposed to be having a party tonight and people are supposed to be giddy and drunk and laid. And Kate and Robbie are supposed to kiss tonight." She stopped, pressed a hand to her stomach, and took a deep breath. "My father cannot step one foot in my home. He will ruin everything."

"Oh."

Kate and Robbie were going to kiss?

"He will *not* ruin my poker night. We're going to dress as carnies tonight. That's the plan. The back-up is animals. Kate's going to be one of those belly dancers. Bubba's the bearded lady, and I was going to dress as the blind hostess. I need him to stay somewhere else, and I'm going to tell him it's my house." She grasped Dani's arm. "Please don't judge me. My dad's not like normal dads."

"Hey." Dani held up one hand in surrender. "I'm still trying to figure out who my dad might be. No judgments here."

"Oh, good." A few tears from relief leaked out. Even Aiden's grin was a little shaky. "All we need is a place—a very nice place—and most of my stuff can be transferred there. I'll hire people for all the moving. Of course, whoever's place we stay at, we'll have to get rid of their pictures and keepsakes, but we can do it. We can do it! I just need your help. You don't have a job. You have time."

Dani took a step back, on instinct.

Aiden rushed inside, producing a thermos from behind her back. Aiden poured the rest of Dani's coffee into the thermos and grabbed her arm again. "We can take my car."

Dani managed to grab her purse and keys before she was dragged outside. "So, whose house are you going to use?"

"That's the problem." Aiden frowned as she gulped some coffee. "I've been thinking about that. My dad's wealthy. He's going to expect a certain type of house and our house won't pass muster."

"He's never been to your house?"

"Hell no! Are you kidding? My father is stuck-up, rich, and thinks mansions grow on trees."

"So, who has a mansion for use?"

"I've been racking my brain, and I can't really—Robbie! Robbie just bought a huge house. That's perfect. He didn't move in too long ago. He probably hasn't had any time to collect furniture, and I'm betting Lori got rid of most of his personal belongings. Lori's the type who would do that. That's great!" Aiden's eyes lit up in anticipation.

"What am I in charge of?"

"Okay—we're going to Robbie's. He should be at the office right now. You charm Kelley Lynn, get his keys from her, and I'll head in to schmooze it over with Robbie."

"Me and Kelley Lynn? No."

"Yes." Her head was bobbing up and down. "The girl's been biding her time before she pounces on you."

Dani frowned.

Aiden continued without thinking, "Everyone knows—Erica knew you were coming back. She made all her friends promise to be really nice to you. Only Julia's the stick-in-the-mud. Kelley Lynn promised, but she thought you needed time to adjust being back home, so anyway, Kelley Lynn will only be *too* happy to help us. She'll probably even help with decorations."

"Decorations?"

"Yeah. Anything Robbie has won't be good enough for Father Dearest."

Aiden raced around a corner, and Dani grabbed the door handle to keep from falling. "Won't your father think it's weird that you give him your house and don't stay there?'

"No. He'll think I did it to spite him." Aiden shrugged. "It's something I'd do. The problem is," Aiden continued, rambling to herself, "is that I need really rich stuff, but I can't afford to buy it all."

"What about your kids' rooms and their stuff?"

"Oh, no. I'll just tell him that they stay at the nanny's house. He'll believe that. He has no clue."

Dani was taken aback.

"We'll need bedding, a few rugs, probably a new set of dishes, um... what else, what else?"

"A chandelier?"

Aiden lit up. "Yes! Of course! Mae has one at the Grill! You think she'd let us borrow it?"

Dani frowned. Uh...what? She'd been joking.

"Okay. Okay. You explain it all to Mae. That's your other job. Would Mae let us use some of her fancy dishes? You know the ones that she pulls out for the 'hoity-toity' crowd? She always says that."

"Uh—" The truth was that she'd probably do it. And she'd definitely do it for a laugh at the expense of some of those 'hoity-toity' folk, but that meant Dani would have to talk to her aunt. The big emotional upheaval that her adoption talk would be hadn't happened yet. She wasn't ready to see her. "Why don't you call Jonah and recruit him for that? I'll be too busy handling Kelley Lynn, and you know she adores Jonah."

"Hmm!" Aiden pointed at her, snapping her fingers. "That's a good idea. You're good at this." Then her eyebrows bunched together in concentration again. "Okay. Plan of attack." Then Aiden punched a button on her car. "Call Jonah." A dial tone sounded through the speakers, but Aiden grabbed an earpiece and popped it in. Dani soon heard, "Hey, I need a favor...well, drop what you're doing. I don't care. This is ground zero time."

Dani was in awe.

"Yeah—still not caring." Aiden rushed over her brother's protests. "Dad is staying at Robbie's house tonight...yes—he'll think it's mine...

shut up. You have to go and talk to Mae. Get her to let us borrow the chandelier and anything ritzy that would impress Dad." Another moment and she interrupted again, "Not caring. You will do this, or you will not be eating at my house ever again."

The call ended soon after that, and she beamed at Dani, parking at the same time. "Mission accomplished. Well, part of the mission." She nodded to Robbie's building. "This is DEFCON one to DEFCON zero. We're going in."

"Do you even know what that means?"

"No."

Aiden smirked in triumph at Kelley Lynn's offers to help with anything. Robbie took a little smooth talking, but after a quick word in private with Aiden, he offered anything and all that he owned to impress Daddy Warbucks.

Dani rode with Kelley Lynn to her own friends and family members. Impressive thread-count bedding was offered. Anything Kelley Lynn asked for, she got. She held everyone in the palm of her hand and Dani was experiencing acute déjà vu.

Erica had operated the same way.

She felt a weird sense of nostalgia, but disregarded it. That was ridiculous.

After they'd gotten added offers of a Jacuzzi and even a pool table, Kelley Lynn decided they got enough. She studied Dani a moment before starting her car. "You've been watching me. There's watching and there's *watching* and you're *watching*."

"People like to help you."

Her hand let go of the keys. She still hadn't turned the car on. "That's not what this is about."

"It's not?" Dani itched for the door handle, but she stayed. She held firm because she was turning away from her running ways.

"This is about Erica." Kelley Lynn leaned back in her seat.

Dani lied through her teeth, "I'm just amazed at how much you've gotten to help Aiden."

"I'm not doing this for Aiden. Those people aren't doing it for Aiden either, or me." Kelley Lynn continued, "They're doing this for Jonah."

Not what Dani expected. "You, too?"

"I dated Jonah for a while, and I remembered him talking about his dad. A real piece of work, right?"

Dani frowned as a few raindrops splattered their windshield. "So, if Dave calls…?"

"Then I'm helping out an old friend."

"And that's Jonah? Or Aiden?"

"No." Kelley Lynn shook her head. "You."

She was stumped again. "Huh?"

"Dave's a bit insecure when it comes to Jonah."

That didn't make sense either. "Just Jonah?"

"Pretty much. A lot of the guys around town are insecure about him. You've seen him."

Oh, yes, she had. Dani remained silent.

"Plus—" Kelley Lynn started the car again. "This is also about all the time that you've been spending with Jonah."

"Really?"

"Really." Kelley Lynn wiggled her eyebrows in a knowing manner. "You think people don't notice? People notice. They talk, too. They've noticed that you and Bannon are spending a lot of time together. And you should prepare yourself, you know."

"For what?"

"You're Jonah's new girl. You're going to be treated differently by a lot of people. People know Jonah. Guys secretly love him and secretly hate him. And all the females—they either adore him in a sisterly fashion because they know they could never have him…like Kate…or they outright lust after him."

"Kate's not like that."

"Yes, she is." Kelley Lynn leaned forward, starting the car. "If Jonah were mine, I'd keep him happy and wrapped around my pinkie."

"Because that's what you do."

Kelley Lynn heard the bite in those words. She turned the car off again. "Is that what the watching's for?"

Dani looked out the window. "You haven't changed much from high school. You and Erica had everyone wrapped around your finger. That's what I remember."

"Not Jonah," Kelley Lynn pointed out. "And Erica couldn't hold him either, remember that? So you one-upped her."

"That's great. That's why I came back—to one-up my dead little sister."

"Erica wouldn't care anymore."

"Or maybe she would. Maybe she'd roll over in her grave." Dani knew she was baiting Kelley Lynn, but she couldn't stop. "Or maybe I should drop the guy who dropped Erica and take my revenge. I could have Jake back."

Kelley Lynn searched Dani's closed features. "I don't know what you want, but I'm not doing this. I'm helping out Jonah because I care about him. If you want to pick a fight with anyone who cared about your sister or Jonah or whomever this is actually about—then go and fight with them."

Dani forced herself to relax, making a concerted effort to loosen her shoulders up. "I'm sorry. You're helping, and I'm grateful."

"I'm not helping you."

"I know. Jonah. You're helping him."

Dani kept quiet through the rest of the afternoon. Aiden was right. Kelley Lynn impressed Dani with her resources, and she pulled out all the stops. By the end, the pool table was delivered, and the Jacuzzi had been rejected graciously since Robbie already had two. All the beds were changed and readied by the time Aiden arrived to Robbie's mansion with a chandelier in her backseat.

Jonah found Dani and Kelley Lynn in the kitchen where they were packing Robbie's non-extravagant dishes to make room for the extravagant ones Mae offered up.

"Hey," Jonah grunted a hello, holding some boxes. "Where do you want this?"

Kelley Lynn pointed to the table. "Leave it there. We'll put it away when you bring all of the boxes in."

Jonah nodded, and as he left to move another box in, he walked behind Dani. His fingers caressed her backside. Dani watched him go, feeling a spark. He glanced back just before he turned the corner, a cocky smirk in place.

She rolled her eyes, but she had to admit that he got to her. She was already thirsting for him, wanting his hands on her body. He only held her last night. Her body was reminding her of that fact.

"Hmm huh." Kelley Lynn harrumphed.

Dani gritted her teeth. "I don't get why everyone cares about my business."

"Are you serious?" Kelley Lynn placed the last of Robbie's dishes into a crate.

Aiden bounced into the room, but stopped short. Her eyes skirted between the two.

"Yeah. I'm serious." Dani ceased caring that Jonah's sister stood in the room. "I'm a little tired of having people care who's in my bed and who isn't."

Aiden's mouth formed an O.

Kelley Lynn snorted. "Get used to it because it's never gonna go away, especially when you have *who* you have in your bed."

Jonah stopped behind his sister. Neither Bannon commented.

"Are you actually doing this for Jonah, or are you doing this for Erica? A little bird told me that Erica made you promise to be nice to me."

Kelley Lynn went still, then slowly moved her box aside before she faced Dani. Her petite shoulders lifted up, taking in a pocket of air. "Okay."

"Okay?"

"Okay." Kelley Lynn nodded. "You've been pissed at me ever since you saw me in the bank. Let's do this."

"Do what?"

Kelley Lynn stopped the riddles. "I'm not doing this for Jonah, and I'm not doing this for you. You're right. It's because of Erica, because of a deathbed wish she forced out of me."

Dani was suddenly wary.

Kelley Lynn shook her head, her eyes grew haunted. "Erica wanted you to feel included and not left out, like what she did to you when you were growing up. That was her dying wish to me. I was supposed to do that." She skimmed over the Bannon siblings. "It's not ironic that the group that never liked Erica welcomed you first."

Aiden spoke, "She's my friend."

Kelley Lynn swept a scornful gaze toward Aiden. "You're friends with Dani because everyone knows about the O'Hara rift. You hate Julia because Bubba flirted with her when you two were having problems."

"What?" Dani's mouth fell open an inch.

Aiden narrowed her eyes. "Julia was a little too friendly, so yes, I'm not a fan. That's not why Dani and I are friends. I like Dani because…"

"Because she's a walking wounded," Kelley Lynn finished for her. "Because she's got what it takes to make your brother fall in love. You know that Jonah likes a challenge, and Dani's the best challenge that came to Craigstown in a long time. *That's* why you're friends with her, and don't even lie, Aiden. You told Katrina that the day that Dani got here. I know because she told me at our bar-b-que that night. She said you gushed how Bryant was going on and on about this 'hot chick he saw driving a Mustang.' You said that it would take someone incapable of life to make Jonah fall hard and fast."

Aiden sucked in her breath.

Jonah remained quiet. He watched Dani.

Dani said slowly, "'Incapable of life?'"

"It's not…I didn't mean…it's not like that, Dani," Aiden finally answered. "Yeah, that's what I'd been hoping for at first, but I consider you a friend now."

"Incapable of life?" Dani asked again.

Aiden frowned.

Kelley Lynn cut in, "It's all over town that something happened to you. Everyone knows it. We can all see it. We don't know what it is, but you *are* the walking wounded. You look like a lost little lamb begging for someone to bandage up your broken limbs."

Whatever 'broken limbs' that Dani might've had healed in anger. She straightened. "Say that again?"

"Please. You know exactly what I'm talking about." Kelley Lynn flushed, but moved back a step.

"I might have taken it before, but you're right. Something *did* happen, and I'm not the same Dani O'Hara who left like a wounded puppy with her tail tucked between her legs."

"I'm not saying you are." Kelley Lynn shifted back a second step.

"You just did."

"You kinda did," Aiden said.

Kelley Lynn stuck a hand on her hip and lifted her chin up. "I'm not here to be on trial. I came to help out. If you don't want my help, then..." She started to slide from the room.

Dani got in her way. "You started this. Don't leave before the fireworks start."

"I didn't come here to be attacked."

Dani straightened even farther, feeling Jonah watching her. "I'm not attacking you, but you don't have to worry about being nice for Erica. For one, she's dead, and two, I don't want your sympathy vote. Not only do I not need it, but I don't *want* it."

The doorbell rang then, and Kelley Lynn heaved a sigh of surrender. "Those are the flowers that Katrina said she'd donate to the cause. I'll let them in on my way out." But before she did, she said, "We're not the enemy, Dani. *I'm* not the enemy. I really was trying to be a friend today, and I didn't mean anything bad when I said that you were the walking wounded. You just looked hurt when I saw you in the bank when you came back. Erica was always a brat. I know that. It's why we were friends. We were childish, immature, and cruel when we were younger, but Erica was hurting, too, you know. We're not the enemy." Her head ducked down. "Not anymore."

The room echoed as her footsteps sounded along the marbled floors.

Two Katrina's Blooms employees brought in the vases of floral arrangements. They were quiet and quick as they placed six vases onto the dining room table.

Once they were gone, Aiden started. "Dani, I—"

"It's okay." Dani held a hand up, cutting off Aiden's apology. "I knew from the beginning why you liked me. Kate wasn't exactly quiet about her obvious delight that I was going to take Julia down a peg or two. I didn't know that you and Bubba went through a rough period, though."

Aiden blinked in shock. "It was about two years ago." She laughed. "Well, that whole conversation kinda came out of nowhere." Aiden glanced sideways to her brother. "I'm going to finish up, but I think we're almost all done." She placed a hand on his arm. "See you tonight?"

He was staring right at Dani when he answered, "Yeah. See you tonight." There was a determined look in his eye, and Dani knew her afternoon of confrontations wasn't done. They waited till Aiden left the room before he asked, "Can we go outside?"

She looked out the window. "I think it's raining."

He grabbed her arm. "Even better." And he half-walked her, half-dragged her out the door. Once outside, he kept going, moving until they were under a veranda. Rain was pouring down on both sides of them, almost forming a complete wall that gave them some privacy.

She let out a soft breath. "Why are you angry with me? Shouldn't I be the one mad at you?"

His hair was wet, and his eyes were stormy. He ignored the bait and slid his hands into his pockets. "How does it feel?"

"What do you mean?"

Jonah stepped closer. "You were Erica's ghost. How does it feel?"

Dani rolled her eyes and moved back, but Jonah caught her elbow and held her firm. He said again, "Don't push that off."

Dani looked from her arm to his hand and wrenched free. "Don't grab me like that."

Jonah crowded her. "You mattered to her. How does that feel?"

"Why are you doing this?"

"You mattered to her."

"Stop it."

"You mattered to her."

"Stop it, Jonah!" And Dani shoved him back. "What are you doing?"

"I want to know how it feels to know that you mattered to someone. You mattered to her. You mattered to Mae. You mattered to a lot of other people—you didn't need to leave for ten years to make people care about you. She already cared about you."

"Where's this coming from?"

The wind picked up, sending bursts of water over. The windows on the house rattled from the rain's force, but they were oblivious. They were caught in their own storm, and then Jonah said, "I want you to let people in. I listened to you last night. You talked about this crazy grandmother. You talked about your two aunts. You talked about all this really heavy shit, but you did it matter-of-factly. And it scared the hell out of me, because I realized last night that you don't let people in. You're shaken by people. You care about them, but you don't let them in. You don't let people in."

"Are you talking about you? About us?" She shoved his chest. His words stung, but she wasn't focusing on that. Her anger helped. She'd cling to that and when he fell back a step, she became the aggressor. She got in his face. "Let's talk about you. Let's talk about the fact that your dad is coming. You didn't say a word. I was spilling my guts out to you last night and not one word about your own family."

He snorted. "Right. Of the two of us, I'm the one who has a sharing problem?" He put his face right in hers. Their noses were almost touching. "Guess what? My dad's coming today. I didn't tell you because I don't give a shit, but you know what else? I'm not going to run away because of him."

A pent-up growl exploded from the bottom of her throat, and she grabbed the front of his shirt. She hauled him close, debating what to do. Push him away. Pull him to her. Hold him tight. Shove him back. She couldn't make up her mind.

As if reading her thoughts, Jonah smirked. "What are you going to do, Dani?"

Her eyes clung to his. She had no idea.

He added, his voice so soft, "What are you going to do if you find out another person cares about you? What are you going to do? Are you going to leave?"

"What are you talking about?"

His eyes darkened, and he clenched his jaw. But he only said, "You know what I'm talking about." Then he made the decision for her. He dug into his pocket and tossed his keys to her. "Here."

Dani caught them. "What is this?"

"You can take my car. I'll get a ride with my sister."

"I'm helping—"

"No, we're okay." Jonah was already turning back to the house. "This is a family thing. We'll manage."

What the hell just happened?

Her head was hurting.

A sane person would want to figure out what happened, but that was the problem. Those were *her* personal problems, dealing with *her* feelings, *her* thoughts, and *her* issues. Nope. She wasn't going there. She wanted to deal with someone *else's* issues, someone whose life was even more messed up than hers.

Her grandmother's.

Once she was back in the mental hospital's lobby, that same blank nametag was placed in front of her. Same Phyliss smiled at her, but different greeting. "Your grandmother doesn't remember your last visit."

"Maybe that's for the best."

The sharpness returned to Sandra O'Hara's gaze when they got to her room. Her grandmother pushed herself off the mattress with her skinny arms that looked like bird's legs. Her muscles shifted and Sandra O'Hara plopped in the lounger beside her bed.

"Well, come on. Bring it over." Sandra pointed to the second chair. "Pull it around. Take a seat." And as Dani did, Sandra pinned her down with an intense stare. "What happened?"

"Huh?"

"Don't play dumb. What happened to you? You look all upset."

"It's my second visit—"

She was cut off by Sandra's snort. "It's your third. That's what Phyliss said." Her grandmother shifted on her seat and reached for a blanket to wrap around herself.

"Right, well." Dani shifted to get more comfortable. "I wasn't really here last time."

"Your mother was."

"You remember that?"

Sandra snorted, pushing off the floor with her feet. She wore hospital slippers, and she began rocking her chair back and forth in a slow and steady rhythm. Dani wondered if this was what she did when there were no visitors.

"It's easier to lie to them than tell the truth." She peered at her granddaughter. "I remember some of it, in patches. Some I don't. I can get legit cuckoo sometimes. From what I remember, you handled me just fine."

"You're no high Mrs. Bendsfield, but it was fine." Dani grinned. She liked hearing her grandmother say the words 'legit cuckoo.' It reminded her of Mae.

"What?"

"Nothing."

"What do I owe you? This is your third visit. I owe you something."

"You promised to tell me who my father is."

"Oh," Sandra cursed under her breath. "I promised you that? Didn't I let something slip last time? Does that count?"

"It doesn't. You called him 'Emmy', but I don't know any Emmy."

"Sure you do. You just don't know their full names."

Dani's eyebrows pinched forward. She frowned. "Are you going to tell me who my father is?"

"No." Sandra plopped her foot onto Dani's lap. "I need to raise my legs. My doc said something about elevating the edema."

Her hands came to rest on her grandmother's feet. "You promised me."

"I'm a liar. Part of the reason why I'm in this place."

"I deserve to know—"

"You don't deserve a goddamn thing." Sandra pulled her feet down and leaned forward. She shouted, "I deserve to have my daughters by my side, but where are they?!"

"One's dead. Another's dying. And who knows when Mae's name is up."

Sandra fell still.

Dani knew she was supposed to stop. She shouldn't talk like that to her grandmother, but she couldn't. The words spilled out in rhythm with her heartbeat. It was speeding up. She was fed up. "You already lost one daughter. Maybe you could begin bridging the gap with your family by starting with me."

"By telling you who your daddy is?"

"Yes!" Dani shoved out of her chair. It screeched across the floor and hit against the wall with a bang. "Shit." She bit down on her lip. She hadn't meant to do that.

"If you pick it up and slam it against the wall, it feels a lot better."

"What?"

Her grandmother didn't blink. "I'm serious. You could even throw it at the window—won't do a darn good. They got 'em covered with thick plastic or something so no one can throw themselves out the window. We just bounce off like rubber birds. It's not a good feeling when you go splat on the floor."

"Are you insane?"

Sandra gave her a 'duh' look. "Yeah."

"You're impossible."

"Impossible and crazy should be synonyms of each other." Sandra tipped her head back and chuckled. "Henri's impossible. Thinks she sees damn angels."

Dani's chest was heaving. No one came to check on the noise, so she retrieved her chair and pulled it back in front of her grandmother.

Sandra murmured as she sat back down, "Henrietta tells me every day that my girls are around. Daniella and Erica. Can you imagine that? Talk about delusional. I don't see things that don't exist. When I'm out of it, I see people from my past. More possible than Henri. She's nuts."

"I'd like to know who my father is."

Sandra sobered, her eyes flicking to Dani's. "You can't handle that yet."

"I can, too."

"No, you can't. It's rolled up in a whole other slew of barrels, and you're barely holding it together as it is. You think this lie is bad? There's a whole bunch more when you find out who he is and his twisted story."

"What do you mean?"

Sandra plopped her feet onto Dani's lap again and settled back once more. "Don't worry about your daddy. He'll come to you when you're ready. I know that much, if I don't know a lot else. Let me tell you about your granddaddy. How about that? He's another story." Sandra chuckled. "Your granddaddy's name is Oscar Bendsfield. Oscar Senior."

Mr. Bendsfield. Dani's eyes lit up.

"That's right." Sandra chuckled again. "Nanery Bendsfield used to be my best friend until her husband up and left her. He didn't leave her for me, so she never suspected a thing, but I hope you don't got the O'Hara curse for stupidity."

"What do you mean?" Dani repeated.

As she talked, her fingers began moving on her lap. Sandra was making the motions like she was crocheting. There was nothing in her hands, but that's what she was doing. "I was stupid. I went back around for more and more. He got me pregnant again and again. I lost the last kid—which is what I think set off my crazy spells. He never made no promises with pretty words and such, and we were never together in the 'official' sense, but I loved him. I kept going back for more and more."

"Does..."

"Does Nanery know?" Sandra nodded her head and grinned wickedly. "She sure does, but she didn't find that out until years later. It took her nearly twenty years before she got told what her precious Oscar was up to outside their cold bed, long before their marriage went stale."

"You ruined a marriage."

She snorted, shaking her head. "The marriage was ruined long before Oscar came sniffing around."

"You didn't help it."

That got her grandma, and Sandra sat back. "Huh. Got a point."

"Marriage is sacred."

"Theirs wasn't. Theirs was just wrong." Sandra's fingers went back to air crocheting. "Sometimes partnerships aren't meant to be. And sometimes they only do bad more than good. Theirs was one of those. They weren't meant to be married, and Oscar knew that."

"Lilies and daisies," Dani announced.

Sandra grew still. "What did you just say?"

"Lilies and daisies. Her husband. My grandfather. He liked lilies and daisies. She told me that two days ago, didn't he?" But Sandra was looking away. That was her answer. Dani stood up slowly. "It was sacred in her mind. Isn't that all that counts? That it was sacred to one of them."

"They just flowers."

"Funny." Dani's voice dripped in disdain. "Those were her words, too."

Sandra O'Hara looked away.

"She cared enough to remember him. She named her son after him." Dani turned away. "Those were my mother's favorite flowers, too. Lilies and daisies. They're my mother's flowers, so don't say they're just flowers. They're more than that. They meant something."

"Why are you doing this? Why do you care after all these years? These are secrets better left buried. They just...they just bring pain to everyone involved."

"So says the one who'd rather have her sins left buried." Dani shook her head. This was wrong. It was another wrong that was being buried. This wrong affected people. The cycle had to stop. The pain had to stop. "You'd like everyone to forget about you, don't you? You *want* to forget what you did, what you did to your daughters. You don't want to be remembered because then you gotta look at your decisions."

"It's not like that."

Dani's blood began to boil. "That's all this family has right now: secrets. I barely talked to two of my sisters growing up, and I don't talk to the one living now. Julia's like an anal, obsessive-compulsive stranger who just knows all my hurts. Secrets got us where we are right now. I think I have a right to find out who I come from!"

"You're going to tear up this family—"

"There's no family to tear apart!" Dani cried out. "We got the same name. That's it. There's no family anymore, and it started with you!"

"Now, I didn't—"

"You told your daughter to give her children away. You told her that Mae could have me, if she cleaned up her act. You acted like we were cattle to give away to the richest owner. You told your daughter, who came to you—knowing that she was dying—you told her to split her children up."

"I gave my two cents. That's all I did—"

"Words have power! I never felt a part of that house. You were a *mother* who told her dying *daughter* what to do. She listened to you. You did that! Not my mother! You tore my home apart, and you did it because that's where you came from."

"I didn't..."

The evidence was right in front of her. "You—"

"No." Sandra bunched up her blanket on her lap and began shaking her head. Her eyes grew wet, and her lips started to tremble, but she wasn't looking at her granddaughter anymore. She reached for a button clipped to the bed. Her hand curled around it. She held it tight, like it was a weapon. "Leave. This is my room. This is my home, and I get to say who comes to judge me. I say leave and don't come back."

Dani couldn't believe what she was hearing. She looked around in exasperation, and she caught sight of a single clove on her grandmother's nightstand. One clove, tucked underneath the Bible, and Dani knew it had been kept for a purpose.

"I always found a clove under my pillow. I never knew who put those there, but I guess it was your mother. She was always worried about me."

"The cloves were for..." Dani scrunched up her face, trying to remember.

"The cloves were to attract my guardian angels. My mother told me one night, and I'm telling you that, too." Dani's mom smiled down

at her, tucking a stray hair strand behind her ear. Her fingers lingered over her cheek, feeling how smooth they were. "You remember that, my little Dani. You see a clove, you remember that I put it there." She lowered her head, resting her forehead to her daughter's, and whispered, "Because I'll be your guardian angel if we're ever separated. I'll be looking out for you."

A clove. That was all it took.

Anything else she'd been about to say died in her throat. Dani couldn't explain it. She stopped. Everything. She stopped pushing for answers. She stopped interrogating her grandmother. She let it all go, and she knew that she was done. Sandra O'Hara was done with her, too. There'd be no more visits. Dani left. Sandra's stubborn face never looked back at her, not after she left the door open, not as she trailed past her window, and when Dani got outside, she turned around and peered up.

The window to her grandmother's room was blank. No one stood there watching.

Dani knew Sandra was locked within herself, and in that moment, she pitied her, but she also pitied herself, too. Her grandmother couldn't physically run, but that was what she was doing.

Dani would never be that person. She was done running.

She'd stay.

She'd stand.

Phylllis watched from the second floor window. She mused, her arms wrapped around herself like she was chilled, "That's a shame. I don't think that one will be back." Then she went back to her desk and didn't give Dani another thought.

Henrietta was in the corner, wrapped in a blanket and rocking back and forth. She looked up, and saw dancing lilies and daisies in the sky. She whispered to herself, "No one will be back. It's going to break."

She saw the rain coming.

Dani parked at Aiden's house, and sat in Jonah's car for twenty minutes.

She couldn't bring herself to go in there. Sandra. Mae. The secrets. The lies. Boone. Even Jake. And now Jonah, as she sat in his car, smelling him, remembering the taste of him, the feel of him on top of her.

She needed to get up. She needed to go. She needed to find him. If he cared about her, he could tell her. She wasn't running. She wasn't going to be another Sandra O'Hara.

But she still sat.

Another car's headlights swept over her and the rest of the cars, driving into the driveway before parking. Two figures stepped out from the car. Boone had come after all, and he wasn't alone. He was holding hands with Jenny as they crossed behind where she sat.

They went inside. The door opened, highlighting the far side of the porch, and Dani saw Kate there. She had a drink in hand, and a koala attached to her arm.

She said once she stood at the bottom of the porch, "For a cop, you're oblivious tonight."

Kate jumped, laughing as she turned around.

Dani saw the darkened spots on her friend's outfit. "Sorry about that."

"No, no." Kate dabbed where her drink had spilled. "It's my fault. You're right. I'm not real alert tonight."

Dani pointed to Kate's arm. "What's with the dude bear?"

Kate laughed. "The carnie outfits fell through. Bubba didn't get them in time, or something. I'm not sure. Aiden said we're going with the animals tonight." She raised her arm. "I'm Koala One."

"Who's Koala Two?"

"Ah. Yes. That's why I'm not the 'cop' tonight. It's supposed to be Robbie, but he's not here yet."

"Oh." Dani leaned beside Kate against the patio's frame. "I heard a rumor you're supposed to kiss?"

"We are." She slumped next to her, holding her cup with both hands. "I think he has to tell Lori that. At least, that's what we decided."

"Gotcha. And if he doesn't come tonight?"

"Then he didn't tell Lori." Kate gave her a pointed look.

Dani frowned. "Oh."

"Yeah."

"I'm sorry."

"Yeah."

"My grandma's alive."

"What?" Kate did a double take.

Dani shrugged. "I thought I'd share in your misery. My grandmother's alive, and she just kicked me out of her hospital room."

"Why'd she do that? Where *is* she? Your grandma's alive?!"

"I pushed her to admit something, but she wouldn't."

A smile ghosted over Kate's features. "Is that code to tell me that I'm pushing Robbie?"

Dani gave her a wry smile. "Robbie asked me one night if I thought Lori would make a good mother." Kate winced, but Dani kept going, "I'm not telling you that to hurt you. I'm telling you that because he's thinking about his future. And I told him if he was asking a stranger that question, he knew the answer."

"He kept dating her."

She touched Kate's arm. "I haven't kept up to date with what's going on, but I wouldn't worry about it. Robbie seems like a guy who needs a little push. And if he doesn't, then he's losing something amazing."

"Oh." Kate frowned. Her hand flicked up to her eye. "Thanks, Dani. Maybe we could stay out here and get drunk? Forget waiting on guys, right?" It was a wishful thought, but Kate laughed as she reached into her pocket and produced a walkie-talkie. She pressed the button and spoke into it, "This is Koala One to Chimp Two."

Static sounded a moment. "This is Chimp Two. Chimp One is still missing in the jungle. What do you need, Koala One?"

Kate whispered over the sound to Dani, "Chimp One is Aiden. Chimp Two is Bubba."

Dani nodded. "Got it." She'd never remember that.

Kate pressed the button again. "Koala One has come across Flamingo Two. Flamingo Two is requesting more coconut juice."

Dani mouthed, "Coconut juice?"

"Booze. And you're Flamingo Two."

They heard a reply, "Coconut juice is on its way, Koala One and Flamingo Two. Good to hear you arrived, Flamingo Two."

Dani took the radio and spoke into it, "Thank you..."

"Chimp Two," Kate mouthed for her.

Dani finished, "Chimp Two."

"Anytime, Flamingo Two. Coconut juice's E.T.A. is two minutes, already en route."

"Over and out, Chimp Two."

"Over and out, Flamingo Two."

Dani asked, "Flamingo Two?"

Kate grinned. "Jonah's Flamingo One, and it's because you're both so pretty."

"If he doesn't come tonight, Robbie is a complete idiot."

The smile vanished from Koala One's face. "Yeah, well, there's a reason why he was given the name Baboon."

Bubba rapped against the door with his knuckles. His hands were full with two glasses. A flamingo sat perched on his face, and its legs spread out down the sides to his ears, holding itself in place like a headband.

Dani burst out laughing.

Kate opened the door, and Bubba handed over two Coronas. He plucked off the flamingo and stood right in front of Dani.

"Oh, please. I kinda wish you'd gotten the carnie costumes." Dani reached for the headband, but Bubba moved her hands away. "Where's your kids? Are they going to be traumatized by all this?"

"They're at my folks. Now, I have to do this just right, Aiden said so." He wiggled his eyebrows up and down. "Flamingo Two has been anxious to meet her owner." Bubba giggled, and it seemed wrong for such a muscular man to giggle like a schoolgirl. He concentrated next, biting down on his lip. "Fancy Nancy is very happy to make your acquaintance."

"Fancy Nancy, huh?" Dani reached to touch the flamingo after he put it on her head.

"Fancy Nancy doesn't like to be touched."

"She doesn't? She's going to bite me or something?"

"Nah." Bubba was biting his lip down. "We'll let Flamingo One do that." He winked at her.

Dani shook her head, grinning stupidly. If this was the start to her evening, she'd come to any party wearing Fancy Nancy. "This is hilarious." She didn't comment on Bubba's other comment.

"This is just the warm-up. We have full costumes still."

"Jonah has one of these, too?"

Bubba laughed again. "He won't wear one of our get-ups, but he still gets called Flamingo One."

"Why do I have to wear this and he doesn't?"

"Because you're cool and fun, and he's not." Kate clinked her drink to one of Bubba's.

"Yeah." Bubba nodded in agreement. "We even bought these two orange hunting pads, you know that you can sit on when you're hunting and they warm your ass up. Aiden sewed them onto this waistband that she took from my old underwear. We're going to make Robbie wear them when he gets here."

Kate's smile slipped. "Thanks for that."

Bubba clamped a hand on Kate's shoulder. "Robbie is a baboon, if you ask me."

"I know." And Kate tried for a smile, but the energy was gone.

He wrapped his arms around her and lifted her in the air in a big hug. He whispered something in her ear, and Kate squealed. Her smile wasn't as forced anymore. Then she stopped, looking inside the doors, and nudged Dani with her arm. She gestured inside.

Jake was right inside with Julia next to him. They were both in the front entryway, and Jake was staring at them. His eyes skimmed over the flamingo with the faintest tease of a grin at his mouth. Then Julia looked up from where she'd been listening to someone else talking. She saw Dani and stiffened immediately.

Dani muttered under her breath, "I don't want to go in there."

And just then, the door opened. Jake walked outside with Julia in tow.

"Jake!" Bubba lifted his arms, but couldn't shake or hug him. He was holding his drink. "You need some coconut juice?" Before Jake could respond, Bubba clamped him on the shoulder with his free hand and moved around. "I'll get you coconut juice. You, too, Julia. You look like you need to get buzzed."

Julia opened her mouth, but closed it as Bubba was already through the door.

"He's on orders to get everyone drunk and to get their car keys." The ends of Kate's mouth tugged upward in a grin, but it slipped as she nodded to Julia. "Julia."

"Kate."

Dani chuckled. She shouldn't, but she couldn't stop herself. She was saying before she completely realized what was going to come out of her mouth, "Man—two people you hate, Julia. You're stuck out here with us. And you have to play nice." She whistled. "That's gotta burn in a special place."

Jake's head tipped upwards. "Oh, my God."

Kate looked away. Her shoulders shook a tiny bit.

Julia sighed. "Nice, Dani. That's real classy."

"I've already gone three rounds with our grandmother. You remember her? She's alive, and she hates my guts right now. I can handle going a round with you."

Julia frowned. "Our grandmother?"

"Sandra O'Hara is alive and kicking, although I guess it could be debated on how 'alive' she actually is. She's not real big on being accountable for anything, but hey. I know where the 'running' trait came from. Did you know how fucked up our family is? Some of it came from her. Shocker."

Julia went unnaturally still. "I don't believe you. You're just trying to play games because you're hoping that I won't press charges against you for burglary."

"You already tried." Dani gestured to Jake and Kate. "But we do have two police officers right here. Feel free to try again."

"It's mine, and I want it back."

Jake cleared his throat. His voice rose in volume. "I thought we were here for poker." He put his arm around Julia's shoulder, turning her back inside. "Let's play some poker."

"I have as much right to Mother's picture as you, Dani."

"No, you don't!"

"How can you say that?" Julia cried out. "You don't know anything about our family—"

"*Your* family!" Dani interrupted, holding on to her drink for dear life. This wasn't the place, but whom was she kidding? Julia would never meet with her one-on-one. It was here and now. She was tired of avoiding. It was time to fight. "It's been *your* family from day one after Mother was buried. Kathryn took you and Erica in and I was pushed out."

"Bullshit. You got Mae. I got Kathryn." Julia couldn't keep the bitterness from her voice.

"Has that been building up over the years?" Dani taunted. "What? Are you bothered you didn't get *both* aunts?"

"This is ridiculous!" Julia hissed. "We are adults, and we are above this."

"No, we're not. We're sisters."

"You're irrational—" Julia started to chide her sister, but Dani cut her off, "Kinda like needing to leave a party so you can obsessively mop the kitchen floor at midnight because it wasn't mopped enough earlier in the day? Irrational like that?"

Julia sucked in her breath—again.

Jake groaned. "Oh no."

Julia's eyes flashed a warning. "Excuse me?"

Dani shook her head. "I'm not going to excuse you. You have to have everything in perfect order. You have to feel needed, all the time. You were like that growing up. I've no doubt you're like that now. I bet Kathryn doesn't need you to remind her to take her pills. She's got her own alarms set to remind herself to take those pills."

"Dani."

She whipped her head to regard Jake. "What? What cardinal sin have I committed now?!"

Jake murmured quietly, "Kathryn's dying. We got the news this past week."

This past week—when Jake was schmoozing with Boone and his family, when Julia was suddenly friends with Boone's new girlfriend.

Dani snorted, hardening over an ache inside of her. "Let me guess. You were never going to tell me. Were you?"

She waited.

Nothing.

Silence.

She got her answer. "I see."

Julia was seething. "You said it yourself. She's my family, not yours."

"You did, too. Your words, too, Julia. You got Kathryn. I got Mae, the only difference is that I lived with her, and she turned you and Erica against me. She chose to love you and Erica, but she never loved me."

"Kathryn told me about her agreement with Mae. Mae got you, and Kathryn got us. It was agreed upon, but Mae took forever to get her life in order, so Kathryn took care of you. You should be grateful—"

"Of what?"

"Jake—" Kate coughed from behind them. "Maybe you and I should go and start up another poker game."

Jake glanced between the two sisters. "Maybe we should."

Kate and Jake disappeared, and Dani shot back,"It doesn't have to be either/or in our family. Why am I the only one who gets that? It never had to be like that."

Julia quieted, but her neck was red.

"You wanna know where that even came from?" Dani cried out. "From our mother."

"Don't talk about her. She doesn't deserve to have her memory dragged through the mud."

"She visited Sandra O'Hara. It was our grandmother who told her what to do, to even talk to Mae about having me." Dani's laugh was empty, even to her own ears. "She took advice from a crazy woman. Okay. She's more broken than crazy, but still crazy. Stubborn, too."

"Grandmom is dead. Kathryn told us that."

"No." She really wasn't. Dani shook her head. "I've seen her three times now."

Julia jerked backwards and held her hands up. She was shaking her head. "I can't do this, not now. I can't—" She choked off her words. The fight left her. Her shoulders dropped down. Her head hung low. Her hands fell back to her side.

"Did you know that our grandfather was married?" Dani kept going. Maybe it was because she wanted to stick it to her sister that she knew more than the all-knowing Julia did. Maybe it was because her sister liked to stick her head in the sand, but she couldn't this time. There was evidence. People were still living. Julia wouldn't be able to deny them away. Or maybe she was saying all this because she was sick of being the only one to hold it? Maybe it was time they stopped perpetuating the cycle?

"Stop it, Dani!" Her head flared back up. Her eyes were wide with panic. "I can't listen to this right now. Not when—Kathryn is dying. She needs me." She rushed back inside, the door slamming shut behind her.

Dani was left alone, a flamingo perched on her head.

"Hey."

She turned around and saw Jonah perched on the steps. "Hey." She touched the flamingo. "I thought for a second Fancy Nancy came alive, or I've embraced the crazy gene in my family and started to hear voices."

Jonah chuckled dryly as he moved up the stairs and leaned next to her. He hoisted himself up on the railing, then lifted Dani to sit next to him. His hands lingered on her waist before removing his arm around her back. She studied him, seeing the pain in his eyes, the bags under them, and the slight crinkle around his mouth. She didn't think they looked like they were there from smiling or laughing.

She offered her drink. "You look like you could use this more than me."

He took it, giving her a half-grin. "Are you sure?" He gestured inside where Julia had gone. "Another one of these and I'm thinking you could go for round two."

His hands were resting on his lap, so she reached and lifted one, lacing their fingers together. "How'd your thing go with your dad?"

Bullseye.

Jonah's lip curled upward, amused at some irony that was lost on Dani. "Your fight with your sister was refreshing." Jonah chuckled again, a twinge of bitterness laced with it. "Beats the superficialness of my family. Aiden just—she lied right through her teeth when we dropped off our dad at Robbie's. He loved the house, said he's going to come more often to visit."

"You think he is?"

"No. We know our lies. Everyone knows them, but we're fake anyway. You and Julia, you guys don't get what's between you. It's refreshing."

She didn't understand that, but at that moment, Jonah needed it to be about him. She looked down to the ground, knowing this next part could be painful. "Jonah, about…"

"Before?"

"Yeah. About before—"

"I'm sorry."

"For what?" Dani lifted her head.

"I pushed you. I'm sorry."

"Oh." Her shoulders shook in a silent laugh. "Everyone seems to be pushing someone today."

"Who were you pushing?"

"My grandma."

Jonah nodded. She already filled him in on her visits, and he squeezed her hand. "How'd that go?"

"Not good. Horrible, actually. I found out my grandmother and grandfather were cheating bastards, and there's some type of curse on our family. The fathers keep leaving, but come back to get the moms pregnant again. Happened to Sandra. Happened to my mom." She hoped it wouldn't happen to her. "Probably a good thing none of us have had children yet, huh?"

His laugh was soft, but sad.

She looked at him, studying his side profile as he was gazing out into the distance. "Why'd you push me earlier?"

"It's not important."

But it was. She felt it in her chest. It was so important, and she needed him to say it again. She was salivating for the chance. She wanted to reassure him, and this time she felt it in her heart. She knew she wasn't going anywhere. She wanted him to see it in her eyes, that she meant every single word.

She whispered now, "Ask me. Ask me again."

His eyes met hers, narrowing slightly. He was looking into her, reading her.

She was letting him. There was no wall, no hesitation this time. She wanted him to know her, not just her body. All of her. A second passed. He was still searching in her. Another second. More. He waited a full thirty before asking, his voice so soft and tender, "What would you do if you found out another person cared about you? If you mattered to one more person?"

"Nothing." She was trying to convey her feelings through her eyes. She wanted him to know so badly. "I wouldn't run. I wouldn't walk. I wouldn't hide. I'd do nothing except stand and embrace it."

His eyes darkened, an emotion passed in them, one that had her heart beating so fast again. "Yeah?" He let go of her hand, but touched the side of her face. He held her in the palm of his hand, and his thumb rubbed over her cheek. It was like he was smoothing away any lingering worries she might have. "What if I was that person?"

She leaned toward him, her eyes going from his lips back to his gaze. Both were pulling her in, making her yearn for more. "Then I'd say, I feel the same." Her breath held in her throat. They were talking in code, but it was out now. She was telling him how she felt, and a second later, his lips were on hers.

This. She turned, wound her arms around his neck. This was everything.

It started raining.

Both were soaked, and Jonah held her hand as they dashed inside. People watched as they moved through the house. A few had a smart comment to share.

Dani was quiet, merely holding Jonah's hand.

Kelley Lynn was right. Kate was right. Their community adored Jonah. The men slapped him on the back with a dirty remark about their wetness. And the women took note of who held his hand. Dani caught more than a few pissed off women, wrinkling their noses and curling their lips in a scowl.

Well. Any secrecy that Dani thought they had was gone now. They were officially a couple. Ducking upstairs, Jonah pulled her into Aiden and Bubba's room. Quilts were strewn across the room, over tables, and even on the floor.

Dani crossed to the window and watched the rain. It was a downpour. It looked like a full sheet was draped over the house, like it could be cut through with a knife. "It's really coming down, huh?" Then she surveyed the room. "Something tells me that Robbie's master bedroom doesn't exactly compare to this room."

Jonah searched inside Bubba's closet. "Probably not." His voice was muffled until he produced a T-shirt and a clean pair of boxers. He laid them on the bed, briskly pulling his drenched shirt off, hanging it over the counter in the bathroom. "I'm going to have to wear my wet jeans. I don't exactly measure up to Bubba's size."

Dani tracked the water on his chest, his glorious and golden and muscled chest. All. The. Way. Down. His jeans cut off her view. His hands were there, and he paused. She was waiting, trying not to lick her lips. He still didn't undo them, and her eyes jerked to his. He was watching her. No laughter. His gaze was dark, almost smoldering, and she felt her body starting to quiver in response.

She lost the battle. Her tongue darted out, wetting her lips.

He groaned. "You're killing me, Dani."

"Sorry." She wasn't.

His voice grew hoarse, like it was work for him to speak. "Stop looking at me, or I'm coming over there."

Her voice matched his. "We're in your sister's bedroom."

"I'm starting not to give a damn."

They couldn't. Nope. But she wanted to. They needed another topic, and then she remembered. "Your family."

"What about them?"

"What happened with your dad?"

"You want to talk about my dad? Right now?" He sounded incredulous, his eyebrows arching up.

"It's either that or everyone's going to know we're doing something else up here."

He closed his eyes. His hand caught and held his neck, and his head fell back. "Shit. You're right. Okay. My dad. You want to know about him." Then he groaned, unzipping his pants.

Dani sat up, but bit down on her lip. She would not say anything to interrupt this. She would not do anything to stop him from changing, or pulling on dry clothes, or telling her about his dad. It was causing a physical ache in her stomach. She rested back against the wall, and forced herself to remain there. She wouldn't cross the room. Would not. No... She found herself leaning toward him, away from the wall.

Jonah was talking as he dropped his wet boxers.

Dani almost fell over.

He didn't notice, pulling on the clean pair. They were baggy, but he tucked everything in as he pulled his wet jeans back on. The dry shirt was next, and once he was covered, Dani slumped back against the wall. She felt like she'd run a 5K, right then and there.

He was saying, "...he's not here to see me or Aiden. He's here because of the Quandrys."

"What?!"

"Yeah." He frowned. "Weren't you listening?"

She groaned. Would he have? But all she said was, "Say it again."

"My dad's here because of the Quandrys. He's working with them. I'm assuming they asked him to come in to talk to me, get me to change my mind so they can build on the river. It's not going to happen, but they can try."

"Boone's here."

"I thought they had their own thing tonight."

So did she. "He's here. I saw him drive up myself. I was sitting in your car." Speaking of, "How'd you get here?"

He smirked. "Hawk gave me a ride. He had to check on something, but he's going to come back. My sister tends to have a lot of good-looking friends. He wouldn't miss this party for anything." He cocked his head to the side, crossing the room to her. "How are you with your ex being here?"

She knew he didn't mean Jake. "It is what it is."

His hand slid around her neck, cupping the back. "You're okay with it?"

Was she? She was having a hard time concentrating with him being so close. She could feel his heat. All she had to do was reach a hand out, just a few inches, and she'd be touching him back. Or she could lean forward, her body wavering. She would close her eyes, and she knew Jonah would do the rest.

She forced herself back. "I'll be fine, but you need to step away because I'm losing the will not to touch you back."

She didn't dare look up and meet his gaze. She breathed out, concentrating on just breathing, but she meant it. If he stayed there, she'd lose the battle in the next two seconds. And then it was time's up, and she found herself going toward him, just an inch. Her hand touched his stomach, feeling his muscles tighten under her touch, and she knew how the rest of those muscles were cut, all deep valleys, all there for her to run her fingers over.

"Okay. No." She pushed him back. "Leave, or when I take my clothes off, I won't be pulling any of your sister's dry ones on."

He laughed, sounding strained. "I'll be downstairs." His lips touched her forehead and she had to will herself not to watch him go. She waited until the door opened, then closed, before she almost collapsed onto the bed.

Too much. Jonah was damned near a weapon himself.

A small grin tugged on her lips. She was looking forward to the end of the night, and with that thought, she sat up. Clothes to wear. She needed some.

Then she heard a knock, and the door swung open. Boone stood there, and he was soaking wet, too.

"Oh!"

"Hey." She straightened from the bed.

He only stood there, taking in her wet state before looking back to the hallway. "I saw Bannon leave a moment ago."

"Uh, yeah." Her lips puckered together. "We were both outside when it started raining. I was just going to change clothes, too."

He nodded, his jaw clenching at the same time. "I see." His eyes were so cold.

"Look, Boone—"

"No." His head clipped to the side. "No." His nostrils flared. Then he left.

She scrambled to her feet. "Wha—" But he was gone. She changed quickly. Boone was angry. He had reason, but he didn't at the same time. He knew she was with Jonah. There were other conversations that needed to happen between them, conversations that she knew both were putting off.

She was searching for him when Jenny seemed to materialize out of thin air. "I'm looking for Mitch. Do you know where he is?"

"You're not the only one." she murmered.

She was looking around, biting down on her lip. "He went out to get my purse. I forgot it in the car, but he was drenched when he came back in. I told him to dry his clothes before he caught pneumonia." Jenny laughed a sickening sound of delight. "Heaven's sake—I wouldn't want pneumonia. I don't even want to get a cold while I'm on vacation."

"He's—" She lied. "He's gone downstairs. There's a clothes dryer down there."

"Oh. Thank you!" But she stayed put. Her eyes switched to Dani's face, suddenly a whole lot more attentive than Dani thought she could be.

"Is there anything else?"

"I know who you are."

"So do I."

Her top lip curled up in disdain. "Mitch told me that the two of you used to go together, when he was in those third-world countries. How he got his heart broken by some slut and you were just a rebound girl. Did you know about the other girl? I don't want you to start thinking that you can have him back. Mitch might not see it, but I know exactly what type of girl you are."

Dani shifted back on her heels. "And what's that?" She crossed her arms over her chest.

"You followed him here." She leaned closer, her face way too close to Dani's, and she whispered, "And that was the *wrong* thing to do."

"You're an idiot."

Her hand was itching to reach up and push Jenny's face away, but knowing this moron, she'd say she was being assaulted. She grew heated, and before she could do something she'd regret, she turned her back and pushed through the crowd. The farther from her, the better.

Turning into the kitchen, Dani stopped short. Aiden was in complete costume. She wore a chimp suit with a pink bowtie on her tail.

"Dani!" Aiden exclaimed. "I knew Fancy Nancy would be a hit with you."

Dani pulled the soaked flamingo off her head. The pink head was drooping down. It looked more like a pink drowned rat. Then she stuffed Fancy Nancy back on. "Yes. Yes, she is." Dani accepted the beer that Aiden held out. "Where's your brother?"

"He headed downstairs." Aiden's smile slipped for a moment, but she brought it back with a forced attempt. "He ditched you tonight, didn't he? Don't take it personally. Jonah's a bit riled with Daddy

Warbuck's arrival. Me—I can let our father's condescension slide off my shoulders, but it bothers Jonah. I'm sure he just wants to forget right now in a poker game." Aiden moved as someone reached around them for a bag of chips. "Which means that I can't play poker tonight."

"How come?"

"Jonah always beats me at poker, and if he's playing seriously tonight—he'll be playing all night," Aiden answered. "Which means that I'm going to be playing hostess all night. No way am I going to lose money to my brother, though I love him wholeheartedly, but money is money."

So Jonah was a poker player? Why wasn't she surprised? "Where's Kate?"

"Probably wherever Robbie is not. If not with him, then at a table downstairs, too. If she doesn't catch the first round of games, then she just creates her own game. Kate's not that good at poker, but she likes to think she is. I told Jonah to be nice to her. Jonah—he can be ruthless sometimes."

Ruthless? Dani tried to imagine it, and she could. She shivered, remembering their time upstairs. She was wondering now if she should've just kissed him and to hell with everyone else. She glanced over her shoulder.

"Looking for your ex-fiancé?" Aiden caught the look and misjudged.

"You know?"

"You told Jake and Kate. That means the whole town knows, but for what it's worth, I didn't hear it from either of them. Dad started in on Jonah when we picked him up from the airport. He was getting interrogated about you the entire car ride to Robbie's house."

"Really?"

Dani's gut dropped to her feet. That wasn't good, not at all.

Aiden touched her hand. "I'm ducking for cover with this one. The big guns were pulled out when they called in our dad. There's no way that I want to attract his attention. He's like a wolf when he gets something in his head. I had to literally bite my tongue the entire car ride. I swallowed some blood."

At that moment, the windows lit up as lightning flashed. The rain seemed to hit the windows harder, and she heard the wind whipping against the shutters.

Aiden murmured, "The storm outside's picking up."

The storm wasn't just outside. Dani gazed around the crowd. She had a feeling there was going to be some thunderstorms inside, as well.

The party divided into two groups: the players and the watchers.

Dani was a watcher, and she sat alone from her group of friends. Kate played with her emotions, getting excited and not hiding her disappointment when she lost, but bowed out before she lost too much. She became a watcher next to Dani.

Aiden circulated the room, played the hostess to perfection. She patted Kate and Dani on their arms whenever she swept past them. It was a nice and loving pat, as if to say, "Hey, how are you doing? I can't stay and talk, but thinking of you."

Jonah was winning, which didn't seem to be a surprise to most people in the room. Dani overheard a few conversations. Most expected him to win. She studied him, and wasn't surprised why. He showed nothing. Absolutely nothing.

Then a spot opened at a different table, and Jake sat down.

A second guy left, and the dealer signaled for one more to join.

Boone stepped forward.

Jake frowned, but didn't say anything. Everyone from Jonah's table looked over. A new player got attention, and no one knew what to expect. Jonah skimmed over him, the unreadable mask still on his face. His eyes flicked to Dani once, but that was his only reaction.

Jenny smiled proudly behind Boone. She flicked her hair over her shoulder, giving Dani a haughty look, then smoothed a hand down his arm. She began to rub at his shoulders.

Kate leaned closer to Dani. "She's a piece of work."

Dani didn't comment. Jenny was annoying, but she was the least of her worries at that moment. Hearing giggling, she lifted her gaze again. Julia was next to Jenny, and the two were whispering together like best friends.

Julia wasn't normally a giggler, but Dani caught the martini in her sister's hands.

"Wonder who's holding Kathryn's hand," Kate muttered underneath her breath. "Isn't that the sole purpose of Julia's life?"

Dani shook her head, changing the subject. "Of the two, who's going to win? Jake or Boone?"

"That's the *guy*?"

"That's the guy."

"Wow." Kate was raking him up and down. "I didn't realize it was him. I thought it was the other guy when we were at Mae's Grill." But she approved. Dani heard her friend's appreciation. "He's not as hot as Jonah, and I don't know. Jake's actually pretty good at poker, but your new guy looks pretty good, too. He looks locked down."

"He's not my guy, and he's angry."

"How can you tell?"

She remembered how cold he'd been upstairs. "I just know."

"Judging by how he's handling himself already, he looks like a contender. He could beat Jake. Too bad Jonah's at the other table. I think the best table would be you against all three of them. You know their tells." Her voice picked up. She was getting excited at the thought. "Do you know how to play poker? We could get you in. You come off as this nice girl, but you've got an unpredictable streak. Jake doesn't know what you're going to do from one day to the next, and I'm guessing neither does your ex. And Jonah—you have to be unpredictable for him to stick around as much as he has. Jonah likes challenges. I love the guy, but he gets bored with girls."

"I'm not playing poker." She didn't know how, but even if she did, wild horses wouldn't have been able to drag her there. She coughed, tugging at her shirt's collar. "New topic, please?"

Robbie descended the stairs at that moment. "We can talk about my screwed-up life." Kate glared at him.

He glanced uneasily around the room until his eyes settled on Kate and Dani. He didn't move toward them. No one budged, and the crowd clapped as Boone won his first hand.

Jonah won at his table.

Aiden stepped next to Kate and Dani. Her face soured. "I could totally take some of those morons, but no—Jonah has to play tonight. It's not fair."

"Why don't you play until you two have to sit together?"

"Because I'd want to go all the way, and we'd just meet at the championship table. It wouldn't be good. Trust me." Someone called her name, and she gave both a forced smile. "And I'm off, playing hostess again!"

"Toot toot." Kate laughed.

Aiden brandished a hand over her shoulder. "Toot toot!"

Dani didn't ask. She knew an inside joke when she heard it.

"Look." Kate tapped Dani's arm. "Jake's going all out in the next move. I bet you twenty to nothing."

And he did. The crowd oohed and aahed. He won the first pot. The loser left, and it was Boone, Jake, and a bearded older guy. There were another three rounds before the bearded guy was forced to leave.

Boone won the fourth pot.

A smattering of clapping and congratulations sounded from Jonah's table. He was deemed the winner, and he stood to stretch. Dani caught his gaze. He looked from her to Jake and Boone's table. She tried to read him, but nothing showed. He nodded to her, then headed up the stairs. Dani frowned, unsure if she should follow him, but she stayed. She was going home with Jonah. They could talk then. She wanted to see who won between Jake and Boone.

"Okay." Kate stole Dani's attention again. "You see this hand—Jake has to be bluffing. He's coming across as if he's got a pair of aces, but I bet that he's got a pair of sixes. He has to. Your guy is cool."

Dani gritted her teeth. He wasn't her guy.

Kate kept talking. "I don't know what he has, but it's got to be better than Jake's hand, and yet—Jake's still pushing."

"Why do you think he's got a pair of sixes?"

"Because when they flipped over the first two cards, Jake tapped the table."

"What's the other card?"

"A king."

"Jake's got a full house," Dani proclaimed.

"How in hell do you know that?"

"Because he's got his full house face on. He looks like that when he's about to burst from the inside. He's excited right now, really excited."

"He's not making a move."

"He's playing Boone."

"What?" Kate frowned and said again, "What?"

"Jake's smarter than people think he is. He plays dumb sometimes, and he's thinking that Boone will make that mistake."

"Will he?"

"Boone knows that I'd never stay with someone stupid. He's not going to fall for it."

Kate's eyebrows arched high. "Someone's going to win because Jake just went all in."

"That's a stupid move. I don't know poker that well, but I know that's a stupid move."

Boone looked up and found Dani among the crowd. His eyes pierced hers for a moment, and a knot slowly twisted inside of her. She saw the decision in his eyes, and he pushed all his money into the pot.

"Oh. My. God." Kate barely breathed. "Winner takes all."

"He's walking."

"What?"

"He's walking away."

"You're not making any sense."

"Yeah, I am." The dealer flipped the last card, and the crowd gasped. The clapping started a beat later. There was a one second delay as everyone realized what happened.

Boone's chair scraped against the floor as he stood up.

"That could've played out for another hour, but man, I haven't seen something like that since Tilly Wade launched herself across the table at Harry Hubbard's." Kate laughed. "Harry never walked the same again."

Jake grinned from ear to ear as his money was collected. He moved to the winner's table. Dani twisted around, looking, and she saw the back of Boone as he was going up the stairs. Her stomach knotted again. She didn't want to have this talk, but it was time. She headed after him, pushing her way up the stairs.

Boone was leaving the kitchen. She headed after him, following him all the way until he turned down an empty hallway.

"Boone."

He paused.

"Can we talk?"

He had no reaction. He didn't look surprised, as he stated, "The back porch was empty earlier."

The crowd's rumble faded to a soothing murmur in the background as Boone led the way out there. He didn't open the door for Dani. He went in and crossed to the far side, sat down on a couch there. He hunched over, just slightly, sliding his hands in his pockets.

She closed the door behind her, but didn't move farther into the room.

The windows were closed over the screens, but it was still cold. The furniture was bare. A table was pushed against a wall. A pile of chips, soda cans, and cookies were on it.

Dani had to move closer, or she wouldn't be able to hear anything. The rain was almost deafening.

"You left that game. You knew what Jake had, didn't you?"

"Yeah."

"Why?"

"Why'd I leave the game?"

"Yeah." He was being difficult. "You walked. Why?"

Boone shook his head, rubbing a hand over his tired face. "Because I remembered why I came to this party. It wasn't for poker."

She knew. Her throat grew thick. "Why'd you come?" she asked anyway.

"It really pisses me off that you're here. It pisses me off that my brother *still* thinks he can order me around. And it pisses me off that I couldn't *not* come tonight." He pushed forward, resting his elbows on his knees. He gazed down at the floor. "I'm sorry. I don't know how to start this. I was so angry when I found out that you lived here." Boone took in a ragged breath. "I came here to get over you, but I can't do that because I'm so fucking angry at you."

Dani expelled a similar sounding ragged breath. "I'm sorry I left you the way I did. I shouldn't have done that. There shouldn't have been a note. I should've been honest when you proposed, and I should've ended things that night. I snuck out. I'm *truly* sorry that I did that."

He regarded her with stricken eyes. Pure agony flared over him but he turned away again. "I still love you. And that's the kicker. I will probably love you for a *long*, long time." His jaw clenched. "I didn't know what to do after you left, so I went home. Drew's been trying to get me back into the business. I used to be the head hunter for them. It's somewhat ironic that they pulled in Bannon's father considering," he glanced to the door, "everything."

"You were a head hunter?"

She had a type. Apparently.

"If my family has a problem sealing a deal, they used to call me in. I assess what the problem is, and I deal with it." The side of his mouth lifted in a twisted half-smile. "Everything was fine until I dug too deep on a job. I fell for 'the problem's' daughter. I was done after that. Drew kicked me out, said I needed to go on a sabbatical and clear my head. I was supposed to figure out what made me tick, then come back better than ever."

Jenny mentioned a girl. "Did you love her? The daughter?"

"No." His eyes held on to mine, for far too long. "I fell in love with you. She just opened my eyes to what else was going on. I looked around, took surveillance, and realized I didn't like what side I was on."

Dani had no response to that. She looked down to the ground.

The door opened. Conversation, yelling, and music filled the room suddenly. Bubba walked onto the porch, then stopped. "Oh." He blinked in surprise. "Sorry."

"Did you come for more of these?" Dani grabbed some soda and chips. She held them out for him.

"Thanks." He took them, then smirked. "Fancy Nancy."

Dani rolled her eyes, but waited until Bubba shut the door behind him. "I'm sorry for what I did."

"You ripped my heart out."

"Boone." She looked down at the table, pulling her hands to her lap. She hunched over.

"You looked like you were drowning after the storm, and I thought I was giving you a future. I didn't know that I was handing you a nightmare instead."

"It wasn't—it wasn't like that."

"You made me happy, Dani. Do you want me to let you off the hook and say that I only loved the idea of you and not you? Do you want me to cheapen what I thought we had?"

"I wasn't right." Her voice was hoarse. The memories were flooding in.

"I knew you weren't right!" Boone scooted to the edge of his couch. "I'm not stupid. I saw things, like when you'd get up the middle of the night and just look out the window for hours. I saw all of that. I knew you had your own demons, but I figured you'd let me in after a while." His voice quieted. "I wanted to make you happy, too."

"I...I..." The waves—she could hear them crashing down again. The crying. Screaming. Her throat swelled even farther. Tears threatened to spill, and she hated it. She hated crying. She hated that just like that a mere conversation could bring it back.

No.

No.

Her vision grew restricted. She couldn't see anything. It was all blurry. Ducking her head down, she inhaled. In, hold, five, four, three, two, one. Out, five, four, three, two, one. In and repeat. In. Hold. Out. Hold. She kept going until the crushing sensation on her chest lifted.

She could see Boone again, and he was waiting.

He asked, "Are you okay?"

She nodded.

"I didn't know you still had the attacks."

"They've gotten better." Since Jonah. She cleared her throat. "You wanted from me what I couldn't give. And you might've thought you were okay with it, that there was no pressure—you'll love me enough for us both, but it never ends like that. I knew that. I was locked down. We barely talked the last six months. Did you know that?"

"I know."

"I kept thinking the reason I felt so awful was from how it ended. I took the coward's way out, but maybe something was wrong with us, and it wasn't just me. I had no idea about that girl, or your family."

"We never talked about our pasts."

"That's what I'm saying. Both of us didn't say anything. I thought that was the agreement, but I was still running away, even after ten years. I shouldn't have been in a serious relationship, and part of me didn't realize how serious we even were. I didn't think we were marriage serious."

"I thought that's what you wanted."

"No." She never gave him any indication of that. She was just trying to survive each day.

"Was it just sex? Was I just convenient?"

"It's not like that. I'm lying there, in a hospital bed, trying to wrap my mind around what I'd just gone through, and you come in with this shiny engagement ring. What was I supposed to do?"

"Tell me that it was too much."

"You were supposed to know I was hurting. You were supposed to know how to comfort me, but you didn't. The other person is supposed to know."

"I'm not a mind reader, Dani."

"Because you should've known about my past. I should've known about yours if a ring and a future come into the conversation. I've been wracked with guilt because I ran, but you were running, too."

"It takes one to ruin a relationship."

"We were two half-people trying to fit together." Dani hugged herself to ward off the chill. "You weren't whole, and I wasn't whole." All the fight left her. Her shoulders slumped down. She said so quietly, "And that was the problem."

Boone gestured toward inside. "So, those two guys in there, would they know? Your ex of how many years? All your childhood. Would he have known? Or Bannon?"

He didn't want to hear the truth. Jonah would've known. Jonah *did* know, even without dating her. Jake would've known, too. But Boone hadn't, and it was because he was hurting like her. Half of him was gone, but that half wasn't missing because of her. She thought it was all her. He was hurting because of what she did, but that wasn't true either. It was him. It was his family. It was what they were doing. That, and probably other reasons she didn't know.

"You were trying to cover up your emptiness with me." She didn't have enough to fill his void. "You needed someone who is brimming with life. Someone not hurting, not trying to deal with their own haunts. That wasn't me." She looked back at the rain. It was so dark outside. "We weren't supposed to be together."

"I'm here for a reason. You're here for a reason. I don't think that's a coincidence." His voice rose. His eyes were brimming with hope. "I love you now, and I loved you back then. Maybe I wanted the future, and I was too selfish to really look at you, I don't know. Maybe what you say is true, but it's you. I don't think it's ever going to be *not* you."

Her eyes closed.

"I love you, and I want another chance."

She exhaled.

Dani stood. "You're not that guy for me."

He held a hand out to her, stopping her. "Okay. I'm not asking for anything. I'm just telling. I'm telling you that I love you." His eyes warmed, becoming tender. "You're always going to be that for me."

This man saw her at her worst. He had been there for her, but it was too late. She was too damaged then, and now—"I'm with Jonah."

"Dani."

He reached for her, but she evaded him. "No. I'm telling you. No."

He wasn't listening to her. She saw the earnest look in his eyes, and her heart sank. She knew what she had to say, but no one wants to hurt another person they cared about. She had, too.

"You are not my future."

Boone left the room, but Dani stayed back. She needed silence. She needed the emptiness to just breathe. Saying those words to someone she cared about, knowing she hurt him took everything out of her. She needed twenty minutes, then she would stand up, then she would keep going.

But until then—twenty minutes.

She got eighteen of them.

"Okay." Aiden burst through the doors, waving her hands. "We've got a problem. A very, very, big problem and I don't know what to do about it."

"What are you talking about?"

"Jonah is at the winner's table right now, and it's him with Jake and Jeffries, and there are flash flood warnings going on right now, but—"

"Are you at a lower elevation? Is water pooling up outside?"

Aiden's terror was evident as she nodded. Her face drained of any color. Her eyes were wide and her bottom lip trembled.

Flash floods happen fast. This wasn't a tsunami, but Dani knew they had to act fast. She shoved her panic aside, all the ghosts and hauntings that were at her backside—she ignored every single one of them. Resting a hand on Aiden's arm, she said in a firm, but gentle tone, "People are drunk, so that means we have to get them out. I'll talk to Bubba. He'll have to go to a neighbor's, see if they have any boats. You gather as many blankets as you can. And flashlights."

"Okay." Her entire body was shaking.

"Aiden."

She had rushed to the door, but stopped and looked back. Dani said, "We'll get through this."

Aiden jerked her head up in a nod. "I hope so."

She left. Dani exhaled and looked over her shoulder to the blanket of rain that pounded the house. She remembered the wind. It was the first thing that slammed against their building. The wind howled, and Dani remembered the anchor that fell in her stomach.

It was back again, but *she* wasn't back.

Different time. Different place. No ocean. No tsunami. No children going to die. And Dani wasn't going to be alone this time. This wasn't that storm. She wouldn't let it happen, not again, but she still felt that same knot start to clench inside of her. It wasn't going to go away until she saw the sun, the clear sky, and everyone was still breathing around her.

The party sounded louder against her eardrums, harsher. The people seemed more drunk, and the giddy laughs were surreal to Dani as she shoved through the crowd, finally stumbling to the stairs.

She heard cursing and recognized who it was. She flung the bathroom door open, and it was. "Bubba!"

He turned, a plunger in his hands. "Uh, yeah?" He wiped his chin against his shoulder. Some sweat clung there. "Can this wait? I'm in the middle of a flooded toilet here."

"What's the elevation for this place?"

"Huh?"

"If there were warnings of flash floods—what's the chance of this house getting flooded?"

He put the plunger away. "Aiden wasn't freaking out about a toilet before, was she?" Then it was like her words registered with him, and he paled. "Oh, my God."

"Bubba—"

"We're not on elevated land at all. Robbie's is probably the best place to go, but that's a ten-minute drive. Is there already flooding out there?"

Hurrying past her, he pushed through the crowd to the back door. He opened the door, and they had their answer. The front lawn was already filled, and water rushed inside. "Fuck!" And then, for a muscular bodybuilder who was man enough to be called Chimp Two, he froze.

Dani didn't. She rushed to close the door.

"Okay." Dani shoved him back, away from the door, and said firmly, "We need boats, and we need shiners. Aiden's gathering blankets and flashlights for everyone, but we need the kind that you'd use to shine deer or portable headlights."

"We don't have any." His eyes were still rooted to the door.

"Neighbors. Who would have them?"

"Eddie would have some. He's a big hunter."

"Good. Do you have waders at all?"

"Uh, yeah."

"Put them on, and go find Eddie. Grab a pair for him. Get all the lights and boats you can."

"Okay." Bubba jerked to reality and surged past her.

Dani hauled him back. "Make sure to come back."

Bubba nodded. "I will."

Kate was heading their way, her arms filled with blankets. "Okay. This is weird. Can you hold these? Aiden dumped them on me and said to bring them to you, but my phone is buzzing like crazy. I need to answer it. What is going on?"

There was no time to mince words. "We're going to flood. No one knows, and I have to get Jonah away from that table without alarming people."

"What?" But then Kate transformed in front of her. Her buzzed/probably drunk friend suddenly became a police officer. The glaze was gone from her eyes, and she nodded, alert. "What do you need from me?"

"Aiden's getting blankets and flashlights for everyone. I sent Bubba to the neighbor's for a boat. It's going to be too late for people to drive their cars home."

"Okay." Kate pulled her phone out. "I'll call our location in. You go and get Jonah." She eyed the water that was leaking in under the door. "People will have to start going upstairs soon."

"I know, but only a few at a time. We don't want a stampede." A round of clapping broke out from the basement. They were wasting time. She had to tell him. "I'm going to get Jonah."

Kate was already talking on the phone, heading to the garage.

They broke for another pot when the third guy left the table. Jonah stood up, and a group of people swarmed him, but Dani slipped through. She caught his hand, and tugged him with her. Once upstairs, Jonah's hands found her waist. "What's going on?"

She pulled him into the first private corner they came across. "There's flash floods, and the water is already coming into this house. I've sent Bubba to get boats and headlights from his neighbor. Aiden is getting blankets and regular flashlights, and Kate went to call the station." She paused, sucking some air into her lungs. "We can't stay in this house. We can start moving people upstairs, but not everyone will fit. What do we do?"

Jonah didn't say anything. He only stared at her.

She took a breath.

And waited.

Then she opened her mouth, but his mouth was on top of hers. His hands cupped both sides of her face, and he half pulled her to him as she stretched to meet him. One moment. That was all they needed. She felt him, reminding herself that he was there. He was solid, and the water coming for them couldn't take him away.

Then he pulled away, rested his forehead to hers, and gazed down into her eyes. "I think I fucking love you."

"I—"

But he stood back, and just like that, the transformation happened right in front of her. He wasn't her Jonah. An authoritative air came over him, and he was now a professional. "Aiden's got a few canoes. We could use them. They'll rock over with the first blast of wind that comes flying, but we're in the middle of summer. The water won't be hypothermia cold, not at first. It will be safe for them in case a canoe tips. They can hold on to it. It'll keep them adrift, if it gets bad." He took her hand and led her through the crowd, heading to the garage. "They built in the worst possible spot. All the water's going to slide down and pool by this house. We're right in the middle of any current that picks up."

Kate was at the edge of the garage, watching the water. Her phone was still in her hand. Jonah ignored her, grabbing a ladder and leaning it close to the canoes.

"Jake's coming out, too."

Jonah nodded to Kate, climbing up the ladder. He began to pull a canoe down from the rafters. "Dani. Kate. Can you grab this?"

Dani deftly caught the nose end of the canoe, and Kate helped her lower it to the ground. They did this with the remaining three canoes. Jonah grinned after the last was pulled down. "Thank God Bubba used to want to be a canoer, huh?"

Kate grunted at the same time Jake joined them. Kate filled him in, and Dani was watching Jonah. He was enjoying this. She caught a small thrill in his eye. He was searching for life jackets. Jake and Kate both joined, looking for anything that could be used as a flotation device, but Dani was rooted in place.

Jonah came over to her, lowering his voice. "What?"

"You're enjoying yourself."

Some of the excitement left him. His grin slipped a tiny bit as he tucked a strand of her hair behind her ear. "Everything will be fine, Dani."

He didn't know. He couldn't say that. "People got stranded last time. They died." It could happen again. He had no idea. "They panicked and stampeded other people. Some of them weren't even given the chance to drown."

The entire grin vanished. He bent closer to her. "That's not going to happen here. We're already way ahead of schedule with security provisions. Part of that is because of you." Then his phone rang, and he answered it, "Trenton!"

Dani heard him talking about shallow boat runners, but the conversation turned technical, so she looked around for what else they'd need. "Bags," Dani stated. "Lots and lots of bags."

Jonah hung up. "What?"

"There's not enough life jackets, but we can triple-bag them—you know—the grocery bags that everyone keeps, but never throws out. We can blow air in them and just put three over each other so they won't break that easily. People can put them inside their clothes. It'll be sort of a life jacket." She spotted a pile of bungee cords. "People can hook these into their clothes and wrap the other end across the canoe to someone else. They'll hold each other up on the canoe if they get too fatigued."

Jonah didn't say anything for a moment. He caught her hand. "Dani—no one's going to die here."

"Not this storm." Her stomach felt like ice had lined the bottom. "Everyone's going to have to be told what to do if their clothes weigh them down—"

"Okay, before you turn into Indiana Jones, Trent's on his way with a flat runner. He and Hawk have a bunch that they're pulling over here. We'll be fine."

"What if they don't get here in time? What if they see other people they need to save and they don't get here? What then? We have to plan. We have to—"

Jonah caught her shoulders. He put his forehead to hers. "You're *not* going to die."

Dani stopped and took a breath. She whispered, "That's not what I'm scared of." She could see the children. They were standing in that garage, watching her, and it was happening all over again. They were depending on her. She was going to fail them.

"What are you scared of?" Jonah kissed her forehead, wrapping his arms tight around her. "Tell me what you're scared about."

Dani's arms hung limp at her side. "People die around me." The ice was spreading from her stomach. It was invading the rest of her, numbing her. "I didn't do anything last time." She gulped for air. She was drowning. "I didn't do anything last time, and they died. This time—"

"—you're doing something."

Dani took her last breath and let loose her demons. "I'm suffocating."

He pulled back and searched her face. His eyes raked her features. "I know."

She couldn't say it. She couldn't explain it.

"I know," Jonah said again. He wrapped his arms around her and said again, "I already know."

Dani's arms slowly reached up and wrapped around him. She held onto him, as tight as she could.

"And you stayed," Jonah added. "With those kids—you stayed with them and you did something. You held onto them. Death is sometimes inevitable. Even if it's for someone who shouldn't die. I know this river and I know that. And I know you. You stayed."

Dani never thought the vision of Hawk, driving a flat runner with three more chained behind him, would bring tears of relief to her eyes.

They did.

He winked at her as he climbed off the flat runner. He anchored the first flat runner inside as Jonah darted across all of them to confer with Trent, who drove the other pair.

"How's it going, Hawk?"

"It's wet." Hawk grunted and turned to grab the pile of blankets that Aiden gathered inside the house's door.

He handed them to Dani, who handed them to Jonah when he returned to the first boat.

"We can hand them out when everyone comes out."

"That's a good idea." But Jonah took one and said, "Before we bring everyone out, we're going to find Bubba." He took one blanket, then disappeared again as Dani heard one of the back flat runners zoom off.

Kate and Jake came over.

"Do you have all the flashlights handy?" Dani asked.

Kate nodded.

Hawk said, "We're going to need five more drivers. Two drivers per boat, one for backup. Just in case. You know anyone who's driven these things before?"

"We can't keep them all together?" Kate asked.

"They'll tip with all that weight. It's just safer if they separate."

Dani offered, "Boone. He knows how to drive a jet ski, and I think he told me once his father owns a place down south, by a swamp."

"That'd work. Who else?"

"I can drive one," Dani said. "I've got experience with this stuff." She flattened her hand to her side, to stop the shaking.

"Huh?" Kate asked, dumbfounded.

"She does," Boone spoke from behind her. He gazed outside. "So this is what's going on."

Kate held up a hand. "Getting back to Dani knowing how to drive one of these things. What'd you mean by that?"

Boone gestured to Dani. "She's had to before, and if anyone knows water, it's—"

Dani cut in, "Jonah, because he's the Water Whisperer."

"Great." Hawk nodded. "Back-ups?"

"Jake can do it." Dani looked to him. "He's driven these things since we were little."

He nodded, stepping forward. "I can do it."

The sound of an engine was coming back, getting closer and closer. Not far from them, the engine was cut, and a moment later, Jonah darted back over to the other three boats.

"Okay." He quickly skimmed over the group. "We're good to go. Flashlights, blankets?"

"Check and check." Jake nodded, slapping a hand to the pile. "We'll hand them out. We don't have enough blankets and flashlights for everyone, but we're hoping that people can sit together and share. Every third person will get a blanket."

"Thank God my sister's a slight pack rat." Jonah grinned and stood beside Dani. He turned to Hawk. "Drivers?"

Dani answered, "Me. Jake. And Boone. We all have experience."

Jonah studied her and briefly studied Boone, but he didn't comment.

Hawk said, "We need two more."

Jonah jerked his head toward the last boat. "Bubba and Eddie. We just picked 'em both up, but both have used these boats before."

"We're good then. We can go."

Jake held up a hand. "Someone needs to tell everyone inside what's going on."

Everyone looked at Jonah. Kate said to him, "You go. They'll listen to you."

"Okay." Jonah nodded to Hawk, and three sets of keys were dished out.

Kate took a blanket and climbed to one of the back boats. Jake disappeared inside, as well as Boone. Dani thought Jonah would follow behind, but he stepped close to her first. "You okay with this?"

She nodded. "I'll be fine. Sure, I was freaking out a few minutes ago, but I've got this. I feel safer with an engine."

He was weighing her words. "You sure?"

"I am."

"Okay." He pressed a kiss to her forehead. His hand touched hers. "Don't get on the boat yet. Wait till I come back out."

"Okay."

He headed inside, and Jake and Boone came out a beat later. Jenny and Julia were in tow, both looking like they were crying.

All the boats were unhooked from each other, and the ones who had drivers pulled out. They waited as one boat was filled, then they would switch places. People began to come out, and though they looked fearful, some were crying. For the most part, everyone wasn't downright panicking like she had. They were able to grab a blanket and climb onto their boats, but not a life jacket.

Bubba's boat came to the side, and he jumped out. Aiden gasped, but caught Dani's eyes. Dani tried to nod at her, letting her know everything would be fine. Aiden swallowed and returned the nod. She pulled her blanket closer around her, and Bubba began to hand out the remaining life jackets. The boats came in close enough so he could wade over to them.

And then they were down to two boats.

Jonah came to stand next to her. "You ready?" His hand touched her hip.

She nodded. "I am."

"Okay." He pressed another kiss to her forehead. "I want you with me. You'll be my backup driver."

The one boat filled up, and Hawk pushed off with Jake as his back-up driver. Then it was only their boat. Dani took a breath, a blanket, and stepped onto the wobbly flat runner.

Trenton sidled up next to them, helping to hold their boat steady. "Hi, Dani!" He was too damned cheerful. "I'd offer a hand, but I'm a little busy."

"Thanks," she said dryly.

"So, how does it feel, Dani?"

"Rather be in bed right now."

Trenton laughed and commented, "Yeah. I'm sure Jonah'd like that, too. I don't think the Quandrys are going to want to still build here anymore. Not when they need to get flood insurance."

This was close to his usual day at the job. She got that, but she asked, "Trent?"

"Yeah?"

"Can you shut up?"

"Sure." He laughed anyway. "Don't take too much to natural disasters?"

"You'd be surprised."

Once they were full, with Jonah in the driver's seat, Trenton turned around to the next boat. He waved, calling out, "Alright. Here we go. Mr. Guy Back There—you're in charge of the back of the boat. Watch the engine for me. Let me know if anything's wrong. Make sure no one falls out, too. Jonah'll take the lead, then Hawk. We've got the rear."

Dani called out, "His name is Boone."

"What?" Boone looked over.

Dani ignored and said to Trent, "You can call him Boone, Trent."

"Will do. And everyone here, I'll let you know the plan how we're going to get you to dry land. We'll be driving at a comfortable speed. We're in no rush. Safety is the only concern here. We'll move at a nice and steady pace. We'll keep each other in our headlights, so there shouldn't be any surprises along the way."

Dani took a moment to gaze around. She hadn't paid attention to when people were getting into the boats, but it was surreal now seeing everyone around them. Boone was closest. Jenny was huddled next to him. Jake and Julia were in Hawk's boat. Aiden and Kate were in Bubba's.

Jonah hopped into the boat now. He took his seat and nodded to Trent. "We're good." He had to shout over the engine's light purr. "House is closed up, and I didn't see anyone left inside."

"Just a day in the office, right, boss?"

Jonah grinned. "A day in the office." His eyes met Dani's, and he added, "For some of us."

Aiden and Bubba were too far out, but Aiden waved. "Love you, brother."

"Love you, too, sis. Everyone will be fine." He stood, his hand on the wheel, and did another quick surveillance of the boats. A moment later, he nodded in approval and waved. "Alright, let's head out."

Then he took the lead. The rest fell in line. The ride to higher ground was slow, but surprisingly uneventful. Jonah veered where he was supposed to veer and everyone fell in line. Each boat followed with six feet behind the other. It was easier to do since the engines were just underneath the surface. There was no wake of waves to follow.

Dani wasn't surprised when they managed to join up with the river. Jonah followed it back to their base headquarters. It stood on stilts, just in case the river rose to dangerous levels, but it was high enough up to outlast any flash floods.

Anyone who was still drunk was sober by the time they reached their destination.

Each boat was clamped into place, and everyone scrambled off the unsteady surface for sure footing. As everyone filed in, they were met with dry blankets.

Dani tapped on Jonah's arm. "Mae?"

His hand grasped hers. "I called when I was looking through the house. She's safe."

"Oh." A wave of relief washed over her. "Thank you."

"I should've told you right away. Sorry. Hey." She began to move in, but he tugged her closer to him. "Everyone's going to be sleeping in the atrium, but we can sleep in my office. It'll be a little more comfortable."

"And not offer such fine luxuries to everyone else?"

"We're going to be sharing with my sister, her husband, and probably Kate." He skimmed over the group. "I think Robbie is inside, too. That should be interesting."

"Does Trenton have an office?"

"Yeah. Why?"

"I'd like Boone to stay there, and Jake and Julia." At his questioning glance, she shrugged. "Family stands for something."

"I'll talk to Trent, but I'm sure Hawk already called dibs on whichever place is the most private. He's got his eye on someone here."

"Why am I not surprised?"

He squeezed her hand once more, but a man approached, saying, "Jonah." And he was off, becoming the leader he already was. That wave of relief was replaced with pride. It was a group effort to get everything together and going, but once the boat showed up, everything could've fallen apart. It hadn't, and that was because of Jonah. Everyone trusted him. They listened to him, and when he said it would be alright, they believed him. Dani knew people were scared, but no one panicked. That was so vital in situations like this.

That was Jonah, all Jonah.

She smiled, her body warming as she watched him talking to a bunch of official-looking people, then she headed inside. Aiden stood with Bubba and Robbie in one corner.

Aiden greeted her, pulling her in for a hug. "Here's Chimp One to Flamingo Two."

Dani hugged her back. "Where's Kate?"

"Doing police-type work. She and Jake both took off right away."

Robbie said, "She was supposed to look for coffee while she was at it. I hope she brings some back for us."

"Maybe us, but probably not you."

Robbie didn't ask for any explanation. He didn't need one. "I broke up with Lori tonight. That's why I wasn't at the party."

Aiden tilted her head to the side. "You should've done it before tonight."

Bubba promptly hit him on the back of his head.

"Hey!" Robbie rubbed behind his head.

"There's a reason why you were named Baboon," Aiden pointed out.

"For my hot ass?"

"For *being* an ass."

Dani caught sight of Jake with Julia and took a deep breath. "I'll be right back."

"May the force be with you," Aiden remarked.

"No doubt," Dani murmured underneath her breath, but she put on a brave face as they turned and watched her approach. She asked Jake, "Did you win?"

"There wasn't a winner. We were waiting for Jonah to come back, and," he gazed around, "you know how that went."

Julia asked, "What do you want?"

Dani ignored the cutting tone from her sister. "You guys can sleep in Trenton's office with whoever else he puts in there. I asked if Boone and Jenny could be in there, too."

Julia looked ready with a sharp retort, but at Dani's words, her eyes rounded. She swallowed, and then only murmured, "Oh." Spying Jenny in the corner, she moved away from Jake. "I'm going to let them know."

There was no thanks, nothing, as she left them. Dani knew not to expect any. She didn't even feel any was warranted. It wasn't her office.

"So," Jake breathed out, "your ex-fiancé walked away from our game before."

"I know."

"I'm trying not to wonder what that was about." Jake chuckled. "But, it's not working."

"It had nothing to do with you."

"I'm aware of that."

Dani stiffened. "What do you want?"

"That's just like you. You immediately go on the defensive."

"Jake."

"No, forget it. I was trying. Friends, right?"

Any guard she had up, thinking he was going in for another attack, lowered. Only halfway, though. She saw he meant what he said, and she rolled her eyes. "I hate you sometimes."

"I know." He lifted his arms in the air and motioned between them. "Can we hug it out?"

"What's Julia going to say?"

"Eh, she can moan or cry, but she knows I love her. She can't get rid of me." He pulled her in for a hug. "I gotta say, you looked good with that flamingo on your head tonight. You should wear it more often. Visit Kathryn with it. Give it to her as a gift."

Dani touched the top of her head. She forgot about Fancy Nancy, but it wasn't there. She frowned. She already missed it. "I wouldn't force a Kathryn visit on any inanimate object."

"Only inanimate objects?" Jake joked. "The animate objects are just fine?"

"Well, yeah. They're animated. They can withstand the Kathryn Glower."

"Because they're animated?"

"They're jaunty and they dance and they stand still enough to feel the full power of Kathryn's Glower." And it felt weird to be laughing with Jake again.

"Jaunty?"

"Jaunty."

Jake looked thoughtful. "You know what else is jaunty?"

"What?" This was her old best friend. She didn't remember the moment when they moved from best friend to more than that, but this was him again. She missed him. She missed this.

"The Chapel of Love." He nudged her arm with his. "Right? Am I right?"

Dani laughed loudly, she couldn't contain it. "I've forgotten. You broke the radio when that song came on. Remember? That stupid thing went off, and you got so mad, you threw a rock at it."

"Well, yeah, because we were in the middle of being—" Intimate. Jake shut up. "Oh."

Dani coughed. "Uh, Aiden's probably looking for me."

"Yeah." Jake nodded.

Dani turned and left, but Jake caught her arm. "Maybe not now, but some day I'd like to be friends again. I mean that."

"Me, too." She went to look for Aiden, but she meant it. She hoped one day she and Jake could be friends again. Not best friends. That was too far again, but maybe family instead?

She joined Aiden and Bubba. Kate was there, too, glaring at Robbie, whose head was hanging down. Jonah came up at the same time. Everyone straightened to attention. He touched the small of Dani's back, saying, "Everything's ready. You guys can bunker down in my office. There should be cots in there, too."

"What about you?" Aiden asked her brother.

He met Dani's eyes. "Save me a place, but I'm going to be up for a while."

The rest nodded and filtered off.

Dani touched his chest. "Is everything okay?"

Bags had formed under his eyes, and he raked a hand through his hair. "To be honest, there's no good way for me to answer that so, get a good's night sleep. For me." He dropped a kiss on her lips, and before he would've moved away, she caught his face. She held him there, just a moment longer. She pressed against him, wanting him to know she cared. She was there for him. He hesitated, just a moment, then he answered back. His lips became hard over her, almost claiming and draining her at the same time. He pulled back, breathing a little heavy, and rested his forehead to hers. "I'm going to slip away tonight, but it's not looking good."

"You don't want to tell me what's wrong?"

He hesitated. "I do. I just can't." He brushed a kiss over her cheek, stepping back. "I mean it. Get a good night's sleep, if you can. Don't worry about me."

But she would. He knew that, too. She watched him go. Trenton met him halfway, and their heads bent together. Hawk joined their group, and a deep frown formed over Jonah's face. Something was going on. Something she was going to have to make Jonah tell her, but later. He wasn't ready to break protocol yet.

Instead of heading to Jonah's office, Dani grabbed a blanket. She went to a bathroom and tried to dry off as much as possible, then she wandered the back halls of Jonah's headquarters. She wasn't moving to a specific target, but she found herself at the freshwater tank. The tank ran the entire wall of the room. It circled around how the river wound along their town and their lands. It was an exact replica of Falls River. And Dani saw the black mussels she helped finance. There were a few real ones sitting in the water. One opened.

A grey pearl was nestled in the sand dirt.

"So this is what your boyfriend does." Julia cleared her throat from the doorway, and Dani's momentary amazement vanished. She looked around, her gaze falling on the tank and then zeroing in where Dani had been looking. Julia chewed at her lip. "Those are mussels?"

"Yeah."

"They're ugly."

"Of course, you'd judge them on their appearance."

"I'm just saying they're ugly. They are."

Dani was tired. Dealing with her sister was the last thing she wanted. She pulled her blanket tighter around her. "What do you want, Julia?"

Julia ran a hand through her soaked hair. She had a blanket draped around her, too, but her hand fell away from holding it closed over her. She propped it on her hip and made sure to drill Dani with her eyes. "Stay away from Jake. I saw you guys hugging before. You have a boyfriend. Leave mine alone."

"You've already tried this trick. It didn't take. Also, get the facts straight. Your boyfriend hugged me. He was trying to put everything behind us."

"Just stay away. I saw the awkwardness." Her eyes flashed in anger. "You want facts? Here are the facts. Jake loves me. He is with me. All true, but he still holds a torch for you. And before you get a big head, it's not really *you* you. It's his past transgressions. He feels a whole ton of guilt about leaving you for Erica, and that was why you left. It's that issue that he can't get over, but since he can't deal with that, he's trying to reconnect with you. It won't work. He's just going to end up trying to hook up with you, and even if you don't, he'll hate himself all over again. I know he loves me, but he feels guilt about you and Erica, too. That's why I want you to stay away from him. For his good, your good, and my good."

Dani was so tired of it. All of it. "Just stop. You're being dramatic." She felt like years were just taken from her. Maybe it was the night, or the last month, or maybe it was everything. "Go away, Julia. Go away."

"You're such a—never mind." Julia moved toward the door, but stopped short and whirled back. "You could have called. Just once. You could've told us you were alive, but you didn't. That was your choice. And that shows me how much you cared. So, why should I be all 'welcome home, sister-who-doesn't-give-a-shit-about-me'?"

"Kathryn knew I was going."

"Yeah, well." Julia crossed her arms over her chest. "Kathryn can be a manipulative bitch at times."

Dani's head reared back an inch.

"What? Like that's news? We both know what she's like."

"Yeah, but." Wow. Just wow. She never thought Julia would admit that.

Julia turned back, but stopped again. "You get on your high horse about how you've been the one left out. Like we did it on purpose, but it wasn't us, Dani. *You* pulled away. *You* pulled away from everyone, even Mae. No one connected to you—"

"I never felt a part of the family."

"Because you put yourself there. We'd be downstairs, and you would go up to your room. You never stayed and spent time with us. What were we supposed to do? You know," disdain dripped from her voice, "it's pretty pitiful that I've gotten to know you through my fiancé." She wiped at a tear. "And I think it's pathetic that you haven't visited your own aunt in the nursing home."

"She wouldn't see me if I did go there," Dani countered. "And you know that. Why would I volunteer for that humiliation?"

Julia waved that off. "How do you know Kathryn would turn you away?"

"Because she's a manipulative bitch!"

"She's dying. She's already lost a niece. I'd like her to feel as if she's been given one back before she goes." Julia let the tears slide down. "She—I thought I was going to be the last one."

"What?"

"I thought—" Julia gulped back the tears, but whispered, "I thought I was the last one. Erica died. We were sure you were, too. I knew Kathryn was dying, and Mae doesn't care about me. I thought I was going to be alone." She sniffled, using the blanket to wipe her tears away. "I still think that at times, so forgive me for being angry when you came back. You expected the welcome wagon, but I'm sorry. You don't deserve it—"

"Julia."

"—shut up." She turned away. "Just, shut up."

"What do you want from me?" Dani cried out.

"I can't touch what you had with him! Okay?" Julia yelled, her hands raised next to her head. "I can't touch what you had with him, and I can't touch what he had with Erica. I can't be either of you two."

Dani quieted. "What are you talking about?"

"It was supposed to have been Erica." A sniffle. "It was supposed to have been Erica who had his children. He loved her, not me. He loved you, Erica, but he never loved me."

"Julia, you can't be Erica. You and Jake are you and Jake. It's not Jake and Erica. It's not even Jake and me. You're you. You're different. Jake's with you because of you. He asked you to share the rest of your lives together. He loves you."

She shook her head, whispering, "Not like he loved you. Not like he loved her." Her hand formed a fist. She pressed it against her chest. "I can't be either of you two. I just can't do it."

"Julia." That's what she'd been thinking? All this time? "You're going to be his wife. You're going to have his children. What I had with him was in our past. We were children. You'll *have* children with him. Don't you get that?"

Tears fell from Julia, and so did a wall to Dani. She could see her sister in a new way, where she saw the hurts and pains. She saw her vulnerability, too. Dani pulled her sister into her arms. "He loves you, Julia. I know he does."

"He loves you."

"He and I were together our entire childhood and through high school. Julia. A person doesn't stop loving someone when the break-up happens. It takes a long time and I'd hope that Jake would always love me." She grasped Julia's face, a hand to both sides, and said fiercely, "But he's not *in* love with me. He's *in* love with you."

"He loved Erica." Julia broke down again. "I can't be Erica for him and sometimes I think he wants me to be her. I don't laugh like she does or make the same jokes. I don't even cook like her. I'm a good cook. Erica was awful, and I feel like Jake wants me to burn the lasagna. I don't want to burn the lasagna."

Dani couldn't contain a laugh. Erica had burned, destroyed, or exploded anything she baked and cooked. Julia had been awarded championships for baked goods eight years in a row. She probably still did.

"You shouldn't have to burn your lasagna. You have *really* good lasagna."

"I do." Julia's hands curled into fists with Dani's shirt. "I felt like I needed to go to confession when I burned the toast."

"Consider it done."

Julia broke again. A fresh cascade of tears. "And they had this ritual where Erica would start telling a story and Jake would finish it for her. They spoke their own language, Dani. How can I do that? I have no idea what he's going to say sometimes. I tried to finish a sentence for him, and I swear, I felt like he hated me in that moment."

Dani cracked a smile, but soothed, patting Julia's hair.

"He still loves her."

"But he's in love with you. That's all you need." Dani felt a headache forming. "Look, you and Jake are going to be fine. I truly think that. And as for this—between you and me—it's our family's fault. It's not ours. We were raised to be like this, and that's wrong."

Julia pulled back, giving Dani a blank look.

"I know we're doing the comforting thing right now, but I've no doubt we'll go back to fighting in a second. It's engrained in us. I don't know how to not fight with you now, so you can mock me. You can hate me even, but we're still sisters." Dani looked away, watching the water. "I'll go visit Kathryn tomorrow. Even if she throws me out, I'll do it."

Julia sniffled, wiping at a stray tear. "That's all I wanted."

"Liar. You want me to apologize. You want me to stay away from Jake. You want me to go see Kathryn. You don't want me at the house—I can keep going, if you want?"

Julia rolled her eyes. "Now who's being the dramatic one?" She groaned. "I know that I love you, and I know that we're sisters, and family stands for something, right? But sometimes, I truly cannot stand you."

The conversation shifted. Dani couldn't explain how it did, or articulate how she knew it did, but she felt it in her gut. Julia wasn't talking about Kathryn, Mae, or Jake. She was talking about the one who used to burn her lasagna.

Dani pulled tight on her blanket, twisting the ends in her hands. "She would've still died if I stayed."

Julia closed her eyes and bent her head.

Dani added, "I don't think anything would've changed if I stayed. I wouldn't have helped because it's how our family is. Kathryn's dying, and Mae won't go near her sister."

"She's a coward."

"It's called stupidity, pride, and just too many ghosts and secrets between us. And we don't even know half of them." Dani spoke the truth, and felt her knot unwind—just slightly—from its hold deep inside of her. It hurt, but it hurt less.

"It would've helped," Julia spoke up. "If you had been here. It would've helped. You could've been at the funeral. That would've helped. I really wanted you there. Even if we hated each other, I wanted my sister beside me."

"For what it's worth, I wish I had known. I would've come back."

"Erica changed a lot." Julia smiled for the first time and laughed even. "I know that I do stupid things. I clean obsessively, and straighten every pencil in the house, but it's because I need my world to make sense. I've had so much ripped from me. I'm controlling and seeing you making Jake laugh, I can't control that. I can't control how much my fiancé still loves you, and I hate that. I hate you, but you're my sister." Her voice dropped. She was so quiet now. "But I don't hate you, and I hate that, too."

Fuck it.

"I knew Erica was dead because I saw her."

She closed her eyes tight. She couldn't believe she was saying this. She hadn't told anyone, but it was there. Erica was there. Dani felt her. The feel of her never went away.

"What?"

"I was in a storm." Her voice was so raw. "Before I came back, I almost died in a tsunami. There were moments I thought I was dead, and there were moments when I wished I had died." Those same breaths that ended. They were never hers, just those around her. "But one night, I thought I was going and then Erica was there."

Julia sucked in some air. Her hand lifted, but Dani didn't look. She saw the movement from the corner of her eye.

"She told me it wasn't my time. It had been hers, but I had to stay where I was." It hurt to speak. It hurt to breathe. "I thought it was a hallucination."

She heard Mae's words again. *You missed your sister's funeral...*

Dani said, "It wasn't. It was real."

"That's how you found out?"

She nodded. "Yeah."

She didn't know what to expect, but then Julia grabbed her hand. She whispered to her, "Then you were the last to see her. How'd she look?"

Dani looked down at their joined hands. Of all the reactions, that was the best one. She squeezed Julia's hand and rasped out, "She looked happy. She was glowing."

Julia snorted. "Figures. She probably looks even better up there." A beat. "What a bitch."

Dani barked out a laugh. Julia joined in a second later and after a moment, Dani sighed. "You were telling me that you hate me?"

Julia rolled her eyes. "Yes. Duh. Always." She was trying not to grin.

Dani murmured, "I love you, too."

Julia sighed too. "I *really* miss Erica." She came to Dani, resting her forehead on Dani's shoulder again.

Dani rested her forehead against the side of her sister's head. "I miss her, too. I miss Mom."

"Me, too." Julia brushed at her face, her blanket swiping against Dani. "Okay, enough of our dysfunctional family bonding." She pulled away, giving her sister one long look. There was no hatred. No loathing. Just sadness and a deep mourning that only Dani understood.

Julia sniffled. "I hate you."

Dani murmured as her sister left, "No, you don't."

"You don't hate her either." Jake stood in a different doorway from behind her.

She didn't ask if he heard it all. She could tell he did. "Are you happy with her?" She pulled her blanket tight around her again.

Jake considered the question for a moment. "Yes, I am. Do I still love you? Yes. I still love Erica, too. I'm not *in love* with either of you, but you know that. Julia needs me, and I need her in ways that I never needed Erica or you."

He stared in the direction Julia had gone, then leaned his shoulder against the doorframe. "Your Aunt Kathryn. She's going to be gone soon."

She looked down. "I know."

He straightened back up. "I don't know if you meant it, but go and see her. Do it for Julia."

"I'm going to."

She'd go to say good-bye. This time, she could.

41

The room was dark except for the light flooding in from under the door. A small makeshift bed was left open for her. Jonah wasn't there, but she curled underneath the blanket, and when she woke—he still wasn't beside her.

She found him in a back room, standing, watching the river through a window.

"What time is it?"

Jonah glanced to her, lifting his arm up. She moved underneath, resting her head against his chest. His chest vibrated as he said, "It's seven."

Dani felt wiped with two hours of sleep inside of her. Jonah got none. He held a steaming cup of coffee in his hand. "How are you?"

"Better." She relaxed against him. "I told Jake that I'd visit Kathryn. Is the nursing home okay?"

"They're safe. The nursing home is on high ground. They should withstand double what the water is outside."

"It's still high out there?"

"It'll go down later today. Most of the town is okay. Some of it's underwater, but the town's square and the north edge are fine. Did you want a boat ride in? I have errands to run anyway."

"Let me go to the bathroom. Got any toothpaste around here?"

"Yeah, there's a staff bathroom. I should've shown you last night. You didn't need to use the regular bathroom everyone else does. We've got toiletries and the like for nights when we stay up sometimes."

"Are there a lot of those nights?"

"You'd be surprised." Holding her hand, he led her down a small hallway, opening a door at the end. "Drownings and rescues—one of us always has to be here and on duty. We pack this place up, just in case." Flipping the lights on, there was a shower. A pile of towels was stacked up on a counter. Jonah knocked on a cupboard door. "You can rummage through here. We keep some extra clothes. You might find something your size."

He stepped back as she went inside. His hand trailed over the small of her back. "I'll be up front when you're done."

She was cleaning up, but then she stopped. She looked at herself.

Her hair had grown. It seemed a little lighter than her dark brown color. It had sun streaks in it now. It was past her shoulders, and she touched it, running her fingers through it. She lost weight before coming home. She gained a few pounds, enough so she wasn't gaunt anymore. She touched her cheek now. She looked almost healthy. There was a glow to her skin.

After the stress from last night, Dani would've assumed she would've looked battered and beat down. She didn't.

Her eyes were—she touched the corner of her eye. The emptiness was almost gone. The loneliness. The haunted look she had when she first looked at herself in Mae's cabin. She didn't look dead anymore.

Her eyes were dark, but there was a little light in them now.

Coming home did this to her. Her home.

Dani smiled, seeing how there was no downward curve at the ends, like it used to do. She would smile, but it would look sad at the same time. That was gone. She touched there, too. Her smile was actually a smile.

Her chest lifted.

She looked alive.

Hearing voices, she finished cleaning, then went off to find Jonah. He was waiting where he said he woud be, and he handed over a small phone. "I nabbed this from the back room. My line is programmed in under star 2. Trenton is star 3, and Hawk is star 4. They both volunteer with me, so this is what we use to communicate sometimes. Keep it hidden. I want to make sure you have it."

She frowned, but tucked it away. He held her hand, leading her back to the door. He said that like someone would try to take it from her, but she stopped thinking about it when she climbed aboard a smaller boat than what they rode in a few hours ago. Soon, Jonah was steering them toward the town's square.

It was another surreal moment. This was her home, and half of it was destroyed. That was what water did. It washed away memories and keepsakes, leaving stains and rot behind. This had happened to her, but now it happened to everyone else, too. This hadn't been across the world. It was right here, right where she was, where her family was.

A deep sadness filled her, but there was another emotion. She was content. She was with Jonah. She was on top of the water. She was surviving.

Dani caught sight of the road that led to Mae's Grill. "Jonah, what about Mae? Can I go see her?"

"She's not there. They were all taken to the town center. Most of the town should be there, and later, people will be allowed to return to their homes to grab keepsakes and stuff like that."

"What do you mean, *allowed*?"

Jonah fell silent and hunched down on his driver's seat. "There'll be an announcement made this afternoon."

"What aren't you telling me?" She gazed around. "The water's high, but a lot of people have houses that might not have even been touched by the flooding. Why wouldn't they go back to their homes? What's going on, Jonah?"

"I don't want to say anything, just in case. Not yet. I'm hoping I'm wrong."

"Jonah."

"I can't, Dani. I'll tell you when I know for sure."

"Give me a coded message. Then decode it."

Jonah chuckled briefly. "Just give me the day. I'll tell you tonight."

She read between the lines. "We're not in the clear, are we?"

"Not by a long shot."

She turned back to watch the rest of the town pass by. "Well, for what it's worth, I'm going to see my aunt. She'll probably not even talk to me, and that's *if* she doesn't kick me out. Your cryptic message is safe with me."

Jonah's jaw clenched, but he loosened his grip on the steering rod. "The dire and doomed visit to the dying Kathryn, huh?"

"Pretty much. You have no worry about me panicking. I'm more stressed about seeing her."

"Trenton said you and Julia got into it last night. You okay?"

"He could hear us? Great. I wonder who else did."

"He shut the fire doors so you were cut off from the atrium."

"Remind me that drinks are on me at Mae's Grill one night as a thank you."

He chuckled lightly, and Dani closed her eyes, letting the sound of his laugh warm her. When she opened them, they were passing one of the cafes in town. The tops of the red umbrellas that covered five or six tables outside the entrance were the only things they could see now. "Look at that." Dani gestured toward them.

"I'm surprised more of the tables aren't gone. Winds were dangerous last night. They picked up an hour after we got to headquarters. We were lucky we got there when we did."

Dani felt a shiver down her back.

Just then, they turned the corner. She noted, "The gas station is still the hookup for drinks."

Two boats of teenagers were drifting around the corner. A bottle flashed as it caught the sun between one hand to the next.

"Don't they have something better to do?" Jonah answered himself, "No, I would've been doing that when we were younger."

"You were the rebellious leader type back then."

"I just wanted to have fun, but, yeah." He grew quieter. "Some things pissed me off."

"Like when you beat up Trenton Galloway."

"He was going on and on about how he was going to 'score' with some chick on prom night, and then he was going to ditch the girl for his real date that night. Made me mad." Jonah fell silent. "He reminded me of my father—just ready to use and discard someone. I saw red that night, but Trent turned out to be a good guy."

"It was just for show."

"No." Jonah shook his head. "Some guys can do some pretty cruel stuff. You never know what consequences can happen from something reckless."

"I was always scared of Hawk." Dani thought a moment. "I still am scared of Hawk."

Jonah laughed, steering the boat behind the local laundromat. "Hawk's a good guy. One-track mind about sex and girls, but he's decent. He sees through a lot of bullshit."

"I'll take your word for it."

Dani glimpsed the nursing home ahead, then the flat runner drew abreast the ground. Jonah cut the engine, hopping out and pulling it the rest of the way on the embankment. He helped Dani get out, placing his hands on her waist and lifting her. She held on to his arms. "Looks like I'm walking the rest of the way."

"You'll be okay?" He nodded to the right. "The town's center is a block down. There shouldn't be any water around it—"

"I'll be fine. It's a block away." She stretched up and kissed him, whispering, "Good luck with your top-secret meeting."

"I'm not—" He stopped and admitted, "I am."

"I know." Dani backtracked up the hill, toward the hospital. "Still rather be doing what you're doing than what I'm about to do."

Jonah gave her a wave before pushing the boat back into the water. He lithely jumped back in, and after a second wave, floored the engine. He was gone from eyesight within seconds.

Dani smelled freshly brewed coffee when the doors slid open. She almost groaned. The receptionist looked up and smiled. Dani saw how tired she was.

"Are you here to see your aunt?"

"Yes." Dani readied herself. "And just so you know, she might have you throw me out. I won't hold it against you if that happens."

She grinned as she stood up, taking a walkie-talkie with her. "Let's hope it doesn't come to that." A pair of glass doors opened behind her. "I'll be right back."

It wasn't long before she came back. "Kathryn said you could go in, but she's not sure if she'll talk to you."

Classic Kathryn. "It's better than what I thought."

"My mom had my grandma barred from her room when she was in the hospital a while back. Every family's got their own ways. You'd be surprised at the families that come through the doors. Yours isn't that bad." She pushed a button, and the doors slid open. "I'm sure you'll have a lovely visit."

Dani wasn't, but then she was heading inside and down the hallway. Call lights were beeping in the background, along with other alarms.

She stopped in her aunt's doorway.

Kathryn lay with her hands propped over the folded-back sheet, dead center over her body. Her rich chestnut curls were brushed, with the curl lying over her shoulders. Kathryn was dressed in a pink silk nightie.

"Hello, Aunt Kathryn."

The eyes stayed closed, but the chest paused on a suspended breath.

There were metal chairs folded up, leaning against the wall. A regular lounger that Dani glimpsed in other rooms was pushed into a far corner. Right alongside the bed was a large white leather chair. It was hard imagining her aunt relaxing in there, but she must've. It was there for a reason.

"I was in a hospital not too long ago, but it wasn't this nice. Then again, this is a nursing home. It's supposed to be like home, right?"

Dani's room had more flowers, a lot more. Kathryn's bedside table was clear except for a notepad, a couple of pens, and an iPad. Her window frames were empty, too. The only flower that decorated the room was a solitary sunflower, put in her bathroom. It was drooping over. A few pictures of Julia, Kathryn, and Jake were put up.

She turned back to her aunt. Still nothing, but she was listening. Kathryn always listened. She had to, in order to judge.

Dani cut to the chase. She wasn't there for the silent treatment. "I know why you loved Julia and Erica more than me. You loved the same man my mom loved, and I'm thinking that I'm a bit too like my mom for you. You couldn't pretend I was yours. Am I right?"

No reaction. She didn't expect any.

"I don't look like him, do I? And that's what you kept in that head of yours. It's why you didn't fight Mae at all, when she wanted to adopt me."

A shallow, ragged breath escaped her aunt's parched lips.

"I've been thinking about it. You and Mom had the same taste in men. My mom wasn't 'right' in the head, as some people said, and you've never married. Those are the types who hold on the longest and you held on, didn't you?"

She remembered Sandra's words.

"You can always ask Kathy. She knows who your daddy is, too."

"Kathryn doesn't like me much."

"That's not surprising. You look like your momma. She didn't like your momma either."

Dani said, "You loved him, too. Didn't you?"

A single tear escaped her aunt's eyelid, but Dani was unmoved. A part of her stopped caring.

"Julia told me I was the one who pulled away, but that's not true. You pushed me away, and a nine year old feels that. A nine year old starts to think something's wrong with her. There wasn't anything wrong with me, was there? It was you. Something was wrong with you."

"You ungrateful—" the corpse hissed.

"I'm not ungrateful, and I'm not grateful either. I'm figuring it all out. That's what I'm doing. That's how everything went down, isn't it?"

"Leave, you ungrateful slut." She muttered as an afterthought, "Just like your mother, you are."

The order was expected. The rest was icing on Dani's cake. It confirmed everything she suspected.

Dani wasn't going to fight the command to leave. Maybe this should've been a longer and bigger ordeal, but there really wasn't much to say. Dani said what she wanted to say. She came. She spoke. It was up to her aunt, and nothing was happening there. No wall was lowered.

She rested a hand on the doorframe. "I'm still your niece, and Julia is not your birth daughter. She's my mom's. You can't erase her DNA, no matter how much you wish you could. I'd like to know who my father is, but I know you won't tell me—not even on your deathbed when you kept it secret for thirty years."

She sighed. "Julia didn't want you to die thinking you only had one niece left in this world, but I think she got it wrong. You wanted to forget I ever existed. Julia's wish did the opposite of what she wanted. You would've been happier if I never came."

"You should respect the dying."

"I know." Dani nodded. "I know I should, but I respect the truth more."

There wasn't much else to say, so she left.

And as the doors opened for her and she stepped outside, the sun winked at her. She had a bigger bounce in her step.

Jonah picked her up and said the town council changed plans. Everyone was supposed to go to the town's community center, and when she walked inside later that evening, it was filled to the brim. She was amazed at how many people just kept coming. The boats left and came back with a new family each time.

Kate found her in the crowd, nudging her and yawning at the same time. "Where'dyoudisappearto?"

"Disperieto?"

"No." Kate raked a hand over her face. "No. Sorry. Where'd you disappear to this morning? I know you slept in the office because I woke up at four and you were curled all cute-like in Jonah's blanket."

"I went to see my aunt."

"Whoa." She leaned back. "For real?" She whistled under her breath. "To be a fly on the wall with that meeting."

"She kicked me out. Nothing much happened."

Kate wrinkled her nose up. "That was anti-climactic then, huh? And speaking of your aunt, because she's kind of connected to my partner, where *is* Jake?" She looked around. "Everyone's supposed to round up for emergencies. It's typical protocol, and I'm supposed to report to duty."

She wandered off, and it wasn't long before Aiden took Kate's spot. She leaned close, dropping her voice. "So, mi hermano called and said that we have to sit tight before saving my home. You know how long? Do you know what's going on?"

Dani wasn't sure what she was supposed to say. "Maybe through the evening? That's a guess. I don't know anything either."

"I can do an evening. Bryant and Amalia are still with Bubba's parents. Thank goodness they live a half hour away. I called to check in this morning. I think I'll have them stay another night, at least. Oh!" Her gaze zeroed in on Dani. "Jonah let it slip you were heading to the nursing home this morning. Was Kathryn in a good mood?"

Dani repeated the same response Kate got, but Bubba came over with a donut in hand. She was saved. Nothing bested the taste of the fried pastry.

Aiden cried out. "They have donuts! I'm over thirty, and my metabolism can't take that, and I really hate this flood even more."

Bubba wrapped an arm around his wife, but Aiden shoved him off. "Oh, no. You're a man. You can eat that donut and not have to spend an hour in the gym. I'm not feeling the warm fuzzies for you right now."

"Chimp Two has been rejected from his first mate. Chimp Two shall maybe look elsewhere for another chimp."

"Chimp Two is welcome to do just that." They were passing the box of donuts at that moment. Aiden moved her head closer, inhaling the greasy smell of them. "Their aroma is just heavenly." Her face tightened up, and she pressed a hand over her stomach. "And I am ridiculously hungry right now." She frowned at her husband. "Chimps probably have great metabolism."

He winked back, popping the last of his donut into his mouth. "I bet chimps could eat an entire box of donuts."

"Maybe donuts are for chimps how chocolate is for dogs."

Bubba shrugged. "You can dream, honey." He smacked her on the butt and motioned behind them. "Come on. I'm sure we can find a weight loss donut somewhere. They're magical donuts. The calories disappear during natural disasters."

They moved off, and Aiden groaned. "Now, I'm the one dreaming."

Dani felt like she was standing at the head of some line. First Kate. Aiden was second. Then Bubba, and they were gone now. She was laughing at her own joke when she looked up, wondering who would be next. The joke faded fast.

Mae came inside the room, the two saw each other.

"Oh." Dani straightened, pressing a hand to her forehead. It was ridiculous, but she had this instant urge to make sure her hair looked okay. That was done before dates, or job interviews, not a talk with the aunt who secretly adopted you years ago. She knew Mae loved her, yet she still felt nervous flutters inside. They increased when Mae walked over, a guarded expression on her face.

Dani murmured, "Hey."

Mae nodded. "Jonah said you slept at the water station?" Bags were under her eyes, and her face looked void of make-up. Her wrinkles showed more, but Mae still looked flawless to Dani.

"Yeah."

Mae watched her.

Dani watched her back.

There was a big topic that needed to be discussed, and Dani was ready to hear the answers, but for the life of her, she was racking her brain how to bring it up. Finally, she blurted out, "I saw Kathryn today."

Mae's eyes rounded. "Really? How'd that go?" She ran an appraising eye up and down Dani. "You still look in one piece. She must not have filleted you alive."

Dani hid a smile. "No, but she told me to respect the dying."

Mae snorted, shoving a hand through her hair. "Please. I don't like to speak ill of the sick or those passed, but Kathryn and loving are two words that don't mix."

There it was. Her opening.

Dani took it. She almost rushed the words out. "Is that why you adopted me?"

Mae's slight smirk fell away. A sudden seriousness replaced it, and her hand slowly lowered from her hair. It went back to her side. "Your mother came to me when I wasn't doing too good." Her jaw clenched, and she looked away. "I... I can't have children, and I wasn't handling it the best way. Then your momma comes along, and here she is. She handed me what I couldn't do myself. She said to get my life right, and I could have you." A tear formed on the underside of her right eyelid. "I never thought I was right enough. That's why I never said anything to you. The adoption was legal on February 26, 2002. I just never felt like I was ready for you, like I was good enough for you to come live with me and then..."

Dani had left Craigstown on February 25, 2002.

She was adopted one day later. One day.

"I was already an adult."

"Like I said, I never thought it was enough. I was enough, but it still meant something to me. Kathryn told me long ago that she'd take care of you until I was ready. I think that's why she was mean to you, because she knew I wanted you."

"Kathryn loved Julia and Erica because she understood them. She didn't understand me. I was different because I kept to myself and I stayed in the background. Erica and Julia demanded her attention, but—" She was repeating what Julia said. It got in her head.

"It shouldn't have mattered," Mae interrupted her. "Kathryn should've loved you equally."

"Like you do?" Dani met her aunt's gaze head-on. "You hardly talk to Julia, but you dote on me. You and Kathryn are both aunts to us and yet, you both take favorites."

Mae paled, but looked away. "I'd like to know Julia. And it ain't right, that I didn't love her. I do love her. We, just, we just stayed apart out of respect to you and Kathryn."

Dani shook her head. Her hands formed into fists at her side. "I've been through a lot. I've held a dying child in my arms—more than one. I've watched someone I loved walk out my door."

She looked at her aunt, and she saw the years of age. She saw the wrinkles, but she saw them in a different way now. This was someone who'd seen her side of ditches, greed, and rejection standing in front of her. Dani knew this about Mae, but it never sunk in. Mae was the one who loved her. Mae was the one who showed her kindness growing up.

But this was different. It was that moment when a person ceased being someone idealized. Dani saw another human who did the impossible, and yet she was still human.

Dani whispered, "You're meant for more. I'm meant for more. Our family—God—we're just wrong. We've been split down the middle, and *no one* has questioned it. No one's tried to close the gap."

She remembered the delusional whisperings of her grandmother. Sandra O'Hara told her daughter to separate her babies to the remaining sisters.

Mae frowned and searched her niece's face. "I'm—I did what I could. I don't..."

"No," Dani murmured. "You were given an olive branch."

"I was given a life," Mae spoke. "You were my reason I got right, Dani."

Dani felt haunted again. It was the feeling she never was able to get rid of. It went away, for moments, but it always came back. It returned once again. There were too many who had passed away. She needed to hold on to those who were living. "When I left, I forgot you were here. You were there, but we were distant too at times. It was in one of those times. Jake became my life preserver. When he pulled away, I sank. I had to learn how to swim by myself, but I couldn't do it here. That's the real reason I left. I wasn't leaving you. I wasn't leaving Jake or Erica or anyone. I left to find myself."

"I know."

"I'm not going to apologize for leaving," Dani stated. "I don't think I can. I had to go."

"You left a girl and came back a woman." Mae stepped close and tucked a strand of hair behind Dani's ear. Her touch was that of a mother's. "You left hurting, but you came back stronger than ever." Her hand lingered there. "Some day, I'd really love for you to tell me what happened to you."

Dani smiled, and it felt right this time. She rested her forehead against Mae's. "Some day, I will."

The room was becoming packed.

Dani and Mae moved to the side as more people just kept coming. Mae was watching all the people pass by, heading to find their loved ones. A new tension settled over the room. "We haven't flooded since '62. That flood wiped everyone out, but they built the dam since then. Folks are upset. A lot of homes weren't touched by the flash floods. They're coming to hear whatever reason why they have to uproot from their dry homes."

"Because it's still raining, and there are still flash floods going on. The water's rising, Mae."

"It's farther north. It ain't that bad around here anymore."

"It's flooding up north?"

"Round about near the dam, but I don't think those folk are being forced out of their homes."

Dani frowned.

Mae gripped the back of her neck, rubbing her lips tight together. "I just don't like being forced from my home. I gotta think a lot of folk feel the same. I don't think they'll sit tight and wait for any announcement saying it's okay to go home. They'll come in, hear any reason that Jonah might have, and probably head back home."

"Whatever reason Jonah has for this, it's not some government controversy. Is that what people are thinking?"

"Folk don't trust the government that well around here."

"Why?"

Mae quieted.

"I want to know why."

"I know that Jonah's got reason, but a while back before Tenderfoot Rush brought a lot of tourists to this region, people were hurting for money. Craigstown was dying, and a lot of resorts tried coming in to help out the revenue. The government said no because of the land. It set a lot of seeds inside people and some of those seeds are still in bloom. Jonah was nearly crucified his first year here when he wouldn't let a big company into town."

"I thought that was actually good."

"Those people aren't thinking that right now. What sits with them is that Jonah didn't let them get more money. They like the water around here, but with being flooded and forced out of their homes—they're not too caring about its quality and such. A lot of resentment is resurfacing."

Talk about doom and gloom.

Jonah didn't speak to the group. Dani didn't think he was even there, but the mayor took the podium and announced everyone needed to stay together in the center. Flooding had increased more and more farther north, and that water would travel south.

Mae's prediction turned out accurate. People stopped listening. Half the people left, and the ones who remained were becoming restless. Dani was playing cards with Aiden and Bubba when Robbie pulled up a chair. Mae had moved to a card game with Barney and Jeffries. Dani could hear their chatter. It became nice background noise.

Robbie turned to her. "Where's Jonah?"

Aiden and Bubba looked up from their card game (they had folded).

"I don't know."

"The mayor didn't really say anything," Aiden spoke up. "Just that we're supposed to sit tight, but Jonah texted me that if we get through the night, we should be okay."

"The water's gone down outside."

"Flooding up north can affect us, too," Bubba said.

"I know, but my home's safe. I built it high enough."

"Nothing's safe," Aiden muttered to herself. "You can't expect anything to be immune to the weather, even if it's got money behind it."

Robbie stiffened. "What?"

"Nothing."

Bubba didn't say a word.

"No." Robbie pushed forward. "What are you talking about?"

"Nothing."

"This have to do with your dad staying at my place?"

"No."

"Or was that some poke at me because I've got money?"

"You've got more than some." Aiden sat up. "You took a pretty penny with that settlement you won." She explained to Dani, "Robbie came to town to help with Julia's lawsuit."

Erica's settlement.

She turned back to Robbie, "And you got partner because of that. You're one of the few attorneys in town. You make more than all three of us together right here."

"Not Dani."

"What?" Aiden and Bubba looked up.

"Dani's got near a million in the bank."

They all looked at her, and Dani asked, "How do *you* know that?" But she knew as soon as she asked. Kelley Lynn. "Never mind. I didn't realize your secretary came back into the bank. I thought she left. I love how everyone is connected in small towns." Her voice dripped with sarcasm.

"You have almost a million dollars?" Aiden cried out. "Where'd that come from? Does Jonah know?"

"Is it any of his business?" Dani countered, but he did know. And she didn't remember him having the same response. "Do you not like people who have money?"

Aiden frowned. "What are you talking about?"

"Is it the money thing? Because you think they'll turn into your father?"

"I can't believe you just said that to me." Aiden sucked in her breath, taken aback.

What she had in her bank account was her business and no one else's, along with the reason of *why* it was there, too. "Yeah, well, my money is personal, Aiden. You don't have a right to demand to know that or command me to tell Jonah."

"I wasn't—"

She was, and Aiden knew it.

"Maybe we should call a breather?" With his hand behind her, Bubba ushered his wife away.

"Don't worry about Aiden. She'll get over it. She's just worked up 'cause her dad's in town. A person can't see straight when they're all riled up inside."

"Yeah, I'm seeing that." Dani gazed around the center. "You think this is some government conspiracy, too?"

Robbie's eyes rounded, but he didn't pretend he didn't know what she was talking about. He lifted up a shoulder, picking at some lint on his pants. "I wasn't here when all that happened back then. Aiden said the town got pretty ugly when Jonah said no to some company's building proposal."

"Mae was hinting some people might be thinking that again."

"Sometimes they think that. You know, the small guy gets worked over by the big guy. Do I think it's some conspiracy? No, but do I think people aren't thinking right? Yes. Some of 'em anyway. Small towns don't like being told what to do, especially when it comes to their homes."

"There's gotta be some reason why we're all staying here."

"They aren't sharing, whatever it is."

"And there's gotta be a reason for *that*, too."

"I think there is, and you think there is." Robbie gestured between them. "But I don't think most of these folks agree with us."

Dani sighed. "Everyone knows each other's business and everyone's got an opinion about it, no matter how wrong they are."

"A lot of these folks didn't get schooling past high school, and if it is, it's from the local community college. They got their knowledge the real-world way. You and I, we left. We saw what else was out there, but people can get set in their ways. The world's a lot smaller than people think. You get humbled when you realize how small you actually are.

Folks who don't realize that, they just have a different way of thinking. That's all."

"That can be dangerous sometimes."

"You're not getting an argument from me."

"I don't have a good feeling about this," Dani murmured as she watched the crowd. More and more small groups were forming. The whispers were buzzing. It wasn't going to end well—whatever was happening.

"There's Jonah." Robbie gestured toward a side door.

He moved through the crowd, stopping to talk to his sister. The crowd moved away from him.

Robbie shook his head. "It's never surprising how they'll turn on someone they used to worship the day before."

"Was this how it was before?"

"I don't know. I wasn't here at that time, but it got ugly. Jonah only had a few friends, but when the report came out that the company actually would've poisoned the water supply, Jonah was hailed as the town's savior." Robbie stood up as Jonah headed in their direction. "The town's not remembering that today." He nodded in greeting. "Jonah."

"Robbie." Jonah did the same and settled on Dani. "You wanna get something to eat?"

"Sure."

Jonah led the way into a private back room where food was waiting on a table. A buffet of meat, cheese, casseroles, bread, and even some lasagna was set out. Another table had drinks such as soda, water, and even some beer.

"What's this?"

Jonah pulled Dani close, murmuring close to her ear, "Even the wealthy get benefits in times of disasters."

"How are we privileged?"

"I got some benefits being the Water Whisperer. The mayor trusts me."

"Even though everyone else forgets to?" She felt a twinge of anger.

"Jonah," a voice behind them boomed with authority. Jonah stiffened beside her. A middle-aged man was crossing the room to them. Dani had one guess—Jonah's father. He extended his hand to her. "Elliott Bannon."

"Dad." Jonah stepped forward. "I wasn't aware that a boat was sent for you."

Dani shook his hand, studying him a moment. "I'm Dani."

He walked with purpose and a stride that told others to get out of his way. His hair was a rich dark brown, but there were graying hints scattered throughout the rich curls. His jaw was firm and pointed that told anyone who saw him that he had a purpose and he wouldn't veer off his course, no matter who be damned.

"You're the O'Hara girl I've been told so much about."

Dani grinned, pulled her hand free and tucked it behind her. "I wouldn't believe anything that you're told from Drew Quandry. He just found out about my existence a few days ago, and he's not exactly a fan."

Elliott took another assessing glance. "You're spirited. That's what Quandry told me, but he wasn't the one filling my head. I heard about your courageous feat during the tsunami. You saved ten children, did you not? You were hailed a hero there. And yet, you're here in Craigstown with my son?"

Dani didn't reply. There was no point. He wanted her to know that he knew her in a way most didn't. The message was received.

Elliott added, "You got a healthy award, too. Near a million, right?"

Jonah stepped between them. "Dani's not going to be intimidated because you researched her."

"True story. My dying aunt is scarier than you.'

"Dad." Aiden was heading their way.

Jonah held a hand up to her. "Aiden, I can handle this."

"You shouldn't have to. Besides, I've got a few more things to say to him than you." Aiden switched her focus. "Why'd you come here, Father? Was it really to spearhead for the Quandrys, or did you decide to call our bluff? Okay. That house you're in. It's not mine. I don't live in a beautiful mansion. My husband isn't an executive for a local business that trades internationally. We have an average home, and I don't care what you think. I'm not moving into the city and working at one of your offices. I'd rather have my home flooded first." She muttered under her breath, "Which just happened."

Dani caught sight of the Quandrys. They were settling in the opposite corner of the 'first-class' buffet. Drew's head was bent talking with another middle-aged man around his fifties or sixties. Dani guessed that was the eldest Quandry. Boone sat at a table with Jenny and another woman. Jenny scooted her chair close enough to nearly be on his lap, but he promptly scooted his chair away.

Dani couldn't help wondering if Quandry, Inc. would still want to build here? Flooding could be damaging. Were the mussels worth it?

A new thought suddenly occurred to her.

Aiden was still lashing out at her father when Dani took Jonah's arm. She pulled him away. Watching his sister, Jonah bent his head closer to Dani. "What is it?"

"That's why he's here."

Jonah looked at her now. "What?"

"He's here to get in your head and mess you up."

"I know." There was movement at the door, and they both looked over. Trenton was there, his hand raised to get Jonah's attention. "I have to go." He pulled her to him, his mouth close to her ear. He pressed a kiss to her forehead. "I'd run from here. Run and hide."

Dani chuckled. "I'll hide behind Mae's skirt."

Mae had never worn a skirt in her life—unless it was a miniskirt.

Mae had enough around ten that night.

Jeffries, who'd been explaining what the dolphin on his wedding band symbolized, turned from Barney to Mae. "What's wrong?"

Dani saw her aunt stand up. "Oh, no." A pit began to form in her stomach

Robbie turned to look where she was. "Huh? What's happening?"

"Mae." Both Jeffries and Barney were waiting.

"Nothing. Everything." She chewed on the end of her mouth, her eyes closed to slits. "This is enough. I'm done waiting. The water's almost completely gone. I'm going to make sure my livelihood is still standing. I'm a bit more worried about that than whatever secret plan they got cooking here."

"Mae." Dani stood, too.

"I'm sorry. I know you're invested here, but I'm going. We're going to be wasting an entire night, and they'll only come in the morning to tell us to leave. I'm going to save myself the wait and leave now."

"They told us to stay here for our safety." Robbie rose.

"From what? We're in the clear. The flooding is up north, and the water's not coming down or it would've been here by now."

"The topsoil is eroding up there. They're worried about what that'll do to the river down here."

Mae could've rolled her eyes, her tone gave the same effect. "The river hasn't flooded since the dam was built. We're fine. We're always fine. I'm going."

Barney and Jeffries stood, too.

"Let's go, guys." Mae motioned and followed behind. Jeffries offered Dani an apologetic smile, but fell in line.

Robbie shook his head. "Huh."

"What?" Dani asked, but her attention had just left the building. If they left, she knew the ones who remained would follow. It only took one pebble to fall down for the whole pile to crash. This so wasn't good, and she had no idea where Jonah was.

"I didn't know Jeffries was married."

"There are some secrets that are just meant to be. I'm sure that's what it is. I've learned that much since moving home." She had to find Jonah. He'd know what to do. "I have to go. I'm not going far. I'll be back." She patted his arm. "Make a list."

"For what?"

"For Kate." They'd been discussing his love life before Mae decided to lead a revolution. "If she's the one for you, start making a list of nice things to say and do for her. Trust me. Tell her she's beautiful and give her gifts. Lots of gifts. She'll melt."

"You sure?"

"Oh, yeah." She gestured outside the center. "I need to find Jonah. I don't have a good feeling about this."

But going outside, she couldn't find him. He wouldn't have been in the center, or he would've found her instead. The town was near vacant. Everyone left for their homes while the others remained inside. She walked around, hoping to see something or someone who might know where Jonah could be.

She found herself in front of the boat store.

"Dani?"

She turned around. "Jake."

"I saw you, and I figured you were out for a walk, to clear your head or some sorts."

"What are you doing here?"

"Folks can't get arrested for going to their homes." Jake shrugged. "I saw you leave. Figured I should try to protect someone tonight."

Dani knew it was time. It was the conversation and the person they never talked about. She knew this talk would happen, and on some level, she'd been waiting the entire time. Almost everything was done. She made peace with Julia, and said her goodbye to Kathryn. It felt right to have this talk now.

It was time.

"Did Erica say anything? When she died? Like—" Dani had no idea.

"No." His eyebrows bunched together, and his head fell abruptly. "She did say some things, but..."

"It's okay." Her throat tightened with emotion. She felt something. Something was awakening inside of her.

"She was so much like you, but she was different, too."

"She was stronger."

"No." His response was swift. "She was different. That's all."

Dani swallowed.

"She was funny. She was sarcastic, opinionated, thoughtful, regretful. She had the hardest times with Aunt Kathryn, but she knew that Kathryn needed her and Julia. She sucked it up and was dutiful." Jake laughed. "That was the only time—or the only person—that I ever saw her be nice for them, not for her. I know that makes her sound like a horrible person, but she wasn't. I swear, Dani. She wasn't a bad person at all. She turned different when she was around Julia and Kathryn, around some of her friends. But that wasn't all of her."

He added, an afterthought, "I wish you would've known that Erica. You would've been friends. It was that Erica I loved."

Dani felt the first tear.

Jake continued, hoarse, "She'd always put cloves in our food. I hated it. They were awful, but Erica said that they had to be in there. They had a purpose and I should just be patient. She loved lilies. She had them in vases all over the kitchen, and she even put up a wallpaper border of lilies in our bedroom."

Jake was allergic.

"I hated them, but—"

"You loved her."

"She was mine. She was a part of me."

Dani drew a ragged breath. "You were my best friend, and I lost you to her, but I've never admitted to myself that it wasn't you I lost that night. It was her. I didn't know her, and we never had a chance. We were never *given* a chance. So much shit in our family."

A hole was there. It was widening.

"Erica kept a wall to the world. She lost her mother, and she had two older sisters. Julia kept it together by controlling everything. Erica told me she had to play along or Julia would've 'freaked.' Her words. And then she had you, but you pulled away before Erica knew what was going on. She was the youngest, Dani. She didn't know better. It was too late when she did."

Dani was already gone.

He added, "You were a kid, too."

"I was broken." Her fingernails curled into her skin. "We were all broken." She looked at him, wiping away her tears. "Is there a time when you get over it? When you start to put it all behind you?"

"Yeah," Jake breathed out as his radio sounded static, then a call from headquarters. He switched it off. "When you learn what's broken you down and you start to rebuild it."

"It's that easy?"

"No, but it's the only way if you don't want to live half-lived."

"Half-lived," she echoed. "I wasn't even living before."

"She saw your mom. When she was close to going, she told me that your mom was there. You weren't. Erica told me you were alive, and that your mom said you were coming home." His voice hitched on a note. "Erica told me you'd be home real soon, but time kept passing. I lost hope. I started to think that she just went crazy in that time, but then..."

"I came home."

He nodded. "She's around, you know. I feel her, and sometimes when I'm not thinking, I'll hear her. She'll call my name like she's just come home. I always know better, but I'll walk down the stairs. I know she'll not be there, but I still do it anyway."

"I didn't do right by Erica, and I should've." She drew in some air, filling her lungs. "I loved my sister."

"She loved you, too."

She missed her sister. She missed the one she knew. She missed the one she didn't know.

"Well." Dani laughed. She needed a reprieve. Looking at Jake, he didn't seem like he had more to say, and Lord knows, she was running empty on the tear tank. "That's over now."

"Yeah, it is. I'm relieved. Been waiting a while for that conversation."

"Me, too."

They leaned against his squad car. "I thought there'd be more tears."

"Way more tears."

"Tons."

"Buckets."

"Waterfalls."

Jake grinned. "Oceans."

Jonah had been right—Jake was the one she needed to talk with. Dani suddenly felt so many words to share with her sister. Maybe she was around. Maybe she wasn't. Dani liked to think she believed in the afterlife, but from a world so cold and bleak, sometimes Dani thought that death just meant rest.

"I'm tired," Dani announced. "I'm really, really tired."

Jake cleared his throat, and then his radio crackled to life. A code orange was called for the Craigstown County.

Jake went still.

"What?"

He didn't move.

"Jake. What?"

It was bad. She felt it in her gut, and she knew it now. She was just waiting to hear the words confirming it.

"A code orange means the dam burst." Jake raised horrified eyes to her. "All that flooding, the erosion—it burst the dam."

"The town—"

"—will be destroyed."

"This is what Jonah was worried about. Those people went home."

"I know. My God, I know. I have to go and warn them." Jake scrambled into his car and gunned the engine. "Get to safety, Dani. Find Jonah. He'll take care of you."

Her nightmare was coming true. The first storm missed her. The flash floods were the warm-up, and now the second storm was coming for her.

The water was coming.

She threw a rock through the boat store's window. There was no time to waste. They would need boats, lots of boats. Her heart pounding, it seemed to take forever for her to reach inside, unlock the door, and take a hammer to the keys' locker.

Her hands trembled as she tried to find too many keys to too many boats. They wouldn't fit. They'd fall. She nearly wept when one sunk in, fitting. Then a second, then a third. She was sweating, and biting down on her lip. She needed more boats than this.

Life jackets.

She needed those too.

Raiding a back room, she grabbed everything she could.

Duct tape. Flashlights. Candy bars. Flares. Even prepaid cell phones. Anything that might be needed. Then she grabbed another round of matches, lighters, and all items that would provide heat.

It took nearly two hours, and in the midst—she heard nothing. She was listening for something, anything, someone, anyone, even as she hit the releases on the boat carriers.

No one sprinted past.

No one was screaming, or crying.

Nothing.

The silence was eerie. It was like the town was in the eye of a tornado. But it was coming. She knew it was coming. The hairs on the back of her neck were raised, and hadn't fallen back down.

The first wave would crush the streets. She was just waiting for it. She did as much as she could before running back outside.

She looked up, and there it was. Her heart stopped. The wave was thirty feet above her, and it was then she realized how miraculous a dam was. She ran inside, just as the first wave hit the pavement. It swooshed past her, filling into the store. The two main windows were still intact, but they'd shatter any second.

She climbed over each boat, and started them.

She couldn't drive all of them, but she looped a rope between a few. She could pull three or four behind her boat. She just had to wait until there was enough water. And then it happened—the windows broke under the weight. The water rushed in, and Dani gunned the engine. She had to get the first boat out of the store. The water was rising fast, so she didn't have much time.

She cleared it. The second did too. The third struggled, and the fourth was caught behind. She gunned her engine again. It was just enough to yank the fourth free. There were more inside that she released from their carriers, but she couldn't corral them all. She'd have to go back for them.

As she drove through town, the people came out.

They were everywhere now. It was such a stark contrast from before, but as she saw people, she gave up a boat. She'd stall. They'd climb up into a boat and unhook themselves from the rope. The only thing she yelled was for them to help pick up others. They stayed with her, helping to pick people up as they all headed to the center.

A wall of people lined the center when they got there. They were standing at the edge of the water.

Dani knew these people were alive, but not in her mind. She was back there with the first storm. These people were waving. Those people had been floating in the water, already dead. The bodies were everywhere.

Dani was mixing them together in her mind. The dead were raising their arms now.

"Dani!" Jonah crashed through the crowd and ran to her boat. He jumped inside, crushing her to him in the next breath. He held the back of her head, holding her against his chest before he kissed her forehead, then her lips. "I thought you were dead. My God." He went back to just holding her, wrapping as much of himself around her. "I tried the phone, but I couldn't reach you and then Jake said you were in the town." He was touching her pockets, but she forgot about the phone. His hand found it, and he pulled out. "The battery's dead."

Dead. She'd never get away from that word.

The town was gone.

Dani pulled away. The center would soon be as well. "We have to go."

"Jonah!"

Hawk and Trenton were running toward them.

Hawk separated, leaping into one of the last empty boats. He revved the engine and swung next to where Dani and Jonah stood. He yelled, "We got a distress call!" He stopped, his eyes flicking to Dani.

She growled. "Who?"

"It's Mae." He said to Jonah, "We can get them if we go now."

Jonah looked to Dani, but she was already pushing him away. "Go. Get her, please."

He was torn, but grabbed her for one more hug. He crushed her to him, and said, his lips brushing against her forehead, "I will come back for you. I will find you. Do not die. Okay? Do not die."

"I won't." She pushed him again. "Go. She's my family."

He did, tearing himself away. Hawk half-lifted him into the boat as Jonah grabbed the edge and swung himself up. He didn't stop looking at Dani. He never broke contact. Hawk turned the boat and left.

Jonah was slowly swallowed by the darkness.

That wasn't real. He'd come back. He went to save Mae. Dani kept reminding herself of that. Then Trenton leapt onto her boat. He was yelling at her. She wasn't hearing him. She couldn't. All she could see was Jonah heading away from her.

There were people streaming around her.

She recognized the looks on their faces. Fear. Uncertainty. Anger. Panic. They were all thinking the same thing: this wasn't real. This wasn't happening.

They were all wrong.

This *was* real. This *was* happening, and it was just the beginning.

She sat down, saying to herself, "They're all going to die." Everyone was going to die.

"Dani, come on!" Trenton was screaming at her.

She half-heard him. People were climbing into their boat. She just sat there. She was the eye of the storm now. She was the middle of the tornado. The winds would ripple. They'd snarl. They'd curse. They'd be angry with her, because it was her that they wanted. This whole storm was about taking back what was theirs.

Her. The water was coming for her.

"Julia."

Dani heard Trenton say her sister's name, then someone climbed into the boat. A second person was behind her. Trenton was saying, "Jake, who else?"

Dani looked up. Her sister was there, but she left? Dani remembered seeing her go...

Julia yelled over Dani's head to Trenton, "The nursing home?"

"It was one of the first to go. It was crushed. I'm sorry." He swept his gaze over both of them. "Sorry, you guys."

Dani sat there.

People were swimming past them, but she didn't know where they were going. There was no hope. For any of them. She was alive, and that meant they'd all die. The storm wouldn't stop, not until it claimed her.

"We have to go!" Jake was yelling.

The boat was moving. They were gliding over the water. Dani knew it wasn't peaceful. Waves and ripples broke over the surface, but she looked down. She saw the calm beneath. She could see them, the dead already. They were in the water, their arms and hair hanging loose. They were content. Their eyes were calm.

They were home.

"My house." Julia collapsed beside Dani. Her hand covered her mouth.

She heard and lifted her head. There it was. Julia's house was completely overcome, but one tree still stood up. It was a rebel, in the path of the water. It refused to sink below. Dani didn't think. She moved, going to the front of the boat where the spotlight was.

"Dani? What are you doing?"

She turned it on the tree, and there was another. Mrs. Bendsfield was tied to a branch, one that Dani remembered swinging from as a child.

Julia gasped. "Mrs. Bendsfield!"

Trenton steered the boat over, and Jake grabbed the older woman. He had to cut away at the rope she used to tie herself to the tree. Hauling her into the boat, Mrs. Bendsfield looked vanquished and depleted. She was soaked. Her arms looked like twigs, and her lips were so blue. She was shaking from the cold.

"Can we go?!" she snapped at Trenton. "I've already watched GoldenEye get swept up by this crush. I don't want to follow my favorite cow."

Julia yelled, "We have to go south."

"Why? That doesn't make any sense. We need to cut across the current. It'll flatten out—"

"Listen to me, Dani!"

It had been Trenton arguing with her. Trenton who was driving, but it was Dani who Julia spoke to. She was so earnest. "We have to go south! I was told that."

"Who told you to go south?"

Her sister sat back down. "You wouldn't believe me if I told you."

"Julia," Trenton leaned closer, yelling over the water, "I am not turning this boat around for more flooding. If we cut across—"

"The wind is too great. If we cut across, we'll capsize and drown." Jake was staring at his fiancée. "Julia, who said that we need to go south?"

"Just trust me!"

"No!"

Julia had the survival instinct of an extinct species. Dani didn't blame them for their disbelief.

"Dani!" She turned to her.

Trenton was waiting. They were all waiting. Somehow it became Dani's decision.

Mrs. Bendsfield screamed as a sudden wave crashed over her. Dani saw her slipping before she could scream again. Dani woke up. She didn't know why, or how it happened, but she woke up. She'd been okay with dying, and then she wasn't.

Suddenly, she was fighting. She had to live.

She surged across the boat and clamped a hand on Mrs. Bendsfield's leg. Trenton was trying to steer the boat toward calmer waters as Dani wrapped the anchor's rope around Mrs. Bendsfield's leg.

"Ahh!" Mrs. Bendsfield's body lifted from the wave's force. The anchor held. It didn't move, and she slammed back down.

"Grab on to a rope and wrap it around yourself. We have to stay in this boat—" Dani was looking around. She thought she put more rope in this boat.

"Unless it capsizes right here and now!" Julia shouted back. "We have to go south. Dani," she twisted to face her sister. "I was told to go south. When have I ever lied to you?"

"You lie all the time." Dani gritted her teeth as she held onto the anchor's rope.

"Okay, but not about this."

"We're going to die because of this, Julia. You know that, right?" Dani wanted to make sure her sister knew what she was saying. That she wasn't going crazy how Dani thought her herself was.

"We'll die if we cut across." Julia slouched over. "We *have* to go south." She yelled over Dani's head, "Go, Trenton. We don't have a lot of time, and we have to get there."

He waited, looking at Dani for confirmation.

She nodded.

He turned the boat and gunned the engine. All of them fell back, then tossed to the right and left from the waves. They were increasing in height and force. Trenton kept driving, but the last wave nearly sent Dani flying from the boat. She wound the anchor's rope around her waist, and it jerked her back down.

Then she looked up. Wave after wave was coming. They were all going to crash down on them, and it wouldn't last. They wouldn't last. Dani was forced with the truth.

"We're going to capsize, Julia. We need life jackets. We need—"

"No!" Julia screamed against the wind. "We need the anchor. Where are we, Dani? Do you know where we are?"

"We're in the middle of nowhere. That's where we are."

"No, where are we? Do you know where we are now?"

Mrs. Bendsfield screamed, "I think I broke a rib!"

Dani glanced around. She was becoming frantic, but her eyes caught sight of a tree. One lone tree that stuck up from the rest, and her heart suddenly pounded to life.

"Oh, God," she murmured, dazed. She stood up. "You're right, Julia. We need the anchor. We need—there should be small heating packs inside that compartment. Grab them all and put them in a closed pocket. Something that can be zipped closed."

"...my ribs..."

Trenton stalled the engine. He leaned toward Dani. "What's going on?"

Julia scrambled up. "Where are we?"

"There's a cave. I'm going over to that tree, and we can follow it down to the cave. We'll have to swim around, but there should be an air pocket inside that cave. There's blankets and dry clothes in there." She twisted to Trenton, smiling so brightly. She had new hope. "It's the cave. Call in our location. They'll have to come find us."

"I can't breathe." Mrs. Bendsfield gasped. "My rib is broken. I can't hold my breath for that long."

"You're going to have to," Dani said. No one else was going to die.

"I'm not going to make it." Mrs. Bendsfield was calm and accepting. Dani knew what she was feeling. She'd felt it nearly the entire time, but now she didn't want to die. She wanted to fight, and she wouldn't give up.

"You can try, Mrs. Bendsfield!" Dani yelled.

"Nanery," she said, a kind smile looked alien across her wrinkled face. "My name's Nanery." She reached and grabbed Dani's hand. "I've got some truths to confess here."

Julia stilled and looked up.

Trenton was on the radio, giving their location, but Dani froze and watched.

Nanery drew in a breath, grunting from the pain. "My husband loved your grandma, but you knew that. He snuck around on me for a while before he up and left, but he came back through town every so often. It's why Sandy had three of them. It wasn't ever told. I never told a soul, but your momma screwed that up. She started coming around—"

"We don't have time for this!" Julia screamed.

Dani shot a hand out to quiet her sister. "Shut up and let her talk!"

Nanery was wheezing, grimacing. There was no blood left in her face. "My boy—I had to tell your momma about who her daddy was. She couldn't take a liking to my Oscar. It wasn't right."

"That's why she was the only one who visited her."

"Sandy used to be my best friend, and even though I hated her, I knew she didn't want her children knowing she was all sorts of crazy."

"What are you talking about?" Julia cried out. "We're going to die—"

Dani rounded on her, "Then I'm going to die knowing the truth!"

Julia shut up.

Nanery coughed before she managed, "I've got all sorts of guilt that eats at me. And one of the worst—your momma."

"What do you mean?"

"Me and her got real tight. I was the only one she could talk to about her momma, but she had the same curse that Sandy did."

"It was a married man." Dani knew.

"He was married, but not happily. Daniella let that right her mind so she wasn't guilt-ridden, but Kathryn stuck her hand into the mix, you see—"

"Kathryn loved him, too."

"He didn't have time for her. It was only Daniella he loved."

"What are you saying?" Julia asked. Her voice was suddenly so calm against the chaos surrounding them.

"Your pop is here. He's been around, but Daniella didn't want you guys to know. She was ashamed. She didn't want her kiddies knowing what a 'screw-up' she was." Nanery coughed again and hissed from the pain. "She knew that Kathryn would take a liking to the two because they look like their daddy, but Daniella knew that Dani would be left in the cold. She didn't know what to do when she found out she was dying."

Julia and Dani stood and waited, hearing their secrets spew from a stranger's mouth.

"I never done right by your momma. My boy took off. He disowned me for keeping that secret so many years. He said he couldn't have a mother who knew he had three sisters and not tell him that. He couldn't ever trust me again, so he took off. I've never seen him since. Suppose now, I won't."

Dani raised her chin. "If he comes back, I'll tell him that you did right in the end."

Nanery's smile was quick. She grasped for her hand, giving it a good squeeze. "Thank you." She slumped forward. Dani recognized the signs. The cracked ribs and the storm, Mrs. Bendsfield was going to die. Her will to hang on was slipping. Dani saw that, too. The exertion was too much, but Mrs. Bendsfield unwound the anchor's rope from her leg.

It was now free from her.

She'd lived a tumultuous life, and she'd die in a tumultuous storm. The poetry wasn't lost on Dani as she knelt beside this woman. "Who is our father?"

"You know him." Nanery smiled. "You've talked to him. He's with Mae all the time."

That was enough. Dani stood back up. She knew.

He wore a white dolphin on his wedding ring. Dani had sat just in front of them with her back turned. She hadn't been listening, but now Jeffries' words came back to her. She heard it all—it's the dolphin that stood for healing and loss.

Jeffries had told her mom about the dolphin.

"I know who he is."

Mrs. Bendsfield continued, "I've run into him a bit, around town and such. He always knew that I knew his secret, and one time he talked to me about it. Your momma didn't want her secret told—that she'd been with a married man."

"He was older."

"He still is old, but he watches you guys. He keeps updates on you, Dani, from Mae and from you, Julia, through Jake. Your fiancé stops in Mae's Grill on a regular basis and talks a plenty of his girl."

Dani was thrown across the boat as a wave rocked the boat.

"Dani!" Julia shouted and reached for her sister.

"I'm sorry!" Nanery shouted now as she stood up. "I could've saved your family. I knew all the secrets, but I chose not to. I'm sorry."

"We have to go!" Jake had been watching the waves. He motioned for them now. "Now!"

"Dani!" Julia screamed into her ear, and Dani reacted instinctively as another wave crashed against them. She dove for something to hold on to, and Trenton gunned the engine. The boat shot across the small divide. The tree brushed against their helm.

They didn't have time for any more deathside confessions.

Dani grabbed the anchor, her sister, and as her hand made contact— the boat was rocked, and this time—it capsized.

All of them plunged into the cold water.

Dani kicked upward, pulled her sister after her, and both gasped their last breath. Trenton and Jake were there. Nanery wasn't.

"We don't have long. I'm holding the anchor—just barely. We're going to fall fast with the anchor—don't fight it." Dani said to the guys, "Everyone has to hold on. Your lungs will burn, but it's the only way. You gotta trust me!" The guys would be fine. She looked at Julia. "You have to trust me."

"I do!"

Dani saw that she did. Julia wrapped a hand around the anchor's rope, and she pulled away from her sister. They were both connected now. Jake and Trenton held on to the rest of the anchor's rope. Each gave Dani a grim nod.

Dani knew their destination, but she didn't know if they'd make it or not. "There's a cave underneath this tree. If I don't make it, you just swim around the cave and go inside. You keep swimming until you clear the hedge. Then you can swim upward, and you'll feel the surface from inside the water." She looked to Trenton. "He knows. He can lead you in, if I can't."

Julia gasped. "Shut up. Let's go." Then she said, "Dani..." She trailed off, treading water.

"I know." Dani stopped her. "I know."

Julia nodded, settled, and Dani saw that her sister was ready.

It wasn't like the last time, Dani thought before she dropped the anchor. It was time. She was going to find out if death called her number.

Dani—

I'm writing this letter, but I have no way of getting this to you, so it's not even really for you. Selfish, aren't I? Well, tough. I don't know where you are, but you're right or I'm right. I don't know which, right now, but this is for me and my mental health. Jake says I need to be 'sound' in the head if I have any way to fight this crap that I have. What Jake doesn't know won't hurt him, right? Wrong. I'm dying and I know it, and he's got to admit it.

You know what? I'm pretty mad at that, too. Seriously. I'm here and I'm dying, and you're the one who took off? I bet you're rich, married, and you already have kids, right?

Jake seems to think you're dead. Everyone else, too, but I just think it's because Aunt Kathryn is spreading that rumor out of spite. She thinks you've left her, and who could ever leave Aunt Kathryn? Obviously someone who's dead. (I'm rolling my eyes.)

She's demented. I know that, but she raised me. And Julia needs her. Jake's scared to death of her. That always makes me laugh. It's really the only moments of amusement that I have lately. I just watch to see how nervous he gets whenever she shows her face. It's so funny how his hand will twitch. He always denies it, but I saw that he sat on his hand today. And his eyes look so strained. Jake's such a guy. He won't admit someone could terrify him like that. Oh, and he has this little jerk at the corner of his mouth. He's got a nervous disorder, but anyway—I'm writing this letter for me because he told me to.

I'm not only dying, but I'm crazy. Crazy and illogical, that's me, but I'm so far gone on the death road that I don't even care. That's kinda funny, too. I can say senseless things like, 'Oh, how the butterflies are so pretty.' And everyone will agree and pat my arm and say that the butterflies are gorgeous. And this is in the winter! I told one guy who I saw that he owned a camel in his future. The guy went out and bought a camel! I laughed so hard when Jake told me that. Jake didn't get it. He just got that cute perplexed look on his face, like he wants to tell me that I'm not making sense, but he doesn't want to hurt my feelings. I love that look. I think that's why I fell in love with him.

But, yeah—that's the other part of this letter.

You took off after Jake broke up with you. He broke up with you for me, but that's a little part of history that I want to set right.

Jake didn't break up with you. I watched you guys. Yes, you were best friends, and you were dating, but you weren't any couple that I've ever seen.

You left him long before he left you, Dani, and you know it. You just put up a wall, and it's amazing he stuck around as long as he did. He did that because he loves you. Sometimes I just hate you. I really do because it's not fair how the man who I have fallen completely head over heels for still loves you. I can't touch whatever part you have in him. And trust me—I've tried! The guy just gets this stubborn look and walks away to get me some water or something. We've talked about you a lot, but we haven't talked about you and him, you know?

Anyway, I'm going to die pretty soon, and here's my confession. I'm not okay that the guy I love with my whole heart still has a part of his for you. I'm not okay with that, and if I were, I'd have to kill myself. I am resolved to it or have reluctantly come to terms with that. I can't touch what you got with him, but here's my shallowness peaking—I'm going to be the girl he loved who died. That's major, and it'll leave its scars. I know that, and a part of me is happy about it. (I know, so morbid of me.)

I'm dying, Dani, and I've known for a while. No one else has. I knew I had cancer before I was diagnosed, but no one will admit that I'm not going to win. I'm not going to be that girl. It'll be someone else. Probably you or Julia or, I don't know. I care, but I don't care.

Anyway, on to more confessions. Did you know that our grandmother is still alive? Of course, now that I'm bedridden, I get told by some guy who's saying he's my uncle that our grandmother is in an asylum. I guess his dad shacked up with Grandmum and spurted Mom, Kathryn, and Mae out. It's pretty amazing what dying will give you. All sorts of people will show up at my bedside and talk all sorts of nonsense that they'd want me to know before I'm dead.

Our uncle is pretty cool. He's come to visit me a few times. He's funny, but he's kind of straight-laced. Not the sort to drink or smoke or have sex, but I'm sure he's had sex. No one can be that straight-laced, right?

But the third confession: I know who our dad is. That's something I'm more pissed about than thinking you're married, wealthy, and have kids.

I'm about to die, any day now, and my dad walks through the door. How unfair is that?! I'm pissed! I'm beyond pissed, and I'm even madder that I can't tell anyone. No one will understand, and if I do say something, they'll just pat me on the head because I'm dying and, of course, I'm delusional!

'Butterflies are beautiful. Yes, Erica, they sure are.'

'I'm going to buy a camel. Of course, I am.'

It's funny, but I hate it right now. I met my father, and no one believes me. They wouldn't believe me, and even Jake—it makes me so sick because he'd think about you first. He wouldn't ever admit it, but I know that in some part of his brain he'd be thinking how sad it was that you left before you could meet your father.

I hate that!

I hate you sometimes!

Julia's freaking out. She's got no one to put lotion on or to pat their heads and swat away the flies. I love Julia. I really do, but some days it's just so tiring. I want to rattle her cage and make her see life. I'm dying, and I have a sister who's living through me! What am I supposed to do? I'm not supposed to be the one saving her life. That's not fair, and it's not right, but I guess it makes sense, huh? I'm dying so I can see all clear-headed and such.

Julia's got her head in the clouds, but you should be here, too. This is your job. You're my sister, our sister, and it's pretty damn cowardly that you ran away. Cowardly and selfish, because even though our family isn't the Cleavers, we're still family. I should be here, too, and you should help with Julia. She's going to need so much help when I'm gone. I'm going to be gone. I'm not going to be hurting. I'll be fricking happy as hell (I'm so going to heaven!), but it'll be Jake and Julia who are going to be empty.

I need you to help. Be there for them. Be the best friend for Jake he needs and, as much as it pains my jealous side to say, he has been missing you so much. I almost think he'd rather still be loving someone who didn't need him rather than go without his best friend. And Julia...God...I know her idiosyncrasies can make a person mental, but man!—she's our sister. She's going to get a wake-up call when I die.

Be a sister. Be my sister!

I'm not sorry that I fell in love with Jake. I love him, and I'm never going to apologize for that, but I am so mad that you can be so petty about that. I lost you! I know that we weren't close, that...I'm learning more and more from Jake that you were struggling on your own, but I lost my sister when you left.

Jake tells me about you on a weekly basis. Not every day, but maybe once or twice a week, and it sounds like you and I have a lot in common. We both put on a show for the world to see. I plastered on the happy and charming face, while you were just contemptuous and didn't need us. That's what I thought for so long—that you just didn't need anyone because you were so above us.

Jake said that I was wrong and couldn't be further from the truth.

I'm sorry, Dani. I wish I would've known the real you in living, but I have the afterlife to appease me. I'll be watching you, every chance I get, and I'm going to haunt your ass so much! If there's a simple breeze that gets you—it's me! I swear it!

I love you, living and in death. I'm always going to love you! Be there for Jake and Julia. They need you. And every time a bird flies by your head, think of me because I probably made it do that, especially if they take a dump on you. That really was me then. (Insert evil laugh with a smile and wink from me.)

Sincerely, in death and still alive for the moment—Erica

P.S. Tell that guy who bought that camel that I'm really sorry. I totally made that up. I didn't mean for him to be spit on, at all.

(I guess camels aren't that nice.)

EPILOGUE

I survived the flood that demolished Craigstown. Both Julia and I survived it. Jonah found all of us. It was an awakening experience to see the bubbles break the surface as the first diver pulled himself upright onto our bank.

I knew it was Jonah before he even showed his face. And it wasn't that I recognized his body or how he moved—I just knew it was him. The first bubble bore his name, and I blinked back tears of gratefulness.

They weren't tears that I was happy to be alive. They were just happy tears, just because.

You see—this story wasn't about falling in love or reuniting with my estranged sister. It wasn't even about me realizing that I'd been cheated by myself and others from Erica.

This story was about me. I came home, haunted, and I fought through the second storm. I needed to fight. And Jonah had been the first to spark that fight inside of me. I was grateful for that, more than I could ever put into words.

Trenton and Jake waited. Julia wept that she was alive as Jonah peeled off the facemask, but his eyes found me first.

He ignored my hysterical sister, as I stood calm. My petty side loved that.

Jonah caught me in his arms and wouldn't let go for more than two minutes.

Julia grew silent, a bit miffed—if you asked me, but how do you gripe to a pair of lip-locked lovers?

Her brush with death had given her some maturity, but I knew then, Julia would always want the attention. That would never leave her because that was just my sister.

And then Jonah gave me a second gift. He whispered that Mae was alive, and my tears broke free at that moment. A fist curled against his chest, and he merely held me longer. My knees were unsteady. My knees were always unsteady around him. I'd grown used to it, but my knees gave out in that moment.

Jonah gave Trenton a side-hug. He gave Jake a tap on the shoulder, but then he swept me up and carried me to a private corner.

Julia and the others huddled with blankets, watching for more bubbles.

We stayed there as more divers popped up. They helped ready the others. Even Trenton. His hands and arms grew weak. He needed help getting the mask on. Then all of them dove back in.

Jonah held me against his chest with his arms around my front. He whispered into my neck, "I—I thought you were gone."

"I thought I was supposed to go."

His arms tightened. He dropped a kiss to my shoulder. "There's a lot that I want to talk to you about, but before I lose the chance to say it—I am in love with you."

The magic of dancing herbs and magical spices burst forth in me.

"Thank you," I whispered.

Jonah laughed. "Not the response I was going for."

"No, I mean—thank you." For giving me that spark back. For being the first one to give that spark back to me. I turned in his arms and grasped his face. "I love you, too."

I had hope.

Jonah helped me get that back, and it wasn't something I could tell. It wasn't a feeling that could be explained. I left home with no hope, and I returned to get that hope again. I had it now, and it took a demolished town to realize it was there—inside me—the whole time.

"Thank you." This time, I spoke to my mother and my sister. They were around. They told Julia to go south, even though Julia would never admit it. All sorts of channels will open in times of crisis, and that's when belief can come flooding in.

Jonah and I swam back out and were welcomed with warmed blankets. Jake grabbed me in a bone-crushing hug before he set me back down and returned to Julia's side. And I knew that my sister changed when she offered me a smile—an actual smile and looked content as Jake wrapped his arms around her once more.

Later, Julia would tell me that she received a phone call. Aunt Kathryn died nineteen minutes before the first wave crashed into Craigstown.

I've thought about that quite a bit since then. And the way I envisioned it—she merely closed her eyes, her hands folded over her chest, peaceful, as the first wave took her body. It was almost a beautiful way to go.

Through the rest of that summer and into the fall, Craigstown was rebuilt. It went a lot faster because of the grey pearls. Those little mussels came in useful when they were needed. In some way, it was like they were meant to be discovered when they were. There were a lot of other heroes hailed from the flood, but I was one of them. I didn't run this time. I didn't *want* to run, and I knew that whatever was broken inside had healed.

You see, I was my own monster. When you don't have hope, something can grow inside of you that will just keep hurting, biting, snarling. You sink farther, and eventually the monster will overtake you.

Some people don't fight back. They might hurt others, hurt themselves, or relinquish the fight for happiness.

I can't explain what happened or how it happened, but learning my family's secrets helped me learn who I was inside. I gained perspective and realized it wasn't me. I wasn't the one who screwed everything up. I wasn't the 'defect.'

It was them.

It was the lies that tore apart my family—that kept my sisters and me from banding together. We stood no chance as children, but now that I know everything—God help me, I was piecing my home back together.

Julia and I started slowly, but by the last brick that cemented Craigstown—she stood at my side. We even visited Sandra together. Mae still wouldn't go, but that's her fight with her own mother.

I just know that if my mom were alive, nothing would keep me from her side. Not anymore.

Boone returned to his own home and to his own story. He did me a favor and took his family with him.

A part of my heart wanted to reach out to him, but the truth was that I hadn't had a heart to give him before. And now that I did, Jonah already claimed ownership. If it hadn't been Jonah, if I'd never survived the first storm and returned home, I couldn't tell you what would've happened between Boone and me. All I know, his name will always be Boone for me, and a part of me will always wish that I could've loved him as he deserved to be.

That just meant that someone else was meant for him. He'll fit with her how Jonah fits with me. How Jake and Julia seem to fit. Aiden and Bubba. Kate and Robbie—yes, finally! And how Mae confessed that she fit with Jeffries.

That's one of my last revelations.

Mae always knew he was my father. He loved my mom, but he folded under pressure and married his wife. He had the dolphin emblazoned on his wedding ring because he truly wanted to make his marriage work.

He tried and failed. My mom was around the corner. Mae was the one who explained it, but she didn't need to. I was aware that life's never simple, especially in adult years.

His story is meant for another time, but it ended sadly and bitterly because when he'd left his wife—my mom had undergone her last round of chemotherapy. He arrived to her hospital room to see her fingers fall lifeless as they were curled with mine.

I'd been sleeping, but I woke up.

I never noticed the big man in our doorway. I just noticed how my mom wasn't there anymore.

Mae told him that the secret was out—that the daughters he'd loved from a distance now knew.

Later, Jeffries would tell me that he kept quiet because he didn't want to do any more damage to another human being. And his daughters were the very last ones he would want to ruin.

I was learning that that's my dad for you, but again—another time and another story.

I always liked to remember that my first words to him as I shuffled into Mae's new bar and took the perch beside him were, "You've been here the whole time."

Apprehension, love, nervousness, caution, all those emotions were rolled together as he stared at me, but all I saw was the love. A father's love and I'm slowly realizing that it's a special entity on its own. I have my right to anger, the right to call him a coward, but I'd just been given a rebirth at life. I wasn't holding grudges.

I didn't have time for that anymore.

And Erica...

It still took me a while to visit her. The cemetery remained intact, and the headstones stood upright strongly.

I thought about that, too, and envisioned that mass of water that crushed everything else. It hadn't touched what lay buried underneath. The tombstones stayed in place and watched everything become uprooted above them.

I sat with my back resting on her tombstone, and I read the letter she left for me. She knew that I was coming back. Somehow, it felt right that she had been the one to know. A bird nearly crashed into me, but after I folded up her letter, I just looked up and grinned.

I love you, too.

I turned and left. Jonah was waiting for me, along with our daughter. We named her Erica Daniella.

THE END

For more information and more books:
www.tijansbooks.com

acknowledgements

There's always so many to thank!

Thank you to all of the girls who admin for the reader group, all the betas who gave me feedback, and all the proofreaders, editors, and Elaine for formatting it. The dedication is so true for me. I want to thank the readers who loved *Home Torn* since I first posted it online for free reading (which will be published in its original version at a later date, in case you wanted to read more shenanigans by the other characters).

I was at a pivotal point in my life where I had to choose between one career path or my writing. I chose to pursue writing, and this was one of those novels I wrote during that time. I remember that time in my life so clearly, and the message I felt while I was writing it was hope. That one word. Hope.

Thank you to everyone, and always have hope in your life!

CPSIA information can be obtained
at www.ICGtesting.com
Printed in the USA
LVHW090245151021
700529LV00009B/31/J